The
Distant
Shore

by
Mariam Kobras

The Distant Shore

by
Mariam Kobras

Book I: The Stone Trilogy

Buddhapuss Ink   Edison, NJ

Cover Art @ 2008 Eric G. Thompson

Author Photo by Sarah Fulford

Cover and Book Design by The Book Team

Library of Congress Control Number: 2011932131

ISBN 978-0-9842035-4-3 (Paperback Original)

First Printing January 2012

PUBLISHER'S NOTE

Buddhapuss Ink LLC and logos are trademarks of Buddhapuss Ink LLC.

www.buddhapussink.com

Acknowledgements

The fact that you are able to hold this book in your hand is proof that serendipity actually exists. In my case, it came in the shape of a black cat that followed me one day on twitter. That cat turned out to be my future publisher, who, with patience, a great sense of humor, and a good dose of friendship, gave me the time and space to shape this story into something you would want to read.

My thanks go out to MaryChris Bradley of Buddhapuss Ink who edited *The Distant Shore*, and taught me to be an author along the way.

~ Mariam Kobras

1

THERE IT WAS . . .

Jon found the letter among the pile of mail he had carelessly tossed on the counter the night before. The corner of the envelope was soaked through from the puddle of milk it had landed in, and it stuck to the counter when he tried to pick it up. With a mug of coffee and the letter in hand, he wandered out onto the deck.

Beautiful morning sunlight greeted him. He felt the fragile warmth of a late February dawn on his face. The sea had a pearly sheen to it as it retreated, the surface quiet despite the gentle breeze. Under his bare feet, the wooden boards creaked softly as the house adjusted to the rising temperature of the day.

It really seemed much too early to be up and about, but he had been restless.

"You're drifting into depression again." Sal had warned him a while ago. They had been sitting on his little deck, "Just look at you, Jon. This is a farce, you living here among shipyard workers and shop girls. The girls aren't even pretty, and the men run around in their underwear."

He had paused meaningfully, staring at the frayed t-shirt his friend was wearing. "Not that they would recognize you; you look just like one of them. You have a wonderful house in Malibu, for God's sake, and you rent it out to Art and live here, in this hovel. One day, one roller too many will shake the foundation and you'll drift out to sea with this collection of clapboard. Then you can sing to the sharks while they gnaw your bones slowly and painfully."

When there was no reply, he added acidly, "But maybe that's what you're aiming for, right? Since you can't do away with yourself on your own."

So here he stood with this letter, wondering why Sal had pressed it on him. He never accepted fan mail anymore: he'd become disenchanted with the unoriginal offers and the repetition of the contents. This one started with the same, old words meant to catch his attention.

"You don't know me, but my name is Joshua."

He stopped reading while he lit a cigarette.

"My mother's name is Naomi Carlsson."

The paper dropped from his hand and fluttered to the ground, where it lay, faceup, on a small pile of sand the wind had blown onto the deck. It fluttered a little in the breeze, grating gently on the rough surface, taunting him.

Jon bent down to retrieve it and read on.

"We live in a small town in Norway called Halmar where she manages a hotel, the Seaside. She said you are my father."

Time stopped. The world around him froze, engraving these images into his memory to be forever connected with this instant: the roiling water slowly retreating, laying bare wet stretches of beach, the seagulls dancing in the air, the single sailboat skimming over the waves.

"I'm sixteen," the letter said, "and I really wanted to know. So on my birthday a couple of weeks ago I finally got her to tell me. It is hard to believe. I don't really like your music, but you are very famous, it seems. How did you meet my Mom?"

"YOU CAN'T STILL be pining for that girl, Jon?" Sal had asked after their third bourbon. "You'll have to get over her at some point. There are so many out there, one of them must be good enough for you. She left you a long time ago without a word, and you have never moved on, still mourning like a lovesick boy."

In the end, it was more like an accusation than a question, and there was no reply.

"MY MOTHER'S NAME is Naomi Carlsson."

As if he could have forgotten her name.

As if he had allowed himself to forget, with those photographs on the shelves he looked at every day.

Gone. One night she had been there, the next morning gone without a word, vanished with all the bits and pieces of her except for the single hair clip on the sink in the bathroom. Naomi. He had stood there and stared at the thing: his brain frozen, his heart numb, and then done what he always did, called Sal and cried for help.

"What do you mean, she's gone?" Sal had asked, "People don't just disappear overnight."

But he had shown up a half hour later, bleary-eyed and cross to be woken again so soon after he had gone to bed.

"For God's sake, Jon," had been his verdict, "she's not dead. She wasn't abducted. Look around, she's taken all her stuff. She only left you, man. Happens all the time." And he returned to his house, and sleep.

As quietly and softly as she had stepped into his life, she had left it again, left in such a way that in all the years he had never solved the riddle of her disappearance.

"IT WOULD BE really nice to get to know you," the boy had written, "if it is true what my Mom told me and she did not just make it up. Maybe she only said it because she is a fan of yours. She has a picture of you on her desk, and all your albums."

This nearly tore him apart. He had to read it again and again until his brain accepted it.

Norway. So that was where she had been hiding herself and their child away from him. It hit him then, the realization that he had been a father without ever knowing it.

Deep inside he felt the nudge, irritating and insisting, and he tried to ignore it while he finished his cooling coffee.

The letter, crumpled in his hand, felt like a captured bird that wanted to fly again, so he opened his fingers and held it up in his palm to stare at it.

The nudge turned into a push, just like that.

He clamped down on it firmly and returned inside.

It was time to start working again, clean the piano and tune the guitar and get some new music written. Sal was right; it was high time to put something out again.

The dust on the piano keys irritated him. He wiped at it impatiently, then gave up; there was no melody in his mind, there hadn't been for a long time.

A shove, nearly strong enough to make him jump, and he rose to pace about the small room.

He could just go. He could just go on his own, all alone, so no one would witness the humiliation and shame when she turned him away like a stray dog, or laughed at him, or had her husband throw him out.

Naomi. She had walked through the big white house like a lost selkie, a mermaid caught on land, a beautiful shadow in his otherwise crowded life. Returning to her embrace after the harsh lights of publicity had always felt like diving into a balmy, azure ocean, being caught on the gentle swell of a wave that would take him away to unknown and peaceful shores.

Jon placed the empty mug in the sink, wiped down the kitchen counter, returned the milk carton to the fridge, and placed the coffee tin on the shelf. It seemed to him as if he were performing a ritual, putting everything in order like putting it behind him step by step, gaining momentum, each act a little faster than the one before, each one making his heart beat harder, until he could feel his pulse on the back of his tongue like the dredge of bitter tea. He stood, his hands on his hips, to look around in the room, until he was breathing freely again and the fog of turmoil had lifted from his brain.

There was an overnight bag somewhere upstairs in a corner of the closet; he had received it as a Christmas gift from his sister a couple of years ago and tossed it there, puzzled by her intent. He never used overnight bags. When he left here, it was always with trunks filled with all the clothing needed for the events he would be appearing at.

On his own, privately, he had not gone anywhere in a long while.

Not even when Sal presented him with an exclusive invite to a film star's private tropical island, stating, "Go, for Heaven's sake. Take swimming trunks and nothing else, get drunk every night, screw every girl you can grab, and come back tan and rested."

So now, this seemed like the right thing to use. A minimum of clothes, a toothbrush, not much more. He would go, find out what he wanted to know, and return. At long last, there would be an answer to the question that had tortured him for years. She would have to tell him, look him in the eye and tell him why she had walked out on him like that, leaving him in misery.

And the boy, his son, the child she had kept away from him, something would have to be done about that, too.

While he stuffed a couple of shirts into the bag, his blood boiled at this thought.

The promises he had made to her, the dreams he had painted for her, and yet nothing had been good enough to make her stay, and she had even taken that from him, his baby. Not only had she torn out his heart and destroyed his soul, she had carried away this secret.

AFTER A MOMENT'S thought, he decided to leave his car in the garage and call for a cab instead. Jon was standing on his doorstep, his bag at his side, when his neighbor stepped out and nodded to him. Mike owned a hamburger grill on the beach in Santa Monica somewhere, but he had never followed up on the many invitations extended to him to stop by for a burger or two.

"Morning," he said. "Nice day, isn't it? Traveling again?"

They knew him, of course. His face was too well known, but the people here had developed a tight-lipped protectiveness about their famous neighbor, and he was never bothered.

"Yes," Jon replied, surprising himself. "I'm off to Norway for a while."

"Supposed to be cold there." Mike judiciously eyed the silk-lined leather jacket Jon was wearing. "That won't keep you warm. Not a lot of luggage either for a trip to Europe."

"I'm not staying long."

"Someone taking you to the airport?" A box of cigarettes had appeared in Mike's hand. He offered one to Jon, who took it with a nod and a word of thanks.

"Nah. Called a cab." It felt rather good to stand outside his house on an early Tuesday morning with a small travel bag and a smoke.

Mike squinted at him in the sun. "Not like you to take a cab. I always see you in that fancy German car or being picked up by one of those dark limousines. Are you lighting out, then?"

"Lighting out?" He had forgotten to pack his razor.

"Yes, man, running away, are you running away from it all? I would, if I were you, run away. At least from time to time." Thoughtfully Mike observed the glowing ashes on his butt. "Must be hard, living in the limelight all the time."

"No, there's this girl…" He caught himself just in time.

Mike, though, was grinning at him in understanding. "Yeah, it's always about them, isn't it? Well, I wish you luck, mate." With a brief wave, he stepped down from the threshold and picked up the newspaper on the way to his car.

"Thanks, Mike," Jon mumbled. Somehow the short exchange had lightened his heart considerably and set things in proper perspective.

There was no anger. Anguish, yes. Anger, no. There had never been anger, only the deep pain of being left alone with those unanswered questions.

"THERE HE IS," Russ said.

He had been looking out of the window from time to time, watching for Jon.

Sal pushed a mug of coffee at him, narrowly missing the stack of photographs still needing to be signed.

"Told you."

"Man, but he is so predictable. Boring, isn't it?" It came out in the British accent Sal found entertaining. "What do you think he'll do?" There was a trace of nervousness in his voice, one that echoed Sal's.

"I'd put down money on him wanting to go there right away. He's been obsessed with that girl from day one, and the fact that she dropped him like that just makes her more alluring. Wait and see."

"Did you order a plane for him?" Russ sipped the coffee and watched Jon, his bag slung over his shoulder, as he walked across the parking lot. "God, will you look at him, Sal! He looks like he's going to sign up with the Navy."

Sal rose from his chair to look outside over Russ' shoulder. "Yeah," he agreed softly.

Their charge and friend, the famous star. There he was, in jeans and a rather well-worn leather jacket, his hair wind-blown and his brow clouded in concentration.

"Pour him some coffee."

"He'll get plenty of that on the plane."

Sal opened the door and greeted Jon with a laconic, "Good morning, my Master. You're early, aren't you?"

Jon set his bag down on one of the cluttered desks, mindless of the papers and CDs piled on it, and took the cup Russ held out. They looked at him expectantly. Russ pointed at the one piece of luggage behind his back, his eyebrows meaningfully raised at Sal, who nodded in return, a small smirk on his face.

"Stop that," Jon ordered, "I know what you're doing, alright? You read the letter, and you know why I'm here, both of you."

Sal nodded.

"I'm going away." It sounded childish and obstinate. "I don't know for how long. And I'm going alone."

"Jon." Sal turned serious, "Are you sure? I'm prepared to go with you. It's a long trip, and you have no idea what you're getting into."

"No."

"Please think, Jon," Russ chimed in from his seat by the window, "You don't know what's waiting for you, there might be legal issues, and Sal would keep his head—"

"Meaning I won't?" Jon interrupted. "Trust me, I will. Oh, I will, Russ. All I want are answers, and if that boy really is mine, there will be plenty of questions to answer." But he knew he was not fooling them. They had been together too long for that.

"Right." Russ seemed to read his thoughts. "So you're going to walk in there and demand your love-child. You're going to make her explain, see your son, and then what? Then what? You'll be stranded in a strange country on a strange continent."

There was no way he was going to let one of them go along, not this time.

He set the cup down on the stack of pictures, spilling some coffee on his own image, ignoring Sal's indignant sniff at the ruined photographs.

"This is private, Sal."

"None of us has ever been to Norway," Russ picked up the argument, "and none of us speaks the language. I'm really not happy about you going there on your own. I don't even think that place has an airport. What if you have to rent a car and drive from somewhere else?" He cast around. "Sal, what's the next big city, anyway? Are there big cities in Norway?"

Sal began moving toward the world map still hanging on the wall over the coffee machine from their tour planning a year earlier, his glasses pushed down on his nose, but Jon picked up his bag again.

"Sal. Stop the nonsense. I'm capable of driving a car and handling a credit card. I'm going now. Call the airport, I want a plane ready in an hour. Find out which…no."

Both men turned toward him, expectantly.

"You don't need to do anything at all. I found her by myself, and I made her run by myself. Now I'm going to find her on my own again and…"

He stopped himself just in time. They would not understand. They would laugh and call him obsessive again, he was certain.

Halfway out the door he heard Sal shout, "You'll need a bigger house when you return with Naomi, you hear me? Better give Art a call and tell him to move out," and the echoing burst of laughter from Russ.

IT HAD FELT so important to convince Sal and Russ he needed to act on his own, and this feeling held as long as the cab sped along the highway toward the airport, but once he stood inside that great hall his courage nearly left him.

He gazed at the people around him. They all seemed to know exactly where they were headed. No one took any notice of him at all. No one rushed up to beg for an autograph or a snapshot taken by a friend or hastily employed stranger as a breathless female hung on to his arm, or tried for an embrace they wanted documented for all eternity.

Jon shifted his bag from one shoulder to the other and made his way to an information desk where a blond girl smiled a greeting at him.

"I need to go to Norway," he said. "As soon as possible."

She began busily typing into her computer as he spelled out the name of the town.

"It is not on a regular flight route. It's a very small place."

"Yeah." He had understood that from the boy's letter alright.

"You could fly via Oslo to Bergen, and then change again."

It was a doubtful suggestion made even worse by the addition, "But there are no direct flights to Oslo from here. You'll have a layover in London—or maybe New York—I'll look, wait a moment." She eyed him speculatively. "Of course, you could always charter a jet."

Pushing a box of flyers out of the way, she turned the screen so he could see it and pointed with a well-varnished fingernail.

"Here it is, Halmar, out in the middle of nowhere, and one of the stops for Hurtigruten post ships. It does have one rather nice hotel, it says. Right on the water, too."

"The name of the place?" Jon asked, but he knew.

"It's the Seaside."

Of course it was, but seeing it on that computer screen somehow made it real for the first time.

"Get me a jet," he said.

He had two hours to kill while the plane was made ready, and he spent them sitting at a bar in the terminal drinking coffee and observing the other passengers. He felt an odd sense of displacement, as if he had somehow stepped out of his life with this mindless and hasty action. The fact that he was out here on his own without being accosted in any way made him feel as if he had become anonymous or invisible the moment he had hailed a cab instead of his limo.

A HOTEL. SHE was running a hotel. The sweet young girl he had picked up in Geneva all those years ago, the same one who had given up her life there on the spur of the moment to be his love and write lyrics for him. She was a businesswoman now.

He wondered if she had stopped writing when she had left him, or if there were songs there, somewhere, just waiting to be sung to the world. From his pocket, he retrieved the crumpled letter from the boy, Joshua, his son, to glean more information from it, but there was nothing.

Not a word about a family, a husband to his mother, siblings.

God, but he hated that thought. Hated that he might step into that place only to be confronted by some blond, giant Norseman who would just turn him around and run him out again. He could hear the mocking laughter even now.

Even worse would be Naomi, standing by, watching silently, letting it happen without a single word to him, and never an explanation, which he needed so badly it felt like a big burning scar down his back.

On the plane, taxiing toward the runway, his anxiety grew into a full -blown panic, and he was on the point of telling the pilot to return to the hangar, but it was too late. The fast little machine was up in the air and pulling away toward the East before he had made up his mind, so he settled down into the deep leather seat and stared out the window at the landscape passing by below as memories roiled in his head.

SAL HAD BEEN exasperated with him. After his move from Malibu into the much smaller place further north, they had sat together on the deck, sharing a bottle of single-malt. Sal, his feet up on the barbecue, had demanded: "So tell me all about it. It's time you talked. "

Jon had thought for a long time. The sun set into the ocean, it grew dark, a warm wind blew over the water, and music drifted over from some campfire down on the sand. "I was waiting in the hotel lobby when she walked in. I knew it was her right away. "

Sal had raised a skeptical eyebrow.

"Yeah, I know. You don't believe in that kind of thing. But it truly happened like that. She was wearing jeans and a white sleeveless top. Her hair was in a braid that hung nearly to her thighs. She had sunglasses pushed up on her brow, no makeup, flat sandals on naked feet."

"You are disgusting."

"Do you want to hear or not? She stopped by the hotel door and looked at me across the lobby, directly at me. There was no searching or uncertainty, she just stood, very still and contained, and looked at me. As if there were no other people in the whole wide world. Everything seemed to center on that look. I got up to meet her as she walked toward me, and I had the feeling that I should open my arms and let her walk right into them. It was that easy."

"And did you?"

"No. I didn't. But it really took some effort. It wasn't like falling in love at all. It was something altogether different and much more powerful. It felt…" He had searched for words. "It felt as if all the wishing and the longing of all the love songs I had ever written were being drawn together in that moment and poured out. I wanted to hold her in my arms and never let her go again. That's how it felt." He had poured some more whiskey. "I couldn't talk. My skin was running hot and cold, my stomach was in knots. I think we stood for a while just gazing at each other. It seemed like a very long time. Then you came. There isn't anything else I can tell you. You ordered coffee, we moved out to the hotel terrace and sat in the sun. It was a lovely afternoon, with sailboats on the lake, waiters serving ice cream and cake and chocolate, and I just sat and stared. I don't know what I had expected, but it certainly wasn't for me to go to pieces."

WHEN THEY LANDED at last in Bergen, he stopped on the steps of the plane as an icy blast hit him. The small seaplane was waiting for him only a few steps away, but by the time he reached it, he was as cold as he had ever been in his life, and his shoes were soaked.

"The flight will be a little rough," the pilot informed him, "I'll take you along the coast so you can see something of the landscape, alright?"

Jon was not quite sure he liked his jaunty approach to the miserable weather. Fear was weakening the drive that had pushed him this far around the globe, fear that he was doing something incredibly stupid and that the outcome would be too much to bear. And here, now, coasting along the shoreline of this rugged country, past soaring snow-covered mountains and over water that was dark grey and capped by white breakers, the Atlantic storm buffeting the Cessna, this fear poured over him like icy slush.

He regretted not having brought Sal, at last seeing the sense in his admonition to take someone with him who would keep a clear head.

The wing of the plane dipped as they passed through a gap in the high hills, past a couple of small islands, and into the bay with the village at its end.

"There." The pilot pointed, but Jon had seen it already.

There was a yellow wooden building with a red gabled roof and white trim right on the water, and behind it, rising into the gentle swell of a forested hillside, the little town itself. A white church with steeples sat nestled among greenery above the houses, looking down on the pier. To the right, just beside the hotel, a small inlet separated the town from a fishing wharf, just big enough to hold five trawlers and a sort of depot.

The landing was not as bad as he had expected.

Using a cigarette as an excuse, Jon lingered in the cold. Here he was, on her doorstep, and now, after many hours of travel, his courage failed him.

The entrance to the hotel lay right on the corner of the pier, the small square of red tiles separated from the water by a wooden railing and a low wall following the curve of the bay to the dock where a couple of yachts rested. From where he stood he could see along the deck at the side of the hotel. There were some folded deck chairs, forgotten now in deep winter, but a reminder that even here there would be days to sit outside and enjoy a semblance of warmth.

The sun had come out, and the wind was not as rough, broken by the surrounding hills, but the temperature was just as vicious, just as bitter. It was so very quiet. A bell was ringing somewhere, a single car passed by, two men strolled along the cobbled street along the pier with the collars of their thick woolen jackets turned up, a flock of seagulls swirled over the choppy water, but that was all. The air was so tart, it stung his nostrils, the light so clear it made him squint. At long last he tossed away the butt.

Seventeen years had changed him from the young man who had just made his first big step toward stardom into the music icon he was now. Yet here he was, just as pathetic as he'd been then, pleading for love from the same woman.

SHE WAS STILL laughing in the elevator.

"Honestly," Christi said in a huff, "if he were the last man on Earth, I still wouldn't go out with him again. A couple of sandwiches made by his mom? That's not a date, Naomi. That's pathetic."

"You might have come here with him. That would have been nice, a date with all of us looking on." Naomi took the tray from her. "I'll take these to the kitchen. You go on up to the rooms."

She stepped out into the lobby, balancing her load through the opening doors, thinking idly how nice these new plates would look with the pale green tablecloths and the table decorations when she noticed the man standing at the desk with Solveigh. He looked a lot like Jon.

In fact, he looked so much like Jon that she just stood, staring, lost in reverie, the old pain a dull throb somewhere below her throat and above her heart where it pinched her breathing. He wore jeans and a leather jacket, his figure tall and well built, his hair a little longer than was fashionable, curled over his collar. For a moment, she allowed herself to linger in that recurring dream of seeing him there, having found his way to her for some unaccountable reason.

Solveigh spoke to him, a sunny smile on her face, and he replied.

That voice she would have known it anywhere, even in the noisiest crowd.

The tray dropped from her fingers and crashed to the floor with an impressive sound, plates shattering, some rolling away to settle down with a melodic ring, some trundling on until they hit the wall.

They turned toward her simultaneously, Jon and Solveigh, to where she stood amid a pile of shards, still as a statue, caught in her moment of shock.

He was by himself. His jacket was too thin for the weather, his shoes, elegant loafers, were wet, as were his jeans, and his hair was wind-blown, and he was still the most beautiful man on Earth.

Jon was moving toward her, an expression on his face she could not rightly interpret—not anger but fear, expectation, and maybe even something like hope, but she could not be sure.

"Get me the key to the private guest room." Naomi said softly to Solveigh, who glared at her.

"I'll take care of our guest myself." Naomi gestured at Jon.

Without a word, she took the key when Solveigh held it out to her and turned to walk down the stairs at the end of the hallway.

Jon followed, with a nod and a brief grin at Solveigh.

SO HARD. THIS was so hard.

How lovely she was, moving before him in the dim light of the corridor, her thick, black braid swinging down her back as it used to, its end well below her waist. She had filled out a little, but her figure was still slim and lithe, her face unchanged.

Naomi unlocked a door to her right. "This is our private guest room. It used to be my son's. Not as luxurious as you are probably used to."

The view was spectacular.

The glass front led out to the deck, and it offered a view of the entire bay and the rising hills on the other side, all the way to the towering mountains in the distance.

"You didn't bring a lot of luggage."

He could not find the courage to look into her eyes now that they were alone, nor think of the words to say to her. There was a big, hidden question in her short statement, and he knew he had to come up with the right answer or lose this moment.

"I didn't take much time to pack."

The room was simple enough, in a typically Scandinavian manner: a single bed with a blue and red patchwork quilt, a wardrobe, a desk by the window, a chair, on the wooden floor a circular woven rug, a painting of a beach on the wall. A second door led into a frugal bathroom. It was very peaceful, serene in its simplicity, cozy despite its bareness.

Naomi returned to the hallway where there was one more door and opened it for him.

Slowly Jon moved through the large space.

There was a kitchen niche toward the back and stairs that led to a sleeping loft to his right. In the center of the room, God help him, stood a Steinway Baby Grand. A couch, deep and comfortable, was turned to take advantage of another view of the bay. A dining table was pushed against the wall, and over it a huge framed photograph of them together.

He stood staring at it for minutes, recalling the day when it had been taken.

THEY HAD BEEN in the garden of the Malibu house, in the arbor with the stone bench and the huge jasmine bushes, to shoot the pictures for the new album. It had been hot and humid, and he had been at the end of his rope, about ready to give up, because life as a rock star was not at all what he had expected. Sal had been upset, demanding he shape up and look his best for the camera, no one wanted to see a sulky bastard on an album cover. The makeup artist kept patting and fussing at his face and touching up his hair, making him want to swat her like an irritating fly.

And just then, right at the moment when he had been about to jump from that bench and tell them all to go to hell and take the whole music business with them and be done with it, Naomi had come up the path among the trees smiling, a cold glass of lemonade in her hand, her hair fluttering around her. She sat with him for a while and talked about small things, like the seashell she'd found on the beach that morning, about that piece of driftwood that looked just like a seal, and would he go for a walk with her later, she was still hoping to find a piece of amber.

He remembered laughing at her then, saying, "Dear love, how often do I have to tell you? There's no amber to be found here," and how she had shrugged in reply and insisted, "There are conifers in Oregon and Washington, so why shouldn't there be amber on the beach in California? It has to end up somewhere!"

He had loved this about her so much, her faith in possibilities and the refusal to give in to common sense when it did not fit her expectations.

On the shelves, all of his records, and more framed pictures from moments he recalled only too well: Sean and Naomi sharing cotton candy; Jon slumped on a stool on stage during a sound check, and Naomi, her fists on her hips, while he grinned sheepishly at her anger, a cigarette between his lips, Sean, Russ and Sal in the background watching them in amusement. Another one where he was on the beach, his jeans rolled up, bending over to retrieve something for her from the surf.

The two of them together, caught by someone's camera in a moment of intimacy where she was in his arms, their lips nearly touching, her eyes looking deeply into his, seeing only each other and shutting out the world around them.

There were more pictures, of a boy.

A baby, a toddler, a gritty urchin of maybe five, a boy in a school uniform. A tall, strapping adolescent in a suit beside a piano, on a stage, bowing to an audience, and if there had ever been a moment's doubt concerning his fatherhood it was blown away, seeing Joshua there.

It was like looking into a mirror of his own youth. He had the same dark eyes and smoldering stare, the same mouth and chin, the unruly black hair. Even the stance seemed to echo his own.

"These pictures," Naomi said, waving at the wall and the shelves, "I put them up recently. After…" she hesitated. "Since I live alone now."

In the corner of the room, where the glass walls met, a desk faced out so she could look at the landscape while she worked.

Jon threw her a questioning glance, but Naomi did not react. She stood, her hands folded behind her back and her head lowered, against the wall, still, withdrawn, and silent.

He looked down at her work, and it nearly broke his heart.

There were pages upon pages covered with poems and lyrics, some of them long, completed song texts, others only one or two verses, and some nearly blank, with only a short phrase or a single word. He saw years of writing, and at least a hundred songs that should have been taken out into the world. "You don't hate me?" It came out more as a statement than a question.

"I don't hate you." There was surprise in her voice. "I never did."

After a pause, she asked, "How did you get here?"

And this was the second big question, its true meaning hidden so well beneath the mundane inquiry.

"I chartered a jet," he replied, which made her nod thoughtfully.

She was wearing a kind of severe traditional dress in black, the bodice tightly laced across her chest, the skirt falling in heavy pleats, with a white lace blouse under it and woolen stockings in flat shoes. It made her look prim and pale, very young and vulnerable.

Create clarity, Sal would advise him, first of all, create clarity. Don't muddle things.

"Is there anyone in your life? Should I leave?"

Naomi looked up at him. "You haven't even taken off your jacket. Your shoes are soaked."

"Well." His soul soared; there was no other way to put it. "I was in a hurry. I wanted to get to you as fast as I could."

Jon crossed the room to her, certain now of what he had to do, the leaden anxiety falling off him finally after weighing on his shoulders for so many hours.

The feeling was the same as in Geneva, the magic had not gone away. She was in his arms again at long last, the kiss a sweet, tentative touch of lips that made him nearly reel with desire and move closer to her. For an endless, wonderful instant, her hands clamped tightly onto his jacket and her mouth opened under his, but then Naomi pushed him back gently.

"Not like this, Jon. I need to understand why you're here first."

"This must be a dream. In a moment, I'll wake up to Sal hammering on the door, yelling that I've overslept and missed some appointment or other, and I'll discover I'm really holding a cushion instead of you, only the cushion would not kiss me back like that, right?"

Instead of answering, Naomi touched his cheeks in a feathery caress, but then she stepped away from him and into the kitchen, where she began making coffee. Her fingers shook as she measured out the grounds.

"Take off those shoes, Jon. And your socks, if they're wet. I can't have you getting sick."

Once she had the coffee machine working, Naomi went up to the loft and returned with thick, hand-knitted, red and blue striped socks. "These should fit you, they belong to…" Abruptly she broke off.

He took them from her, and the cup of steaming coffee a moment later, and sat on the piano bench where he could watch her as she moved around, evading him.

"Naomi."

Her shoulders drew together, and he hated it, hated to see the fear in her.

"Come here, talk to me. We've found out we still like to kiss, but I want to know."

The socks were indeed comfortable and warm, the coffee a welcome fortifier for his chilled bones. He realized he had never even looked at his watch since he had landed in Bergen and had no idea how late it might be, the light here being no help at all.

"Know what? There is nothing to know."

The black dress was too much to take. He had never seen her in anything even remotely like it, and he hated it.

"I got a letter. From Joshua, from our son."

Naomi stood very still, waiting for his next words.

"He wrote to me. He asked if I'm his father."

When there was no reaction he rose and went over to her.

"I know I'm his father, seeing those pictures over there is proof enough for me. But, Baby…"

The smallest gasp escaped her at the stupid endearment, but she did not turn to him.

"He shouldn't have done that." Her voice wavered a little. "I asked him to let it rest. But he's just like you, he can't let well enough alone, he has to poke and worry at things until he finds what he wants."

"I want to know why you left me, Naomi. I want to know, and I have a right to know. The sooner we start talking, the sooner we will know how we're going to do this."

"Do what?" Her eyes were wide and dark with trepidation.

"Well, you didn't really think I'd come all this way on my own just for a few stupid answers, did you? For that, I could have sent Sal, or maybe a busload of lawyers. You were mine, and you still are, I can see it. It's right there in the way you look at me. Don't deny it."

"No." She said it very softly, but without hesitation.

"Why did you run like that, Naomi? Why did you leave me like that, without a word, without a chance to clear things up? What have I ever done to make you do that? I want to hear, and right now. And the child, Naomi, God, our child, yours and mine…"

"Jon…" In vain, she tried to free herself from his hold.

"No Naomi, I've waited and wondered for so many years, but now I won't wait one minute longer. I'm here. I want to know."

The tears came, silently and slowly they spilled over and ran down her cheeks, and Naomi wiped them away with the back of her free hand.

"Nothing."

It came out like a sigh, so low Jon thought he had misheard.

"You did nothing, Jon, nothing to make me run from you. It was not your fault."

He had been ready to hear many things, but this shocked him more than any of the versions he had conjured up over the years, the many imagined wrongs he might have committed, or, a possibility he had always pushed far away into the darkest dungeons of his mind, another man.

Another man who had won her away from him, receiving her smile, touching her, holding her during the night, hearing her soft whisper when she was in his arms.

"You met someone else." His voice was dark with hurt. "You met someone you loved more than me. Was that it?"

He went over to the shelf to stare again at the images of their past, happy faces in a carefree time, lost forever. The bitter insight that his journey had been in vain added to the fog of jet-lag and made him feel the exhaustion of his long flight, and brought the coldness back to his limbs. Sal's words with their cool common sense rang in his ears, and here, seeing her like this, he had wanted everything again, right away, without reserve.

"There wasn't anyone else, Jon."

The words did not register at first; he had lost himself in the memory of that day when she had folded him into a neat parcel on that stage for smoking just before the show. How fiercely he had loved her then, seeing the concern for him in her furious face, and the reaction of the others who had bowed to her will and put out their own cigarettes hastily enough. She had been queen that evening, so much younger than any of them and yet leading them on a leash like puppies.

"Never anyone else?" Jon could hardly believe what he had heard. "Never anyone else, Naomi? No one? Not one?"

"Jon."

She touched his wrist to catch his attention. Her tears were gone, but her face was still pale and wan. "You should know better. How could I ever love anyone else after you, after having been yours?"

He had her against the wall in an instant, his hands on her body this time, holding her tightly, the kiss hard and deep, punishing. Miraculously, she melted into his rough embrace, moaning softly when his thighs moved against her, moaning into his mouth in the way he loved so much. His hands slid over the stiff, unforgiving linen of her dress to her breasts and cupped them, but there was too much fabric for his taste. But again she pushed him off, with an effort this time, though.

"Jon. No." It did not sound entirely convincing.

This time he did not let her go again. "Tell me, Naomi. You want me, you love me still, and me, I'm just crazy to get you in bed right now. I want that awful dress off you, and I want to make love to you so badly it's killing me. I need you in my arms again, I truly do. I know I can make all the pain and every bad memory go away if you'll only let me, Baby, so please, tell me what happened so we can go on from here!"

She was pleasingly mussed, the braid no longer neat and straight, her face framed by escaped curls, softening her features. Against her weak protest, he reached for the ribbon and freed her hair, unraveling the strands until the long locks sprang back to life and fell over her shoulders like the black curtain he had always loved on her.

"You honestly don't remember?"

For the life of him, he could not recall any incident that might have driven her away, as hard as he tried.

"We gave the concert that day, and what a success it was. There was the party at the house later, and we all ended up in jail." His memory of that night was foggy. "We ended up in jail, but Sal got us out the next morning, and I went back to the house and you were gone. There was nothing left of you, nothing, not a note, no explanation, just an empty house."

And my broken heart, he thought.

Naomi sank down on the couch, her legs pulled up against her chest, her arms knitted around them.

"You really don't remember, do you?"

Jon couldn't tell if there was a trace of accusation in her tone. Dismally, he shook his head.

The concert, and the many thousands who had attended it, and he, Jon, up there on the stage, singing to the thunder of their applause, took the final step into stardom, the great breakthrough he had been working so hard for, and here it was, on a warm July night in Hollywood. At twenty-seven, he had it all, at last. His face was on the front page of magazines, on billboards, on posters all over the city. He was handed from one glitzy party to the next. There was not one opening night, premiere, or event that he missed. Everywhere he went, he was the celebrated centerpiece.

"We had stopped living, Jon. Your career, your fame, was all that mattered. You were moving away from me a little more each day. But the thing that really made me flee was the night of the concert, and I knew I had to go, and not only go but vanish completely from your life if I wanted to save my own. And the baby's."

"Ah." He returned to his perch on the piano bench. "So you knew you were pregnant before you left. And you didn't tell me."

Again, the cruel pain of being cut off.

"I never had a chance." She tried to hide it, but he could see she was crying again.

She had meant to tell him, she went on, right after the concert, but there was never the right moment for it. After the performance they had celebrated, first backstage, and then, with an ever-growing crowd, at their house.

"There were people everywhere, Jon, there was no chance to get you alone at all, and…" There was no way to say this without hurting him again.

"And Jon, I was waiting for you to…I don't know, make more of me than I was. I was only your little lovebird, your plaything, and I did not want you to marry me because I was pregnant. Even then, at twenty-one, I had that measure of pride." She held up her hand to stop him when he sat up straight in indignation. "Don't say it. I know you loved me. And that was not the final reason, either."

For him, it was quite enough. He hung his head to stare at his knees and his folded hands.

"The night of the concert." Her skirt had tangled around her legs and made it difficult for her to rise from the couch.

Jon rose and went to sit beside her and clasp her hands tightly. "Oh no, you're not going anywhere, Naomi."

The resistance was weak at best, as if all the fight had gone out of her once she had decided to talk to him, but for good measure, he sat down beside her and pried her stiff fingers from the fabric to hold them in his.

Outside, darkness was settling over the bay, clouds lowering themselves onto the hills and the water like a thick grey blanket closing off the view.

"Baby." His voice nearly broke on the love word and the strength of his feelings. "Please, Naomi, something happened. Something scared you so much it made you make that decision that night. You were unhappy, and then something happened to push you away forever."

Gently he laid her hands against his chest to warm them. "But Naomi, look at me. Please look at me."

She raised her eyes to him.

"You should know better, love. You should know you can talk to me about anything at all. Tell me what happened that night, I beg you. If I did something to turn you away, I need to know, so that I can set it right."

"But how can you not remember, Jon?"

She could not hold herself together anymore. Helplessly he watched her crying bitterly, unable to find the words to comfort her or ease the pain for her. At least she did not pull away from him again.

"I recall the party after the concert."

Jon tried to conjure up that evening.

Everyone had been there. There had been people in the house, in the garden, even spilling out onto the beach and through the open gates into the street. No one had taken control, and even Sal had said to let the world see how famous he now was, and to hell with everything else, at least for this one night. A bit of notoriety could not be all that harmful. Art had brought Wes along, and Jon could remember standing in a corner of the porch at one point and accepting the pills offered with the promise that he would be able to party all night on them, and hey, he was going to have the surprise of his life when he took his girl to bed later. The only drawback, Jon had found out soon enough, was that he felt more than drunk; he was delirious with his success anyway, and now high on drugs and alcohol, and somewhere at that point his memory simply vanished into a mist. It did not lift until the following morning when, hungover, he had stepped out of the police building into a blinding dawn and right into Sal, who gave him the harangue of his life.

He remembered being in the cedar grove with a girl, a stranger, kissing him wildly, her bare thighs wrapped around him, her hands on his crotch. He was ready to give in to the temptation of a quick, hot encounter but had pulled away because she was not the right one.

He had found her in the kitchen, sitting on the counter, feet dangling, a glass of Coke in her hand, chatting with Russ.

"We ended up in bed, yes?"

Naomi forgot her own misery for long enough to shoot him an impatient glare and huff at him. "Of course, Jon. We always did."

This made him grin in delighted embarrassment. "And you remember that night, Babe, and I don't. So tell me." Gentle encouragement only, which nonetheless made her retreat again into that stillness he had begun to hate.

A terrible fear was growing in him that she would offer him a vision to destroy him, confront him with a truth he had locked away so safely he had never been able to retrieve it on his own. Wild suspicions boiled up in his mind, apprehension making his back prickle with sudden sweat. He had hurt her; in his drunken, drugged state, he had dragged her off, taken her away to the solitude of their bedroom and done things to her, forced and abused her, driven her away, after she had seen the darkness of his true soul.

"The drug raid," Naomi interrupted his panicked fantasies. "Don't you recall the drug raid, Jon?"

"Drug raid?" And there it was, as if she had unlocked a door for him.

The reason they had gone to jail. Here was the memory he had never called up from its lair.

She was speaking again, in a dreadful, tortured monotone, revealing to him what he should have known all along. "At some point you came to me in the kitchen, and we went upstairs. You were so hyped and so wild, you could hardly wait to get my clothes off, and I laughed at you, and Jon…"

Slowly her head came up.

He could hardly believe his eyes; despite the tears and grief and turmoil, there was something else in her face, a softening of her lips, a faint flush in her cheeks, her gaze, wandering to his mouth. Desire, despite everything that had happened and the long time that had passed, there it was, plain to see, easy enough for him to recognize.

"And we made love. I was loving you, Baby, say it. It isn't hard at all to say."

He could see it now, could recall it in shattering clarity.

Her hair spilled on the pillow, her arms reaching for him, lips receiving his feverish kisses and whispering his name. Passion had been riding him wildly, full on fame, drink, and pills as he had been, and she had been his, no reserve, no other thought, nothing.

He made an effort to clear his mind of the all too delicious image.

"And then they raided the house, the police," he tried, only to be interrupted by her.

"They raided the house Jon, yes. Someone had called the police, and they stormed into our bedroom while we were…"

She caught her breath, searching for words, so Jon added softly, "While we were having sex. There's no shame in that. You can say that, surely."

"They turned on all the lights, there must have been ten of them, and they pulled you away from me, and…Jon, you fought them, and you bellowed, there is no other word for it, naked as you were. Don't you remember that?"

Dismally, he shook his head.

"They made the crudest jokes, and when I tried to cover myself up one of them took the sheet from me, and I sat there, exposed, while you raged and screamed. They wondered how many girls you had done that night, and one asked if he could come back after his shift to have a go at me. It was awful."

She paused, her eyes on their hands. "There were cracks about the little chick in your bed until one of them found your jeans and a shirt and they took you away, and everyone else they could get their hands on, I don't know, most of the people must have fled by then. I didn't dare move from the room until everything was quiet again." Her face flushed as the shame of that night overwhelmed her. "One of them said to just leave me there, I would be of little use and looked harmless enough, and another considered asking for my driver's license; I seemed to be minor and maybe they could get you for that."

Jon could just see it.

He could see her wandering around the deserted house after everyone else had vanished, all by herself, scared and crying, his sweet girl. What a terrible mess there had been in every single room, the beds used and the sheets soiled, every bath reeking of vomit and worse, the kitchen a sticky, filthy place, spilled drinks and overturned bottles everywhere, food on the floor, the fridge door wide open, the shelves raided. The living room had looked as if something had exploded and smelled like a pit.

It was growing dark outside. He could see lights twinkling across the bay where single houses stood sprinkled like little beacons of life in an otherwise empty landscape. On a small island at the mouth of the bay, a lighthouse had begun casting its bright ray in a ponderous rhythm, highlighting spots on the hills and passing right over their window.

Weariness was catching up with him, his stomach growling with hunger. He had not had a cigarette in ages and wanted one badly now. It would have to wait though, all of it, for a while.

"Naomi, listen to me. If I had remembered, if I hadn't been such a stupid, self-centered bastard, don't you think it would have gone differently? Do you really believe I'd have left you alone there?"

Deep down he felt the budding fury at what she had told him, the understanding of her shame and fear, but the sense of his own failure was stronger still.

"Do you think I'd have allowed that? Would have allowed them inside our bedroom, to see you like that? Not on my life."

She gazed at him for a long time as if she now saw him clearly. "I'm going to change." Naomi said.

So many questions and so many things to talk about, but when she returned from the loft in a red wool skirt and a cream cashmere sweater, Naomi stopped him with gentle fingers on his lips.

"Not now, Jon. Get some rest. I'll send down some food. You should sleep for a while. You look tired. Anything we say now will become unreasonable, and then maybe we'll get hurt when it isn't necessary. Also, I need to get back to work."

"But tonight, Baby."

The braid was back, but now tied off with a jaunty red ribbon.

"I never want to see you in black again. You looked like a widow. You aren't a widow, and I don't plan to make you one for a long, long time."

She made him promise to return to his room, eat something, and relax, and please, no smoking in the rooms, he would have to go out on the deck for that. This made her look at him critically. "You are going to need other clothes. So senseless, Jon, a silk shirt and that thin jacket? Didn't you think?"

"No."

Naomi had been on the point of leaving, but this made her turn around again.

"One question, Jon, before I go. What did you expect to find here? I mean, you just drop everything and come here—what was your plan?"

"There was no plan. I'll do what I have to do to get you back. I'll do it. That's all."

THE MESS SHE had made when she dropped the tray had been cleared. Solveigh was back by the desk talking to some guests. In the dining room, Christi and Sven were busy setting the tables, sadly not with the new plates she had been so proud of when she had unpacked them only this morning, fresh from the factory in England.

"Do you know at all what you're doing?" Solveigh rounded on Naomi. "Don't you know who that is? Why did you put him in Joshua's old room? The suite is free, and you hole him up down there? And what is someone like him doing here anyway, and in the deep of winter? You can't leave him there, the impression he will get! Why is he all on his own, I ask you? Those people never travel on their own!"

Naomi busied herself with the computer until Solveigh ran out of breath and questions.

"You changed your clothes, and you were gone for nearly two hours. What's going on, Naomi?" She was a pretty Scandinavian girl, with frizzy golden hair, a complexion like a porcelain doll, rosebud mouth, and blue eyes like the summer sky. Her hourglass figure was the perfect first sight for anyone entering the lobby.

"I was tired, I took a nap."

"And then you change out of your work dress, why? In all our years together I've never seen you in private clothes during your shift."

"Spilled coffee on it." Naomi tried to turn away, but Solveigh stepped in her path.

"How many of those do you have? Three, four? All of them, you spilled coffee on all of your dresses? Come on, there's something fishy going on here."

Naomi went around her and into the kitchen, letting the swinging doors close rudely behind her, but Solveigh followed her. "And why did you drop those plates? We've been waiting for them for months, and you were all excited when they were finally delivered this morning, so what made you drop them?"

Andrea stopped chopping carrots to hand them muffins and coffee and listened to Solveigh's interrogation with raised eyebrows.

"Cook a steak, Andrea," she ordered, "Medium, with fried potatoes and mushrooms. A really nice one with bread and butter, please. A slice of apple pie, and vanilla sauce. Don't forget the coffee, and have it taken to Joshua's old room. Do it right away, our guest wants to rest after his long flight."

That silenced Solveigh for the moment.

"You're so going to tell," she said finally. "I'm going to make you. Anyway, he can't stay down there forever. At some point he'll show up, and then I'll just ask him what he wants here in this godforsaken corner of the world."

"Do that, Solveigh." She heard Solveigh gasp at her calm offer and felt a surge of elation at having shut her up so neatly for once.

Naomi, with little to do at this time of day, rested her elbow on the desk and stared out into the darkness and the curtain of snow.

It had only been one kiss after all, on that summer afternoon all those years ago.

She had left the hotel terrace with him when he offered the stroll, and followed him along the tree-shaded promenade on the shore of Lake Leman. They walked past the wooden pier with the paddle boats and the ice cream vendor, the bells on the sides of his cart ringing out their merry signal to the children down by the swings on the narrow stretch of lawn. The fountain's spray had cast a rainbow over the water as it danced in the breeze from the mountains.

They had talked about little things, like the breakfast he had eaten, and how different it had been compared to what he was used to, especially the French coffee. How he had expected to be served a bar of chocolate, but there had only been croissants and jam.

She had laughed at him and explained that breakfast was not such a big deal, but lunch was generally nice, and then he could always have his chocolate for dessert. That had been the moment when he had taken her in his arms.

That kiss had changed everything for her. He had been so careful, shy even, barely touching her lips at first. When she did not pull away, he had brushed his tongue over her teeth until she opened up to him.

Jon had not let go of her hand on their way back. There had been little talk, not even when they returned to the hotel where Sal had been waiting impatiently. Without resistance, she had followed Jon onto the bus. The members of his band had been there, a loud, high-spirited group commenting on the sights they passed as they went through the city. One of them had his guitar out and played snatches of melodies and crazy riffs. The girls in the back row chatted about their shopping trip earlier in the day, someone else had covered his head with a towel and reclined in his seat, his hands folded over his chest, his long legs stretched out into the aisle.

"What am I supposed to do with you now?" Jon had asked. "I can't let you go. I'm afraid you will vanish and I'd have to spend days searching for you, and I can't because I have to go on to Paris from here. You have to promise not to run off."

He took her up on the stage and ordered the man sitting at the piano to watch her and to not let her leave at all costs. Then he picked up the microphone to sing his songs to the empty, sun-drenched space.

"He made you sit up here?" Sean had begun playing the next song while talking.

"Does he do this often? Bring girls onstage?"

He had laughed out loud at that. "No, never."

"Are there many girls?" A stupid and unnecessary question, but it had popped out before she could hold it back. Sean had pointed toward Jon, his tall form moving with the rhythm of the percussion.

"What do you think? Look at him!" He patted her shoulder in a friendly manner just as Jon turned to look for her.

"Don't touch, Sean," he called. It came out rather imperiously. "Don't touch what's mine."

Sean's laugh had changed into an amused grin. "Oh, so that's how it is. Alright then."

This had been a little too much for her.

Sal, sitting in the first row, waved to her and she clambered over the edge of the stage to join him.

"Tell me about yourself!" he shouted over the music as he handed her a can of cold Coke.

There was not much to tell, Naomi replied, but then painted the picture of her life for him, of skiing trips to the mountains in winter and balls at the yachting club on summer nights, sailing on the lake on cool mornings with friends. And yes, she lived with her parents right here, actually on the lakeshore not too far from their hotel, in an apartment that looked out over the water. Jon broke off the sound check a short time later after a rather tart discussion with his musicians.

"Oh my," Sal commented acidicly as he rose from his seat and brushed off his pants, "Look at him. All wound up because you're sitting here with me and chatting away as if he wasn't there anymore. I'm going to find something to do before he rips me apart, the jealous bastard. Farewell, lovely one." And he walked off; whistling the same tune Jon had sung only moments before, only coming from him, it sounded slightly off-key.

JON SHIVERED AS he stared out into the early darkness in a mixture of wonder and awe. He was cold, even with hot food in his stomach and the quilt pulled up to his chin. The bed was awkwardly narrow; in fact, it was so frugal that lying on his back, there was barely room for his arms. He turned onto his side to watch the beacon of the lighthouse. From upstairs he could hear the muted sound of people talking and laughing, occasionally a chair scraping and footsteps, some heavier than others in sturdy boots, crossing right above his head.

"Nothing," she had said, as easily as that. He had done nothing to send her away; it had not been his fault. She had kissed him and let him hold her to prove it—not quite long enough for his taste, but it was a start.

Jon, trying to change his position without falling out of the bed, marveled at the ease with which she had accepted him back, as if she had expected this to happen someday, or had even been waiting for it. He was certain now that he had done the right thing in coming here without thinking about it. Maybe, just maybe, there was nothing here that could be treated rationally at all, just like all those years ago.

The blue light of his cell phone blinked from where it lay on the bedside table. He considered ignoring it, but Sal would keep calling him every fifteen minutes until he finally gave in.

"Hey," he heard his manager's voice as if he were standing next to him. "Where are you, man?"

"In bed, Sal." Jon cursed himself immediately for it.

"Alone?"

Yes, that had been the reaction he had expected.

"Alone, Sal. It's afternoon here. I'm just resting. That was a long, mean flight. And the last stretch, in that little plane, flying through a storm, was no fun at all."

He could hear Sal's breathing on the other end, then a circumspect clearing of his throat. "You really did it, Jon? You're not kidding me, are you? What did she say? What does she look like?"

"Much the same, really."

And it was true, not wishful thinking at all, as if time had passed her by while she was hidden away in this tranquil place.

"What did she say when you walked in? Come on, Jon."

There was no way he was going to talk about this with anyone, not even Sal.

"I'll call you, Sal. When I'm ready, I'll call you. Don't worry about me, and don't call me. Not for anything at all, you hear me? I'll fire you instantly if you do."

He hung up before Sal could ask more questions.

Squirming again on the bed, it came to him that this had been his son's room, and was probably the same bed he had slept in, maybe even the same quilt he had used. He sniffed it carefully, but there was only the clean smell of detergent, which made him feel like a pathetic fool again.

Jon wondered where the boy was; his *former* room, Naomi had said. That meant he didn't live here anymore, which was another explanation he wanted very badly. Twisted into an awkward bundle, the covers tangled around his legs, he fell into an uneasy sleep.

FOR A MOMENT, just before she entered her apartment, Naomi had the eerie feeling she had only been deeply immersed in one of her recurring daydreams which would bring Jon to her, let him unravel the veil of obscurity she had woven so tightly around herself. But then she opened the door and saw that indeed her life had changed.

His shoes still stood under the piano bench where he had taken them off at her demand, the damp leather jacket lay over a chair, her desk light was turned on, and her lyrics sheets were spread out, half of them on the piano, the other half over the dining table. On many he had scribbled comments or added a few lines, finishing with a quick stroke where she had given up, changing a sequence where the rhythm was awkward, a word where the rhyme did not work. She read some of his notes while she gathered the scattered papers, deeply moved by his fast insight into her moods and intentions and the implicit manner in which he had taken possession of her work. On a couple of sheets, he had even drawn a few quick staff lines and sketches of tunes, hearing the melodies in her verses as he read them.

It had been like this before.

Behind her on the shelf, together with all the other recordings he had put out during the past twenty years, was the one they had made together: the only album with a rose cover, and all of the songs on it had her words in them.

She showered and changed into her prettiest nightgown and made some tea before she settled down on the couch.

He would come, and reclaim her. Aside from locking him out, there was precious little she could do to prevent it. She had made sure the door was unlocked. All he had to do was walk in.

She felt a little like a bride waiting for her new husband, excited, expectant, fearful. This one night, she promised herself, she would not think about the future nor dwell on the past.

Her eyes on Jon's shoes, Naomi drifted off.

IT SEEMED TO be dark most of the time, Jon noted when he woke to the sound of waves slapping against the deck. He had forgotten to reset his watch and cell phone, and there was no clock in the room.

In the hallway, silence greeted him. The lobby, which he could partially see from where he stood, was only sparingly lit, and there were no sounds at all, which told him it had to be night.

Her door was unlocked, and seeing her asleep on the couch, her face resting on her hand, Jon knew he would not give up this fight, no matter how long it took or how hard it would be.

"That bed," he said softly when Naomi opened her eyes to look at him, "It's very hard and narrow, Baby. Will you let me sleep in yours tonight?"

The sheets were fresh, even new, pristine and white, the covers turned down, the pillows in lace covers and flower-scented. On the small night table stood a bottle of red wine with two glasses and a bouquet of nodding roses. She had wanted this too, he understood.

Very gently he slipped the straps from her shoulders and let her nightgown drop to the floor where it pooled in folds of ivory satin.

He undressed, letting her watch, watching her in turn as her eyes traveled from his face to his chest, then deeper. He had passed forty a few years ago, but he was in good shape, slim and well-muscled, nothing to be ashamed about in that department.

She allowed him do as he wished, spread her hair on the pillow, kiss her ever so gently, brush his fingertips down the hollow of her throat.

"I'll make it real now, Baby," he said. "Don't be afraid, my love. I've dreamed of this moment for so long. Don't be afraid."

As if it were an act of prayer, he unfolded her limbs, and her body welcomed him, arching against him in a sudden, hot surge of passion. Jon caught her, sensing her rising need, his movements gentle and slow, and whispered all those words to her he had wanted to say through all the years, her breathless sighs the loveliest sound he could imagine, her hands on his skin the touch he had missed more than he had even known, and the look in her eyes the sweet surrender he craved.

"Yes, Baby," he breathed. "You and me. Always was, and has to be, forever." Here it was, the deep truth he had always, even in his darkest moments, held on to, the proof he had been right.

They lay together for a long time afterward, their limbs entangled, her hair wrapped around them, lips touching, skin to skin, overwhelmed by the intimacy they had regained.

"You know we are absolutely insane. We should not be falling into each other's arms like this. It can't last. I'm afraid it won't last. I will wake up and find it was just another one of those dreams in which you come to me and which always leave me hot and bothered and—" His deep kiss silenced her and took her breath away.

"I'll make you as hot and bothered as you can take, any time you want, my love," he promised darkly. "Just say the word and turn down the sheets. Or, at the least, clear the table."

Desire welled up in her again, he could feel it. His mouth close to her ear, he asked, "I take it you are thinking of that table at the studio in LA?" and caught her in a wild embrace when she gasped.

NAOMI WOKE, WARM and cozy, wrapped in the quilt by loving hands, sunlight on her face, the scent of coffee in the air. From below she heard the soft tinkle of the piano. Still drowsy, she listened to the experimental notes, the short phrases of melody, to Jon as he mumbled to himself and the soft bubbling of the coffee maker. She felt deliciously languid, unwilling to rise from her soft cocoon, so she lay and dozed, her head buried deep in the pillow, until she had to admit the day had started and the hotel staff would probably be in upheaval if she did not show up at some point. Lazily she stretched, savoring the mild ache in her muscles, wrapping the sheet around herself before heading down the stairs.

Halfway down, she stopped. He had not noticed her yet, bent as he was over the piano keys, intent on what he was doing.

It looked so right to see him sitting there, in jeans and an unbuttoned shirt, barefoot, with glasses, please God, scribbling on the paper in front of him with one hand while playing with the other.

Composing, creating, singing softly to himself.

Jon looked up at her, a smile spreading on his face. "Ah, this is surely how a bride should look after her wedding night. You are lovely. That is the most becoming dress I can imagine. Come here."

He pulled her onto his lap and handed her the coffee mug from which he had been drinking.

"I found this," he said, tapping the piece of paper in front of him. "How do you do it? Does it just pour out of you? It's incredible."

His hands went down to the piano keys. "I don't even need to think, the music is right there in your words. It feels a little like stealing from you. Listen."

A slow, measured melody emerged with his playing. "I can hear the strings and the harp right here, then, for the second verse, a cello and horns. It should be airy and a little transcendent, there's this fairy touch to it. Oh, and here...oh yes."

For an instant he drifted away from her and his surroundings, caught up in the music he alone was hearing, letting the tune flow through him. She shifted, and the sheet parted, revealing a length of leg. His gaze dropped to her naked thigh, his hand following a little slower.

"And what are you trying to do, distracting me like that? Really, Naomi, here, on the piano? You are one shameless girl."

"Hot and bothered again? You'll have to deal with it on your own Jon. I need to get to work. But first I want a shower. Alone."

He watched her walk away, dropping the sheet halfway to the bathroom. When she returned she was dressed in a smart cream-colored business suit, her hair done up and in high heels, a delicate string of pearls around her throat. She leaned over to kiss him.

"Don't look at me like that. I have a business meeting this morning. I do own more clothes than that black dress and a sheet."

For a long time after she left, Jon found it difficult to concentrate.

THEY WERE TRYING to find a new pastry chef, and had four interviews scheduled for this morning. Naomi sat with Solveigh and Andrea, trying to keep her mind on the task at hand.

"I want to know what you are up to," Solveigh murmured as the third applicant left. "And don't even dream of disappearing like that again. You are so telling."

Naomi smiled vaguely at her. "He's Joshua's father," she whispered.

Solveigh spilled her coffee.

It was entertaining to watch her after this revelation. She could not go on asking because the door had opened again as the last candidate entered the room.

They cornered her in the kitchen.

Solveigh was scandalized. "You are joking, of course."

"Have I ever lied to you?"

"Naomi, do you know who that is? You should not be joking." Solveigh tried hard to maintain her composure.

Naomi was enjoying herself. "He's a musician. A very, very good musician, true, but in the end, only that. And I'm not lying. "

"What are you talking about?" Andrea was nearly shrieking by now. "What's going on here?"

Solveigh solemnly repeated what Naomi had told her.

"Only a musician?" Andrea cried, "Are you out of your mind? Don't you know he fills concert halls with twenty-thousand people? Do you know how many women out there would die just to meet him? And you call him a *musician?*"

Naomi took a muffin from the tray behind her and bit into it. "It's what he does. I've seen him at it only this morning. And I've been to his concerts. They are very nice."

"So how come…" Solveigh pushed, and she told them her tale at last, though she left out the gruesome details of the drug bust on that ill-fated day so long ago. As it was, the story was fascinating enough for them. They sat for quite a while, drinking coffee, nibbling tea cakes, and talking about the music star Naomi was hiding in her apartment.

"But how will this go, Naomi?" Solveigh said. "He walks in here out of the blue, and you let him? You let him push aside your life like that? Have you thought what Joshua will say if he shows up now and wants to play father?"

These were words she did not want to hear. She got up and brushed crumbs from her skirt. "Jon will be here for a while. I guess for a quite a while."

I REMEMBER WHEN that picture was taken." Jon was sitting on the couch, his feet up on the coffee table, papers all around him. Naomi glanced at the photo.

What a wonderful estate. A wilderness with dark, cool arbors and winding paths leading to the beach, and a lone stone bench, standing in the shadow of some tall jasmine bushes. They had often sat there on balmy California nights, listening to the far-off sounds of life.

"You saved me from myself that day," he said. "You saved me just by sitting with me and touching my hand. I was ready to give up. You were the only real thing in my life, the only thing that had any true meaning. And I wasted it. In the end, when it mattered, I didn't keep you safe. I left you all alone. I failed you."

Naomi was wordless, stunned.

"You were always there for me. I should have asked you to marry me, and I didn't. It never occurred to me, even though I loved you more than anything. This is a shameful, terrible thing to admit. What happened was my fault." He was still looking at the photograph. "It never crossed my mind you could have been lonely or unhappy. I failed you." At last he looked at her. "I'm trying so hard to find the right words to say to you. I've been sitting here watching the ships come and go. Reading your lyrics—I haven't made it through even half of them—they're all so sad and broken-hearted. They've shown me how much I hurt you. I'm so stupid, Naomi. After you left I wondered and wondered why you had gone away. I just couldn't figure it out. How can you ever forgive me for all that wasted time?"

"You are here," she said. "What more is there to say or do? You came as soon as you knew where to find me. After all, I was the one who ran away. Who knows, we might have been divorced by now. Driven apart after a bitter struggle, used up by your fame and the crazy life we would have been living. You, always surrounded by adoring females, trying to resist the temptation, and me, laboring to find myself in the turmoil that surrounds you, failing. And Joshua? Unraveled by life in Los Angeles and by us. All of us, a psychiatrist's dream."

"But here we are." Jon pulled her into a tight embrace. "Not divorced. Not tired and disgusted with each other, but full of sorrow for what we think we lost. It seems to me, put like that, we are better off this way. At least we have a future to look forward to."

"We also have a past. We have Joshua. We have the time we spent together, that's not wasted. And you came, and we've just spent the most glorious night together." Fear fluttered in her stomach like a moth. "Or is this your way of telling me that you're leaving, Jon?"

His kiss was tender and lingering. "No, my love. It's my way of telling you that even in the light of day I've made up my mind. I'm not letting go of you ever again."

His hands moved on her back, cradling her firmly against him.

"I'm going to ask you to marry me, Naomi. Not today, not yet, I don't want you to think I'm acting on an impulse or pushing you. But I will, soon. This needs to be forever. Everything else will work out somehow. But this, you, I'm not letting go."

"I won't live in Los Angeles again. Ever."

Jon nodded, gazing at their surroundings, as he had done all morning. "Then I'll stay here. I can write music here at your piano just as well as anywhere else, and at least I'll have the certainty that you'll come to me when your job upstairs is done. It's that easy, Baby."

He waved his hand at the space around them. "I've been going through your work and messed up the place. You'll have to live with that from now on. I'm going to invade you, good and proper."

His eyes sparkled at the double meaning and Naomi drew a deep breath, steadying herself, so intense was her longing.

She changed into her regular work clothes and returned to find him bent over her lyrics once more, murmuring, humming, tapping a rhythm with a pencil, totally oblivious to the spectacle of the mail ship right outside the window. It passed so close to the deck he might have merely stretched out his hand to touch it, but he did not seem to notice. She had been wrong.

"You know, the weirdest things happen in this place. I've been watching the bay while I was reading your stuff." He indicated the small pier that lay around the corner from the hotel. "There's this depot or storage thing over there, with the parking lot in front, and all the time cars drive up, stop for a little while with their motors running, and then turn around and leave again. I can't figure out what they're doing."

"Those are the women who wait for their men to return." His observation moved her inexplicably. "They are fishermen's wives. The men are gone for weeks on end, and after a while, when they are expected back, the wives drive by to look for them. There's always the great fear they might not return. So…" It seemed so poignant suddenly, even though she had been witnessing it for years. "So they wait and hope and get into their cars and come here."

He watched her patiently.

"They are afraid as they drive through town, because they'll only find out if their husbands are safe when the boat returns. Everyone who watches them go by knows what they are doing, and yet no one talks to them. It's just so hard. While the boats are at sea, they listen to every weather report. When there's a storm warning, the wives meet in a café down by the fishing sheds, full of fear…"

There were goose bumps on his arms. He had missed this almost as terribly as their love. This was Naomi, writing, even though she did not know it, the story unfolding as she told it, and through her telling the melody grew in him, following the rhythm of her words.

She drew a deep breath. "It's just the way life is here. It's a hard life."

Lyrical, even when she was only explaining daily life. This was the thing that had first caught his attention. It was just the way she put things, speaking directly to him, hitting a nerve or touching the pulse of music that was always in him.

Or, he thought, maybe the two could not even be separated. Maybe it was this web they wove again and again, creating a time and place made of love, music, and poetry. It was a spark of insight; something he felt should not be seen or understood except in rare, transcendent moments like this one.

The ship had begun its stately, spectacular turning maneuver in the narrow harbor basin, its shadow casting a gloom on the room.

Naomi glanced toward it. "Let's go up for lunch. Andrea will burst if we don't show up. Those girls are nearly out of their minds with curiosity about you."

"TELL ME," SHE asked over the broiled cod, "How much did you pay for your solitary flight across the Atlantic?"

He shrugged. "No more than it was worth."

The wine was excellent, the service unobtrusive, the restaurant a very pleasant, restrained place. All in all, this hotel was a surprise, a lesson in good taste and restfulness. Jon liked it.

"I wasn't going to miss one hour more than I absolutely had to. I wasn't going to miss last night for anything." He took her hand, and she did not pull back.

On their way back to her apartment, he laid his hand on her waist. "I can hardly wait to pluck those silly ribbons from your tight little bodice. What happens once they come off?"

To his disappointment her dress did not fall from her when he loosened the lacing, and he watched as she very unromantically unzipped it from the back, laughing at him.

They lay on the bed, talking for a while in hushed voices as the sinking sun pouring in through the windows, touching each other's bodies with gentle fingertips, rediscovering their closeness. He made love to her in a slow, leisurely way, savoring her sighs and the way her body moved against his.

"I love to make love to you," Jon said afterward. "You have a way of giving yourself over so completely, it's so enticing and sensual, but it's also such a deep expression of trust. I love to see your hair spill all over the pillow, the way you say my name, the way you touch me. I love you. That's all, really. Always have."

She lay beside him and looked at him with large, luminous eyes.

"The boy," Jon began, and here it was, the subject they had both avoided so carefully.

"Yes."

"Where is he, Naomi? Why isn't he here with you?"

He was in Oxford, Naomi said, he had been admitted to a special education program for highly talented young musicians. She went to see him whenever she could, but he was doing fine. In fact, he was doing exceedingly well.

"He's your son, Jon. Music is in his blood. Leaving you was the most terrible thing that ever happened to me. But coming here, running this hotel, has given me such a peaceful life. Joshua grew up here. There was time, and space, to write and think. When Joshua was very small, he used to sing along when I played your music. He started on the piano when he was four, and he loved his lessons. I could hardly tear him away from the stupid thing." She gave him such a sweet smile that his heart turned over. "I sometimes imagined it was you as a small boy, he was so intense in his music. When he was ten he wanted to learn to play the guitar too. If it hadn't been such a joy to watch, it would have broken me."

He saw the brief hesitation.

"I nearly gave in, then. I could see how much you would have loved to know him. To have him around." She drew another deep breath. "When he was twelve I sent him to school in Geneva. It was very, very hard, but there was nothing more I could give him here. He needed to go to a school that specialized in music education, and he was with my parents. He had his first audition when he was thirteen, and last year he got the scholarship offer from Oxford. He's a real prodigy, you see. I'm insanely proud of him."

"As you should be, as I am, too. I can hardly wait to meet him. We'll have to go to England soon. But not yet. First, it's about you and me. When we go to see Joshua I want it to be us, together, not just father and mother, but truly us. I told you before, I want you back. I mean it, Naomi."

Her shoulders tensed. He knew he was pushing her again, but he could not help himself. Those words he needed to hear could not come soon enough for him. Outside, a large sailboat slowly glided like a huge white swan on its way to the open sea. The unfurling lengths of sail made snapping sounds in the wind. Happy shouts could be heard from the deck, and Jon, sitting up from his comfortable position, marveled at the hardiness of those sailors going out in the deep of winter.

Naomi did not reply.

In a lighter tone, Jon asked, "So what did Joshua say when you told him? What do you think he will say when we meet?"

"Oh, he's seen you. We were at your concert in London. We had really good seats. Third row, right in the center. You looked down often enough."

It took a long while to digest this. He had not seen her, but he felt as if he should have sensed her closeness, even amid the many thousands of others.

"And what did Joshua say?"

There was laughter in her eyes. "He said you were a chick's man and no self-respecting teenager should be forced to listen to you. He thought your shirt was disgusting. I didn't think it was that hot, either. And the tickets were incredibly expensive. You should be ashamed of yourself. Sean was good, though. I love his bone-dry rendition of *The River*. It's really sexy. And he looks sexy playing it."

"You little beast. You were truly there and never tried to see me? You were just sitting there, watching me bawl out my heart, and never did anything? And then you talk to me about how sexy Sean is? I'll fire him immediately!"

THE SUN HAD long set behind the mountains by the time they picked up their conversation again.

"It was so unreal, seeing you up there. You were a stranger, yet so very familiar. I had the memory of you deep in my heart, but I never thought there would be a second chance for us."

At last he could let go. "I longed for you all the time." Her head rested on his chest, her hair tickling his throat. "When you walked into my life that day in Geneva, everything seemed to fall into place for me. It all made sense suddenly, the struggle to express myself, I finally knew why it was like that for me. You gave a meaning to it all, a sense of connection. You gave sincerity to my music. There was never any room for shallowness with you."

She kissed him softly on the corner of his mouth. "The shirts were the worst. I hated those shirts."

6

THEY ARRANGED THEIR new life in Naomi's corner apartment as if it were a slow dance, watching the ships and the wharf life, waiting for the arrival of the mail ship every other day. Jon still counted the cars that came and went to the depot, fascinated by their sad regularity, and started to watch for the fishing boats to return as well. The weather took a turn for the worse, bringing higher temperatures and rain, accompanied by ugly winds from the sea and a dark, brooding sky that hung low over the bay, blurring the landscape into bizarre images. But much more than the snow that had come before, it drove Jon to work. He had shifted the baby grand so he could look toward the ocean while he composed, his back to the room, and he spent hours sitting there, deep in thought. This cold, stark atmosphere fascinated him. It seemed to express the feelings in Naomi's lyrics so much better than the pristine snow had done.

They spent their days in a simple pattern that laid itself around his shoulders like a fine, warm blanket, giving him space to find his inner harmony again, making it a delight to compose tunes to go with Naomi's words.

Naomi reclined on the couch, most often wrapped in a quilt, her laptop on her knees, her thoughts far away, her eyes sometimes looking right through him, which amused him. Jon marveled at the repose in her, the simple acceptance of him, no discussion, no turmoil, no questions, as if she had been waiting for him all her life, ready to take him back.

For a brief time, they did not talk about it, but lived only in the present and celebrated every moment.

Solveigh never called. They were left alone, a fact he noted with gratitude. Naomi checked on the hotel routine daily but was sent away again with the advice to enjoy herself as long as it lasted.

"You're walking in a dream, Naomi," Solveigh said at one point. "You should know it will not last. He will return to his old life, he has to, and you will break. That's not just any man you're hiding down there. He belongs to the world. Be careful."

Naomi went away with a shrug.

THEY WENT TO Bergen. The colorful houses around the harbor seemed to gleam in the early morning light, even the fish market looked scrubbed and new. Jon, who had been all over the world, had very rarely taken the time to actually see the places. Here, he had plenty of time to enjoy the atmosphere of a foreign country. They strolled through the town, hand in hand. Naomi showed him the old wooden houses along the waterfront and the few elegant shops Bergen had to offer where he bought more clothes and everything else he needed.

He was hesitant at first, walking among the many tourists, but they were not approached which surprised, and then irritated him a little until he began to enjoy the freedom of being in the open without security or camera flashes going off in his face.

At the market Naomi made him eat a fish burger, which she called *fiske boller*, and boiled shrimp directly from the vat. No one took notice of them. They enjoyed total privacy sitting on the wooden bench beside the stall, their fingers greasy, the table littered with prawn shells. It was such a rare luxury for him, he reveled in it despite the uncomfortable wind blowing over the cobbled plaza.

On their flight back, Jon said: "Next week we'll go to England. I think it's time. We need to make this whole now. We'll spend a couple of days in London, on our own, and then we'll go see Joshua."

She nodded silently.

"Did he truly call me a chick's man? What's that supposed to mean, anyway?"

Naomi bit her lip as she thought of a fitting reply. "It was so funny. I made Joshua come down from school to go with me, and he was really bitter about it. He asked all the time if it truly had to be you, and if I wanted to go to a pop concert could it please at least be Springsteen or the Stones. Or even better, wait for the Proms."

Jon, a drink in his hand, gazed at her without interrupting.

She stopped briefly to look at him, at the wonder of seeing him before her.

"I had taken him to Claridge's for tea, and he was so indignant he forgot about the cakes in front of him. I was much too nervous to eat. I was going to see you."

She could not explain even to herself why all of a sudden she had been so driven to see Jon in a concert. He had been around a number of times before, traveling through Britain and Europe on his tours, but here it was: she wanted to see him.

They had all been there, right before her. The band had walked on, taking their places, adjusting their instruments; Jones and Sean, chatting, had come close to the edge of the stage to sort out some cables but had not taken notice of the audience. Then they had started their intro and Jon walked on.

It had been almost too much to bear. Joshua had squirmed in his seat. But Jon had been wonderful, powerful, radiating a very masculine sensuality, sure of what he was doing, at one with his music, in perfect harmony with his musicians. Then, her own words, returned to her. It had become very quiet in the great hall, Jon standing close to the piano while Sean played to him.

"Come to my secret garden, my love, in the middle of the night..." His eyes closed, singing softly, almost painfully, following Sean's haunting melody. He had seemed so lost in the song, the thousands of watchers forgotten, as if he were reliving special moments, as if he were all alone up there. The intensity had been nearly too much.

She had cried, mourning what she had given up. It had felt like a leave-taking, a final salute, and it had broken the last shards of her heart.

After the concert, she had bought the tour-book and a photograph, accompanied by Joshua's acerbic comments. She had been a little embarrassed at doing such a thing, but she felt she needed something to keep this night real for her when she was home again.

So when on his birthday he had asked her again about his father, she had told him. Joshua had come to Halmar for the weekend. They were sitting on the couch with tea and almond cake. He was sixteen, and she knew he had a right to know. Of course he did not believe her.

"Wow, Mom, how? Was I an accident? Does he even know?" he had asked after a few minutes of thoughtful silence.

It was then that she had lied and said it had been a one-night thing after a concert. And no, he did not know and she did not want him to. She wanted him to let it rest. Which he had not done, obviously.

"He said the ladies all wanted to get laid by you."

Jon blinked at her. "Such insight from a child." He paused. "Anyway, if Joshua is that good, you should have sent him to Juilliard. They have great programs for young students, and it's the best music school in the world." Jon was taking the guitar he had bought in Bergen out of its case. The instrument pleased him, it was far better than he had expected to find here.

There was no answer from Naomi. She seemed preoccupied with what she was doing, and so he went to her, only to find her staring at the package of pasta in her hand.

"If I had known, Baby, he could have lived with my family, my mother, and gone there. He still can! He should, in fact. But why didn't you send him to Juilliard, Naomi?"

Again, the still withdrawal he hated so much, and the tightening of her shoulders that was like a rejection of him. She tried to move away, but Jon didn't let her. "Oh no, you don't. We're going to talk about it, just as we are going to talk about everything else. We've skipped around all these issues so carefully, but at some point we need to unpack them. No more secrets, no more hiding. If we are going to make this last, we need honesty, and trust. So tell me why my suggestion makes you turn away from me again."

It took her a while to reply, and when she finally did her words came out in a dry, clipped manner. "I manage this hotel, Jon. And I get a salary that makes it possible for me to send Joshua to Oxford. It's hard, but I manage. I couldn't afford Juilliard.'"

His hand dropped from her arm. Jon took a deep, mortified breath, at a loss for words. But, as was the way with her, once she had overcome the initial hesitation, she went on more easily.

"It's my responsibility. It was my choice to let him go to Oxford. It works well enough." And, with a glint in her eyes, "There is enough left for me to fly to London once in a while to see my favorite singer, even though his ticket prices are outrageous and his taste in shirts is atrocious."

"Well enough," he repeated slowly. "I'm sorry, Naomi. I truly am sorry for the pain I caused you. You should not have been alone. We should have been together. I don't believe that divorce crap you said the other night. I know we would never have parted."

"No," she interrupted him, caressing his face, "no. Don't fuss. It doesn't matter. Everything is fine now. Please, Jon. Don't be sorry for the past. If I can get over that drug bust, you should put away the guilt for the lost time too." Then, with hesitation creeping into her voice, "It *is* fine, isn't it? Because, really, after seeing you buy this guitar…" He had begun to kiss her, barely touching her lips, while she was trying to speak. "And talking to you about that concert, now I think I would like to see the guys again. I miss Sean."

Jon moved closer, knocking her into the counter. "You'll have to stop this Sean talk. It really drives me mad. What is it about Sean, anyway? He has a beard."

"Oh, but it's a very neat, trimmed beard. And I told you, the way he hits the piano keys is really exciting." She giggled softly when he lifted her onto the table, the dire mood of just moments ago broken.

"Well, I can do that, too. I'm not that bad at the piano myself. Don't go on about Sean, I'll have to take some really drastic measures to get him out of your head otherwise. It's my fault, I should never have let you meet him."

She laid her arms around his neck to return his kiss.

"You worry too much, Jon." she whispered against his mouth, sweetly, enticingly.

Very reluctantly he let her go again when she pushed against him, realizing how deftly she had turned him away from the subject that really mattered by teasing him about Sean again.

"We will have to talk about money and all the other stuff soon. You know you and Joshua are my responsibility, and I want you to be, very much. So we'll ask him if he wants to change schools."

She nodded silently.

A few melodious sounds escaped the strings as he laid the instrument back in its case. "If he would like to go to Juilliard, we could get an apartment in Manhattan. Would you like an apartment in Manhattan, Baby? Maybe one with a view of the Met?"

There was no reply, so he turned. "Naomi?"

She was still sitting on the table, fiddling with her braid, absentmindedly watching the cars on the pier. "You need a studio. I'm thinking we could convert some of the rooms."

Yes, that too. It almost seemed to him as if they were moving toward building a new reality. Abruptly, he rose and left the room to see Solveigh. It was time to set things in motion. He was gone nearly two hours.

7

JON WALKED INTO his room when he returned from his talk with Solveigh.

The place looked sadly neglected. They were in Naomi's apartment most of the time, sharing that space in complete harmony, never getting in each other's way or feeling crowded. He relished that and saw it as a sign that they could indeed make a life together. It seemed to him as if all the things that might have kept them apart had been pared away.

Jon wondered, as he searched for his cell phone, how much of that was a result of them being here in this isolated place, where the outside world rarely intruded or diverted them from their own, small existence?

"Hey." Sal's voice sounded raspy. "Do you know what time it is here? And it's a Saturday, Jon."

He had forgotten and this filled him with satisfaction. California seemed like a different dimension.

"Sal," Jon said, going out to the deck for a cigarette. "I need you to do some things for me. Listen up!"

"Do you know," Sal interrupted, "that hotel your lovely lady manages belongs to her family?"

Jon stopped in mid-breath. He hadn't of course, and she had not mentioned it once. More secrets. How well she kept those until he stumbled on them.

"Yes, whatever," was the best he could come up with, which earned him a derisive laugh from Sal.

"Yeah, you didn't know. I bet you didn't find the time to talk about a lot, right? Hey, you didn't need to go all the way to Norway for that, Jon."

Jon could hear the hissing noise of a coffee maker and the soft murmur of a female voice in the background. He was beginning to feel the cold even though he was wearing one of the sweaters he had bought in Bergen, a colorful, hand-knitted thing with a high collar and sleeves that were slightly too long. Sal would have a laughing fit if he ever saw him in it, not to mention the thick woolen socks he'd become so fond of.

"Shut up, Sal. Just do as I ask, and do it quickly."

"Yes, my Master, so I shall. As always. Say hello to Naomi, will you?" A brief pause, then: "How is she doing, Jon? How does she cope with you being there?"

Just fine, Jon wanted to reply, but didn't. Just fine, and she loves me. She's mine again, and this time she will be forever. But he did not say it because he knew Sal would have another biting reply that he did not want to hear.

BEING WHO HE was and doing things the way he was used to doing them meant they flew on a private plane to London. At the airport, a limousine and driver were waiting for them.

Jon shrugged her dubious look away. "Do you really expect me to do this driving-on-the-left-side-of-the-road thing?" was all he said.

It was a lot warmer in London than it had been in Halmar, and a promise of spring was in the air. The first touches of green on some of the trees broke the monotony of a city in winter, and gardeners were busy planting blooming shrubs in neat rows along the paths in the hotel garden.

"I look like a Norwegian farmer," Jon said as they walked through the lofty hall with the marble columns and dark green carpeting. "I definitely need city clothes. And you?"

Naomi stopped on the broad stairs leading down to the busy street.

Bustling life greeted them, the noise, movement, and smells of the big city as it launched into its daily rhythm. The traffic just outside the hotel was stalled by a construction site across the road, three red buses had stopped right in front of them with taxis trying to find their way around, drivers shouting and blowing their horns in a futile attempt at movement. If she leaned forward just a little, Naomi could see the grand facade of Harrods and a good stretch of Brompton Road. On the other side was the curve of Knightsbridge and the green wall of Hyde Park. She felt as if she was right in the heart of London.

THE CAR TOOK them the short ride to Bond Street, and Jon dismissed it until further notice.

"I'm going to buy clothes," he stated. "Enough to last me for a while. I just don't feel like having someone pack up my stuff back in LA and send it here. It's kind of nice to start out fresh, don't you think?"

She was not going to spoil these precious, enchanted days by voicing her worries and doubts, so she sat and watched as he ordered the shop girls around, picking out shirts and shoes, a new black leather jacket, and fine cashmere sweaters that looked a lot more natural on him.

There were, on a display right next to her, a couple of purses, and she picked one up, enjoying the touch of the fine leather and the exquisite stitching.

"Hey, Babe."

She had not seen him, absorbed as she was, and returned the thing to its place guiltily, as if he had caught her in an illicit act.

"Is there anything you want? That purse? You want it?"

Naomi shook her head.

"Naomi, don't be ridiculous. If you want that bag, it's yours and you know it. Hell, Baby, anything you want. Please?"

She drew up her shoulders and clamped her hands in her lap. "Later. I want to go to Harrods for some tea and maybe…"

Jon looked at her for a moment. "All right," he said very softly, then went to pay for his things.

Back out on the street he took her hand and began walking. It was a busy time of day, with many people around, strolling, chatting, moving in and out of guarded store entrances. They walked past all the big labels until Jon stopped in front of Tiffany's.

"This is it, then." He turned to face her, right in front of the liveried valet. "Will you marry me? And soon? Will you set a date, right now, no more waiting?" His fingers gripped hers tightly. "Please let me set this right. We should have done this all that time ago."

The valet was trying very hard not to listen, but Jon was oblivious, bent on getting the answer he wanted. She opened her lips for a reply, but nothing came.

"Don't be afraid," Jon urged. "It'll be alright. You know we can't walk away from each other anymore. You know this is the only possible future for us."

Silently she shook her head at him.

"I just can't let you go, Naomi. I don't care where we live or if I never release another song, but I don't want to give you up ever again. You're afraid of living in Los Angeles, I understand that. So we won't go there. But I want you with me. And if you don't want to marry me, fine. I'll just…I'll just hang around."

"Oh, but I do."

It took a moment to register.

"You're so stupid sometimes," Naomi said. "What did you think? You promised it would be okay, so I'm going to take your word for it." And, after a pause, "Anyway, I won't ever get to see Sean again otherwise, right?"

For once he chose to ignore her teasing and repeated his question. "Will you marry me, Naomi? "

"Yes, I will."

"Well then."

She protested, overwhelmed by what he was doing, but he would not listen. "You are my fiancée now," were his words, "and as such you should be wearing my ring. So let's buy you a ring."

They were seated in a discreet niche and served champagne by a black-clad salesman while trays of diamond rings were displayed for them.

She let Jon pick one. "It's your promise to me," was her reason, "so you should be the one to choose."

Afterward, looking at it, she had qualms. But it was his choice, and it looked like the statement he wanted to make. It was a large diamond, the platinum band set with smaller stones all around, a glittering, luxurious thing of incredible beauty.

And even though she had never thought it possible, something changed between them. The moment he put that ring on her finger, so solemnly and slowly, the feeling shifted. There was a sense of closeness, of belonging, and he gave her a look he had never given her before, and with a proprietary pride in his expression, he escorted her through the door.

"SO, WHEN? SET a date, my love."

Back outside, Naomi stood in the cool sunlight, dazed and breathless. Again and again she gazed at her ring. She couldn't think, much less come up with a wedding date.

To give her time, he suggested lunch.

Over cocktails Naomi said tentatively: "But how will it go, Jon? You know you can't just leave your real life like that. It's a pretty dream, but it's not a true option. I can't live in Hollywood, I just can't. I'm not made for that kind of existence, and you can't give it up. You're famous, you're needed—"

"I'm needed." He opened the menu. "A few months ago I turned forty-four. I've given my youth, my creativity, and my love to my career. You, I gave you to my career and my fame and wealth. I have achieved everything, career-wise, anyone could dream of. Hell, I can't walk down a street without being noticed, I have so much money I don't even know how to spend it all. But what's it all worth, I ask you, if I have to do this alone? If there is no one to do it with? Who will love me for the songs I come up with, if it's not the one I want in my life?"

"Everybody loves you, Jon." She swirled the cherry in her drink.

"Yes."

Naomi looked up at him, startled by the bitterness in his voice.

"Everybody loves the star, Naomi. But me? I don't think there are a lot of people who really care about me that much. Sal, he's a good friend, but in the end he loves the money I make for him more. Sean? Well, yes. My mother, and my brother and sister; they see the normal man in me. Or at least I hope so."

He took a sip of his bourbon and lit another cigarette.

"But it's not the kind of love I want, Babe, and you know it. You." He smiled at her. "You have always refused to judge me by who I am when I'm on stage. That day in Geneva, when you walked into that hotel lobby and looked at me, there was nothing of that in your eyes. Truly nothing. And that's why I need you so badly, and why I love you. Because you see me, Jonathan Stone, and not the centerfold from some girl's magazine."

He shrugged, his humor winning against the darker side of his thoughts. "On the other hand, you also refuse my life, my house, the parties and the glamour, which of course is going to turn me into a Norse country-rat with woolen socks and terrible sweaters, but so be it."

"You are such a goof." Naomi sighed. "For you, everything is easy and simple. But it won't be like that, Jon. Your life will reclaim you, and then you will have to decide how far you're prepared to go."

But in the end, it did not matter.

The ring threw its radiant sparks at her, reminding her she had made a promise.

Strolling through Burlington Arcade later, reality caught up with them when a couple of women, standing next to them in front of a shop window, recognized Jon and nearly became hysterical. Graciously he allowed them to take photographs, posing with them and smiling into their cameras while Naomi withdrew into the comfort of a bakery where she watched the women as they hung on his arm and twittered like excited birds.

Her husband. She could hardly wrap her mind around that concept.

Her husband. She wondered how many had passed through his life and bed over the years and how long they had been allowed to stay. She was quite certain a good number of them had been willing to become his wife. Jon, rid of his fans, came to find her, a sardonic grin on his face. "Hiding from the crowd, Baby? You know you don't have to. I'd rather have the world know I'm not up for grabs anymore. Maybe then I'll have some peace."

"You know you won't." The marzipan cupcakes looked inviting, but the chocolate tarts also seemed very luscious.

She had said it so coolly and matter-of-factly that Jon forgot his next words for a moment and just watched as she bought the cupcakes.

Back outside, he took her hand in his, his fingers on her ring. "It's like this, Naomi. You are going to be my wife as soon as I can get you to set a date. If it were up to me, we would fly to Las Vegas today and get it done and over with so you couldn't have second thoughts and run off again, but that's not how we are going to do it."

Naomi had been on the point of biting into her cake, but this made her halt and wait for him to go on.

"We're going to have a proper wedding," he said while the pulse of London flowed around them, "With a proper service and a feast with the families and our friends, and you are going to wear a white dress for me. And our son will carry the rings. We'll have the band play for us. Oh," he added when she opened her mouth to reply, "and a wedding cake. A huge one, three tiers, with red sugar roses on it."

"You're crazy."

Jon shrugged. "No. I'm not going to marry you in a small, clandestine ceremony and announce it afterward as if I feel guilty about it. I'm proud of having won you, and I'm going to show it. I want it to be a statement."

"You are crazy."

He did not react to this, but tugged her forward instead. "Come on, you silly chit, I'll get you that purse now. The one you were cradling as if it were a precious newborn."

Her protests were drowned out by one of the open, old red city busses, tourists glued to its windows.

Striding into the store, he announced, "My fiancée saw a handbag here earlier. Please wrap it up for her," and when Naomi started to interfere he said to her, "Not a word. This discussion ends here. If you go on I'll force you into every single shop up and down this street and into every single piece of clothing I fancy for you."

"This is not why I came to London with you, Jon."

He waved her objections away. "You've refused to talk about money until now, and so we will do it now and then never again. Listen well, Naomi."

She was so unwilling. It amused and irritated him how she turned away and looked down the street as if she could make the subject disappear by ignoring him.

"I want to do this, Naomi. You and Joshua, you are my family, and I want to care for you. I want to give you all I have. A few pieces of luxury are the least I can do, and they're only the beginning. So please, Baby, let's just browse through these stores and you pick anything you like. And I mean *anything*. Just for the fun of it, just because it's nice, because we happen to be here and are having a good time together."

When no response came, Jon wrapped his arm around her and drew her close.

"Listen, Naomi. I have a fortune. But I've not spent a lot of it for fun. There never seemed a good enough reason. Here, now, with you, I want to have that fun, and in a grand way. Hell, Baby, this is what I dreamed about! You, allowing me to wrap you in silk and satin and furs and put beautiful jewels on your skin, and take you out and show the world the one I always wanted will soon be my cherished wife."

"I'll be your wife, Jon. But I don't need this. Really, I don't."

"There's Prada, right across the road! Why don't we go there and look at what they have."

"Jon!" The orange shopping bag in her hand felt like lead, like a manacle she did not want at all.

"No, don't give me that." His tone had lost all lightness as he forced her to look at him. "No more. I've had it with your reticence. How will it be once we're married? Will you refuse every gift I give you, and insist on living your own small life and not accept anything from me, just to keep your distance?"

"Everything here is so unnecessary and expensive." She knew it was a lame argument, and was in fact capitulation.

"Yeah, Babe, so am I, expensive, as you so kindly reminded me when we were talking about the concert and the ticket prices. Nothing good comes cheap, it's that easy, and you shouldn't either. Will you let me take you shopping now?"

Her reluctance was so entertaining, but under the pleasure he felt, watching Naomi try on the things laid out for her, there was a sting of hurt at her refusal to let him take care of her.

When she stepped out of the dressing room in a flowing blue evening gown, so beautiful it took his breath away, he urged her, "Take that one!" but once more she shook her head at him.

"You don't trust me." It slipped out before he could stop himself. "You don't want anything from me because you are afraid it will give me a hold over you, is that it? You don't want to feel obligated so you can slip away again as soon as things get rough."

The sun was streaming through the great bow windows, glinting on crystal vases with hothouse flowers, catching the highlights in Naomi's hair and glowing on the satin of the dress. She stood before him just as she'd done when he'd first arrived in Halmar and those plates had crashed from her hands, so still and withdrawn, listening to his words.

"Why did you agree to marry me, Naomi, if everything is so disgusting to you?"

How thin the veneer of happiness truly was, how deep and troubled the maelstrom lying in wait under it. He had been hasty and impetuous, trying to force fate once again in the direction he wanted, and here she was, handing him her deepest reservations in a Prada gown. How he'd rejoiced when she permitted him to put that ring on her finger, and now, over a stupid dress, the pieces were crashing around his feet.

"I don't like Prada very much," Naomi was saying in a low voice, "If you really want to please me, take me to Valentino."

"What?" It came out stupidly.

She shrugged her pale, perfect shoulder at him in a cool gesture of disdain. "I want Valentino," Naomi repeated and returned to the dressing room, leaving him behind in mystified silence.

JON WATCHED IN bemusement as she picked outfits for herself in a calm, sure manner, as if she never wore anything else, and how she easily dealt with the question of matching purses and shoes, the two shop assistants nodding and doing her bidding while she sipped coffee and chatted with the store manager in Italian, the words slipping from her lips like a fluent, graceful melody, accentuated by small gestures of her hands and flashes of a bright smile.

"Well?" Naomi asked him, dressed in a cream suit with a short, square-cut jacket with a dark-blue border on the pleated skirt. "Do I need evening gowns to please you, or can we go now and get some tea?"

"I didn't know you spoke Italian."

She gave him a strange, distanced glance as if she had to measure her words.

"My mother is Italian, Jon."

He had not known. Sal's words rang in his memory, when he had so gleefully told him about the hotel.

"I thought you were Canadian." She looked a lot more natural in the hand-tailored Valentino than she had in her jeans and felt jacket, moving as easily as if it were a second skin, and the navy high heels did not seem to bother her in the least.

"There are a lot of Italians in Canada." With a brief glance she picked matching kid gloves from the choice the shop girl was holding out to her and asked her for a shawl.

"So your family lives in Canada, your parents are in Switzerland, you run a hotel in Norway, and your mother is Italian."

The shawl she chose was a soft, blue cashmere thing, and she didn't look at the price once.

"You never told me anything about yourself or your family."

It sounded a little like an accusation, but she only shrugged, her back to him, and wandered over to the evening gowns.

He watched her hand go to a rose chiffon dress and then quickly pull back. "You'd look lovely in that," Jon offered, not sure why she hesitated.

"I won't need it in Halmar."

And here they were, back full circle to the question of their lives, over a simple thing like a piece of clothing, the easiness and joy gone out of the day like the light of a dying candle.

He reached over her to bring it down from its place. "I'll take you to places where you'll be able to wear it, Paris and New York, to the Met. There will be plenty of chances for you to dress up."

But not Los Angeles, and he could hear those words quite clearly without her having spoken them. "And I promise, not Hollywood. You don't have to go there, ever. We'll live a private life from now on."

"It won't work, you know." She took the gown from him and went into the dressing room with it.

He took her to Bulgari a few steps down the street against her hissed protests. He simply stated that she needed some jewelry now that she had proper clothes, and very lovingly picked out earrings and necklaces, laying them on her himself with a dark twinkle in his eyes and an amused pursing of his lips at her protests.

"If you don't stop I'll buy you a Rolls next, chauffeur included, and have you driven through the streets of London like royalty. Shut up already, you crazy girl, and let me have some fun."

Over tea at the hotel, Jon said, "Go on, tell me you don't like being spoiled. Look me in the face and tell me, seriously, that you aren't looking forward to wearing those things. Tell me it was better for you being alone and running around in that black nightmare outfit every day, going to bed by yourself at night, with no one to tell you he wanted you the way I do. Go on."

Naomi had ordered brandy with her Darjeeling. She was exhausted and shaken.

"I hate you," she answered, and shot him a furious glare when he laughed at her.

BUT IN BED that night she wore the diamonds he had chosen and nothing else. To see her naked, sprawled in sensuous curves on the white sheets with those jewels on her creamy skin, took his breath away. She lazily pushed her hair aside like a favored, indulged odalisque, regarding him with measured, languid eyes. There was only the soft golden light of the bedside table playing over her body, casting enticing shadows, hiding secret places, revealing others as she moved slowly and invitingly, the glittering stones sliding over her breasts only enhancing her nudeness.

"You…" He had to start again. "You should not do that. You might get more than you asked for."

"Really?" A soft, teasing drawl. "Is that possible?"

It was a real challenge, but in the end she seemed well satisfied.

DESPITE THE FACT that he could order anything he liked, or stay as long as he wanted—even in their nicest room—Joshua rarely went to The Old Inn. It would certainly please his mother if he went more often, but he felt awkward claiming special treatment. He liked the thatch-roofed, half-timbered building and the large garden with the old apple trees, but in the end he preferred living on campus with the other students.

He sat on the low wall near the garden to wait, basking in the surprisingly warm sun, his mind still on his last class, his stomach growling in anticipation of the nice lunch he would be served shortly.

A massive black limousine drove up and stopped in front of him. A chauffeur got out and opened the door for an elegant man in a dark blue suit who held out his hand to the woman in the car.

"Hello, Joshua." His mother smiled at him, holding the well-groomed stranger's hand.

Joshua jumped up, gaping at her.

"Mom, you look beautiful." He hated how his voice cracked in surprise.

She came over and kissed him on his cheek. "That is the nicest thing a mother could hear from her nearly grown son. I've brought someone to meet you."

The diamonds at her throat flashed as she turned back toward Jon.

Joshua's attention shifted to her escort, the car, the driver. It took a moment for him to take it all in.

"Do you know who I am, Joshua?" Jon asked.

"You're the guy with the great band and the bad shirts. You're my father. But what are you doing here?

Jon laughed out loud. "That's the best description of me I've ever heard, I think. Your mother could not have put it better. You wrote to me, remember?" Jon came forward. "So now I'm here. You said you wanted to meet me, didn't you?"

Joshua had no reply. He stepped back, putting a little distance between them, and stumbled into the wall behind him, but Jon reached out and held on to his shoulder, steadying him. For a moment it seemed as if he would shake him off, but then Joshua managed a mumbled "Thanks" and a crooked grin.

They entered the inn and took their seats at a table in a quiet corner, where they were served a light white wine with fresh bread and butter. Jon scrutinized the menu and asked Naomi what she wanted.

Joshua was still staring at his mother and this man who was his father. His parents. These beautiful, poised people who smiled at each other and whose hands touched frequently across the table were his parents.

His mother, how radiant she looked in that suit and wonderful jewelry! She smelled nice too, like flowers, and she seemed happy.

"Why are you here? Was it truly my letter?"

Jon took a deep breath and told him in well-considered words how he had taken the very first chance to reclaim his lost love.

Joshua looked at his mother. "You said it was a one-night stand after a show."

Jon glanced at her, but Naomi did not return his look, her head lowered over her folded hands. "Your mother lied to you. She lied to you because she thought you should grow up in peaceful surroundings, and I was not able to give her that. And she never told me because she knew I would not let her go. She did the right thing for you, but it was a terrible thing for me. And for her. If I had known about you…" He broke off and looked at Naomi, who had tears in her eyes and grief in her face and posture. "If I had known about you, I'm sure I would have changed our life, I'm sure we could have…" He faltered. "I loved your mother very much then, and I still do. Will, always."

Joshua said nothing.

"I came to find your mother the day your letter arrived. Immediately."

None of them had much of an appetite, but they gave their orders to the waiter, who stood patiently to the side.

"But that must have been weeks ago. So what happened in the meantime?"

Here was the hard part. Or maybe it wouldn't be so hard after all.

Joshua raised his eyebrows, making him look exactly like his father.

"I've been with your mother in Halmar. We needed to figure out where we stood before we came to see you."

His hand caught Naomi's.

"Yeah," said Joshua, "and so? You either love my mom or you don't. It's easy, isn't it?"

He was going to love this boy, Jon thought to himself. Joshua sat, waiting for a reply, his dark hair in his eyes, lips slightly pursed.

"Put like that, it sounds easy. But there's more that I haven't told you yet…" With a short look at Naomi, he continued, "What I haven't told you yet is that your Mom is more than just my love. She was also my lyricist. My best songs have always been the ones with her words. She's written a lot while we were apart, and now we've begun working together again. Besides getting reacquainted."

Now *there* was a nice, useful euphemism.

Joshua stared at his mother quizzically.

"We did not just meet after a concert," Jon said in a measured tone. "It was never a fling in the dressing room. It was a carefully set up meeting in Geneva because I wanted to use her lyrics. But we fell in love, right then and there, and she came with me to America. We were together for nearly three years. You are not the product of a dressing-room tryst, Joshua. You come from parents who loved each other deeply, and still do."

"If you loved her so much, why didn't you try to find her sooner? You hurt my Mom."

Jon took a moment before answering. The food had arrived and was excellent, as was the service. He noticed how the manager hovered behind the waiters, watching them carefully, almost anxiously, and how he shot a glance in Naomi's direction, as if waiting for her approval. She did not react.

"I was devastated when your mother left. It was as if she had vanished into thin air. She's very good at hiding herself away. We were both hurt, Joshua. The important thing is that we are back together again now, because of you and your letter. We want to focus on becoming a family, the three of us, instead of looking back on what we can never change." Jon paused.

Joshua turned his head away. Studiously he looked out the window, but Jon could see how the corners of his mouth quivered, and he could have sworn there was the glimmer of tears in his eyes. His heart was heavy. In an effort to lighten the mood, he said, "I brought you something. It's in the car. I thought you might like one of the guitars I bought in Bergen the other day. It's a koa twelve-string and very special. Your mom says you're a great guitarist."

There was no response for quite some time. Then, after folding his napkin into a tight, perfect square, Joshua answered, "Thank you. That's very kind."

"It's the kind of guitar I use during my concerts." This meeting was more difficult than he had expected, and for a moment Jon felt as if he was bargaining for Naomi with a very unwilling male relative of hers. In a way it was amusing, but he was much too scared of the outcome to crack a joke about it.

"Mom made me go to your concert a while ago, and I saw the guitars you and your band were using. You had nice instruments." Joshua stopped as the memory came back to him and he put the pieces together.

"You cried!" He turned accusingly toward Naomi. "It wasn't the heat in that hall. You were crying. You sat there and looked up at him on the stage and cried."

She pressed her hands together in her lap, but Joshua went on, oblivious to her distress.

"And she bought that ridiculous picture. I made fun of you. And I made fun of mom for buying it."

There was a long silence while Naomi sat, her eyes lowered to her clasped fingers, her ring cutting into the skin. Jon was looking at her, but she could not face him.

"But Naomi said you liked the music." His voice was steady enough.

"The music was great." Joshua's tone had changed, the moodiness had vanished. He tackled the food. "But you made it really hard to concentrate on it with that shirt and the lighting. It was too much."

They began at last to talk about music, about Joshua's studies and the band he played with, the composition he was working on and his daily life at Oxford. Telling Jon about all this seemed to make him forget his misgivings.

Jon felt his heart turn over at the growing joy in his son's face when he described the latest band rehearsal, and how he had walked in on the orchestra, purely by chance, because he was looking for a book he had forgotten in the auditorium, and they were practicing a piece he had written.

"Can you imagine," he said, his eyes glowing and his cheeks flushed, "how that felt? There was this whole group of grownups, all of them really good musicians, and they were playing *my* music. That was the first time I'd heard it played, and it sounded just like it had in my mind, when I wrote it."

Jon wanted to cry. He wanted to cover his face with his hands and cry for the lost time, for the many moments they had missed when they could have had these conversations and shared the joy that music brought to both of them.

"I'm sure," he replied, and he could hear his voice crack on the words, "I know how you felt. It's the instant when you realize you have created something that others appreciate. And it just feels so good. It's all you need to make you go on, and it makes the struggle worthwhile."

Joshua, the corners of his mouth turned down in a way that made him look just like his mother, shrugged his shoulders disdainfully. "Oh, it's no struggle. The melodies are just there. All you need to do is write them down."

And here, Jon realized, was true talent. His own son was more of a composer than he himself could ever hope to be. For the first time ever, he knew how it was to feel proud of a child.

A waitress came to clear away their plates and bring coffee and pastries.

Joshua began to ask questions. How did it feel to perform in such huge venues? What was it like to be so famous and live in Los Angeles? Could he meet his musicians sometime? And: "Are you going to be my father from now on?"

"I've always been your father," was Jon's reply. "I just didn't know it until I got your letter."

Joshua turned his eyes accusingly on Naomi, which made Jon touch his arm.

"Don't look at your mother like that. She did what she thought was best for you. And it probably was. You might have turned into a spoiled Hollywood brat, and I like the way you are just fine. And yes, I'll be in your life from now on. Your mom and I are finally getting married."

That silenced him for a while.

"Joshua…" Naomi said.

"Why did you cry, Mom? At the concert? You could have just walked up to—" he searched for the right word—"to my father and told him you were there, if it meant so much. If you wanted to marry him, you could have done it that much sooner."

"Let it rest, Joshua." Jon answered for her, "It's going to happen now, and that's all that's important."

Joshua looked from one to the other. "So it truly was my letter, right? You're here because of my letter."

"Yes." Jon replied.

And finally, at last, the hint of a smile crossed the boy's face.

SAL TRIED TO keep his eyes open as he listened to the string of requests coming from the other side of the ocean. Once again Jon had called at a god-forsaken hour, and Sal struggled hard to refrain from making any really snarky comments. At least this time Jon had found him in bed alone.

"Jon, what time is it over there?" He kicked free of the sheets "It's the middle of the night here. You've got to stop doing this, you crazy bastard!"

It wasn't really the middle of the night, he realized when he glanced at the clock, but it was still too early for him.

"About three in the afternoon. Stop whining, Sal. What is it with you, don't you work at all when I'm not around to kick your butt?"

That was rich; Jon was the one who often had to be prodded and pushed into working! Sal found himself wide awake and wondering if this might be the right time to mention the offer they'd received a couple of days ago. It was a great offer and he had wanted to accept it on the spot, but had managed to wheedle a week out of Harry before they had to give an answer.

"Listen, Jon. Since we're talking about work, Harry called and asked if you would do a movie soundtrack for him." He padded to the kitchen to start some coffee and search for his cigarettes. There was no reply, so Sal pushed on, "It's a great script, and from what I've heard the film will likely get an Oscar nomination. We could be in on that. Harry kicked the original composer out and now he needs a replacement. Would you consider giving him a call? Please don't say no because you're busy honeymooning."

All he could hear was Jon's breathing and some obscure background noises, as if he was standing out in the street, but no reply came.

"You want me to come over to Norway anyway. I could bring Russ and Sean and we could discuss it, or even start working, and then finish it when you return—"

"I'm not returning Sal."

This made Sal pause.

The coffee tin was nearly empty. He would have to go out for a cup, which made him curse silently and dampened his spirits considerably on top of his growing irritation at Jon. "Yes, whatever. But don't let this thing pass, Jon. This is too good, and if you come up with something great you might even have a chance for a nomination yourself again. It would be good for you, running for an Oscar. You might build a tour on that next year. With new songs."

Four years had passed since he had put out a new album, an eternity in their business where hits came and went on a daily basis. Sal wanted a song back on the charts very badly. Or better yet, an entire album. It wouldn't be easy with a movie soundtrack, but it could be done.

"It's now or never, and you know it. Come on, you know you want this, Jon. I know you do, it's just what you've been waiting for. Take it as the motivation to get back in the swing again! You have what you pined for all this time, right, the girl is back with you, so you might as well start working again." How he hated having to prompt Jon into composing, but this chance wasn't one he could let slip away, even if it meant dragging the whole band to Norway.

"So what's the deal with your elusive maiden?" he asked, "She wants you to stay with her in that God-forsaken wilderness? Seriously Jon, you aren't going to do that, are you? I mean, come on, man, your life is here."

"My life," Jon echoed, musing. "Yes, my life."

"Don't give me the songwriter bullshit, Jon, not at this time of day. I want that deal, and you should want it too. Regardless of what's going on over there in Norway."

The cigarette did not taste half as good without coffee, which made Sal irritable and very impatient with Jon and his romantic issues. He opened the balcony door to let in the early sun. From the street below, he could smell freshly baked bread, and, sadly, coffee.

"We're getting married."

Sal wasn't sure he had heard that with cars honking and a police siren screaming by. "I don't think I understood you just now. There's too much noise here. Did you say you're getting married?"

He knew it was a stupid question and would only earn him a sarcastic reply. He nodded to himself when Jon replied, "You heard me. Don't give me that crap."

It was rather lame; he was used to better comebacks from Jon. "I'll be over in three or four days," Sal responded after a pause, "And I'll bring Russ and Sean. And you, I want you to think about that soundtrack, Jon. I'll send you the specifics later. Check your email, will you? For once? They do have computers in Norway, don't they? You know, the Internet? Please tell me they don't use snail mail for everything still? Or do they still have outriders carrying the letters?"

"Shut up, Sal. And get your ass over here."

Sal could hear someone talking in Norwegian near Jon, and the soft silver sound of laughter that he remembered only too well. His stomach plummeted. He wondered how she looked now, so many years later, if she still was as lovely as he remembered her.

"Hey, Babe," Jon was saying, "Want to say hello to Sal? He's a bit speechless, so it's a good chance for you to knock him over."

And the way his voice changed when he addressed her, with the dark, soft timbre that captivated his female fans and made all the difference between a good singer and a great star.

"Hello, Sal."

She sounded exactly the same, as if time had stood still.

"Hello, my dear," he answered shakily. "How are you coping with him around?"

"Just fine, Sal. He's being a good boy."

Jon growled softly, "Careful, little beast, I can hear what you're saying!"

It was too much for Sal.

IT HAD TURNED warm, and the landscape around them had changed so quickly. Jon stood on the pier and stared at the sudden green in amazement. He had the impression that nature was in a hurry to gather as much strength as it could before summer was over again. It was as if the ground was pushing the grass and flowers up in a frenzied attempt to soak up as much as it could of the sudden, fierce sunlight. The sky was full of birds. Flocks of geese and ducks passed overhead, their cries echoing from the hills and water as Jon watched them fly north, heralding spring. The little town seemed to come to life too. Tables and chairs appeared outside the café across from the hotel. The flower shop set blooming pots under their awning, and people turned down the collars of their jackets and left their woolen caps at home.

It was Saturday morning and Naomi had slept late. She opened the door to the deck and walked out in her bathrobe, a cinnamon roll and coffee in her hands. On the water, a couple of white yachts drifted lazily toward the ocean. The post ship had just arrived and docked at the pier; gulls were flying around it, screeching and fighting, hoping for tidbits from the guests leaning on the railing. A hum of well-being seemed to drift on the wind, mixing with the salty scent of the sea.

Jon, in one of the deck chairs, took the coffee from her, and she sat down in his lap. She leaned into him, her head against his shoulder, enjoying the warmth of both the sun and his body, listening to his heartbeat and his breathing.

"Are we going away on a honeymoon?"

"Would you like to? We could, certainly. Where should we go?"

He wrapped his hand in her hair and tugged at it playfully. The bathrobe had fallen open to reveal her legs and bare feet, but she didn't mind. They were alone on the balcony, hidden from the outside world, set apart from daily life.

"I don't know." Naomi wiggled her toes. "Truly, I can hardly wrap my mind around the wedding thing yet. I'll believe it when it happens. It seems very unreal. *You* seem unreal."

He tugged a little harder.

"Stop!" she protested, "I know you're here; there's barely a moment when you let me forget it. But still..." Her head was bent back and her lips beckoned, the robe slipping from her shoulder to reveal the top of her breasts.

"You look just like Scarlett O'Hara," Jon said approvingly, "right before she gets ravished by Rhett. All we're missing is Atlanta burning in the background."

"That's so like you," she replied, breathless, "You would burn a city just to get your way. Think of all those poor Coca-Cola shareholders."

His grip on her hair tightened, pulling her back a little further. He leaned toward her, nearly touching her lips, a dangerous sparkle in his eyes. "The things you say just to get a little ravishing, you impossible girl."

Naomi strained toward his kiss but he held back, stretching out the moment, reveling in this sweetest of tortures, waiting for her to plead a little, wanting her to need him, if only for a kiss, for a touch.

There was a knock on the door, and Jon, without looking up, called, "Come in!"

She struggled harder then, but he didn't let her go. Embarrassment made her squirm, and she hit his arm in a futile attempt to make him release her, but Jon grinned and held her tightly to claim the kiss he had wanted all along.

"Oh look! It's *Gone with the Wind* all over again," Sal said dryly.

"It's Sal!" She pushed at Jon. "Let go, look, it's Sal!" And then, when she could look past Sal, "And Sean and Russ! Jon, Sean is here!"

"I know, Baby."

Naomi flew into Sean's embrace, surprising herself with her emotional reaction at seeing these two.

Sean clasped her tightly. "Hello, darling. Such a hard time you gave us. It's good to see you well and back in Jon's arms where you belong. God, but you're still beautiful."

"Jon," Sal drawled, "are you sure it's you she was after? It seems to me there's a little sideshow going on here." He hugged Naomi when she turned to him.

"Hey, Babe. So here, in this God-forsaken dead-end, somewhere in Norway, we find the solution to the great mystery. And we hope to hear everything explained before the day is out."

"You will." Jon laid his hands on her shoulders. "But give the lady time to find some clothes first. Here, have some cinnamon rolls."

STILL RUBBING HER hair after her shower but finally dressed, she returned to the deck, where they had settled in the sunshine.

"Right." Sal bent down and opened his briefcase. "You see, I'm not really here for our favorite pop star. I'm here because of you. There's something we have to talk about, that's why Jon called me over. So here I am, following my Master's orders, as always."

"Oh for heaven's sake, Sal." Jon gave him a pained look, but Sal ignored him.

"Listen, Naomi, there are a few things to put in order, and we'll do it right now, before we all get sentimental and drunk. Jon, take Sean and Russ and go do something. Go get that blonde's phone number for me."

"Oh, no." Russ raised his hand. "That one's mine. *I'm* getting her number. She's my kind of girl."

Naomi looked wildly from one to the other, upset by what was happening. Jon kissed her lightly when he got up to leave, "Don't worry, everything is fine. Just listen to Sal. I'll be right inside."

Sal put a thick manila envelope down on the table, which Naomi opened with trepidation. Inside were three debit cards in her name and a thick sheaf of legal documents. Perplexed, she held the cards up. "What am I supposed to do with these? We aren't even married."

"Oh, no, no. These have nothing to do with Jon." Sal said, with a nod toward Jon, who had returned to listen, leaning against the door frame. Then he conceded, "Well, in a way they do, of course, because he performed the songs, but these are for your accounts. You have your own money, you see. The thing is, we never knew where to send it, and none us ever thought of giving it to your parents. I guess Jon always hoped...well, whatever. So we just held it for you." He shrugged apologetically. "But here it is now, all yours."

"For what? Why do I get money?" An awful, ugly thought crept up in her, something so bitter she could hardly say it out loud. "Are you trying to buy me off, Sal? Is that it? Do you want me to let go of Jon?"

"Baby, no, for God's sake, no!" Jon caught her and held her, his arms tight around her. "Don't say such a terrible thing! Sal, please, if you can't do this properly, let me—"

"I'm sorry," Sal said quickly, "I thought...Naomi, this money I'm talking about, these are your royalties. You wrote the lyrics, remember, for the Garden album? We were very meticulous. Half the net proceeds went into your account. I've been looking after it all these years, as your de-facto business manager, but it's yours. Please sign these and take it. And some advice: spend it before you get married. Because then he'll have to pay for you ever after. Nice, huh?" He laughed. "Let her go, Jon. I don't think she'll run. She just needs to sign these things."

She sat again, but Jon remained behind her. From inside, they could hear Sean trying out the new melodies he had found on the piano.

Jon touched her hair. "Go ahead, Naomi. Sign those things and shut him up. Everything is in order, I promise. It's my fault, I should have told you. But I wanted it to be a surprise, I wanted it to come from Sal and not from me so you would see it truly is a business transaction and not something I'm giving you. It's yours. You earned it, every penny."

Naomi leafed through the papers. There were bank statements, shareholder reports, calculations, and all kinds of other documents. "I own stocks?"

"Well, yes." Sal shifted and lit another cigarette. "We couldn't let the money just sit idly in the bank, could we? But we picked solid stocks, as you'll see."

"How much do I own?"

He pushed another sheet toward her and she stared at the number.

Silence descended on them like a cloud. Sal, satisfied with his delivery, smoked while Jon waited, rather anxiously, for her reaction. Naomi was still looking at the papers, leafing through them again and again. At last she looked up at Jon and said: "I don't want your money. You don't have to pay me for those lyrics; I wanted you to have them."

"Ah." Sal held up his hand to stop Jon, who was about to reply. "You're such a sweet, innocent child, my dear. Who do you think pays all our salaries? Forget about the love and art stuff for a while, and what you'll see is a big business machine. We're all on Jon's payroll." His eyes twinkled at her. "You're his writer. You're truly entitled to half the net earnings from those songs you wrote together. Every time he goes on stage and performs them, every time you hear one of them on the radio, and every time some chick buys one of his CDs, there's money rolling into your account. That's what it's about in the end, Naomi. We make money, a great deal of it. And you do too."

Naomi shook her head, stunned by what was happening.

"You earned it. Forget the romance. Think business. Those songs wouldn't exist but for you."

They waited for her to say something, but she didn't. There was nothing to say. When she had cried so bitterly at the London concert listening to Jon sing Secret Garden, she had in fact, been making money.

"You truly never thought about this, have you?" Sal asked. "You really did it all for love."

This at least she could answer. "No, not love. It had nothing to do with falling in love."

Sal grinned at Jon. "More like all the love songs you've ever written coming together and pouring out?" He got a sharp glare in reply.

"Yes, in a way." She pondered his words. "But no, it's the other way around. When I heard Jon's voice, it was more like having to write all those songs, to hear him sing them. Something like that."

"God, you are one sappy couple." Sal rose. "Sign the papers, Naomi. Pick up your cards and tuck them away."

"Do I own Coca-Cola shares?" The question had just popped into her head, the funny side of this whole thing finally asserting itself in the midst of all the confusion. Sal could not figure out why that rather sensible question should make Jon laugh so hard.

"Why yes, yes you do. Coca-Cola is always a safe investment."

"And you were going to burn Atlanta just for a kiss," Naomi said accusingly to Jon.

10

AFTER SHOWING SAL, Russ, and Sean to their rooms, Naomi found Jon on the deck, his bare feet on the table, his eyes closed, his face turned toward the sun. There was a steaming cup of coffee on his knee and a cigar in his hand.

"You know," he remarked, "if I close my eyes very tight and ignore the cool breeze, this could almost be California."

"You won't say that in October when it gets dark at two in the afternoon."

Something in her voice bothered him and he looked up. Naomi stood well away, regarding him with that inner stillness, her hands folded over her skirt, her posture almost formal.

"Baby?"

"This money…"

He put the coffee down on the table and the cigar in the ashtray, and closed his eyes again.

"You knew Sal was coming over with those papers."

There was no answer.

"Jon."

He stirred. "No. We're not having this discussion, Naomi. If you don't want the money, give it away. But it's yours. It's not a gift. Every penny of it is accounted for. It's a huge amount, but that's only because so much time has passed and nothing was ever spent. So no, we are not going to talk about it."

Sitting up, he held his hand out to her. "Come here. Sit with me. It's not important. It's just money, for God's sake."

She didn't move.

"Oh, come here, you Coca-Cola shareholder. I won't burn your city, I promise." He lunged for her and grabbed the hem of her skirt. Naomi resisted, but he didn't let go.

"Besides, I probably own more shares than you do. So I'll outvote you."

Reluctantly she let him draw her closer and pull her down on his lap.

"So tell me. I really thought you would be pleased. There's some disappointment here. After all, I made Sal come over for this."

It was so hard to refuse him, nearly impossible. "In London, you took me shopping and made me buy all those things, and I felt so bad about it."

"Ah."

"You tortured me, Jon, you forced me to spend your money when you knew I really didn't want to, when it would have been so easy to wait until Sal slapped down those papers on the table and I could have bought them myself."

"But that's the whole point. I wanted to give you those things, and I wanted to enjoy doing it. Now you don't need me for anything anymore, and I worry that you will push me away again at the first opportunity. For just one day, I wanted that feeling of caring for you, of being able to look after you the way I should have and didn't. Is that so hard to accept?"

"But if I had known about the money, Jon, I would have bought the bracelet to go with my diamond necklace." It came out a little sulkily, but he could feel her relenting and softening against him.

"That's not going to happen," he replied sternly. "No buying diamonds on your own. That's my prerogative. How will I ever get to see that naked vision again if you aren't wearing jewelry that I gave you?"

"You are never serious. I'm trying to make a point." She sighed, exhausted by his stubbornness.

Jon's hands were caressing her face ever so lovingly, his fingertips following the lines of her cheekbones and jaw, pushing into her hairline and trailing down her throat to the hollow at its base.

"My sweet beauty. I know. But it's not something you should worry about. I did what gave me pleasure. I'm indulging my wife-to-be. I'm entitled to it, it's my right. Don't you know I'd give you anything in the world?"

"I know." She leaned into him. "But I'm so used to looking after myself, that it is hard for me to let anyone, even you, do it for me."

"Yes," Jon said after a moment, "That's my fault. I can't turn back time, so you'll just have to get used to it now. Please let me spoil you, Naomi. That was the point of that shopping trip in London. I knew you would be able to buy anything you wanted soon enough, but I wanted to spoil you a little, nothing more. We're getting married. So I have the right to buy you nice things, just as I reserve the right to see you stretched out on my bed with nothing on but that necklace, like a painting. God, that was a stunning sight."

HE HAD DONE it so neatly. She marveled as she walked upstairs to make the bed at how easily he had managed to turn away her concerns and make her give in again, accepting yet another piece of his life with her barely noticing. Step by slow, careful step, he was relentlessly pulling her toward him, into his existence. She found herself unable to resist him and the temptation. Bringing not only Sal but Sean and Russ here had been such a clever, insidious move, well calculated to weaken her resolve. It almost angered her..

"It's still much too cold," Jon called, coming in and closing the door behind him. "I hope it does get warmer at some point, or I'll freeze solid. Do you ever go swimming in the sea in summer? I can't imagine the water getting warm enough for a dip, it looks so forbidding. In LA, we'd be out on the beach by now."

The quilt dropped from her hands at those words. Her heart heavy with dread, she made her way back down to where he was bent over the piano.

"I'm not going back to California, Jon."

She said it so softly that it did not register with him right away and he mumbled, "Sure, Babe," without looking up.

"And I don't want Joshua there, either. I'll fight you over this, but he will not go to Los Angeles with you. I never wanted money from you; I never wanted anything from you except your love. Not your life, not your wealth or your fame, and I don't want any of that for Joshua either. That's why I told him you were a brief affair. You are a public person. I will never be, not if I can help it. I want the freedom, to live my life the way I choose, not how others want it."

Once spoken, it sounded a lot harsher than she had meant it, and final in a terrible, painful way. Jon had straightened up but had not turned toward her, his shoulders rigid and his head bowed as he listened to the verdict she was delivering so quietly.

Silence fell between them like drops of molten lead, searing away the joy of the morning, burning the skin on his face and neck.

He tried to let the words she said wash over him in a desperate attempt at safety and the assurance that his life would not be torn asunder, but it didn't work. She had struck too deep.

"You hate me that much." The words came out before he could stop himself. "You hate me so much that you told our son such a sordid story, Naomi. What have I ever done to you to make you strike me out of your life so brutally? God, I never knew you had it in you to be that cruel." He gripped her shoulders tightly.

"I know that drug raid scared you badly, and you wanted to hide and run. I took you for granted, I admit that. But what else, Naomi? Was that all? I want to know, because if we are going to make this work, I need to hear the whole story from you, the truth. I don't believe that one night, horrible as it might have been, was enough to send you away like that." There was dark doubt in his eyes, and deep grief. "You gave Joshua that image of us, of me using you in a dressing room as an after-show whim, a mindless, cruel moment of release and nothing more, and he carried that with him. His mother, a young, innocent girl, only a few years older than he is right now, used and tossed away. No names asked, no love, no tenderness. When in truth…in truth…I loved you more than anything when he was conceived."

For the first time ever, he felt anger at what she had done welling up inside him, and bursting out of the hard place where he had hidden it away.

"You are going to tell me. I have a right to know. So spill." And dear God, here she was, caught in his tight hold, crying again, and the day had turned bitter gray despite the sunshine and the warmth.

"I ran away with you. You know I ran away with you, don't you?"

More or less he had known, but he had not bothered to ask. She had been there, with a travel bag and a passport, and that had been all he had cared about. "You had a right to go where you wanted. So why not come with me to LA if it pleased you?"

That was exactly the point, and she had no idea how to explain. "But I had nothing, Jon. I came away with you, and I had nothing of my own. We were living at your house, everything was taken care of, and I had nothing. I just drifted through life."

"You had *me*." His voice was rough with disappointment. "And I would have given you anything you asked for."

Naomi pressed her lips together, helpless against his anger, unable to find the right words.

"And that's just not true, Naomi," Jon went on, "You were working, and working hard. Should I have paid you a salary for writing those lyrics? Would that have made you feel better? I was under the impression that we were a couple, and I wanted to share everything with you."

"But we never spoke about it, Jon."

"What was there to speak about? You were there with me, you lived with me, we shared every moment. You were my life, for heaven's sake!" He could not see a good enough reason for what she had done.

"But that night, the night of the drug raid, Jon, I realized that I was totally dependent on you. I didn't have one penny of my own. I couldn't even afford to take a taxi anywhere without raiding the housekeeper's stash. There was not a single soul that I could talk to, other than you and Sal, and you were in jail and Sal was busy getting you out." A ragged sob shook her. "I had just turned twenty-one. You were well on your way to world fame, and there I was, only the girl you were…"

"Don't you dare! Don't you dare say that, Naomi."

The breath went out of her in a troubled sigh, but she did not try to get away from him.

"Any other woman would have been overjoyed at getting pregnant in that situation, it would have meant having a hold over me, and you run? And you don't just run, but you hide yourself away so I can never find you? Just because you wanted your independence? You and your stupid, childish pride. Me and my useless brain. I never realized. We had everything we wanted, and we could have done whatever we wished." Finally he understood, even as he spoke. She had never asked for anything, but he had never offered. "I should have paid you a salary." But that didn't sound right either. "I should have asked you to marry me. Yes. Then you wouldn't have felt like a kept woman. Would you have married me then, Naomi?"

"How should I know, Jon? Probably, yes; certainly if you had asked before I got pregnant."

His hands dropped from her. He sat down on the couch, drained.

"Good grief, and so getting you pregnant was my death blow? So I have to be glad it took nearly three years, or you would have left even sooner, and only because I never gave you your own checkbook?"

Furious herself now, Naomi threw a pillow at him, which he caught with one hand and returned to its place. "That's not it and you know it, Jon! I didn't want your money. I wanted to be myself, to find my own worth, my own place in life!"

"Ah, Baby," Jon replied sadly. "But you had all that. Didn't you see that? Didn't you see how valued you were for what you wrote? Didn't you see how much I loved you? You had it all."

11

NAOMI WAS HEAVY-HEARTED. She knew she could no longer put off the phone calls to her family. So when Solveigh was finished with her daily report she locked herself into the office and phoned her uncle first. Carl listened to her tale in bemusement and without interrupting, and only when she told him about the upcoming wedding did she hear him sigh, "Very well, my dear. If this is your decision, then I will accept it. But Naomi…"

He stopped before she could ask him to.

The talk with her parents was harder.

"You are too old to fall for that rock star of yours again," her father said, "as soon as he walks back into your life." And why did he, anyway? Had they not they hidden her away well enough? And what about Joshua? Was she going to expose the boy to the drugs and party life of Hollywood and risk his talent and education? Had she learned nothing in the last seventeen years? What about her responsibilities to the family? How would her life be from now on? Didn't she have any self-respect and pride?

"You are useless," he told her. "You know what we expect of you and what you should be doing. We let you come back to us slowly and gently enough, but Naomi, you are throwing everything away again. You have a choice of important, wealthy men who have made a place for themselves in real life, in real positions, and you know you were meant to marry someone else."

His disappointment was nearly more than she could bear.

Her mother cried, afraid to see her hurt again. To her, Naomi had confided what had really happened the night of the drug bust. It was hard, and she felt the deep shame of it all over again, but it was necessary to make her mother understand that it had not been Jon's fault.

"Oh, but it was," Lucia Carlsson said. "If not for his lifestyle and notoriety, there would never have been a drug raid at that house at all.

What does he want now? How did he ever find out where you are? He will make you unhappy all over again. He will destroy you. You took so long to heal; in a way you never did. And now, what? He is back with you for a few weeks and you lose your head again like a star-struck teenager. You will break and be destroyed, and I do not know what to do about it."

Naomi wept bitterly. She hid in the office as long as she could, then slipped out and walked toward the fishing depot. There was little traffic and the boats had all gone out. She stood for a long while at the water's edge and looked at her hotel across the small bay. It was the first thing that met the eye for anyone coming in from the sea. It was well-cared for, a proud place, her haven when everything else had failed.

Her family could not keep her from being with Jon, but they would never be happy about it, and might never let go of their distrust and anger. She had not even told her mother about the wedding; she just couldn't find the words.

Her parents would never understand what bound her to Jon.

"Our biggest mistake," had been her father's bitter words when she had fled back home, "was that we didn't watch you better when you were young. And this, Naomi…ruining your life for a singer, for God's sake. You should have finished university. You should not be pregnant and alone. At the very least you should be married and cared for, with the child. Not abandoned and left to fend for yourself."

But she had never tried to explain, had never told them the truth.

IT WAS QUIET in the lobby, only Solveigh was at her usual place between the reception desk and the office. She nodded toward Naomi when she walked in from the sunshine with her jacket drawn tight around her, arms crossed in defense.

The door to her apartment stood slightly ajar.

"…no way," Jon was saying, "This is how it's going to be. Sal, you need to accept this. I'm not even going to discuss this with you."

It was delivered in a tone she had never heard from him before, adamant and fast, hard. Her hand rested on the door knob, her heart beating wildly.

"Do you know what you're doing, Jon?" Sal was saying. "You're putting yourself out of touch with everything that's been important to you. This is not your life. This is just a short reprieve before life claims you again. And then what? Are you going to drag her back to LA, tear up everything she has built here for herself? You broke into her life without thinking about the consequences, and you've shaken it completely. What do you think will happen once you decide to pick up your career again? Take care of the boy, but don't destroy her. She deserves better than to be dragged away and burned up by your life."

His tirade was ended by the sound of the deck door being pushed open and the flick of a lighter.

"I came," Jon replied in the same cold, dry voice, "I came here in the hope of solving the riddle and to win her back, if I could. Well, I did. I'm not giving her up. If it means living and working here, so be it. It's not a bad place, and my love is here. If you can't take it, you'll have to find another job. That's it."

"Is the sex that good?" Sal asked, in a mean, tough tone.

Another pause, then, in a soft breath, "You can't begin to imagine. But that's not all of it, and you know it."

"For Christ's sake, Jon! Listen to yourself. You've taken leave of your senses. You're ruining your career over a girl!"

"He's trying to protect you," Sean said coming up behind her. "Sal is. Don't worry."

He laid his arm around her shoulder and hugged her in a friendly, comforting way. "He's worried, and he wants to make sure you'll be okay. Come away."

He led her back up to the lobby and out through the front door onto the street. Naomi was too upset to speak. She sat on the pier wall, drawing ragged breaths, so close to tears it hurt. Sean stood patiently by her side, squinting into the sun to watch a sailboat far out on the water. A couple of cars drove by slowly and stopped in the parking lot of the hotel, and two families scrambled out and went inside after sorting out their children and luggage.

"Is it true, Sean? Will he want to return to Los Angeles?"

"I can't answer that, Naomi."

Miserably, she hunched her shoulders. "I can't live there, Sean. Never again. If Jon returns, then he'll have to go on his own. I love him beyond all reason, but that I cannot do."

Sean laid his hand on her shoulder again. "Don't worry, darling. Trust him. You should have always have done that, you know, even back then. Whatever happened that night, I'm sure he would have set it right."

"I talked to my parents today."

She turned her head to look at a flock of gulls swarming over the water, their screeches echoing off the hills. "It wasn't easy and it was definitely not nice. My father said some very unkind things. I didn't expect them to be thrilled, but this…I needed some space, so I took a walk. Then I come back to that scene downstairs."

He sat down beside her and took her hands in his. "You don't get the gift of a family very often. So many lives end up lonely, and I know how lonely Jon was, despite all the women who threw themselves at him. He needs you. You have no idea how much."

There were voices from the lobby.

"You're holding the wrong girl's hands," Jon called from the door. "Find your own, Sean. This one's mine."

"There you go." Sean rose from the stones. "Possessive, arrogant, impetuous, and altogether much too domineering. But he's all yours, if you want him."

Jon went over to them. Sal seemed to be deep in thought as he wandered off to the newspaper stand down the street.

"Baby? What's up? You've been crying. What happened?"

She tried to pull herself together and not make a total fool of herself with Sean and Sal around, but she wanted to be in his arms so badly, to feel the safety and assurance that everything would be alright.

"I phoned my parents. That's all. It's okay."

She could see that no one believed her. "I'm fine. Just a little tired. I'll go down and rest a bit, and I'll be fine."

Jon came after her, as she knew he would, as she wanted him to.

As soon as the door closed behind them, before he could say anything, Naomi turned to him with a sob. "Hold me. Please."

She allowed herself to sink into his embrace, letting him catch and cradle her, his lips on hers, soft, comforting, healing. Her body melted into his, needing the feel of solidity and security he gave her.

"Please," she said, her voice small and broken, "Please say you'll never leave me. Please tell me you love me. Please."

"Naomi." Gently, he held her away from him so he could look at her. "You know I love you. You know I'll never leave you. What happened?"

She shook her head, refusing to answer, and kissed him with a fierceness that caught him totally unawares. "Love me. Don't make me beg. Love me. Claim me, take me, make me yours."

He took her to bed, still bewildered by the terrible need in her. Afterward, she lay in his arms in near fainting passivity.

"Baby," he whispered, "I love you, you know that. I'll never let you go. I promise. I'll tell you every day, every time you need to hear it."

Jon let her rest against his shoulder for a while before he asked again. "What happened today? I truly love making love to you, but I would prefer to do it for happier reasons than to stop you from crying."

Her head lay on his chest, he could not see her face. "I told you, I phoned my parents today to tell them about us."

The hand playing in her hair tightened as she told him.

"He said I was useless, and that I had no self-respect or shame." And after a thoughtful pause, "Well, I guess it's true enough. I'm useless, because I'm in love with you."

"Yeah, Baby," he said caressingly, "I felt it, right there, a moment ago. And I tell you, it feels so good. And I'm okay with you being useless to all others if it means you love me."

"You are a silly man." She knew he was trying to ease her pain, but she could feel from the tension in his body that he was annoyed, very annoyed.

GENTLE HANDS WOKE her in the gray light of early morning.

"I hate to leave you when you are so sweet and desirable," she heard his voice close to her face, "but I need to go. Take care, my love."

Before she could reply or even reach for him, he was gone. Bewildered, she sat up and stared at the closed door, alone again in the silence of dawn. Fear welled up in her that he had left her, dropped from her life as suddenly as he had entered it, and she rushed, barefoot, over to his room. All his things were there. Back in the apartment she saw he had even left his reading glasses behind on the piano, and her hammering heart calmed down again. Sal had gone with him, she realized over breakfast, but no one knew why or where. They had simply vanished before anyone else got up.

The weather was bad. A storm had been brewing over the ocean and now it had moved inland, bringing sleet and high winds, and grew worse as the afternoon progressed. She imagined his plane flying along the coast, buffeted by gusts, sight nearly impossible, and her beloved in it.

"What's wrong?" Sean asked when he saw her standing, staring out the window, the coffee pot she had meant to bring to their table in her hand, forgotten.

"The storm. It's much worse out on the water. I wish I knew what Jon and Sal are up to."

"Don't worry." He took the pot from her. "Those two can take care of themselves just fine. They fight like cats and dogs, but nothing will happen to them if they're together."

"I remember," Russ said suddenly, "four years ago when we were on tour in Australia and got into a sandstorm on that plane."

"Hell, that was a real pisser!" Sean yawned. "We were flying from Sydney to Perth on the equipment plane, and man, that thing shook like a maple leaf in November. Rodney barfed, remember?" He grinned broadly. "We had been at that fabulous steak place before we left, and *wham!* He lost that ribeye right there on the plane. And guess, my lovely, what the Master did? He slept through it all. Never batted an eye. Woke up just before we landed, as fresh as you please, and wanted to know why we were all so green. Rodney nearly hit him. That same night we had our concert in Perth, and I swear Rodney missed more than a couple of beats. Jon made fun of him all the way back to States. So don't worry about him. He'll be back. I have a feeling that a little storm out there won't keep him away from you."

He gave her a wink and poured more coffee.

"Yes, that's what happened," Russ agreed. "Poor Rod. He never heard the end of it. When Jon was done with him, we took up the running gag. I don't think he ever ate another steak after that."

"I've never seen Jon mean or making fun of anyone." Naomi picked up the plate, empty now of cake. "He would never do that. You're making this up to put me at ease. That's all."

Back in the kitchen, she leaned on the counter, breathing hard and fighting exhaustion and fear. She realized she didn't even know Jon's or Sal's cell phone numbers, but there was no way she was going to admit this. Russ would laugh his head off.

The unreality of the situation hit her, the isolation and timelessness of the past weeks, the many things they had not talked about, practical, day-to-day things. While sharing so much else, they had pushed away much more to make room for their own small bubble of dreams.

There was nothing she could do but wait and worry.

"Do they need more coffee?" Andrea eyed the machine doubtfully. "It's nearly dinnertime. Maybe drinks would be better now?"

"They can get drinks themselves if they want any. I'm done serving them for today."

The apartment was cold and dark when she opened the door, the rain a constant splatter on the panes, the deck awash with foaming seawater. Despite the sandstorm tale, she was frightened. Russ and Sean didn't know how a gale could blow over the mountains and the ocean, either of which a plane would have to cross to get from anywhere to Halmar.

For a while she sat at her desk and went through her lyrics, reading his annotations and corrections, turning her words into his song.

She remembered sending a bundle of lyrics to Los Angeles, to the manager's address on one of the albums, and how she had wished for Jon to receive and use them. That day in Geneva was burned deep in her memory. She remembered her excitement and her mother's cautionary words, her agonizing over what to wear and how to do her hair, and walking out of her home with her heart beating hard. She remembered seeing him there; sitting on one of the deep couches at the hotel, gazing directly at her, shining like a beacon so there was no one and nothing else anymore. He rose and took a few steps toward her, and she moved closer, mindlessly pulled toward him. The way he had looked into her eyes and at her mouth had been frightening, exciting, and altogether delicious. For a moment she had thought he was going to reach for her, but he had not. They had stood, speechless, staring at each other, the magnetism so strong it seemed to vibrate between them.

Then Sal had come.

The ringing phone woke her from her sublime reverie.

"Baby." Her heart missed a beat. "Don't worry. We're on our way back."

For a moment she couldn't speak, still too caught up in her memories.

"Naomi?" There was worry in his voice. "Are you okay, love? We're good, but the storm is keeping us in Oslo. We flew in an hour ago, and we're stuck. Miss you so much."

"Where were you?" She could hardly control her voice. "You frightened me. You can't run away at dawn and not tell me where you're going!"

"I'm sorry, Babe. Don't be afraid, all is well. We'll talk in the morning. I promise. I had to take care of something, and it's done. I won't ever leave you like this again. God, but I miss you. You were so sweet and warm this morning. It was so hard to get out of our bed."

"Well then, see to it you return. And soon." She was faint with longing.

"Will do, my love. But please, don't sit all alone waiting for me. You are all by yourself, aren't you? Again?" There were voices in the background, and motor noises. "Everything is fine. If we can, we'll be back tonight. The plane is sitting here waiting for the storm to die down. I must go now, Baby. Go and look after Sean, he'll be pining for you. Love you so much."

"Jon!"

He was gone again. Confused but relieved to know at least where Jon and Sal were, she returned to the kitchen and poured herself a glass of bourbon from the bottle they kept for emergencies.

"Don't drink so much of that." Andrea took the bottle from her with a shake of her head. "It's not good for your complexion."

"I was so worried about them. But Jon just called."

"Ah." Andrea put a couple of cheese biscuits beside her glass.

THAT DAY IN Geneva.

Jon had called a break, and Sal had left her before Jon had come down from the stage and chased him away.

"I don't know what I'm doing here," she said carefully, from a well-kept distance. Aren't you supposed to be preparing for the concert?"

"Oh, but I am. We are. Don't worry." He had jumped up and pulled her with him. "Let's find some coffee."

They had walked through the hallways beneath the grandstand, and at one point he had turned to her and kissed her, lingeringly and softly, her back to the whitewashed wall. Voices had drifted toward them from around corners, laughter and shouting, from the parking bay further along, the rumble of trucks as they were moved around.

"You're going to be mine. Oh yes. I'll do whatever I have to do, but you're mine. I won't let you go." A murmured promise, a stroke of breath on her cheek.

And yet, that day, her reply had been: "That's not how it works. I'm nobody's own. I sent you some lyrics, but that does not make me yours."

"Really." He moved closer, until their bodies touched. "Tell me again. And tell me in a way to make me believe you."

"I'm not yours," she had repeated, battling her desire. "And I'm not going to be in your bed tonight."

There had been surprise and delight in his eyes. "Right, my flower. Let's do the concert and see how the night goes. Just promise me you won't run."

"I'm not one of your groupies or one of the girls running after you."

And her astonishment when he had drawn back, his dark eyes serious and thoughtful, all play and flirting gone out of them.

"I'm sorry. I didn't mean…that's not what I want you to think."

Sean's voice had echoed from somewhere down the hallway to them, and Jon had sighed.

"I don't know what to say. When I first saw you I wanted to reach out to you. You are not one of those girls. I have a feeling there won't be any other girls anymore. Please tell me you won't go away."

There he had been: the famous singer, the rocketing star of the worldwide music scene, pleading. Black mane nearly to his shoulders, dressed in jeans and a faded t-shirt, holding her hand, waiting for a reply.

"I'll stay." Naomi had said.

She had stood at the side of the stage with Sal and Russ during the concert. The music had been so loud and insistent, it went right through her body and made her breastbone vibrate. Sal and Russ had been joking, commenting on the girls glued to the edge of the stage, screaming their heads off and reaching for Jon. From time to time he bent down to touch one hand or another, but he always stepped back again before any one of them could hold on to him. Sean, right behind him at the keyboards, had always been in close communication with him, the band around and beside him a well-tuned unit, in complete harmony with their singer and each other. They had belted out one song after the other, the huge audience singing and jumping and swaying to Jon's music. In the short intermission after he had introduced the band and they'd played their solos, Jon had come over, grabbed her around the waist, and kissed her. This time there was a wild and heady promise in that kiss, and it left her breathless and in turmoil when he walked out again to launch into the rocking, suggestively erotic version of the "River" song they had rehearsed earlier in the afternoon.

After the show there had been a party. The band never seemed to get enough of their own playing, so they had usurped the empty ballroom of the big Geneva hotel, opened the piano, and gotten out their instruments. Jon had held her close but had never given her the feeling he was pushing her. At some point he asked Sal to order the limousine and had taken her home, making her promise to be with him again the next day, to be ready when he came to pick her up at noon.

SHE DIDN'T KNOW where to turn with the memories that had come flooding back, thoughts and pictures she had kept under lock and key for so long they had faded like an old sepia photograph. It made her realize it was truly possible to destroy something wonderful and special simply by deciding to forget it.

For an eternity she had refused to think of those first days with him, the whirlwind speed with which he had grabbed her from her life and taken her away on the tour across Europe and then back home to California where they came to rest in the big house by the sea.

Being alone at this time of night in the apartment felt strange now and reminded her of the long years she had lived like this, the first to show up in the morning, the last to go to bed at night, always by herself. She would walk into the silence of her room, sit down at her desk and most nights come up with a few lines, stare at the darkness outside and listen to the solitude that wrapped itself around her like a taunting, silky mist.

Naomi stood inside her door, missing the caress and the inviting, softly spoken words that would seduce her and tempt her and heat her blood and never let her be lonesome.

This was what it meant to have found the love of her life. She would grasp this feeling of longing and put it down in words and then put the paper down before Sean and Jon. And they would make a new song.

HE NO LONGER dressed in t-shirts and sneakers, but wore a silk shirt and a leather jacket. His hair was a lot shorter, the shoulders wider, his whole body better toned, and as he climbed out of the water-taxi with Sal on his heels he looked better to Naomi than he ever had back then.

Exhilarated to see him, angry and relieved, she shouted across the pier: "Don't ever pull a stunt like that again, you useless punk! What were you thinking?"

Jon laughed at her as he strode forward to draw her into his arms and kiss her.

"Is that my woman, yelling at me like a fishwife at the top of her lungs? You taste good. Andrea made cinnamon rolls, I take it?"

He kissed her again, harder.

She embraced him fiercely. "Don't do that again, or I might pick one of the others to warm my bed."

"Oh." Sal came up behind them. "Please. Take me. I've always wanted someone to shout at me like that."

"Sorry, Sal." Naomi released Jon. "But I'm afraid it would have to be Sean. I need sensitive men in my life. Like this one here."

"Yeah, sure." Sal shrugged. "I never get a chance with the quality women. Someday I'll have to figure out why that is."

Jon gestured back toward the plane. "Look, Baby, I brought some people to see you. Go say hello."

Her parents. She was stunned.

"What did you do? What have you been up to, Jon?"

He grinned easily. "You were unhappy, and I didn't like to see you unhappy. So I went to meet your parents and talk to them, and I think they're relieved to realize I'm not the monster they thought. Oh yes, I also bought you that bracelet you wanted." His hands were still on her waist, holding her firmly.

"You are truly and completely insane." Naomi peered around his shoulder. "You can't have been to Geneva and back in this time. What did my parents say when you walked in on them? Oh Jon, the terrible things you do."

"Well, I told you all about the jet thing when I first came to you, remember? It's easy, really. And darling, don't fret. Everything is fine."

How could it be, she wanted to reply, seeing her father's stern face and the silence in her mother's eyes, receiving a cool greeting from them in reply to her softly spoken welcome.

HE LED THEM to a table in a far corner of the restaurant, close to the large bay window and well away from any listeners, dismissing Russ and Sal with a small wave of his hand.

"I'm only going to discuss this once," Jon said when coffee had been served and he had made Naomi sit down beside him. "Your parents have to realize how serious I am about you."

Her father nodded without looking at her, his hands folded on the tabletop, and her mother stared out at the post ship as it came into the harbor. Unhappiness was painted on her face, and a sad compliance.

"Part of yesterday we spent at a Swiss lawyer's office," Jon went on, "to set a few things in order. I won't go into details now, but Joshua's set financially, and so are you. I've also put my will in order. Your parents are satisfied with the arrangements."

Naomi jumped from her chair and retreated from them, afraid of what was to come next.

"Sit down, you silly girl." Jon smiled at her fondly. "It's time you came to terms with the hard facts of life."

"No." Adamantly now, and with a swift step away when he tried to reach for her, "If you people think it is necessary to haggle, then fine. I'm not going to be part of this. I don't want your money, and I don't need any contracts. It's you who wants to get married so badly. Loving you has nothing to do with your wealth, and you know it. Take care of our son all you like, but leave me out of it."

They stared after her as she walked away, coffee cup in hand.

"Naomi, come back here," Jon called, but she did not return.

Andrea was in a deep discussion with the other cooks when she walked in and sat down on one of the kitchen stools.

"Bastard," she hissed under her breath, "Thinks he owns me body and soul and pulls these incredible stunts and then expects me to fall into his arms with happiness. Thinks he can have everything with those dangerous eyes of his and his music, but not me, oh no."

With a shake of her head Andrea dismissed the others.

"Thinks it's a grand idea to go to Geneva and pluck up my parents to bring them here, and not even tell me. Thinks he can bring back a few diamonds and get me to—"

"Go on, I want to hear you finish that sentence." Jon threw open the swinging door with verve. "Say it out loud, Baby."

"You!" She rounded on him. "I'm not going to finish it! Make me if you can! You run off like that and come striding back in my door and tell me how much I'm worth to you?"

He was in a fine mood. Without much a word he grabbed Naomi's hand and pulled her with him before she could protest. Back in the apartment, when the door had fallen into the lock, he pushed her against the wood and demanded: "Go on. I want to hear the rest of that sentence."

His hands were on her body, holding her firmly and touching her in an incredibly arousing way. Naomi struggled against both him and her rising lust.

"No. I won't. Make me if you want to hear it."

"Oh, I will." Jon moved against her until she gasped. "And I get the feeling you'll love it, my little beast. God, but you drive me crazy. I want you so when you get like this. Come on, tell me. What was it with the diamonds?"

When there was no answer he kissed her, his tongue moving in her mouth in a slow, suggestive way that made her knees buckle.

"Finish that sentence now?"

She was furious. "Oh, alright! Here you are! You think you'll get me to lay myself down on your bed naked again."

His breath quickened and his grip grew tighter..

"You think you'll get me to yearn for your kisses and touches and your soft song when you know I am at your mercy and delirious and weak and aching for you. You want me to beg you to never stop and to never let me go and and please, never let the light of dawn inside the room again so the night might never end. You'll get me to tell you how

I love you and how I long for you all the time, and you'll make me tell you all my secret dreams."

Here, with him breathing hard, his body straining toward hers, Naomi pushed him away and said firmly: "But that's not how it works. You'll never get me to sign contracts and accept money or your obscure transactions. Forget it, my friend."

He laughed in surprise and frustration.

Seriously, and a lot calmer, Naomi went on: "I don't want any money from you. Take me for what I am, don't buy me. We were happy together before Sal showed up. Please don't make the world think I've brought you to your knees and bled you out. I know I'll get anything I could possibly desire from you and probably more, but don't do this." After a brief pause, she added, "It might make me run off with Sean, you know, to experience the true sense of music, without all your commercial bullshit."

"In a minute," his voice raspy with passion, "I'll have you flat on that table over there, and this time, my dove, there'll be no mercy. I'll drive this Sean talk right out of you if there is no other way to stop you."

"No. In a minute we'll be back upstairs to explain to my parents why we vanished all of a sudden, and you, my love, will be on your best behavior. No more sex talk once we're back with the adults. And nothing more until bedtime either."

He drew a very deep breath, watching her carefully as she put her clothes back in order and redid her braid. "I don't know how I survived without you. How could I have forgotten? You could always do this to me. Make me want you so bad it hurts, make me want to possess you and have you close all the time."

"Let's go," Naomi said. "I don't want my father to get the wrong impression. Besides, if we keep this up much longer, I'll take you up on your offer. You know, the Sean talk, and the table, and so on. And by the way, you've tried that before, and it didn't work. Guess you'll have to try a little harder next time."

Jon tried to catch her, but she was gone.

WHEN THEY SAT down again with her parents, Sean came over with the lyrics she had given him only that morning and laid them down before Jon, who read them briefly.

"Listen," Sean offered, "I've been over these, and I've come up with a nifty little melody. I'd like to give it a try, if it's okay with you, Jon?"

"Oh, if Naomi gave them to you I expect she wants you to work with them, and not I. Sal handles her contracts, so check it out with him."

Which caused her father to raise his eyebrows.

"We see to it that everyone gets his or her share, here in our little group. Naomi has received every penny she made for her work." Jon paused for a sip of coffee, clearly savoring the moment.

"Of course, if I had known earlier where she was, there would have been no need for her to wait so long for it."

Naomi was on the point of walking off again, but this time he was ready and held on to her. There was a tinge of bitterness in his words and in the way he clasped her fingers, the sorrow for all the misspent time welling up again.

"You see, I really would have preferred to take care of Naomi rather than just take care of her money. I know I failed her badly, but I never got a second chance. You are a very unforgiving family. I'm glad you can find it in your heart to accept me now, because I can't give up your daughter. There never was another."

"That's really hard to believe." There was a small, doubtful smile on Lucia's lips."There must be a huge choice for you."

"Yes, there is." He shrugged. "But it's a choice that I made long ago. I, for my part, don't have to reconsider."

"So how much did you make with your songwriting?" Her father turned to Naomi, which made her wilt where she sat. "You know I love to talk about money, and your man here is rather good at it."

She shook her head, refusing an answer, but beckoned to Sal who had entered with Russ.

"My father wants to talk business. You do it. I'm sick of it. First you come and dump those papers in my lap, and then you let yourself be dragged across the continent to help buy me off my family. So finish it. Close the deal, and then tell me how much I'm worth to the Master."

"Oh, he didn't tell you?" Sal took her seat when she rose. "You're getting half of his property, the romantic fool. On the day you become his wife you'll be filthy rich. You'll own something like a quarter of a billion."

HE WANTED TO go after her, but Sal held him back. They stood in the lobby, Sal holding his arm, Jon angry because he wouldn't let go.

"I told you," Sal said. "I told you it would be a mistake. You don't understand her as well as you think, my friend. You refuse to see the purity in her, the uncompromising love she holds for you. All this, it means nothing to her. You may think it's great fun to spoil her and shower her with gifts, but it's not what she needs. Open your eyes and look at what you've got, Jon. Don't ruin it. You're pushing her to her limits." He shook his head. "All the sex in the world or soft, sweet songs won't stop her from running if she can't take the rest. You should know better."

Surprise washed over Jon. He looked at Sal for a good long while, but Sal did not budge. "I won't let you ruin her life again."

"Maybe," Jon said slowly, "Maybe Naomi is looking to the wrong man, Sal? Could your heart be in this a little deeper than it should be?"

"My heart is my own, and only for me to know. I don't go for complicated women, as you should well know." Sal let go of him and took a step back. "But I won't let you destroy the best thing you've ever had, in every respect. She makes a better person of you, and we all know it. You pined for her for seventeen years, and you're putting it all on the line."

"I meant well." Jon knew he sounded defensive and petulant. "I thought it would please her if I got her parents to accept me."

"Yes, and the gesture was truly grand. For her father. But not for Naomi."

Sean came out of the restaurant, Lucia a few steps behind them. "Problem?"

"Oh, Jon messed up again." Sal lit a cigarette. "Our girl is out there being miserable, and he hasn't a clue what he did this time."

Jon turned on him, but Sal only shrugged, unimpressed. "Go write a song, for God's sake. That's something that nearly always turns out right. Or go sing something to the hills, maybe they'll understand what you want. But otherwise, shut up. Let other people repair what you messed up."

Sean sighed and began to move toward the door, but Lucia held him back.

"I'll go. I think this calls for a mother-daughter talk."

NAOMI WAS LOOKING at her ring when her mother sat down next to her on the pier wall, turning it on her finger so the beautiful stone caught the light and sparkled with all the colors of the rainbow.

"I never liked it here." Lucia looked out over the water toward the ocean. "Sometimes even Geneva seems too cold for me. Why you chose to come here I will never understand."

There was no reply.

"You know," Lucia went on, "when you came home all those years ago, so torn and hurt, we thought he had done something truly terrible to you and you had fled from Jon. I hated that man and his voice on the radio whenever I heard him sing."

"Mama, stop, please."

"He came to your father yesterday and laid down all those documents to show him how very, very serious he was about you. He asked our forgiveness, and he asked for you as his wife. He was very solemn about it, and all he wanted in return was for us to be present at your wedding. That is all. It was a compelling gesture, and it softened even your father. You can always impress Olaf with money." She smiled wryly. "But that's not important. It was meant to overwhelm your parents and bring them around to the idea of their daughter marrying the man they held responsible for her sad and secluded life up here in the cold." She took a deep breath before she went on. "Does he know at all who you are, Naomi? Does he know what he is getting by marrying you? Have you told him?"

A small, stubborn shake of her head.

"Child, you can't let him walk into your life blindly like that. It is utterly unfair to him. He needs to know. You have to tell him. He thinks you are virtually penniless, when nothing could be further from the truth. Why do you keep your real life from him like that? It's not as if we were criminals, Naomi."

Naomi, her lips pressed together tightly, watched a couple of tourists walk by.

"You need to relent, Naomi. Do not throw away what fate has given you. You are getting a second chance. If throwing all that money at you will make your father accept you marrying Jon, then that is a small price to pay. It is only your pride that has been hurt." Her mother gave her a gentle push. "Go, dear. He is desperate because he cannot fathom what he did wrong. He so wanted to please you."

When she returned to the hotel lobby, she got the strongest feeling of being thrown back in time, but this time she walked right up to him and into his arms, the way she had wanted to back then, in Geneva.

"Right, then," she said. "Take me away to your concert, and then convince me to go to your hotel room with you again. Find another dark and empty hallway to do it, too."

"So will you come this time?" he asked, folding her into his embrace.

13

"YOU NEED TO tell him," Lucia had said, and Naomi knew she was right.

Sean and Jon would make some music tonight, like the old days, a small, private concert for family and friends meant to show her parents who they were.

Jon had retreated to Joshua's room for some practice after lunch. When he opened the door to her knock, she had the weirdest sense of deja vu, as if she had been transported back to another place altogether. This could have been any hotel room in any city in the world, right before a concert, with him preparing for the performance. He stood before her with his guitar in his hand, a deep line of concentration on his brow and a faraway look in his eyes, but his face lit up when he saw her.

"My love. What a nice distraction."

Naomi gazed at him through the open doorway, mesmerized by the moment. She had geared herself up to talk to him about her family, but seeing him like this blew it conveniently out of her mind.

"What's wrong?" Her silence disturbed him. "Has something happened? Talk to me."

Spellbound, that was the word for it, far out of time and place, somewhere else altogether. For an instant she had seen him as the public perceived him. The star, so far removed from everyday concerns that he never appeared to be truly real, but remained a vision and an object of desire. An icon.

"I know why I love you. But why do you love me? What do you see in me? Why am I that special to you? You could have any woman in the whole wide world, but you want me. Why?" She blushed at her own words and the way she said them, like a star-struck teenager.

He smiled softly. "Well, not every woman. There are those who prefer Robbie Williams or even Mick, though I could never understand what anyone sees in him."

Jon put his guitar aside and pulled her into the room. "Don't stand out there as if you had no right to be here. What's wrong with you?"

"Why me?"

"Baby, what do you need to hear? You know you are my one true love. Come here." He laughed in surprise.

The door closed behind her, and she looked around. There were music sheets on the bed, a half-empty water bottle and an ashtray with a cold cigar in it on the table right next to his glasses. Naomi picked up the papers on the bedcover and laid them aside so she could sit.

"I stood in the doorway and looked at you and saw what all the others see. It was the weirdest moment. For an instant you were that strange, faraway star who has no place in a normal girl's life and who has no time for a normal girl in his life because he can have his pick of movie stars and models."

"Ah." Jon sat down beside her. "That. Honestly? I don't know. So many women think they're in love with me because they see me on stage or listen to my songs, but they don't know me at all. They see the illusion created by Sal's maneuvering, the lighting technicians, and the band's music, and, my dear, the shirts you deplore so much. It's true that many would like to get closer…but I think they would be rather disappointed, don't you agree? Besides, who said you were a normal girl?"

He picked up his guitar as Naomi settled back against the headboard. She watched as he played, his back to her, head bent to listen to his melodies, singing in an undertone. A pleasant drowsiness crept up on her as she listened to his voice, its perfect modulation, the dark timbre, the compelling sound of it.

He seemed lost in thought, but Naomi was content to wait and push the dreaded truths her mother insisted she tell him far away, as far as she could, and let time solve her problems for her.

He would not mind. He would not turn from her.

"I loved your lips first," Jon said suddenly, "and the way you looked at me. Sweet, trembling, soft lips and a cool challenge in your eyes. God, what a mixture. Your lips, begging to be kissed, while you sized me up to see if I was worthy of you. You were so reticent and cruel that day. Such a lofty, cool way of putting me in my place you had. 'That's not how it works," you said to me, just like you did this morning, you fiend. I remember I wanted the ground to open up beneath my feet and swallow me, I was that ashamed."

He moved around so he could see her at the other end of the bed.

"You sent that sheaf of lyrics to me in Los Angeles, and there was no letter or explanation to go with it, just a terse 'sing this'. How Sal laughed! 'This is one cool number,' he said. And then into the lobby of that hotel walked the loveliest girl, the essence of all I had ever dreamed and written about, and she walked right up to me and I know I'll have to make her mine, just like that, and, please God, hold on to her, because this is perfection, she is perfection, made for me." He fell silent for a while, as if reliving that day.

"Mine. My very own. And of course the next night, when you finally let me love you…"

Naomi's breath caught.

"I knew there would be no way back once I had you in my arms," Jon said. "I would just drown in the terrible need I felt for you, and it would hold me prisoner forever. Even back then, my love, back in Geneva, you could have asked anything of me. It would have been yours. I would have given up the music, my singing, and my life. I wanted you that badly."

She shook her head slightly, embarrassed by this unexpected outpouring, the way he put it, so final and dramatic.

"I remember laying you down on that bed, you were so lovely and soft and virginal, I remember you were afraid, but also ready for me, oh, I know you were. And I remember that first time, oh God yes, and you moved toward me with those gentle sighs of yours and gave yourself over so unconditionally. It was like no other lovemaking I had ever experienced. It was so much more. It felt as if the universe itself had opened to welcome us into its embrace." Jon tugged on her hands to get her to look at him.

"It still feels that way to me, Naomi, every time we are together. It feels that way when you walk into a room and I see you. Now that I have you back, I feel the unbearable emptiness of those years without you. I was selfish and distracted and uncaring. You should never have had to endure what you did, and I should have fought a lot harder to find you again…" His words trailed off.

Silence sat between them. Naomi did not want to talk about the loss again. The thought of all that wasted time was too much to bear.

Jon shifted closer to her. "Come, Baby. Come and let me kiss you. Let me love you." His eyes wandered to her lips. "Come to me."

It was so hard, and the compulsion so strong. Every fiber in her wanted to give in, but she resisted.

"No. No. Singing before pleasure. We'll see if you can convince me later. And it might not even be tonight."

"You're killing me." Jon sighed. "Really, Naomi. I so want you now."

"Not happening." She slipped off the bed, but he looked so distraught that she gave him a peck on his brow before she left.

She returned to the lobby to find Solveigh ordering Russ around as if he were nothing more than a bellboy, totally oblivious to the fact that he normally ordered around a host of people himself.

"Your hair is down," Naomi commented, "You never have your hair down."

"Well, now it is. Russ thinks it looks nice." Solveigh fluffed her golden curls, as an engrossed Russ watched.

Sal, coming out of the dining room with Sean, whistled at the sight of them.

"You look exactly like you did that day in Geneva," he said to Naomi, "What are you playing at here? Are there any girls left for me, or are Jon and Russ taking up all there is? What about me, the guy who makes the money for them? Left out in the cold as usual?"

"To each what he deserves, Sal."

Solveigh laughed at her acerbic response, but the moment the words were out Naomi knew she had hurt him. Sal nodded slightly. He lit a cigarette and walked out into the street, where he stood watching the few clouds in the clear blue sky.

Naomi followed him out into the biting air. "What's wrong, Sal?"

He took a moment to reply. "It's okay, Naomi. I know you meant it as a joke. We don't always get what we want in life, at least not all of us. And it's okay, but sometimes we don't find out what we want until it's too late."

"But Sal…" Naomi was at a loss. "Then you need to say what it is you want. You always seem so tough and contained. What do you want?"

He turned to look at her, smiling a little, his wild locks blowing in the breeze.

"We'll be hearing some great music tonight. Has Jon done some vocalizing? Is he prepared to sing?"

She knew she was missing something, but she could not figure out what it was.

He reached out to put a curl of her hair in order. "You look so good. I never thought I'd see you again. You were like a mirage…there and then gone."

"Sal." Jon's voice, cool, calm and distant.

"You need to keep your soul," Sal whispered so only she could hear him. "Keep it intact. Don't give yourself away completely, no matter how seductive the prospect seems."

She heard his words, but she did not know what to do with them.

The men stared at each other over her head. Jon had a dark, calculating expression that scared her.

Sal walked away from them.

"You're jealous of Sal! I can't believe it, Jon. You should know better! I just don't believe it, shame on you!"

It seemed as if he woke up from a disturbing dream when he looked at her and his face lit up a little.

"Why are you out here?" she asked, "Everyone else is inside."

He looked at his watch. "Waiting. What people do when they're standing outside a hotel. I've asked for another musician. Should be here any moment now, he just called."

After a moment she left him to it.

THERE HAD BEEN no announcement, but in a community as small as Halmar, word spread quickly that there were famous musicians staying at the hotel and that they would be performing that night.

People began to drift in, settling down for a bite or a glass, happy to share the comfort and food of the restaurant and each other's company. Being who they were—neighbors, shop owners, friends of hotel staff—they never even asked if they were welcome. They just hung around patiently, ordering one cup of coffee after another, or after a surreptitious glance at their watches, stronger drinks.

"What's the Jonman doing out there?" Sean asked when she joined them.

Naomi threw up her hands. "Waiting. Smoking probably, and I don't know what. Having stupid, unnecessary words with Sal, would you believe it, about Sal talking to me in a way he did not like, the jealous bastard. Really, Sean. Have you ever heard anything more ridiculous?"

"He's afraid of losing what took him so long to get back, Sweetie. He isn't sure of you yet. You were the only one to ever walk away from him. You were the only one he ever wanted to go after, and he had to wait a long, long time before he could. You don't walk away from the Master." The first slow melodies shaped themselves when his fingers moved over the piano keyboard.

"The Master," she repeated softly. "Like hell."

The music ended abruptly.

Naomi heard Russ' soft "Well, slap me sideways till I cry," as he turned to look at the doorway, where a young man stood in the entrance, guitar case over his shoulder and travel bag in hand. It was Joshua, in a grey shirt and leather jacket just like Jon's, his dark wavy hair a little too long, his stance so much like his father's it was almost comical.

There was pride in Jon's eyes, and satisfaction. He watched Naomi embrace Joshua. His oldest friends were at his side, and they were on the verge of going out to play to an appreciative audience. He thought of the thick collection of new songs waiting on the piano downstairs and felt, for the first time in a long time—maybe for the first time in his life—complete. Everything came together for him in that moment. The feeling was one he had searched for in so many songs. *Belonging.*

Sean began to play again, starting off with a lively song from their early days.

Jon did not wait for a long introduction. He sang with the abandon and verve of a glad heart, with the rhythm and easiness of long practice, the guitar coming to life in his hands.

Sitting unceremoniously on the low coffee table in the lobby, Joshua unpacked his own instrument and began to tune it.

"Dad phoned last night and told me he would send a plane, but I couldn't get away sooner. There was a class this afternoon I could'nt miss. Sorry. But it was cool to be picked up in a car and then flown here in a private jet. He said he brought my grandparents here today as well, that he wanted them to get to know him. Wow, Mom, this is so cool. He's much better like this, just listen! He doesn't need a big stage. He goes all Hollywood in the concert hall, and here he's so honest and..." he searched for the right word, "straightforward, yes?"

"Dad?" Naomi repeated, "When did this Dad thing come about?"

Joshua shrugged as he plucked a few experimental chords. "It's what he is, right? I don't like calling my parents by their first names, Mom. That's fake coolness. I always wanted to know who my father was, but this is so much better than anything I could have dreamt up. Thank you, Mom."

"My pleasure."

He joined Jon and Sean, falling right into the song they were playing without missing a beat. He even sang along, his young voice a nice addition to Jon's clear baritone. From where she stood, Naomi could see her parents sitting with Sal and Russ, her father staring out at the water, bored and impatient, her mother smiling at Joshua. She caught Sal gazing at her, but he looked away when their eyes met and poured himself another drink. Russ was busy with Solveigh. He even ignored Jon's little introductory speech, totally smitten by her cloud of golden hair and sunny smile.

From the piano came the solo she knew only too well, the River, and Sean was playing it just the way she remembered: cool, dry, jazzy, suggestive. Jon raised his chin at her, challenge in his smoldering stare, enough to make her hot with yearning.

They performed well into the night.

14

JON THANKED THEM gracefully after their last song, then came over and pulled Naomi down the hallway that led to her apartment. The light was dim and the noise of the restaurant seemed far away. Someone called after them, but he didn't stop until they were nearly at the door to the guest room. Then he let go of her hand and spoke to her in a low, enticing voice.

"My pretty lady, I saw you sitting there all by yourself, and I thought we might get to know each other a little better."

She stepped back against the wall as he used his body to corner her.

"After all those songs, I need some love. I'd hate to go home alone on such a night." Song lyrics, he had never used something like them on another woman. There had never been the need. "Let's go somewhere quiet, and let me hold you. Come, my lovely dove, I can feel your need, your sweet lips are trembling with desire and I can hardly wait to taste them."

Naomi let the words hang between them for a few heartbeats.

Then she said, "That's not how it works."

Jon was speechless.

"You don't need the seduction routine to get me in your bed, Mr. Stone."

He had the eerie feeling of being in some venue after a show, with a strange girl he'd invited backstage for a few hours of mindless amusement.

"You can have me wherever you want. I've been yours for so long I can't even think of another."

He took her into the guest room with all its disorder, the faint smell of cigars still in the air, music sheets all over the place and a half-empty coffee mug on the bedside table.

When he had her on the bed, he made love to her with the passion that had been building in him all day, along with the drive from the songs he had sung.

"Tell me. Tell me you are mine alone."

Naomi gasped.

"Tell me. I need to hear you say it. Tell me there'll never be another for you!" His hand dug into her hair. "I want you to be mine. God, how long I've wanted this! To sing to you and then make love to you, pour all my love into you, imprint you with it. Mine, oh yes."

"I'm yours," she managed. "You know I've always been yours. There has never been another."

"Oh, the thought is with me all the time." His words came in a rough tumble; there was a raw vulnerability in them Naomi had never expected to hear from him. "I see you every morning, every day. You are real and you let me hold you and love you, and still I'm afraid I'll wake up one day and you'll not want me anymore, decide I don't fit into your life, and send me away."

"That's absurd. I've given you no reason to fear such a thing. You aren't thinking I'm serious about Sean, are you?"

He couldn't tell if she was joking. "I saw you with Sal out there on the street, and I saw how he looks at you. It brought back the memory of how he was always around when I was too busy or too hyped for you."

She pushed him aside and sat up. "You can't mean it! Do you really believe I would run off with Sal? Are you out of your mind?"

There was no prompt reply. Tentatively Jon reached out to draw her back to him, but she retreated to the edge of the bed.

"No, no, we'll have this out now."

Jon watched as she pulled the bed sheet toward her but did not wrap it around herself, rather sitting before him in wonderful nakedness, her hair falling around her body like a dark curtain, its ends curling on the linen, her skin glowing softly in the dim light.

"You are so beautiful, it breaks my heart just look at you. So lovely. Why aren't there dozens of lovesick men around you? Why did they let you remain alone? Did no one ever try to pick you, my sweet rose?"

A gentle silence descended on them. The beam of the lighthouse washed over the bay, and all was quiet.

"Jon, don't you know no one else could ever stand up to you? Didn't I tell you clearly enough that no one could hold my heart, not as long as you are alive, not ever? I tried to love someone else a couple of times, but then there you were, your voice on the radio, somewhere, anywhere, and you would have me tied up again, unable to touch another. Yours. I was yours before we ever met. And you know it."

Gradually she came closer again, drawn by the need to be touched. He laid her back down, his hands on her body, finding places to caress and strokes that made her breath catch and her eyes close in bliss.

Naomi sighed. "I love when you possess me with all your power and look down at me and I can't move or breathe or think, and you, so strong, relentless, hard and forceful."

"I know, my little beast," Jon whispered in her ear. "Oh God, yes I know. And how I love it. It drives me over the edge, the way you yield to me."

"Never doubt me again. Never." She took hold of his chin and made him look into her eyes. "I should not have left that night. I was young and stupid and frightened and out of my mind. Now I would come after you, into your gritty little prison cell, and give you hell. And I would get Sal to hire a whole office of lawyers to sue the police department for seeing me naked while I made love to my man."

"All right, Baby. Tell me about it." He smiled at the bravado in her voice.

"I was only your little lovebird, and I never took a step out of that house without you. My life centered around you completely. I had no life of my own."

Jon thought about her words. He laid her head back on his chest and drew his fingers through her hair, smoothing it down.

"This time," Naomi went on, "it was my decision. I could have thrown you out right away. I could throw you out now, but I chose not to do so, I chose to cast my lot with you and your crazy life." She sat up and gazed down at him. "I did not like the stunt you pulled on me with my father. For a moment there, I hated you and your arrogance. Oh, I appreciate the sentiment, but it was pushy and manipulative. I would have liked to have been informed. I like all those things about you in our lovemaking, but you overdo it with the money thing."

There was no reply. He merely watched her intently.

"I know you are rich. Of course you are. It would be a terrible shame if you weren't. Of course I know I'll get whatever I want from you and probably a lot more, but not like this. Don't push your wealth at me. My love for you, it was never about wealth and fame. I wanted *you*, your songs, your music, the magic we can create together. You, in my bed.

You, loving me the way you do…" Jon saw her face go soft and dreamy with the memory of their lovemaking. "And then you dare to question me, you miserable punk," Naomi said, blasting the mood away. "You make love to me until I'm ready to scream, and then you have the nerve to demand promises and vows from me? Well, how's this for a change: no more lovemaking until we are married!"

"Are you out of your mind?" Jon sat up straight. "You aren't serious! You can't be! Tell me you aren't serious. No, you're joking."

A small, wicked smile appeared on her lips. "Well now that I see your reaction I think I am serious. It will be fun to watch you live with it."

"You'll get yourself into trouble." He caught her in his arms. "You might get kidnapped on your way to your apartment and be ravished in the hallway, or abducted to a strange bed and assaulted by a desperate, starving man."

"I might just take the risk for that experience." Naomi mused. "It sounds like fun. I rather like being ravished by desperate men, being the Coca-Cola shareholder that I am."

"Oh, Miss Scarlett, don't play games with me." Jon kissed her wildly. "You know what happens when you do this."

"Yes." Her arms went around his neck. "Cities get burned."

15

THEY WERE ALONE again. Only Russ and Sal had stayed behind to help Jon start work on the soundtrack, with Sean promising to be back in a few weeks.

Naomi watched Jon escort Joshua to the water taxi, his hand firmly on the boy's shoulder, talking to him in a low voice. Joshua laughed at what he said and even hugged him briefly before he climbed in.

Her parents, that was harder. Jon never left her side while they waited for their transportion, and even though her father was civil enough, promising they would be back for the wedding, she could see that it was said with reservation.

Lucia took her hand and assured her all would be well, but Olaf glowered at his wife, and she fell silent again.

Naomi could have sworn she heard Jon mumble "Bastard!" as her father got into the plane, but couldn't be sure so she let it rest.

How much things were going to change became crystal clear when Sal said he would be leaving shortly to meet the movie people and also, with a doubtful glance at Naomi, start working on a tour for next summer, if she and Jon were okay with that.

Naomi, a bright gleam in her eyes, nodded. She wanted a tour. She wanted to get out into the world again. She wanted to fly and live in the music. And she wanted to work with Jon on the soundtrack, despite her fear of having to deliver lyrics on demand again. Yes, she wanted it.

He had presented it to her so circumspectly after her parents had left, the excitement over the project wearing off fast with the realization that it would take him back to Los Angeles a lot sooner than he had ever imagined, and he had no idea how she would react. But there had been no reluctance in her response. She wanted to write for him. About returning to California she had said nothing.

When he asked her where there might be room for a studio, she only shrugged.

"Come with me," she said, and led him to the elevator and then all the way up to the attic. It was cavernous and dusty, with a few pieces of furniture stacked in one corner, lit by a few small windows but otherwise gloomy and very quiet.

"Have fun," he heard the echo of her voice in the large, empty space. "Play to your heart's content. Tell me what else you want."

"A nice smooth table," came his instant reply. "Large enough, the right height, sturdy, made from the finest wood."

"Jon." She had wandered away to open one of the pigeonhole windows. "You are so crazy. In fact, you are the craziest bastard in the whole wide world."

"Why would you say such a mean thing, my little beast?"

He had discovered the light switch and turned it on. A single, tired bulb lit up in response. "I'm a man who needs a lot of inspiration, is all. And I'm lucky, because I know where to go for inspiration."

He heard her soft laughter drift across the huge room, elusive as a fairy tinkle. She came back and put her arms around him, fitting her body to his, and listened as he told her about the work they would soon be doing.

"What book is this movie based on? You didn't say."

They returned to the apartment where she made coffee for him. It had become a ritual, a simple domestic task that brought them back to the basic reality of life.

He told her it was something or other about Captain Ahab and a wife of his, a love story he thought, he had no idea, and neither had Russ or Sal.

Naomi looked at him disdainfully. She put down the tin of coffee and went over to her bookshelf to take out a thick volume.

"Here, you illiterate punk." She dropped it into his hands. "It's one of the most beautiful books ever written. It's sad and happy and it does tell a great love story, but it's much more than that. And you're telling me you are going to write the music for that movie? But Jon, that's wonderful! I'll have to tell Solveigh right away. She'll love it. And I promise, you'll like the book."

He was skeptical, but he spent the rest of the afternoon on the couch reading.

"You know," Jon said much later, scandalized, "they eat their dead friend. This is gruesome."

It made Naomi smile. "Wouldn't you do everything to survive if you were shipwrecked in a little boat with a dead body and not much else?"

There was no swift reply. She turned to face him. "If you weren't prepared to save your own life, how far would you go to save mine?"

He did not respond.

"Tell me, how far would you go? Would you make me eat human flesh to save my life? What would you do?"

"And what would *you* do?" he asked back. "Have you asked yourself?"

"Sure!" This was easy. "We read that book years ago, Solveigh, the others, and I, and we had that discussion way back then." A flutter of her hands. "They were a little taken aback at my reaction. I told them that if I were in that situation with the one I loved, I would force-feed him if necessary. I said I would probably cut out pieces of myself to keep him alive."

Her coffee cup was empty, so she got up for a refill. Jon watched her walk past him and return to her desk.

She shrugged a little. "And if the situation was hopeless, the dead body completely eaten and no water left at all, then what? Would you be able to kill your beloved, to save her from suffering a slow, gruesome death?"

"You aren't serious, are you? This is strictly academic?" There was, well hidden beneath her sweet face, a steely core that scared him.

"Well, obviously it is, since there's plenty of food and drink in the fridge, and Andrea would never let us go hungry, and we aren't sitting in a tiny boat right now. But, you haven't told me what you would do. Eat or not eat? Kill or not kill?"

As if to underline her words, she popped a chocolate cookie in her mouth.

"Really, Naomi." He looked at her full of incredulity and a good measure of disgust.

"What? You brought it up, now finish the thought."

"I can't tell you," Jon said, deeply uncomfortable. "I don't want to even think about such things."

He fell silent for a while, staring out at the rain.

Naomi returned to her writing, amused by his reticence. "You see, that's the difference between men and women. Women are simply more romantic. At least in thought, we would willingly give our life for the one we love. You guys, you can't even theorize about such a thing."

"Oh, but that's a totally different discussion!" There was relief in his voice. "Giving my life for you or making you eat the most disgusting stuff to ensure your survival is easy. But killing you to spare you suffering…" He shook his head. "I would not give up hope until the very end. I would never give up hope." His tone took on a new quality. "I didn't give up hope, *ever*. Even in my darkest hours, when you seemed as lost as the drowned sun, there was always the dream of hope, the faintest flicker, and the belief that fate could not be that cruel. And when I felt all hope had gone, there would come a moment when it crept back in like a hurt little mouse lying on my doorstep. I refused to believe it was all gone; that would have been lethal. And see where it has gotten me. No, my love, no mercy killings. Not for me, not for you."

Jon regarded her back and bent head, the way she did not react to his words. "And you? What about your hope?"

For the longest time there was no answer, and he began to think that she was so deep in her lyrics that she had not even heard, so he picked up the book again, stretched out on the couch, and resumed his reading. He thought the story was romantic, liberating, and sometimes even funny, but also disturbing and stark, full of harsh weather, with many difficult partings and lost loves. It was a lot more than he had expected, and he could see a theme for the music shaping from the atmosphere of the book. The ocean, ever present, the loneliness, the many wonderful characters living and breathing in it, and the growth and liberation of the heroine would be wonderful to put into a soundtrack.

"None." Naomi's voice came across the room, so low he almost didn't hear it. He hadn't realized how deeply his words had touched her until she spoke. The book sank from his hands as he waited for her to go on, but nothing else came.

"Naomi?"

"Hope was not in my dictionary." There was a bitter undertone in her hushed words, the sadness and withdrawal back in the set of her body.

"Baby…"

"Don't." She rose and swiftly walked to the door.

"Don't go!" he called, but the door fell shut and she was gone.

It took him a moment to decide what to do before he went in search of her.

Solveigh was in the lobby chatting with Russ, but Naomi was nowhere to be seen.

Solveigh only shrugged. Naomi had walked out with Sal a moment ago, and they had taken the van.

Russ tore his attention away from Solveigh. "Let's have a beer and talk about that movie. They'll show up at some point, and then you can find out where they were." A malicious twinkle appeared in his dark blue eyes. "And what they did."

Jon was on the point of walking out, but Russ held on to his sleeve. "Jon, don't be a fool. Stay here."

Solveigh leaned on the counter. "You shouldn't be so anxious. Naomi doesn't even register the existence of other men."

Her blouse was cut low and loose and showed her cleavage nicely as she bent forward to put some pens in order. Russ looked in appreciation, and Jon's sense of humor returned to a degree seeing his friend so besotted.

"Jon." She took his arm and led him away into the dining room. "You may be a great singer, composer of the greatest love songs this side of the sun, but you are as stupid as any other guy about girls. I take it you had words and Naomi decided to take a break, and now you fear for life, love, and future. She'll be back, and if she really gets fed up with you, let me tell you, it will be you who goes, not Naomi. She'll never let go of this place."

Russ had followed them, listening to Solveigh's speech in amusement.

"Sit here." She pulled out a chair. "Drink a brandy and smoke a cigar. Talk to Russ about your stupid movie or the tour or whatever it is you people talk about, and give it a rest."

Stunned, Jon sat in the indicated place and waited for her to go on. Solveigh brought over a bottle and three glasses and dropped down next to him. Russ stood beside them, curious what she would tell Jon next.

"I've known Naomi for nearly all the time you haven't. You still have the vision of that sweet, innocent young girl. But she's been through a lot, not the least of which included raising your child by herself. And she has always, as long as I have known her, been a totally independent soul. Don't destroy that by being dumb."

He hesitated for a moment before he reacted to her words. It was easy to find an answer, but he didn't want to sound too possessive, too jealous, too needy.

"You are one lucky person, Solveigh. You are the one I really envy, because I didn't get the chance to be with her all that time. Believe me, it was not my decision, and I think you know it. So…" He was so close to confessing his innermost fears, but he broke off.

"So," Solveigh finished his sentence for him, totally unmoved, "so you live in constant fear of doing or saying something wrong and alienating Naomi again."

She poured liberal measures and pushed the glasses across the table. Russ sat down next to her, taking her hand in his and playing with her fingers. She gave him the sunniest smile, a vision of gold and rose and sparkling blue eyes.

"So what was it you said that made her go out with Sal?" Russ' eyes never left her.

Jon was too confused to think up an excuse or a lie. "I told her I never gave up hope."

Solveigh's attention turned to him, and it seemed as if the sun had turned from Russ to him. "Oh. What a wonderful, wonderful thing to say. No wonder you are such a success with the ladies."

"Well, I also asked her how she had fared, hope-wise." Once said, it sounded childish and possessive.

Solveigh again said, "Oh," but this time with less zeal. "That must have been tough for her." She saw the question in Jon's face. "But you know she never talked about you, we never knew who Joshua's father was. Naomi was always so self-contained and silent, a good and kind person, but she never talked about herself. We never knew what she did in her apartment down there when the shift was over. I recall she went to London last year to see a concert, and that was a major event…Oh!"

Naomi had told him that Solveigh was smart.

"She went to see you! Oh. And did you meet her there, then?" She looked expectantly at Jon, waiting for his answer.

There was no elegant way to tell her the stupidity of the whole thing.

"She…" he began, then started again, "I didn't know she was there."

His hand gripped the glass tighter, the bourbon sloshing dangerously.

"I should have felt her presence. I can't understand why I didn't see her. She should have stood out like a torch, a beacon, the sun itself, I don't know. I should have noticed."

"Well." Solveigh cleared her throat. "Here you have the difference between song and reality. It's not important."

"Not important?" He couldn't believe his ears, but she only shrugged.

"Yes, totally unimportant. It finally made her tell Joshua who his father was. She gave way, you see. She knew he would never let it rest. It was rather clever. She turned it all over to you, so there could be no disappointment. If you did not react to Joshua, well, then nothing would have changed for her, and if you did, then all would be right."

She rose to greet some guests entering the hotel, but before she walked away, she said, "What you did, of course, is spectacular beyond imagining. Unheard of, like something out of a love story or a romantic song. If only for that, she would never leave you. No woman would. Let her have her beer with Sal and enjoy her evening, Mr. Pop Star."

THE WEATHER WAS miserable. Sal had no idea how she managed to find her way through the rain and darkness, let alone stay on the winding road without dropping into the fjord below. Her driving style didn't exactly inspire confidence, either. Naomi took a last turn before they entered an unlighted gravel lane just as he was on the verge of asking her to let him out, saying he would gladly wait for her here in the cold, dark, rain. She stopped outside a house that had been hidden by the dense trees on the side of the hill.

It would be only a moment, she said, jumping out of the van, and he could wait if he wanted, but Sal was too curious.

She had brought him to a carpenter's shop, and he watched from the entrance as she ordered a table, specifying in great detail the type of wood, the size and height, and while he smoked in the cold wind he allowed himself the luxury of staring at her, for once without Jon breathing down his neck.

She wanted fries, she announced when they were back in the car, and there was really only one place to get them. Again she took them through the night, this time in a wild hurtle down the mountain.

"You do know where you're going, right?" His hands were clamped so tightly around his seat that they hurt.

Naomi only laughed.

By the time they reached the gas station where, she declared, they made the best fries within a hundred miles, Sal was shaking so badly he could hardly pick a cigarette out of the pack.

"What's wrong with you?" he muttered. "Do you want to kill yourself and take me with you? Just to piss off Jon?"

She had been about to step inside but now whirled back, hair flying, and laughed again, the sound echoing over the open space.

Sal's breath caught at the sheer exuberance in her expression. He coughed, the smoke scratching in his throat, and waved her forward, too shaken by her loveliness to speak.

"I'm in a really good mood," Naomi said when they were back in the car, greasy paper cartons in their hands, "I'm not reckless. I've been driving along these roads for ages. I know every turn and pothole. Don't be such a coward, Sal."

"And where does this sudden good mood come from?" The fries were indeed excellent, better than many he had eaten in the States.

She shrugged. "No reason. Just happy with life, happy with the way things are going."

"Naomi." His heart skipped every time he spoke her name. "Are you happy about the soundtrack, happy about the tour?"

"Yes." Careful not to drop anything on her clothes, she squished more mayonnaise from the little plastic container onto her fries and licked her fingers. "I'm happy. A little scared that I won't be able to deliver what Jon wants from me, but happy."

"But you know we'll have to go back to LA, right?"

Incredibly, she shrugged again. "Yes. I know. We'll go."

Sal forgot the food in his hands. "Just like that? After all the pain and terror and misery and the hard times you made Jon go through, now you tell me you will go back?"

"Do I have a choice?" Her voice took on a distant quality, and she turned her head away. "Do I have a choice, Sal?"

"Of course you do." His appetite had vanished. Sal placed the fries on the dashboard. "You don't have to go anywhere, Naomi. You have a life here, you can stay right here, safe and secure and peaceful, and no one can make you go back if you don't want to go." And, after a moment: "And no one can force you to give up everything for his sake."

Naomi gave him a long, inscrutable look before she replied.

"Sal," she said very softly, "what in the world would I want in Halmar if Jon's not here? I'm with you instead of him now because I needed to collect myself or go to pieces with the love I feel for him. I'll never let go of him again. Never. We should never have parted in the first place, not for longer than an hour, not ever, and that's why we're going back now."

In the parking lot of the hotel, turning off the motor, she added, "And California? I'll go to LA with him. I'd go anywhere on Earth with him. I'm not fond of LA, but if that's where Jon needs to be, then it's where I need to be too. It's that easy."

"WHERE DID YOU two run off to?" Russ asked when they entered, taking the burden from Jon.

Sal sat down. "Oh, Naomi wanted to go see someone, and she wanted company. She told me the Master was busy reading and she didn't want to disturb him. Said it was my job to escort her instead."

"So where did you go, love?" Jon asked, drawing her close.

She picked another fry out of her container and daintily bit off half. "I needed to see our carpenter. He lives outside of town, so I didn't want to go on my own."

Russ looked at her questioningly, and she shrugged slightly. "Needed to order a table. I wanted to pick the wood myself, and I think I did well, right, Sal?"

"Really nice," he conceded. "Rosewood, would you believe it? She spent a fortune."

Naomi shrugged again. "It's my gift for your studio. I hope you'll enjoy working on it."

Jon's hand tightened.

"A table for the studio? Did we ever have one in LA? I don't remember a table." Russ looked from one to the other.

"Hell, yeah. Can't do without a table in the studio. I need it badly." Jon relished the shiver that ran through her body.

"Well, if you say so." Russ looked dubious. "You're the Master."

16

SAL HAD FLOWN back to LA a few days earlier, and life was settling into a new sense of normalcy. Naomi was at the desk, checking out some American guests.

"There's certainly been a lot of music here," the woman was saying. "It's been nice, but I do wish they had played more songs that we know."

"Yes, well, they are trying out some new songs and…" just then Naomi glanced up from her work and saw Art walking in the door.

There was a shout of laughter from Art, who had a bright grin on his face. He came toward her and slumped on the counter, grinning at the strange woman. "You have no idea who was playing that music, do you?"

He hadn't changed much. There was some grey in his blond hair and a few laugh lines around his mouth, but otherwise he seemed the same man that Naomi remembered so well.

"Shut up, Art," she said.

"You weren't this outspoken earlier in your career," he crowed.

She pulled herself together and sent the guests off. Only when they had left the building did she turn to him.

"What are you doing here? Did anyone ask you to come?"

Her tone was unfriendly and defensive, but his grin only widened.

"Baby Girl. You are lovelier than ever. And yes, the good Sal sent me. I had so hoped for a warmer welcome. Whatever did I do to deserve this much animosity?"

"I will tell you right up front because I want you out of here. And I don't want your goblin's grin within a thousand miles of my home. You brought those drugs to our house that night! So out you go."

The grin fell from his face, replaced by a questioning look and a quick drumming of his fingers on the counter.

"Drugs? Nah, no drugs. Wes had the stuff on him all the time, and we used it alright, but I never owned any drugs, just like your man. We were always partying, and there was reason enough. What is this all about, Naomi?"

Naomi vanished into the office without another word.

JON FELT OUT of place seeing his producer, manager, and musical director sitting in the attic room—now a brand new studio—that looked out onto the stark Norwegian landscape with its strange light and brisk wind. It was so different from his studio in downtown LA. Motes of dust danced in the slanting sunlight falling through the panes. It was quiet, and the air smelled of the ocean and fresh timber from the new floorboards.

There was a profound feeling of peace and the slowing of time, a gathering of energy and the essence that meant music to him, a silent sound that hung waiting in his mind, ready to be called forth when the moment was right. He had always needed solitude to compose, an atmosphere that would let him concentrate, at best a place that would channel inspiration and let him hear the harmonies evolving from the source deep inside him. He could see himself working here, writing the soundtrack he had promised to deliver.

"Hey," Sean said softly. "You seem ready to work. I know that look on your face and I've missed it for the longest time."

Jon pulled himself out of his reverie. He had been pleased at first to see Art, but when he had walked into Naomi's office and noticed her shuttered face he had recalled her reservations. She had refused to talk about it, refused to talk to him at all, saying she was too busy to worry about him and his cronies right now, and to please leave her alone.

"Yeah. About ready. But before we get down to it, there's something that needs taking care of. Art."

The manager nodded and stood up. "Coming. I guessed we'd have to talk after Naomi's warm welcome."

"NICE PLACE," ART commented as they made their way down. "A bit far off the beaten track, and a long ride from any city that deserves that title, but very nice. Do you really want to live here?"

"It's where she is."

"You know that drug raid had nothing to do with me, don't you?" Art asked when they had reached Naomi's door.

"It's not me you need to convince. It's Naomi. She's the one you need to talk to."

"Ah," Art breathed. "Finally tamed. Never thought I would see the day. Domesticated. Purring like a kitten under the gentle caress of the little woman."

Naomi was sitting at her desk, her back straight and stiff, her hands folded in her lap, staring out at the water, waiting.

"Hey, Naomi." Art stopped right inside the door. "Maybe you'll give me a second chance and talk to me?"

"You've been in so many of my nightmares, Arthur Kennedy." She rose from her chair. "You'll need to do a lot of talking to convince me."

Jon moved toward the kitchen. "I'll make some coffee."

Art watched him start the ritual of brewing coffee as if he had never lived anywhere else, finding the things he needed without looking, moving in the confined space with ease. Jon took a pink mug out of the cupboard and filled it, mixed milk into it, and put it in Naomi's hands.

Art had to wait a moment before Jon could tear his attention away from her.

"I don't know what I did to earn your hostility, but I would like to clear the air and be back in your good graces again, Baby Girl." He could see her demeanor soften somewhat at his words, encouraged by a smile from Jon.

"No one," she answered, "truly no one has called me that in a long, long time, Art. I had completely forgotten about it."

"Well." He shrugged at her. "It seems you aren't that much of a baby anymore, my dear. You've gotten your shit together just fine. Got your old man in line, too. It was high time someone took him in hand, and I always thought you would be the one. So tell me why you want me out of here so badly. What have I done to deserve your hatred?"

He saw her draw a breath to answer, but then reticence took over again and she looked toward Jon, who waited patiently for her to gather the courage to do her own talking.

"You blame me for the raid at the house. But I don't know why. Why don't you tell me what happened that night to make you think so?"

Art watched her closely, fascinated by the fact that she was the one who had held their star's heart for so many years. She was pretty enough, short, the top of her head well below Jon's chin, slim but not bony, with clear, white skin. Her eyes were dark and large, her black, curly hair sensational, no two ways about it. Her beauty was fragile but then again not; there was a distinct Mediterranean flair too. Art could not fathom Jon's obsession with this European female, but he recognized that having her back had done him a world of good. Jon had not been so at ease with himself in a very long time.

"I can't tell you," she replied into his thoughts. "I won't tell you what happened. But the reason it happened was because you and Wes had those drugs on you. I wasted sixteen years of my life because of you. I could have been…" A small, helpless gesture toward Jon. "We could have had a life together. We might have been together. But for you and Wes, none of this would have happened."

Art's hands dug deep into his curls, as if pulling his hair would bring some kind of atonement. "I would gladly take the blame for that night if it would change anything. Hell, I will take the blame! If it helps, I will tell you I had those drugs and it was my fault we all went to jail. I should have kept Wes from bringing them to your house. I didn't. My fault. So throw me out."

But despite his words, he did not move away from his spot. He observed her reaction closely, the way she stood so still and withdrawn, gazing at him from those velvety black eyes, lips soft and vulnerable, and had a fleeting glimpse of what it was that seemed so alluring to Jon. It would appeal to him, the elusiveness and the withdrawal. It would be a constant challenge to decipher her.

But he received the surprise of his life.

"Baby," Jon said with some amusement, "don't give him that look. I know what you're thinking, so give the poor man a break. Tell him you forgive him already."

His tone was so unstrained and easy. Art had a hard time remembering when he had last heard him like that.

"Right." He cleared his throat in bewilderment. "I'll get on my knees and plead if I have to, but please let me stay. I need to witness this wonder you have wrought. Peace and domestic bliss in the Stone household. Where's your son, just to make the picture perfect?"

Naomi took her empty cup to the counter, where Jon picked it up again to put it in the dishwasher. Art could not contain himself any longer; he broke out in loud laughter.

She threw up her hands in exasperation. "What's so funny, Arthur? Haven't you ever seen Jon put something in a dishwasher?"

"Hey. Don't talk about me as if I were an idiot, please. Tell Artie what he must be told and be done with it. Sean and Russ are up there waiting for us, and I really can't afford to lose another day. So let's get on with it." But Jon's face was bright with hidden glee as he said this.

THE MOVIE SOUNDTRACK had come together overnight when Jon, in a bout of furious creativity, disappeared into the studio for nearly twenty-four hours, not even calling down for food or coffee.

They had written it in little more than two months, a nearly impossible feat, and he had no idea how they had done it. For years and years he had written nothing but songs about lost love and dreaming of finding it again, preferably with the one he had lost in the first place, songs about wanting to belong, about forgiving and understanding, or even meaningless funny tunes about things like a night in a bar, driving down a country road, or drinking a bottle of scotch with a friend and drowning in maudlin reminiscences, but never anything of great musical value. Nothing he considered important enough to signify real creative growth. The inner peace, the quietness he needed to listen again to what was inside him, was back. Had come back, if he was honest, in the jet that had brought him here, as if the knowledge of where he was going had been enough.

In a flurry of activity, they finished the last preparations for the trip to Los Angeles. Art had ordered a private plane that would take them from Halmar directly to California.

He laughed at Jon over breakfast, when he told them about his first trip coming here. How he had gone to the airport all by himself, not even knowing where Halmar was, and how he had taken the water taxi from Bergen, not knowing Halmar even had an airport, albeit a small one.

"Big enough for a small jet," Solveigh remarked a little acidly.

"Yes, well, I know that now."

There were quite a few things he had discovered, both about himself and the world in general. Things he had either forgotten over time or never bothered to find out before, like the fact that life outside of his home country held a kind of freedom for him that he could not have in the States.

It rained miserably when they left for the airport, as if Norway was sad to see them go.

Solveigh, leaving her hometown for the first time, said good-bye to her parents on the tarmac. Russ stood beside her, assuring them he would take good care of their daughter and would not let her come to harm in the big city. He received a stony glare from her in return.

Jon watched critically as the luggage was loaded. Now, minutes before they were to take off, he was having qualms. The thought of Naomi in LA frightened him, and he was about to turn around and tell her to stay behind when she walked out of the little building, her arm in Sean's, a magazine in her hand.

"Ready, honey?" she called. "Time to go?"

He was shaking in his shoes at her volatile moods. Here she was, dressed in sweatpants and a comfortable shirt, sneakers and thick socks on her feet, ready to spend hours on a plane as if she had never done anything else in her life. There was nearly nothing left of the prim, pale, black-clad hotel girl he had found when he had come here.

He could just see it. For an instant, the curtain blew open and he could see a vision of their future, traveling, seeing places, giving concerts to huge crowds, and in between, writing, creating, loving.

She smiled at him and vanished into the plane.

THEY FLEW INTO the night, leaving the sunset behind them, the cities far below twinkling up at them like a second sky. Joshua sat by a window, staring down until he fell asleep with his brow pressed against the cold glass. Naomi started to rise, but Jon held her back. "Let me." He settled Joshua back into the broad seat and covered him with one of the blankets provided by the attendant.

"You look cozy," Jon remarked when he returned. "As if you had spent your whole life flying across the Atlantic."

"I can do some simple math. It's a terribly long flight."

This was something he knew all too well. The last time, he had done it alone, and it had seemed to take an eternity. Now here they were, going back, and he prayed it would all turn out alright.

He had asked her before they left if she wanted to stay at a hotel rather than in his house, but Naomi had only stared at him in surprise.

Of course, she replied, she wanted to see where he lived. Not "had lived." It disturbed him, the way she said it unconsciously, as if there was, despite all the protestations of faith, still a measure of disbelief that he would stay with her.

"Maybe," he said in a hushed voice, "bringing you to California wasn't such a good idea after all."

"Didn't you clean up before you left?" She eyed him in mock suspicion. "No fresh sheets? When did you have your last lover there?"

"Naomi." Jon was scandalized. "Why would you ask such a thing?"

"Well, come on!" she shrugged. "Don't tell me you never took anyone to your home. Did you always book a hotel?"

"That does it," he said. "I'm not taking you there. We'll stay at a hotel. You're right. I can't take you to that house. I won't have you sleep in that bed."

She drew up her legs to lay them over his knees.

"A little late to realize that, isn't it? No. I want to see it. I want to see where you spent your life. I want to be part of it, even if only for a day. We'll ask Art to put up Joshua, and you and I are going out there." Her look grew pensive. "It might have been my home…"

"No." This was easy enough to answer. "Never. We would have stayed in Malibu. I would never have moved you out there. It wouldn't have been safe for a kid. It's a place for lonely people, not for families."

"You are so ridiculous. Why did you move there, then? Why did you move out of the Malibu house? Who lives there now, do you know? Who bought it?"

It was very quiet in the little plane. Solveigh was asleep with her head on Russ' shoulder, Sean, way up front, was working, his laptop open on his knees. He was typing furiously with Art next to him looking on with great interest.

"I didn't sell it," he said after a while. "I just moved out. After you left I didn't want to stay there. It was too lonely, too big, and every corner reminded me of you. But I couldn't make myself sell it. It would have been too final. Sal used to say I was obsessed with you and should let go, but I couldn't. I always thought somehow that as long as I held on to the house there was still some chance that someday you might return there…I don't know."

There was nothing to say. All those years had wandered past them in slow, unfaltering steps, but this had not changed, a constant of irrational dimensions, a monument to loss, the inability in both of them to let go.

Holding on to that house had been just as foolish a gesture as her going to that concert. It was a way to keep reality from turning into nothing more than memory.

Jon laid his head back against the seat and closed his eyes, his hands on her legs, and Naomi let her thoughts wander.

FROM THE LIVING room it had not been possible to see the ocean; there had only been the green wilderness and the many blooming bushes and the meandering path that led from the terrace down to the high fence and then the beach. It was a mansion still waiting to be inhabited, elegant in its way, but not yet imprinted by the owner's taste.

There was only one corner that had seemed lived in, and that was the room with the piano and the guitars and the cluttered shelves, full of folders and books, music, records, and a stereo. But even this had been a spartan, undecided place. The bedroom led out onto a covered roof garden that stretched nearly the width of the building, but it had been sadly unkempt. From here, the view of the sea was spectacular. Jon had told her that she was welcome to do with the house whatever she wished. After all, it was supposed to be her home from now on, and he wanted her to be comfortable. But other than buying a new bed and a rug, she had never found the courage to change anything at all.

Naomi opened her eyes again when he touched her face lightly.

"What are you listening to that makes you go all dreamy?" he asked when she took off the earphones. He heard his own voice from them. "Oh, shame on you." With a smile, he pried them from her hands. "You have the original right next to you and you listen to the canned version?"

"I can't hear you sing right now," she replied. "And it wasn't the music that made me dream. You never told me, who lives in the house now?"

Jon shifted so he could look straight at her. "Why do you ask? You ran from that house, and I seem to recall you saying you never wanted to return to it."

"Did you?"

"Return to the house? Yes, often. But not without always recalling the morning I walked in and found you gone. I still have that hair thing you left behind, the only thing you didn't take."

"So why did you return if it was that hard for you? You aren't answering my question. Who lives there now?" She dug her heel into his thigh until he held her tightly.

"Stop that! I'm only wondering why you ask now. Does it matter? I rented it out to Art. He lives there with his girlfriend."

Art had offered to take the house off his hands when it became clear he was unhappy there and wished to leave. Sal suggested he sell it, but Jon could not bring himself to do this. He did not want to stay there, but neither did he wish to let go of everything it meant to him.

"Art?" Naomi repeated, disbelief in her voice. "Art, of all people? Why would you do that?"

"Oh, for God's sake." He sighed. "I didn't know you blamed him, all right? And I felt better knowing someone was living there who would take care of the place. Why is it so important? You don't like it anyway."

"I never said I didn't like it." Abruptly she sat up. "I only said I didn't think I wanted to live there. There's a great difference between the two. I loved that house, and you know it."

Jon gazed at her in confusion. "So you don't want to live there, and yet you don't want anyone else to have it either. So what's it going to be, a museum of lost love? Naomi, please. That house is worth a fortune. I can't let it just sit there. Now that we are together again, I can sell it to Art if he wants it."

"No. It's the one place where I was really happy, with you. I don't want it sold."

"But..." He was tired from the long flight now and could not follow the twists and turns of her mind. "Well, what are we supposed to do? I'm not a very good landlord, I don't care for that kind of obligation. Let him have the old thing and be done with it."

"No!" Naomi had no idea where the sudden vehemence of her emotions came from, but now that she knew the house was still Jon's, she felt she did not want to let go of it. "What happened to my bed?"

"Naomi," he sighed. "You are doing it again, turning me around and around with your wild, jumping thoughts. God, you profess to hate something like mad and say that you will never go there again, and then when the mood takes you, you can't wait to go back."

"Well, don't complain. After all, I'm here on this plane because I'm able to change my mind."

"I need a drink."

Naomi took the glass from him as soon as he sat down again. Alcohol on a plane, she informed him, was death for the complexion, and he needed to keep his nice and firm. There were too many females who would mourn if his skin grew old before its time. He plucked the glass from her again, a pained look on his face.

"The bed," she reminded him. "What about my bed? Is Art sleeping in it now?"

"Of course not." He sighed, closing his eyes in a mixture of exasperation and amusement. As if he would ever allow anyone else into that bed. It was hers, and it was still in their bedroom, the only room he had demanded remain unused by Art and Sue.

"How unkind." Naomi pulled up the blanket and wrapped it around herself. "You denied them the nicest room in the house."

Jon nodded solemnly. "So it was. So it is. And it's mine."

18

IT WAS A small place; he had been right about that.

"For God's sake, Jon. I don't believe this. Why?" She could hardly envision him here, in this narrow wooden house on stilts, wedged between a dozen or more others, a long, tiring drive from the city.

Jon went to the glass door and stepped out into the warm breeze of a California morning.

"Why? There is no why. I couldn't stay in Malibu. After you were gone, I wanted to get away from it all. I wanted to be by myself, and after a while I came to like it here. It's peaceful." He gave her a crooked smile. "In a way it's a lot like Halmar, only I decided to live by myself and not have friends around me."

There were no people on the beach, the tide was too high for that. Water and sky filled the view.

The deck was nice enough but sparsely furnished with a couple of Adirondack chairs, a barbecue, and a low wooden table. A pot in the corner held a withered lemon tree. A lone glass, forgotten by the cleaning woman, stood on the floor beside one of the chairs next to an ashtray, its contents blown away by the sea wind. On the railing, a row of stones, varying in shape and color, were lined up in a contemplative mood. Between them sat a number of seashells of different kinds. He had brought her collection with him, a foolish, sentimental gesture and a very loud statement.

Naomi picked up one of the rocks, a roundish thing nearly fistsize, and turned it over in her hands. "You said you never cared for my 'debris.' You used to laugh at me."

"Well, yes." He took it from her, toying with it. "It seems some things took on a different meaning. I found them after one storm or another, and I thought, she would like that one. She would make up a story about where it came from and why it ended up here. She would wash it in the surf and dry it on her skirt and say, 'Poor little stone, so lost and battered, I will keep you close and cherish you. You will like it in my garden and feel right at home.' I always imagined you were talking about me, using the wordplay about my name. So I started collecting them myself, wanting to…" He put it back in its place. "Oh, for Pete's sake, this is so disgustingly sentimental. I shouldn't be telling you this at all. You should not be seeing this place; it will give you the totally wrong impression."

But when he tried to pull her back inside she resisted, still intent on the stones. One after another she touched them and looked at them closely. There was one among them that had streaks of turquoise in it, a silvery granite pebble not much larger than an egg, and one that was nearly white, round and perfect like a snowball. Another was jet black and jagged, the size of a human heart, with a crack down its center, and one was a red sandstone shard, flat and smooth, as if it had lain in the surf for ages.

"I think," she said gently, "I'm getting exactly the right impression, and it's no use trying to hide it, my love. It was my fault you decided to hide out here in this lonely place and collect rocks from the sea when I should have been keeping my most precious stone close to my heart, not letting it flounder in the tides."

Jon went inside to see the driver off while Naomi remained alone, looking out over the water, listening to the surf and the wind and the wild screeching of the seagulls. She closed her eyes and let the warm sun shine on her face. The air, the smell, and the sounds put her back in a past she did not want to relive. And yet, as she stood there by herself on the small wooden veranda above the waves, she let her mind go its own way, her thoughts turning around the little collection of stones. She felt the words rolling around in her head as if they were pebbles in the surf. The poignancy of it all, the dried-up lemon tree and the used glass by the chair, and on top of that narrow ledge, those stones that cried out to her in loneliness and loss.

Wordplay, he had said, on his name.

There were only fragments at first, but they fell together into verses almost instantly.

Jon stopped in the doorway when he saw her with the notepad from his desk. "Those are verses. You're writing verses."

"Go away." She felt embarrassed at having been caught. "I can't think. Go make coffee."

He retreated without another word.

Carefully, he held out a mug to her, not daring to come any closer. "Naomi. My beloved. Anything you want, it's yours. But I beg you, that must be mine."

She grinned up at him, pencil still poised over the paper, the satisfied gleam of achievement in her eyes. "You are a greedy bastard. But it's yours. After all, they're your little rocks. I never knew why I picked them up in the first place, but you did. So here you are."

There was a little pause in which she listened to her mind.

"I think there is more to say. We really need to go back to the Malibu house. What do you think, would the Los Angeles police value a song about their work?"

"YOU DID THIS to punish yourself, didn't you?" she asked when they had finally retired to the bedroom, the balcony door wide open to let in the evening breeze.

Jon lay beside her, drowsy and relaxed, his arms under his head, body stretched out long on the sheets. "Not punishment; retirement. I can do what you did as well. Withdrawal. What made you think you were the only one taking damage that night? How did you expect me to go on when you dropped out of my life like that?"

She rolled over on her stomach and propped her chin on her hands, feet crossed in the air, locks tumbling all around her. "You frighten me. Ever again, you frighten me. Look at you, beautiful male that you are. Killer voice and musical grandmaster. You are not supposed to suffer for any one woman."

He opened his eyes halfway at the hushed sound of her voice. "You. Beautiful. Stunning. So gifted. You sit down and scribble for five minutes, and out comes a song to break hearts. You, who could go out there and write for anyone, and you pick me. Once again, you pick me and put up with me."

"The stuff I write is only good because you make it good. It's only words. They mean nothing without your music and your voice." Her hand trailed across his chest.

"I love the lyrics about the stones. I just love them. I've never read a more precious declaration of love, and I adore the way you played around with my name. *Our* name, soon. Yours too. My wife. I can still hardly believe you consented to be my wife. Truly, truly mine, at last.

From the moment I first kissed you, that's what I always wanted. I knew right away I would find my peace only with you. Promise me. Promise you'll never leave me again. Whatever happens, never leave. Please don't go again."

"Oh." A soft giggle. "So now here I am in the bed that has seen so many others, and you have the nerve to demand such a promise from me? No shame at all? Tell me, how many? Did you keep count?"

Jon groaned.

"No, come on. Confess. I want to know. Otherwise when I go down to Rodeo Drive with Solveigh tomorrow I'll have to look at every one of the stylish woman and ask myself which ones you laid out here on these sheets for your amusement."

"Laid out for…" This made him sit up, wide awake, taken aback by her choice of words. "But Naomi, you have a way of putting things sometimes…I don't know what to say. You don't seriously expect me to discuss this with you, do you?"

Of course she did. And yes, were any of them famous? Did he have a hot affair with an actress? But no; she answered her own question with some wickedness, she would have read or heard about that, right? So he must have been really discreet.

"Baby." He twisted her hair around his hand. "Stop. Here I'm trying to tell you how badly I love you and you go and start keeping score? What did you expect, that I lived like a monk? I never cared for being alone."

"Oh no." She struggled against him. "No lovemaking in this bed of yours here. Not with me. And anyway, I'm going to get my hair cut if you keep this up. Stop pulling!"

"Baby, if you get your hair cut I'll divorce you before we ever get married, I swear. I love your hair, I love how it tangles around us when we are really at it, and it turns me on to no end when it sticks to our sweaty skin, all those lovely black tendrils on your perfect white breasts and framing your face."

A soft, enticing threat, his body moving closer to hers, touching her.

"I was on the point of falling asleep. You woke me up with your teasing. So I think you will have to deal with it now."

"Dealing like crazy." There was laughter in her voice, he could feel it rippling through her, a tantalizing vibration against him.

"You see, Baby, you see what you do to me. I want you all the time, even when I'm so dead tired. No one else has ever done that to me, could ever measure up to you. You, all you need to do is lie here beside me in your t-shirt, and it's enough. You are not supposed to do that. You should not be so alluring and exciting all the time. Just hearing that laugh of yours makes me go wild. And look, your lips are parting in that way that tells me you need to be kissed right now, oh yes, kissed deep and good, and then you'll sigh a little into my mouth, and then I'm lost. You do it all the time."

"God. All those words. You talk too much. All the time, talking yourself into trouble, when really you should save your breath for singing. Whatever am I going to do with all the songs that still need to be written if you ruin your voice talking?"

"I'll sing them, never fear," he whispered. "On my deathbed, I'll sing to you if you want me to. My last breath, it will be a song to you. Even if no one else listens to me anymore, if you want me to, I'll sing my love to you."

IN THE BRIGHT light of the morning, a coffee mug in her hand, Naomi stood again on the deck and looked out across the ocean. She tried to imagine him with Joshua's letter, reading and rereading it, the turmoil he must have felt.

When he came down the stairs, she asked, "Tell me, how was it when you got the letter? It was here that you received it, was it not?"

Surprised, Jon stopped on the last step. His eyes wandered to the kitchen counter where she had put his coffee. He had not thought about it at all since he had returned. Incongruously, he recalled the splashed milk on the countertop.

"I stood right here. It was early morning, and the beach was fairly empty. I had no idea what to expect, and it hit me like…"

Naomi watched the emotions play over his face as he let the memory return.

"I dropped it. It fell from my hands, and I just stared at it, unable to collect my thoughts." He shrugged. "That's all. I grabbed a few things and left. Called a cab and just walked out of the house. The next morning, I was with you. As soon as I realized what had happened, that was all I could think of. Finally, after all that time, I wanted to find out why you had left like that. I was scared, and yet I had some hope."

Slowly he put down his cup on the railing, right next to the stones.

"I think I left my coffee out here, too. It's a wonder I remembered to close the door."

NAOMI REFUSED THE limousine. She had discovered Jon's Porsche in the garage beside the house and insisted he drive them downtown. Jon looked at her in exasperation, but she smiled at him so sweetly that finally he gave in.

It was such a simple thing, driving to work on an ordinary Wednesday morning right into the heart of LA, but it gave her an inordinate amount of joy to sit beside him while he drove, sunglasses over his eyes, shirt half open, his bare feet in loafers, elbow resting on the car door.

Naomi gazed at him as he maneuvered the car through traffic, singing along with the music under his breath, relaxed and at ease, free. In this moment, he had it all, and he looked it, radiating contentment like light.

"Baby?" he asked when he noticed she was looking at him, "Something wrong?"

"I can't stay at the studio. I'm taking Solveigh out shopping. We need some California clothes. She'll love it. I want shorts. And sun tops. Oh, and a bathing suit. I can't believe I forgot to bring one." The car swerved a little as his concentration wavered, and she laughed.

IT WAS JUST as she remembered it.

The band was there, chatting and tuning their instruments, Rodney massaging his hands and shaking out his fingers, Sean fiddling with his keyboards, Jones and Joshua discussing guitars and testing strings and picks, the background vocalists humming the new melodies. There was a full orchestra, ready to start on the movie soundtrack. Jon, Russ, and Art had gone into the mixing room to discuss the proceedings with the conductor and the director of the movie. Solveigh was sitting on the table, dangling her legs and sipping fruit juice from a large plastic cup.

"I love it here," she declared. "They have these freshly pressed juices in all flavors, and the servings are so huge. I'm not going back to Norway. I'm a Californian at heart. Being born in Norway was a mistake of Mother Nature."

The look Jon gave her when he saw Naomi sitting down on the edge of that table nearly made her faint. Through the glass panel separating the rooms, he was staring at her. Art was talking to him, but it was obvious he was barely listening. All she could do was return his stare, right into his eyes across the distance that separated them, and endure the terrible, sudden desire this moment woke in her. She saw his lips move and knew he was not speaking to anyone close to him but was mouthing something at her, sharing the same memory.

"Are you alright?" Solveigh eyed her anxiously. "You have the strangest look on your face."

Russ was only too pleased to give Solveigh his credit card. He urged her to have fun and buy herself the prettiest bikini she could find, patting her behind fondly as he said it.

"Give me your car keys." Naomi held out her hand when she went over to kiss Jon goodbye.

He hesitated.

"Come on. It's that or I'll rent a Ferrari, and then I'll be driving it all the time, and you can try to catch up in your inferior little German car."

With a sigh he handed over the keys. "If I'd known you would go all wild on me, I would never have brought you back here. I hate the thought of you going off by yourself like this. I would prefer that you had a driver and a closed limousine. I should get you a Rolls. With bullet-proof glass."

She gave him a tight, suggestive embrace that made him respond in surprise and with some fervor. "Don't be afraid. We won't go where there are bad boys. I only want to spend some of your money. You like me to spend your money, right?" He nodded. "So give me the card, sweet boy. Solveigh needs to see the expensive stores, and I need to see Solveigh ripping LA apart."

His eyes twinkled as he handed over the same card he had used to pay for his lonesome flight to Norway. In a slightly threatening undertone, he told her to remember, no jewelry on her own.

"Ah." She turned the plastic in her hands. "Here I have the no-limit thing in my hand, and you tell me that now? Too late."

"Baby, you come home with new diamonds, and you'll see what happens to you. I'm telling you, you don't want to find out."

"Promises, promises. You are setting a high standard for yourself." She left before he could come up with a response.

19

NAOMI FELT APPREHENSIVE as Jon drove up to the gate of the mansion that night. The driveway was lit up and looked like a silver ribbon leading into the jungle that was the huge front garden. From the road, only the red roof of the house could be seen over the swaying bamboo groove and rambling jasmine bushes. Nothing had changed. The place seemed untouched by time, as if it had fallen into a long slumber, awaiting her return. It frightened her a little to see this immense testimony to hope and how everything seemed to turn on her presence.

"Here we are." Jon turned off the engine when they reached the house but didn't move, awaiting her reaction.

He watched her look up at the white façade, the graceful entrance so brilliantly lit up. The curtains blew lazily in the open French doors, as if waving an invitation to enter. Palm trees swayed in the wind with a dreamy rustle around the deep porch.

"It's just as beautiful as I remembered."

The shopping trip with Solveigh had transformed her into a scantily dressed beach beauty, utterly tempting, and as she climbed out of the car in her shorts and tiny top and tossed her mane over her shoulder he gazed in admiration at her bare legs. His heart had nearly stopped in shock when she had walked into the studio late this afternoon, seeing her like that, her hair loose and visibly shorter, her feet in red high-heeled sandals, giving him a sultry glance over the rim of her sunglasses. It had been difficult to work after that.

Art's girlfriend Sue was a little abashed at having Jon as her guest. The fact that he was also the owner of the house didn't make it any easier, but Art broke the tension by saying, "We're going to let you do your thing, Sue and I are going to sleep. Make yourselves at home." He laughed at his own joke.

"No way." Naomi embraced first him and then Sue. "You are staying right here. I'm sure you have some Irish whiskey stowed away. We are going to sit on the porch and enjoy the evening for a while."

They talked in low voices, swirling the ice cubes in their glasses and watching the smoke of the men's cigarettes vanish into the blue night. After a while, Naomi asked Sue if she could walk around the house. Sue offered to accompany her, but Naomi declined; she needed to do this on her own.

The kitchen was different. A wall had been taken down and replaced by a counter. The huge living room didn't look uninhabited anymore, with different furniture and paintings on the walls and books, flowers, and magazines on a low table.

Outside the bedroom Naomi stopped, hand on the knob. Here it was, finally, the one place she had so wished never to see again, and yet she found herself here voluntarily.

The door to the roofed terrace stood wide open to let in the night breeze. It was the same room, with the same canopied bed and blue carpet, and yet it was not the same. Naomi let the memories wash over her.

There was the corner she had fled to, naked, frantic with fear, and right here Jon had stood, raging at the police while they handcuffed him and made their dirty jokes. Slowly she retraced the steps she had taken that night, down the stairs to the big hallway and into the kitchen once more, to the living room and Jon's studio. The front door had stood open, so she opened it and stepped outside.

Only the Porsche was out there, and the faint light from the garage. The cicadas were singing their nightsong, and the rhythmic surf in the distance was pounding like a heartbeat. There was peace, tranquility, and the murmur of familiar voices.

Try as she might, she could not recapture the turmoil and panic of that night. She stood here now, looking back at that night in an almost clinical way. She saw herself, lonely and helpless, amid the debris of the party. Still a child in almost every sense, and she understood what she had felt then, even felt sorry for that young girl, but she could not relive her feelings anymore.

This insight surprised and saddened her immensely. The time she had thrown away and wasted made her want to cry.

She heard footsteps, then Art appeared. "Oh, it's you. Are you done remembering? What happened back then, love? What was so bad that you felt you had to leave Jon like that?"

To her surprise, she opened her mouth and drew a breath to answer before she could stop herself.

"Reliving it now, it seems funny. But back then I was so scared and beside myself, so raw from the crazy life we were leading. Artie, I had nothing. All of you were gone, and I didn't even have enough money to buy a plane ticket. I had no idea what to do, what was to come. I was twenty-one, and really still a kid. A pregnant kid."

"Yeah." He fumbled for cigarettes in his jeans pocket. Before he could light one, Naomi went on. "The police came into the bedroom. They were crude and shameless and scared the living daylights out of me. You should have seen Jon when they pulled him out of bed. He was so furious!" With amusement she watched as he dropped his cigarette. "They made crude remarks about the rock star and how they would like to watch as he did his little chickie, the one who was naked and crying in the corner of the room, and maybe they could have their turn with her afterward. Jon was drunk and high that night." She turned to look Art in the eyes. "He had forgotten, Art. He didn't remember it at all, he was that doped up. So now you know why I hated you so much. And I wasn't going to take it anymore, and so I ran."

He bent down to retrieve his cigarette and lit it. "I'm not sure if you had stayed that you would have been able to change anything. Things can look different in retrospect. You understand that even though you regret your choices, the alternative would not have been good either and would not have been a situation you could have lived with." He shrugged his lean shoulders with resignation. "Sometimes there are only bad choices, and you hope you make the least painful one. Seems to me you made the right one, even though now you mourn the lost time."

"But Artie," she protested softly, but he only shook his head.

"No, really, Naomi. Maybe it wasn't necessary for it to be so very long, but for Jon, it was the right thing to happen, maybe for all of us. It shook him badly, made him grow up overnight, and he was finally ready to take on the responsibility and make his own decisions. He was beside himself, but in a weird manner, it as if someone had taken away his favorite toy. Only after a while did the loss seem to take its toll, and he became introspective and thoughtful and then moved out into that hovel to be alone. Sal was furious, but I think Jon made the right decision. He needed to grow up, and in the end, it was you who forced him to do it." Art shrugged again, but this time in a slightly malicious manner. "You did him a big favor. Whatever he is today, he is because of you. You forced him to take a step back and look at his life outside of his professional success. A person can get lost in fame, you know, and leave their soul behind. He found his because of the pain." Gently he touched her arm. "And, love, don't fret. You two have all the time in the world."

Naomi sat down on the top step and drew up her knees. Art crouched down beside her. They did not speak for a while, watching the moths dance around the lamp beside the stairs. They sat in companionable silence, both lost in their own memories.

The music had flowed around them all the time, the tunes Jon created dominating everything. They had bowed to it and its wonder, and the magic he could do.

Naomi plucked a blossom from the bush beside her and rubbed it between her fingers until only mush was left. "What do you think, Artie, will he be able to live in Halmar with me? Or will it make him unhappy in the long run?"

"I can't see any reason why it shouldn't work, unless you prefer the nicer weather here. And really, now that you have chased your demons away, why shouldn't you both be happy and split your time? You have a house here waiting for you to return."

"No," she demurred, "It's yours now."

"Ha!" He laughed merrily. "Take the big old thing off my hands any time you like. Sue wants to live in the hills. She wants us to move up to Napa and get a vineyard, have a horse, a couple of dogs, and some kids. Just say the word, and we're out of here. Really. I've been more of a caretaker than a resident."

Art got up and brushed off his jeans. "I'll tell you what. Don't make any decisions right now, just let it roll. You'll be staying for a while, so get the feel of it and don't think. Have some fun, and show the city who's the boss now." He pulled her up. "Let's go back inside, before your old man thinks you've deserted him again."

Joshua had joined Sue and Jon, a huge container of ice cream on his knees. He was listening to their exchange about some award ceremony where another singer had spilled a glass of beer all over Jon's suit just before he was to go on stage and receive a prize, and how he had sent Art up instead and hadn't been able to make up his mind whether he was furious or relieved by the whole thing.

"You were furious." Art interjected. "I remember the way you smiled. Shark's teeth."

Naomi wandered off into the garden.

It was dark under the foliage of the trees and the overhanging bushes; the white tiles under her feet shone, leading her along until she stood before the gate where she could look out to the sea through the mesh, out to the surf that had picked up with the tide. There would be new debris for her to sift through in the morning. But for now, the beach was empty, silent, dreaming in the moonlight. Just the kind of night when they could escape from the house and go down to the water all by themselves.

Off to her left, deep amid the oleander, was the stone bench. It stood in an arbor all by itself, a hidden, secret place with only a small pebbled trail leading to it. The marble was cool under her legs as she sat down, the tendrils of the bushes tangling in her hair. The quiet was so deep and dark that she could hear her own breathing. Here the cover for their album had been shot on that hot day when Jon had been so exhausted from the load laid on him with his sudden, frightening fame.

She heard the footsteps before she saw him.

"Hiding, Baby? Alone here in the dark you look like a fairy in the moonlight. Very alluring and lonely. I think I'll go with you to your fairy kingdom and be doomed."

He had always been able to create magic moments like this with just the right words.

"Not hiding." She made room for him on the bench. "Thinking. Remembering the day they took those pictures for the album and how tired and lonely and distressed you were. "

Jon drew her close, his hands warm and firm on her waist.

"Tired and distressed, yes. Lonely, no. You were right here, so no, not lonely. How do you feel about being here now? Is it bearable? Have you been through the house?"

"Yes." Her fingers touched his chest where his shirt was open, trailing over his skin. "Kiss me. Do you know how to do that?"

"Do I know how to kiss you? Are you crazy?"

He kissed her lingeringly, sweetly, his arms tightening around her. It was just the way it had been. They had spent here so many nights in this secluded corner, talking and exchanging caresses.

"I was in our bedroom," Naomi said. "It looks nearly the same, but the fear and the shame were nowhere to be found. I walked through the entire house trying to find that fear and shame, but they weren't there. All I found were sweet memories of times gone by, and a much nicer kitchen than we used to have. Really, maybe we should forget about the whole future thing and just cherish the lovely memories."

"You are utterly out of your mind." His grip loosened in shock. "Ah, you are joking! Little beast, that's not a nice thing to do. You could kill me, I'm old enough to have a heart attack from such a scare."

She laughed out loud. "You silly man. You won't have a heart attack until I say so. And anyway, if you don't give yourself a heart attack with all the exertion you get in bed, then it certainly won't happen from a little shock. Come on. Let's get back to the others, poor Joshua will think we ran away."

On their way back she remarked how the garden had not changed at all, and Jon told her he had told Art not to alter anything and not to take down the towering bushes. Art had complained that it was nothing but a couple of tiled paths through a wilderness, good for nothing but keeping away onlookers. He very much wanted a real garden with lawns and roses and a swimming pool. But Jon had been adamant. No, this had been Naomi's favorite place. They could rebuild the kitchen all they wanted, but the shrubs were staying put, and the cedar grove as well.

You couldn't even see the beach, Art had argued. What good was such a huge property in Malibu if you couldn't see the surf?

Sit on the balcony, Jon had suggested; the water was perfectly visible from there. But don't touch the master bedroom or the roof terrace. Those were the conditions.

Sell the damn place, Art had said, and be done with it.

But he could not bring himself to do it, and so here they were, and his wildest, most fantastic dreams had come true. She was with him again, laughing, wrapping her arms around him, moving against him as they strolled under the cedars, her bare waist warm and silken under his hands, her lips willing and open to his.

"Will you let me take you to bed now?" Jon asked, a little breathless from his thoughts and the feel of her naked skin. "Will you sleep with me in that bed again? Will you let me finish what we started before we were so rudely interrupted the last time we lay there?"

JOSHUA HAD RETIRED when they returned to the house; Art and Sue were busy clearing the table and didn't even look up when Jon bade them good night.

In silence, Naomi followed him up the stairs, excitement and some feeling she could not name growing in her, not trepidation or fear, but something that seemed almost like it, a notion that this was the last, final step she had to take before all that had happened in the past few months became reality and lost its dreamlike quality. It was the place where she had last seen him before she had run away. It was the last image of him that she had carried with her.

She never knew if Jon shared that feeling or realized what was going through her mind, but he took her hand in his and stood for a moment before he led her inside. Willingly she entered with him, but as the door shut softly behind them, she asked, "Do you think we could lock it this time?"

20

"GO BUY SOME evening gowns," Russ told them over lunch a few days later. "We're going out. Harry invited us to a movie premiere. You want to meet Brad Pitt, don't you?" he grinned like a schoolboy when Solveigh's face lit up.

Naomi, without even looking at him, held out her hand to Jon, and he laid his car keys and credit card in it with a small sigh.

"Don't get too used to that Porsche. I'm getting you a Rolls and a bodyguard today. Your days of flirting with strange men from a convertible are numbered, my dove." The words were spoken lightly, but she knew there was a stark reality behind them.

Rising, she kissed his temple. "Don't worry. You'll be too busy staring at me in my new gown to care about cars. But if you really want to buy a Rolls, make it silver, please, with tinted windows."

IT WAS THE perfect evening for a grand Hollywood party. The sun was setting by the time they arrived at the luxurious resort in the hills, and the palm trees along the road swayed gently in a refreshing breeze. The sky was the color of a turquoise Egyptian beetle, mixed with the peach and rose of porcelain and spring flowers, as beautiful as a Turner painting.

"Are you ready?" Jon asked when the limousine stopped in front of the well-lit entrance.

"As ready as I'll ever be." Flashlights exploded around them as they walked to the entrance, waving to the spectators and the press.

The ballroom and garden were filled with celebrities and those that strove to be among them. There were legions of photographers and beautiful women. There were flowers and music and a luxurious buffet. Liveried waiters with large trays of champagne and saucy maids in scanty costumes carried platters of appetizers and finger food, circulating easily among the guests. Hundreds of white blossoms floated in the pool beneath the twinkling lights strung in the palm trees.

"Very pretty." Solveigh gazed at her surroundings critically. "We could do that, on the bay. But where would we find enough well-toned and tan boys to serve the booze?"

She was mildly scandalized by Naomi's new dress—a silver creation with a nearly transparent chiffon skirt—and told her so, saying she was only wearing it to provoke attention, to which Naomi shrugged coolly and replied, "Of course." After a moment, she added, "If he is going to flaunt me in public, then they should have something to talk about. No Norwegian country girl for my Jon, Solveigh."

He was not far away, talking to Harry and Russ, his posture easy, hand in his trouser pocket, photographers circling him like birds waiting for crumbs to drop from his fingers. Some of them veered toward her, speculating expressions on their faces, but none dared come too close.

"Yeah, at their peril." She heard a well-known voice behind her. "They don't dare touch what's his. It's like belonging to a mafia boss in a way."

Sal grinned at her like a hungry shark. "You are stunning. He has turned you into a proper LA girl. Where has all your sweetness and clarity gone, the pure light I loved so much in you?"

"Do you really think an expensive gown and some makeup could corrupt me, Sal? You mustn't have a very high opinion of me. What a pity. And here I thought you were my one true champion. And where have you been all this time?"

He reeled a little under the assault. "Have you taken the time to inform your fiancé about your family yet? Or are you still sitting on that dirty little secret? I had quite a chat with your mother, my dear."

"Shut up, Sal." Her shoulders drew up in discomfort, but he laughed. "Yeah, like hell. I want to be around when he finds out, or when someone else tells him." He tossed the cherry from his drink into a flower pot. "But I think you're safe for a while yet. The poor, besotted fool does not give a damn about who you are. If ever there was proof of love being blind, Jon is it. And seeing you like this, I can see why. But don't count on it to last forever, honeychild. I might even spill your secrets myself if you don't own up soon. I'm not letting him walk blindly into marriage with you."

Before she could reply, he walked off to hail a man standing beside the pool, only to be replaced by Solveigh, who asked, "And where is Brad Pitt? They promised, didn't they?"

They were standing in the doorway to the garden, gentle music drifting from the band on the other side, where a dance floor had been placed beneath a white pavilion.

Beautifully dressed women floated by, some casting glances at Naomi, some drifting toward Jon, but he never reacted. He turned to look for her and smiled to see her with Solveigh, obviously at ease with her surroundings. Naomi gave him a tiny, secret smile and moved her hips slightly so he could see her legs through the thin material, and any concentration he might have had for the conversation around him vanished. Even as he walked toward her, she came to him, her body moving gracefully with the swirling skirt.

"Dance with me?" Naomi asked. "I would like to be in your arms a little, even if only on the dance floor. Do you think we could get them to play something nice?"

"I'll make them, if it's your wish." Here it came again, the single, half-raised finger to get the attention of an attendant, who was instantly by his side to hear what Jon had to say. He did it unconsciously, without even realizing how incredibly arrogant it might appear to onlookers.

He was so used to being obeyed right away. The music changed, the band picked up the charming tune of a slow, dreamy rumba rhythm that fit wonderfully with the sultry dusk of the Los Angeles evening.

He pulled her a little too close for decorous dancing, but she did not mind at all, loving the feel of his suit through the chiffon and the warmth of his body against hers.

"Sal said you are ruining me with all the glamour and wealth. I think he'd rather have me hidden and lonely in Halmar. What do you think?"

It took him some time to reply.

"He has a point. I'm scared to death someone will come and try to take you away from me, and who knows, maybe there's somebody out there who will appeal to you. Someone not as dumb as I am, who won't spook you again and again." A brief pause, then: "So yes, I like to see you safely tucked away where no one gets to see you but the locals who know you as a withdrawn, reticent girl, and those elderly Minnesotans who go there to explore their roots and are much too old and tired to get it up sufficiently to meet your high standards and please you."

"Stupid! How can somebody as brilliant and successful as you be so stupid at the same time? You drive me to tears with your stupidity."

The music changed into something faster and funkier and Naomi stopped dancing. She excused herself and left him with Russ and Art.

IT TOOK HER a while to find him when she returned from the powder room, and when she did she stood very still, hidden in a doorway, watching the picture presenting itself to her. He was in a quiet side room of the hotel, quite apart from the party, talking to a woman in his low voice, leaning close to her and touching her hair in a tender, thoughtful way.

"No. That's not going to happen, Sophie. I'm only here for a short while, and then I won't be coming back for a long, long time. You need to let it go, dear."

"But surely," she pleaded. "surely you aren't telling me it's over? You can't mean it, Jon. Not after what we had together. You can't just drop me like that, you're breaking my heart. It can't be because of that Norwegian girl? What's so special about her? She's older than I am. If you want to live somewhere else, we can go together, darling, please…"

"Sophie, I can't. I've made a commitment, and I will stick to it. She's the mother of my son, and I will not leave her."

"A commitment," she repeated with a bitter laugh. "Yes, well, pay her handsomely and then pull out. You can't mean this. We belong together, and you know it."

Naomi took a careful step back and waited for his reply.

She heard him sigh. "I'm sorry. I can't. I'm tied to her in every way, and I would not leave her for anything or anyone in the world. She's the one I will marry, and that's it. It's as final as my last breath."

The stranger grabbed Jon's sleeve, but he moved away.

"Don't do this, Jon," she begged. "Don't leave me. Come back to me. We were good together until you left, and I've been waiting for you to return. You don't need to marry her for a grown son's sake. Just pay her off and keep her quiet. Don't sell yourself like that. You haven't seen her for how long? Twenty years? You can't tell me you truly love her; it's only your hard-headedness. If you need to, live it out, then come back to your senses and to me. You know your place is here, not somewhere in the Norwegian countryside."

There was no response from him.

"Tell me, Jon," she heard Sophie's voice. "Tell me to my face you never cared for me. Do it, and I'll walk away from you right now."

He took a long time replying. "You were the best thing that happened to me in a very long while, Sophie."

"Ah." Her head went down. "But it wasn't enough. I'm worth more than a brief call from some airport or other to tell me it's over. Well, you are no better than all the others after all." There was no response, so she plodded on. "And now what? You go back to that Norwegian village and marry a hotel clerk? Is that your future, Jon?"

"Yes." Naomi closed her eyes at the firmness in his voice. "Yes, Sophie. I'm going back just as soon as I can. I will not stay here a day longer than necessary."

Naomi retreated, wildly upset and at a loss what to do. For a while she stood, watching the bustle around her. She felt as if she were standing outside a snow globe where people were swirling to the sound of music that had somehow gone out of tune. From the corner where she was standing she could see Jon, hands deep in his pockets, return outside into the brightly lit garden and the company of Art, who asked where he had been hiding. She did not follow. Instead, she made her way slowly to the bar inside and Sal, who was sitting there by himself nursing a drink. He pushed his glass in her direction without a word and watched as she took a big gulp. They were quite alone; most of the guests had chosen the garden and the balmy night air.

"So. A moment of peace amid all the turmoil, eh? And you pick me to share it with?"

Her head swiveled toward the noise of the party.

"Where did you leave the Jonman?"

A small shrug of her shoulders, a slight tightening of her lips.

From the corner of his eye Sal could see Jon coming toward them, his step easy and his smile bright, but he saw how Naomi's tension did not slip away from her.

"There you are, Baby." Jon's hand caressed her bare back. "I was looking for you. Want to go home? Enough of the tumult?"

She glided from her perch directly into his arms. "No, let's dance some more."

His smile widened in delight as he led her away. Sal, alone again, held up his hand to order another drink.

21

IT TOOK FIVE weeks to finish the recording, and Naomi relaxed into the rhythm of their life in LA. She didn't go to the studio with Jon every day but preferred to stay at the house, enjoying the beach and the sunshine. Most of the time she was on her own in the huge mansion and spent many hours wandering through the rooms, imagining how she would redecorate them if she came to live here again. The roof terrace outside the bedroom was the subject of most of her attention. Often after Jon and the others had left she went back up there and stood staring at the unused space, turning it into a lush outdoor room in her mind. A place for her to work, lounge, and look out over the sea. A retreat.

Sal, at her request, brought her a stack of tabloids every day, which made Jon ask if she now had a new interest in Hollywood gossip. Sal inquired acidly if she was waiting for pictures of her chiffon dress, but she gave no explanation, so he sat patiently while she leafed through them, only to discard them quickly.

"You've been very lucky so far," was Sal's verdict, "and you know it. You need to tell him."

Again, her shoulders went up in that gesture of denial he had come to know so very well, and he let it drop.

Jon took her down to the little beach house a few times, at her request, and Naomi pocketed the stones from the porch to bring them back to the garden of the Malibu house, where she placed them by the stone bench with all the others she had collected

Standing once again in the house where he had spent so many years in solitude, Jon recalled the day he read Joshua's letter and his feelings then, just to keep them alive in his heart, along with the miracle of its outcome. He knew he would not be coming out here again, having decided to sell the house.

It felt strange to have time on their hands to stroll down Rodeo Drive together, just the two of them, just like in London. Jon talked seriously to her about writing for others and of the offer from Harry to write a movie script for him, but she demurred.

"I started writing because of you. You know it. I was vacuuming my room, and despite the noise, I heard this voice on the radio that made me drop what I was doing and sit down and write those lyrics, for you to sing them. And you did. You do. That's all, Jon. Don't push me."

He shook his head at her, but she continued, "Think about it. I know what you go through to put a new album on the market, the talk shows, the cameo appearances, photo sessions and fan clubs, interviews, God, the touring! Just imagine, we would be apart most of the time! Why can't we just settle down, write some beautiful stuff, raise a new family, and sit in the sun?"

He mulled it over while they were sitting in a beach restaurant over cocktails, swirling the lemon in his glass.

"It is good to be here. And I want to return. But really, I think we need to go home now. I feel restricted here, and under constant observation. Don't you like to be able to just step out of your house and meet only friends and neighbors, no fans or photographers?" As if to emphasize her words, a flashlight exploded in their faces.

"We're going," Jon announced abruptly. "Pack some things, we're leaving tonight. We'll go to New York."

She was too perplexed to rise. "What do we need to do in New York? I don't want to do any sightseeing. Really, Jon, if we can leave then let's head home!"

He rose from his seat. "And so we will, but on the way we'll stop in New York."

"Why, for God's sake?" Exasperated, she ignored the photographer who was hovering just outside, waiting for another good shot.

Jon tossed some money on the table. "Don't you want to see where I grew up? Where I used to live before I became a star? Don't you want to meet my family?"

He loved the look he got from her, open-mouthed, speechless for once, and how she followed him without resistance to the car and let him drive her home.

Joshua was delighted at the news.

"Does that mean I have cousins I don't know yet?" he asked on the plane. "And more grandparents, too? Uncles and aunts?"

One uncle, Jon explained, and an aunt, and sadly, only a grandmother. But yes, there were cousins of both sexes, and close to his age. And, he added, his gaze on Naomi, he thought it was a good idea to meet them before they came to Halmar for the wedding.

"You really are such a self-absorbed bastard," Naomi said after Joshua had plugged in his earphones, "You vanish to Geneva to kidnap my parents, and you never even think to tell me of your family. And now, a few weeks before we get married, it suddenly occurs to you to visit your mother?"

He grinned at her. "You never asked."

She could not decide whether or not to be furious at him.

"Does she even know you are getting married? Does she even know where you were for the past five months? Did you talk to her at all, Jon?"

He shifted uncomfortably, knowing very well she had caught him out once again. Naomi would not let this rest, and he would get a hiding from his mother, too.

"Well, yes and no. I called her when we arrived in LA and told her I had found you again. I thought it would be a nice surprise to drop by with you and Joshua—"

"Oh, for heaven's sake, Jon! That's not the way to do things! You can't just dump us on her and say, 'Hey Mom, this is my future wife, and by the way, here is your grandson.' She'll have a heart attack! God, but you can be so stupid sometimes!"

"Yeah, yell at me." He did not look at her. "I know. Only there never was the right moment, and really, little beast, I've never gone through this before. It seemed like such a good idea, showing up with you, surprising them all…"

Naomi threw up her hands in exasperation. "At least book us into a hotel. We can't show up on her doorstep and demand shelter as well."

"Did that," he replied, relieved that he had done something right at least.

SINCE THEY WERE in New York anyway and had a day to kill before Jon's mother would see them, Joshua insisted they visit Juilliard, a request that surprised Naomi. "You take him, Jon," she said, "I'll take a stroll down Fifth Avenue. I know you'll be talking about music the whole time anyway."

She could see he didn't like the idea of her alone on the streets of Manhattan very much, so she told him not to fret, and please, could he maybe stop treating her as if he were a sheik from the Middle East and she one of his harem?

His eyes twinkled in appreciation. "Yeah, Baby, now that is a nice thought. I could build you a palace with a wonderful garden and buy you some nice, strong, good-looking eunuchs, and you would lie around naked all day by your pool, nibbling figs and honey cakes, and I could come around whenever I want, and you would be there, and I could have you anytime. Oh yes, what a lovely fantasy. And I would have all those incapable men stand by and watch. Ah, and they unable to perform... Me, the only one to give you pleasure, and you, on your silk cushions, the heat of the sun on your skin, and I would put a diamond-studded anklet on you to proclaim who you belong to..."

"Like hell." A smile played around her lips. "As if you could. You would hate the idea of other men, eunuchs or not, seeing me like that. And anyway, an anklet alone wouldn't do at all. There would have to be a lot more, and chiffon skirts as well. And oh, don't forget the steady supply of chilled champagne. And some ladies to keep me company, preferably well versed in singing and entertaining. And at least one of your strong male slaves would have to be very accomplished at massage. Rose oil, too."

His breathing quickened a little and his concentration drifted for a moment away from the orange he was peeling.

"Oh no." She laughed at him. "Don't even think of it. I'm going out. You, wake up your son and take him to that school and shake up the poor professors with your appearance. God, but I wish Solveigh was here! It would be so much more fun with her around."

But Solveigh had declined to return to Halmar any time soon. For her, Los Angeles was heaven, and she could not bear to be parted from Russ. Jon had commented on it over their last meal together, offering to advise Russ on how to propose and buy an engagement ring, and Russ had been more than willing to go right then and there to get her one, but Solveigh had refused. Blushing very becomingly, she had said, "Not yet. And certainly not with Jon in tow. I can do without his comments." It had not been, they noted, a rejection.

For the first time since she had gone to London to see the concert, she was all alone in a big city, free to do as she pleased.

The high-rise buildings of Manhattan cast shadows on the streets below even though it was noon, and a cool wind blew through the straight canyons. The noise was deafening, even worse than on Oxford Street or around Piccadilly in London. It seemed as if a police car or an ambulance came tearing past almost every minute, their horns and sirens blasting their way through the incredible traffic. The smells of a hundred different types of food assaulted her. Hot dogs from street vendors and all kinds of Asian cuisines, the delicious invitation of a deli at every corner, the scent of fresh bread from the bagel shops and cake from the pastry counters, coffee and the aroma of fruit juices, all mixed up with the stink of exhaust fumes and the evil blasts that rose from the grills of the subway system. The fast movement of the pedestrians confounded her, and she stared in amazement at elegant, executive women, dressed in grey suits with leather laptop cases slung over their shoulders and sneakers on their feet, thick socks over their nylons, rushing past, phones to their ears, seemingly always on the run.

She loved it. With a paper cup of coffee in her hand, she stood on the sidewalk and breathed in the turmoil, listened to the noise around her, and had the eerie feeling that the city was talking directly to her, telling her its stories in a rhythm all its own. Staring at the people around her, without realizing it, she began to make up stories about them and their lives, their secret wishes and dreams. For the first time ever, words fell together for her without the constant hum of Jon's music in the background, words shaping themselves into something more than lyrics, running on and on, weaving a ribbon of many colors. Coffee forgotten, Naomi listened to the plot unfolding in her mind, quivering at the possibilities. A novel? She hardly dared touch that thought yet. Very carefully she tried to step back from it, but it would not let her go, clinging to her like a needy kitten.

"I need a new laptop," she said out loud, and a man walking past her at that moment, a well-groomed stranger in a hand made suit, gave her an amused glance.

LATER, ON THEIR drive through the city and across the Brooklyn Bridge, Jon told them about his childhood, how he had grown up in the same house where his mother still lived with his sister and his two nieces after his father had died and his sister, Valerie, had kicked her husband out.

He looked at Naomi and Joshua while he talked, seeing his own family, feeling a deep pride to be able to present them to his mother, a lovely bride and a gifted son, the whole package. Finally he would settle down, in his mid-forties, and enjoy his achievements.

His mother had been a teacher, he told Joshua, and had worked at a high school right here in Brooklyn. His father, who had died five years ago, had been a surgeon. They lived in the house his great-grandparents had built. His mother, Helen, was retired, but his sister had followed her professionally and was now a music teacher at the very same school a few blocks from home.

"And my uncle?" Joshua asked. Jon grinned at Naomi. "He's a doctor, like our dad. The family tends to follow the same paths. Except me, I'm the vagabond of the bunch."

"They sound so normal." Joshua frowned. "Just a normal family."

They stopped in front of a three-story brownstone on the corner of a rather quiet street, directly opposite a small Italian restaurant with a red and white awning. Getting out of the car, Naomi could see the river and the promenade not far away, and the skyline of Manhattan across the water. It was a nice view, and she thought it would be romantic and exciting to walk there at night and see all the glittering lights from the skyscrapers of the city.

"I grew up here," Jon said. "My childhood, my youth, my first guitar lessons all happened here." He pushed his hands deep into his jeans pockets. "And I used to stand here, staring at Manhattan, just the way you're doing now, and dream of making my career over there, standing on the stage of Radio City Music Hall or Madison Square Garden. A star."

The woman who opened the door was not what Naomi had expected at all.

"Well, don't just stand there in the street," Helen said briskly. "You might as well come in. Jon, don't be so mindless. Stop dreaming, for God's sake."

"Yes, Mother," he said meekly.

Naomi would not have described her as formidable, but there was something of it in her; of middle height and slender, with straight, chin-length silver hair, startling blue eyes, and very fair skin, she looked nothing like her dark-haired son. Any qualms Naomi might have had about her own clothing were blown away, seeing her future mother-in-law in a jean skirt and apple-green knit jacket over a pink t-shirt, an incongruous and wild mixture. "You could have stayed here with us," she said to Naomi instead of a welcome. "I would have told him right then how stupid he was. No need to keep one of my grandchildren away from me for so long."

"I never thought there was anybody who could stand up to him. If I had known about you earlier, believe me, I would have sent him home to you to have his head bashed."

Naomi loved the house. The dark hardwood floor of the hallway shone like auburn hair in the slant of the evening sun, the walls were lined with family photographs, and a vase of flowers sat on an antique sideboard.

Helen tilted her head like a curious bird and eyed Naomi speculatively. "You are not what I expected. I never thought he would have the guts to pick a woman who would not be starry-eyed by what he has made of himself."

"Mother!" Jon's voice from behind her sounded painful, and Naomi enjoyed it enormously.

"Oh, shush!" Helen waved her hand at him. "You are the reason for all this upheaval. Since you are here early you might as well light the barbecue. Your brother and his family will be here soon, and you know Kevin is useless with the thing."

Naomi soon found herself in the kitchen. Joshua had received a warm embrace and some kisses from his new grandmother and then been told to go out in the garden to find his cousins and aunt. From the window Naomi watched as two young girls came running toward him, a woman following with a basket of tomatoes.

"My daughter, Valerie." Helen had begun washing potatoes. "And her girls, your new nieces." She paused, then added in her tart, lively voice, "Of course I want to know everything about you. He never said much, being the way he is, but I know he suffered enormously through the years. Then, all of a sudden, he vanishes from Earth, and now, out of the blue, he calls to tell me he is dropping by with his family? Informing us we had better get ready to travel, that he intends to get married finally, and in Norway, of all places! Go on, I want to hear."

She pushed the paring knife and the bowl of clean potatoes over, indicating that Naomi should start working.

"He doesn't come here often, leading the life he has chosen, and he rarely speaks of it. Doesn't have to either, we can read it in all the tabloids anyway. But you, now, you have been a rather well-kept secret. And the temerity of it, presenting me with a grown grandson! I should have clobbered him instead of sending him out to light the fire."

"He didn't know," Naomi replied defensively. "I never let him know. I hated that life, and I didn't want it for my child. That's why I left him."

"Well, good for you." Helen tossed more vegetables on the table.

"Don't clobber him, I beg you. It's not his fault." She had never in her life peeled potatoes, and now she was afraid of making a fool of herself.

"Oh, and protecting the self-centered bastard! Really, my dear, you should protect yourself if you intend to stick with him. He'll eat you up without a second thought if it suits his purposes. I never thought a son of mine could be so self-absorbed and willful."

Jon walked in just then, his shirt half open and the sleeves rolled up.

"Ma, I need the lighter fluid. Where did you put it?"

"It's in the garage," Helen replied without turning. "Don't spill it on your clothes."

"I won't, Mother."

At which point Naomi broke up in hysterical laughter, the tension she had felt washing off her in a sudden rush of relief.

"Yeah, laugh all you like." He shot her a dark look, petulance in his voice. "Didn't think I could light a freaking grill?"

Naomi looked up just in time to see a grin pass between mother and son before he left again.

Helen sent her off to have a look around the house after commenting that cooking didn't seem to be her strong point. Naomi shrugged her shoulders in defense.

"I grew up in hotels, more or less," she began her feeble explanation, but Helen waved her away wordlessly.

It was cool and dim in the silent rooms. Opening doors and peering into them seemed a little intrusive, but when she walked up the carpeted stairs she found a gallery of photos from Jon's life, on stage, receiving honors, a Grammy, another Grammy, and an Oscar; Jon, standing godfather to one of the girls; with his siblings; with his father.

On a sideboard on the landing, the Oscar statue itself. She touched it reverently, wishing she had been there when he had received it, in that colossal moment of glory.

One flight further up she found Jon's old room, untouched by time. A boy's refuge, with posters on the walls, a bed with a patchwork quilt, the pennant of some football team over it, and rows and rows of music books from all kinds of artists.

She sat on the bed absorbing the atmosphere of the place, imagining him at the desk with the view of the restaurant on the other side of the street, making his first attempts at songwriting, searching for the melodies that would make him famous.

"Ah, here you are." Jon peered through the half open door. "You shouldn't be here. I'm not sure I like you unearthing my secrets."

"Afraid I'll find the naughty magazines under your bed?" She made room for him on the quilt. "Tell me, Jon. Tell me about your life here, and the first songs you wrote. It must have been here, in this room."

"But you know all about that. There's no big secret to it. I got my first guitar, I took lessons, I found I could express myself in music, and I started to write. It's that easy."

But it was not true, of course.

It had been a hard and bitter struggle, first against his parents, who wanted a proper career for him; with school, because he never seemed to have enough interest or concentration for it; and then the true, painful fight with his inner self, the process of learning how to reach deep inside and find the melodies and words he wished to communicate to the world.

"First," Jon said thoughtfully, "there's this itch, or maybe an ache, like a very irritating, persistent, nagging mosquito bite or a headache, I don't know. You need to pick at it all the time, it just won't give you any rest, and it feels as uncomfortable and annoying as anything you can imagine. So you worry and work at it like a dog with a bone until all the meat is gone and you're left with only the basic thing, the gist of what it is that you want to say with this particular song. But you know all that! Why am I telling you?"

"Because I asked."

"It's different for you; you get the spark, and then you sit down and belt out whatever it is you want to say. Which I admire greatly, as you know. But I have to dig and sweat and grovel and humiliate myself most of the time before I can drag it out. Often it's not what I thought it would be, and sometimes I can gnaw at it forever and it still doesn't come out right."

He wandered over to the desk and looked down at it, clean and orderly now in a way it had never been when he had inhabited this room. He moved his hand across the wood. "I used to sit here and stare out of the window, and instead of studying my Latin I would have one of those yellow legal pads in front of me, scribbling disgusting, sentimental lyrics, a young boy's fantasies of his one perfect love, the one you would recognize in an instant, one glance, and know for sure she was the right one."

"As far as I can see, you're still doing it today," Naomi murmured, but he heard her.

"Of course!" He turned back to her with a smile. "Of course I am, because it still confounds me that such a thing is possible. I've never overcome the miracle of our first meeting in Geneva. That is a bone I've been chewing on for years now, and I've still not found the marrow. It's irrational and confusing, but there it is: it has never left me alone, this thought that I'm not entitled to receive this special grace. And maybe there's some truth to that because I lost you soon enough, wasn't able to hold on to you. I knew it had to be you, and yet I did nothing to make sure of you. My punishment and I accept it."

"Here you go again." She sighed. "You are such a hopeless fool. A romantic, hopeless, and wonderful fool. Let's go back down. I want to meet the rest of your family. I love your mother, by the way."

"Told you." His grin was wide and quite smug.

22

THIS WAS NOT what she had expected at all. Surrounded by his family Jon seemed reduced, somehow toned down to normal size. Just another grown son and brother who lived far away and had come to spend the weekend at home. He was tending the barbecue and discussing baseball with his brother while their teenage children sat in the shade of a tree. The sound of their young voices drifted over as they talked about school, movies, and music.

Naomi received an unrestrained monologue from his sister Valerie, who told her in no uncertain terms what she thought of a woman who would keep a child of the family away from them, and when Naomi replied, "But I did not even know you existed. He never talked about family back then!" she very unceremoniously went over to Jon and hit him hard on the shoulder.

"What was that for?" he cried in mock outrage, rubbing the injured arm. "I come home and what happens? I get beaten up by my own sister. They're here now, aren't they, so what's the fuss? I had to get things settled first!"

"You conceited bastard. And now you tell us you're getting married, and I don't even get to do any organizing?" She refused him the ketchup when he tried to reach for it.

Jon's brother Kevin popped open another bottle of beer. "Yeah, man. And then showing up here like that, the audacity of it all. Hey, Mom, I'm in town, and guess what, I'm getting married in a few weeks. And oh no, not here, but in Norway. Drop everything you're doing, and no, I don't care that you have tickets for the Met for that weekend. What? *La Boheme*? Vastly overrated. Nah, what's a couple hundred bucks for a ticket, they pay that every day to see *me* perform."

Joshua and Kevin's son Ethan ran past them into the house and returned a moment later with a couple of guitars. They began to sing together softly, then more raucously as they gained confidence.

"Leave him here with us for a while," Valerie begged, "We'll bring him back when we come over for your big day. We have so much catching up to do."

Once more the terrible, deep hurt cut through him, and he wondered briefly if it would always be there, if they would ever be able to outlive their burden.

"Of course, if he wants to," he heard Naomi's soft voice from behind him. "I'm so happy to have found you. Even if you weren't related to Jon at all, I would love you as my family."

"YOU TRY NOT to become what you do," Jon said much later, when the grill had cooled down. "But it takes constant reflection. I know you don't want to hear this because your credo is 'you made your bed, now lie in it,' but that's not the whole truth. You choose what you want to do; the life that goes with that choice catches up later. The lack of privacy, the constant need for security, the tabloids and paparazzi lying in wait for the most embarrassing moment to snap your photo and run. That I could do very well without. But I could never do without the music."

Naomi had the feeling they had discussed this before and often. There was a mild but pervading accusation in the air, of him not seeing enough of the family.

"You are all successful in your professions," he went on. "And you strive for perfection in what you do. But perfection in my job means success with the masses, or it would be for nothing. If no one wants to hear my music, I might as well go out and flip burgers. The only thing we can do,"—he took Naomi's hand and pressed it—"is try to be as good as we can."

Kevin asked Naomi what she did for a living, and when she replied that she ran a small hotel in Norway, Jon laughed at her.

"She runs a hotel, right. She makes her millions by writing my lyrics. Did it back then, is doing it again now. Watch us; there will be a series of albums with her lyrics. Running a hotel, yeah, Baby."

"I did," she insisted, "And I did it well. Our restaurant is famous all along the west coast. I only wrote in my free time."

"The way you write, my love, that is all that's needed." Jon kissed the tips of her fingers one by one. She drew them back in embarrassment.

Helen returned from the kitchen with two bottles of champagne. "It seems we have ample reasons to celebrate. My lost sheep back in the fold, and still sane enough, it seems. Or sane again? No matter; bring out the glasses, Val, please."

"Whole again," Jon said in a low voice. "Oh yes, whole and healed."

Dusk fell slowly in the garden. A mild wind blew in from the river, bringing the sounds of boats and ships with it, and the scent of sea water. Naomi lifted her head to breathe it in, wondering how it could vary so much in different places, and if it might be possible to recognize a shore simply by its smell.

"You wanted to be famous even when you were still in school. You always wanted to stand out." Jon grinned at Valerie and her accusing teacher's tone.

"Of course. The same way Kevin wants to be chief of surgery or you want your own private music school."

"You never understood." She waved at him disdainfully. "You could never be a teacher. A teacher's success is seeing her students turn into successful people, into doctors and lawyers and engineers and more teachers. Famous musicians, like you. Great cooks, like Naomi."

Naomi woke from her reverie. "I'm not a cook. I hardly know how to peel a potato. I haven't cooked anything but coffee in my life. Jon does the cooking if we do it at all."

The laughter that followed her statement was so loud that she looked around in confusion.

"Really?" Helen said. "He cooks? I never thought he could. Jon, you really do the cooking in this new Stone household? You are a dark horse. I'm definitely coming to see that!"

"Yeah, thanks, Ma." Jon opened another bottle. "You never think I can do anything useful at all. That's so encouraging."

"We can debate all you like about being useful, my dear." Helen took the open bottle from him to pour herself. "I don't care how useful you are to the rest of the world, but you certainly aren't much use to us if you're never here. You could have come home to lick your wounds, but no, you elected to hide in that shack by the ocean, all by yourself for all those years. I guess being with your family wouldn't have satisfied your dramatic streak."

Naomi coughed to hide a giggle, but he knew, of course.

"Laugh all you like. It wasn't funny. I was lonely and confused and sad, and I'm not going into that again. I don't have the time for it. If you want to wallow, go ahead, and don't forget the ice cream buckets and the pizza to go with it. I want joy and happiness back in my life. But me? I'm not going to waste another moment mourning those lost and lonesome years."

"Hey man, you're right. But promise to show up at home a little more now that you have a family. And who knows, maybe there'll even be more family some day?" Kevin raised his glass to Jon.

"Hush!" Helen reprimanded him sharply.

"No, it's okay." Naomi blushed, but no one saw in the growing darkness. "I don't mind you asking. I can imagine…" She reached out to Jon, who caught her hand and rested it on his knee. "I can imagine…" But she couldn't finish the sentence.

"You want another grandchild, Mother," Jon said instead. "You're mad at me because I never took care of Joshua, so now you want me to raise another child, and you want to be there to see a child of mine grow up."

Helen carefully gathered some crumbs into a neat little pile.

"Mom, I'm sorry." His voice was pained. "I promise, we will not cut you out of our life. It was never meant to happen like that."

"For goodness sake, Jon! It's not always all about you. Or maybe, come to think of it, it is. I don't know why you thought it would be a good idea to retreat from us and only show up every couple of years or so, usually when you were passing through anyway, and then only for a cup of coffee. You truly could have come home for a while and taken a rest here."

Naomi was thinking much the same thing, and she gazed at him expectantly as he took his time in answering.

"I needed to be there. I couldn't move away. It was unbearable, but still…"

"No!" Naomi knew what he was going to say before he drew his next breath. "No, Jon! Don't say it, please. Please. Please don't lay this burden on me, or on yourself. Come on, let's clear the table."

She began piling the dishes into stacks, the plates ringing dangerously with her abrupt movements.

Jon gripped her wrist. "Put that down. You have a terrible habit of dropping things when you're agitated. I'll do it. Sit."

Silently, the others watched as he carried the tray inside, his tall figure moving carefully through the door.

"What was that all about?" Helen asked, "I've never seen him like that."

Here it comes. She knew she would have to supply the answer sooner or later, so it might as well be now.

"He was going to say…" Naomi tasted the painful words on her lips, trying to put it in such a way that it would not sound too pathetic. "He was going to say he had hoped I would show up again at some point."

She swallowed the bitterness in her throat and took another sip of champagne. "I went to see his concert in London last year."

"Oh." There was relief in Helen's tone. "So you did go to him, in the end."

Naomi chewed on that for a while.

"No," she admitted. "I stood with a group of fans and watched him walk by. But I didn't try to reach out to him."

This was greeted by another lengthy stretch of silence. Kevin, eyeing her thoughtfully, opened another bottle of beer.

"So…are you getting married because of the boy? It doesn't seem necessary; I know Jon would take care of him anyway."

It felt like a knife, this sensible and sober question, and she drew back into herself, probing the pain, a sharp, searing thing driven right into her center.

"Kevin," Valerie said.

Naomi rose and moved away from the table, her arms wrapped tightly around her waist. "I'm sorry, I'm so tired. It must be jet-lag. Please excuse me."

She met Jon on her way into the house and went right past him. "Baby?" he asked, but she only shook her head.

"I think I'm going to retire. I'm truly exhausted. Will you stay here? I'll take a cab back to the hotel."

He stopped her. "Hey! Wait! Why are you running this time?"

"Nothing, love." She tried to evade him, but he only held her closer. "I'm tired."

"There's something wrong here, and I want to know what happened. I'm not letting you go that easily, and you know it."

"Jon." She laid her arms around him. "Why, exactly, am I marrying you?"

"Oh, I don't know. Maybe because I'm good at making you write? Or because you like a certain stupidity in your men? Perhaps because you love me beyond all reason?" His body moved into hers suggestively. "Or maybe because I'm the only one you really want all the time, and you just can't do without me? Are you getting weak right now, little beast? Do you want to get ready for me when I come to you later? Will you put on your diamonds and lie there and give me that outrageous, inviting look of yours, so tempting, so sweet?"

He kissed her in earnest then, right there in the hallway of his mother's house, unconcerned that his family might see them. Holding her very tightly against him, he savored how she melted into his embrace.

"Well," Helen remarked from the garden door. "This certainly doesn't look like a business arrangement to me. Or at least it's not the kind of arrangement Kevin had in mind. Stop it, you two, or at least find a more private place."

THEY RETURNED FOR breakfast, at Helen's insistence. Jon grumbled all the way over the bridge, saying it was way too early to think about eating pancakes when they should still be in their nice, big hotel bed together. Naomi gazed out the car window at the Hudson below, and the mesmerizing skyline of the city in the early morning with a strange, new feeling of belonging, and for once, she did not respond to his ribald words. It was a rainy, windy morning, the water choppy and capped with white foam. A couple of barges made their way upriver, gulls in their wake, the men on them as small as toys.

A crowd of words danced in her mind, all of them striving to catch her attention, lining themselves up into rhymes like little soldiers ready for her inspection, and for an open-mouthed moment she even thought she could hear a melody weaving itself around their neat rows.

She turned to Jon just in time to see his amused gaze before he leaned back again and said, "Anyway, my mom's coffee is so bad it tastes like old dishwater."

It wasn't true of course, as she had suspected. Joshua sat between his cousins in pajamas he proudly announced had been his father's, and he had slept well in his old room too, and could he please stay here a while longer? After all, he was on summer break, and anyway he felt he wanted to attend Juilliard if they would have him, and not go on in Oxford. And live with his grand-mom, who was so much more fun than the family in Geneva and Toronto.

Naomi shot him a brief, sharp glance, and he shut up for a moment before adding, much in the same tone Jon had used in the car, "Besides, the bed at Oxford really sucked."

Valerie suggested a walk to the Promenade to stretch their legs when it stopped raining. She wanted to chat without Jon sitting on Naomi's shoulder all the time. Jon shot her a glare and took a breath to reply, but Naomi swiftly planted a kiss on his lips and pulled Val away.

"I'm going out with Joshua then!" he called after her. He made it sound like a threat, but she ignored him.

Walking beside the tall, sturdy woman she felt insignificant and exposed, all the more so since Val, in her outspoken manner picked up her harangue about the lost family as soon as they had left the house.

Naomi didn't even try to argue. Val's hurt was hidden well under her brisk voice and the glasses she pushed up on her nose until they almost looked like goggles, but it was still visible enough.

"A boy," she said, leaning on the railing of the promenade, "a son of Jon's. Our superstar, and here he is, with a grown son and an almost-wife. And a normal, simple woman too, not one of those wealthy, made-up ladies that normally swarm around him. How did you do it?"

"I didn't do anything." Valerie's vehemence made her smile; it was a brisker version of Jon's. "It just happened. We ran into each other…"

"You don't run into Jon Stone," Valerie interrupted. "No woman runs into him and gets to stay. There must be something different about you. He obsesses about you like crazy."

This felt a little uncomfortable and she let it pass.

They had turned back to the street where Helen lived when Naomi stopped dead in her tracks. Val stopped to see what Naomi was looking at.

"Oh, you've discovered the Miller house. Pretty, isn't it?"

It was. Naomi had a vision of them living there, right on the promenade, with the spectacular vista of Manhattan skyline from her bedroom, so close to his family, so near to the city, she felt it had been waiting for her. It was huge, set well back, with a yard of its own, surrounded by an old cast-iron fence overgrown with ivy and wild rose vines, a white three-story building from the last century.

"There would certainly be plenty of room there for everything you creative people need," she heard Valerie say. "And even though it's right here on the corner, it could be secured easily enough."

"Is it for sale?" Naomi asked.

Valerie pushed up her glasses. "How the hell should I know? But does it matter? Jon always gets whatever he wants."

JON COOKED DINNER for them just to prove he could do it.

He announced that he had booked a box at the Met for the following night so Kevin could see his *La Bohème* after all.

"And it wasn't easy, let me tell you. But I had the office take care of it. What good is it being a star if you don't get any of the benefits?"

"I bet you paid a fortune." Valerie took the bowl of pasta from Joshua to carry it outside. "The thing has been sold out for months."

Jon cut the bread into neat little diamonds with care. "You just need the right contacts. Whatever. We'll be going to the Met tomorrow. And I'll take you all out for dinner afterward. We'll practice celebrating. Get out the nice clothes."

Watching Naomi while they sat down for dinner, with Kevin home from work and the kids finally pried away from the piano, Jon was pleased. She fit in with his family as if she had known them all her life, and the mild derisiveness his mother and sister treated him with was like a natural habitat for her, a way to deal with the life and circumstances he had to offer. Sitting in his mother's garden, chilled white wine in their glasses and plates heaped with food, he felt a deep satisfaction settle in his heart.

"So did you get to see the Statue of Liberty? Did you go all the way up?" Naomi was asking Joshua.

"No." He shot Jon a glance. "I changed my mind. I wanted to go to Juilliard once more. They gave me a private audition. I played for the masters."

Naomi almost knocked over the wine bottle in her excitement. "How did it go? What did they say?"

She saw Jon's small, satisfied grin and knew.

"You got accepted! Juilliard accepted you!"

"In a manner of speaking." Joshua squirmed a little in his seat. "They want to see more of my compositions, but yes."

"You could live here," Helen suggested. "Your father's old room is yours, if you like. There's the piano, and I would be so happy."

Joshua glanced at his mother. "If I had my choice, I would go to Juilliard. But it is even farther from home than Oxford."

It didn't hurt as much as she thought it would. "Not that much farther. And I would feel good knowing you would be with family and not alone on a campus. But how did you do it? They don't give private auditions just like that, do they?"

He said that he didn't know, but somehow it had helped to have Jon along, because the head of the school had welcomed them himself and been exceedingly friendly.

Kevin gave Jon a knowing look, but got no reaction.

JOSHUA PREFERRED STAYING at the house to the hotel, which gave them the kind of liberty they had not been granted since they were in London on their own.

It had turned warm again, with many tourists out for a stroll, just like them.

"I like it a lot better here than in Los Angeles," Naomi stated. "People here are interesting, and somehow it seems more…more European? They don't seem to be so shallow and self-centered. There's more of an intellectual depth. And the music scene! Will you show me the places where you started out?" Something else occurred to her. "You never told me how you came to work with Sean. Where did you meet? Was it here in New York? Or after you moved to LA?"

He motioned her into a bar, where they sat in a quiet corner and ordered some wine. "Funny you should ask that. Just the other day I was thinking that really, besides the band, I don't have any friends at all. It's a lonely business." He paused, toying with his glass, deep in thought. "Sean and I met when I was just starting out. He was playing a nightclub, sitting in a corner tinkling away on a battered piano while the people around him talked and drank and paid no attention to him at all. I had one of my very first public appearances there, God, I remember I was so nervous and hadn't the faintest idea what I was supposed to do. There was a tiny little stage with barely enough room for the stool and the mike and me, and I had only a handful of songs in my bag. And there was Sean, with long hair and a ragged shirt, a cigarette hanging from his lips, and he said, 'Hey, you look as if you've never sung to an audience before. Let me tell you, they won't listen, no matter what you do.' But they listened alright, at least after the first song." Jon grinned in reminiscence. "Then Sean came up to me and said, 'Give me that music.' And he played along with me and it worked beautifully. When I went to Pittsburgh for my first real gig, I asked him to come along. One day we were doing a stint in a club in Greenwich Village, right here in New York, and during the intermission Sal walked up and offered to manage us. God, we were so young."

He sat in silence for a while, watching the other customers. It seemed like an enchanted moment. Either he was not recognized at all or the other people had collectively chosen to ignore him.

"From then on, we rapidly climbed the ladder to success, and a few years later, with the band complete, we had our first European tour, after doing two huge rounds through the States. I will never know why, but Sal had the idea of including Geneva. Everything was settled and the dates fixed, and then he calls me one day from the office, very excited, to tell me about an envelope he just received." A small, thoughtful smile appeared on his lips.

"He ordered me to come down right away because he had something to show me, and he thought I would enjoy it. So I went, even though I had other things on my mind. I wanted to go out and hang in a Hollywood bar and maybe find a date."

Naomi raised her eyebrows at him. "Really. Trying to find a date. You? Having trouble finding a date?"

"Don't interrupt. Now I'm getting to the best part." A small wave of his hand brought the waitress over. Jon asked for another bottle of wine and some snacks. "I walk into the office, and there's Sal, and he makes me sit down and hands over those fateful pages. Suddenly my stomach was tied up in knots, my heart skipped a beat, my palms were sweaty, and I think I stopped breathing for a moment."

"Jon." She laughed a little, embarrassed by his tale. He had never told her about that day before.

"Well, that's how it was. I recall it as clearly as if it happened yesterday. Sal hovered over my shoulder, asking what do you think, what do you think, I can just hear your music here, oh, whoever she is, she has plunged right into your heart and found you. And that was the truth of it."

Their wine arrived in a silver cooler.

"I took those lyrics home, the need for a date forgotten. Every time I had to stop at a red light I looked at them. The melody was right there, I could hear it so clearly. The song was ready by the time we were on the plane, the band was toying with it even then, on the flight. Sal had set up an appointment with the author and wanted to meet her but I said no; I wanted to do it myself, and alone. There was some magic here, and I didn't want to ruin it by having my manager around. So I sat in that lobby, not knowing what to expect, and then, through the sunshine, comes this wonderful vision, this girl in jeans and her silly little white blouse. That's when I realize those lyrics were written from the soul, from one that reaches out to mine and touches me in a way I had never thought anyone could. Yes, and I knew I would have to hold on, even at the price of my life. Hold on to that beauty, that lovely, graceful beauty, with my soul residing within. Mine, my very own, made for me."

His recital made Naomi shift uncomfortably on the leather couch.

"I called Sal," she said, changing the subject. "There's something I need done before we get married, and I need him for it. He's coming here tomorrow. And Jon?"

He curiously looked up at her tone.

"No more sex before the wedding. I want to feel like a bride when I come to our marriage bed."

Jon laughed.

23

NAOMI WAS LESS than happy when Jon informed her that Russ had called and needed him back in Los Angeles for some changes to the recordings, but there was little that could be done. Jon offered to take her back with him, but she firmly refused. She had spent enough time gallivanting around the world, and it was high time she found her way home. Joshua was not ready to leave New York yet, and Helen had a few appointments to keep before she could travel, so two days later they went back to the airport, where they boarded separate jets and flew off in different directions. She watched the Gulf Stream with him aboard taxi onto the runway and take off, turn in the air, and speed off to the West, then boarded her own and settled down for the flight across the Atlantic.

THE AIR WAS so different in Norway. Even the sky felt lower. It was a rainy and cool afternoon, and Naomi stood at the entrance to the Seaside, trying to imagine how Jon must have felt that day before he stepped inside for the first time. She tried to capture the sentiment that had driven him to make that lonely trip across oceans and time and seek her out. The magnitude of his act washed over her, unfathomable and utterly driven as it had been.

Christi came out to meet her, a wide smile on her face, followed closely by Andrea. It felt good to see their faces again and to be welcomed back to the place she had come to think of as her home.

The apartment was clean and airy. Someone had put flowers and fruit on the table and opened the door to the deck. For the first time in a long while, she was alone again here in Halmar, back in the timeless quiet and solitude of her former life, and she let the feeling of peace wash over her, the stillness settling around her after the turmoil of the past few weeks.

With a sigh she dropped down on the couch and sat for a while, purse still in hand, and stared out over the bay and the mountains, hung now with low, grey clouds that were drizzling a fine, misty rain down onto the landscape. The slate grey water, capped with little white breakers, sloshed under the deck, making a rhythmic, sucking sound.

The certainty that she was in the one place where the world could not touch her made her relax, and even though she had slept on the plane for quite a while, drowsiness overwhelmed her.

When she sank into her bed, tired from jet-lag and the excitement of the past days and weeks, she stretched out her hand to the empty side of the bed where she had come to expect warmth and comfort and tried to figure out what time of day it was in LA now. This going back and forth across continents confused her, and she fell asleep while mulling over time zones.

IT DIDN'T TAKE too long to do a new recording of the song Sean wanted changed. Jon was in fine form after his visit to New York. Life had been very good to him of late, and with this sentiment he strode into the studio and belted out the tune with a verve and conviction that left the band silent with astonishment, Sean nodding in satisfaction. They spent a few hours listening to the now completed soundtrack with Harry, who was pleased with the outcome, and discussed the release date with Russ and the representatives from the record company over a couple of drinks at a bar on the waterfront.

Jon's heart was not really in the project anymore.

"Do what you think is best," he said to Art and Russ. "I know you'll do the right thing, and it will be beautiful. Just send me a couple of copies when you're done. I want to go."

They looked out into the sunset, all of them exhausted after the furious work the past few months. Sean, Russ, Art, Harry, and Jon toasted each other on a production well done.

"And now," Art announced, rubbing his hands, "Christmas, and then we get ready for the tour." His phone rang.

"Sal," he mouthed at Jon and then listened to what was being said to him.

Sal had just arrived and wanted to talk to Art and Jon right away. He didn't have much time and needed to return to New York immediately.

"And it couldn't wait until we meet in Halmar in a couple of weeks, or be done over the phone?" Jon asked in bewilderment. Art shrugged. They broke up the gathering and drove to the house to meet with Sal and hear what he had to tell them.

"Do you know," Sal said instead of a greeting, "who it is you are marrying, Jon? Art, I need a triple bourbon, if you please." He dropped onto the couch and pushed his hair off of his forehead.

"Yes?" Jon eyed him a little doubtfully. "I thought I did, until now. Why do you ask?"

Sal gave him his best shark grin. "What do you know about her, then?"

Obediently, Jon recited everything he knew about Naomi, which, he admitted, was not extensive, but he had been satisfied that it was enough.

"Let me help you," Sal interrupted gleefully. "Do you know where her family comes from? How much has she told you about them, the secretive little thing?"

"Canada," Jon answered. "At least that's what she said. Most of them live in Toronto. The hotel belongs to her family. Her parents are in Geneva because her father's job is there. "

Oh yes, Sal picked up the tale with relish, and did he know why that was so? Because he managed the family's finances from there, and it was worth the trouble to have someone do this, as there was so much to manage. Had he ever heard of the Hiltons? Well, the Carlsson empire was not quite as large as that, but they owned a cute little row of hotels in Canada and Scandinavia, and the Seaside was only a very minor chapter of the book, the family's hobby horse, so to speak. Her Uncle Carl had managed it himself for a while as a favor to the family. They had been prepared to go to that length with Naomi because, Sal said, she was one of two heirs to the whole empire. They needed her and would not allow her to drift off again after her disaster.

Jon had known for a while that the family owned hotels, but not the extent of it.

"Her mother told me a bit, but man, that family is circumspect. They might as well own a Swiss bank for all the secrecy!" He laughed out loud at his own joke. "So you understand, they gave her this sweet little sanctuary and hid her away there with her uncle so you would never find her. You are dealing with a tight-knit and powerful family here, Jon, and your sweet rose has chosen to step out of it because of you. You will have them sitting on you soon enough when you wed their daughter."

He took a big gulp of his drink and held out the glass to Art for a refill.

"Oh, and by the way," he finished with a flourish, "it's old money. Really old, like they were some kind of big-ass landowners or nobility in Norway some hundreds of years ago, before they decided that Canada was much too empty for their liking and lacked guest houses of a certain standard."

Art sat across from them and looked from one to the other. "And you know this how? And how does it concern Jon? It doesn't really change anything, does it? So her family is rich and owns a bunch of hotels. What of it? Why should it matter? Jon has a few dollars socked away, and he's not nameless, either."

"Yes, Sal," Jon echoed, "how did you come to know all this?"

"My friend," Sal said expansively, "your Baby Girl has asked me to manage her finances, and I had a very, very long talk with her father. The old bastard is one tough bird, and he knows everything about money management. And let me tell you, he is still none too pleased about the whole thing. He'd really prefer to see her go back to Canada and take over her duties instead of languishing in Halmar with you making music. But her mother has worked the female Carlsson magic on him, and he is compliant, if not happy. If you, my friend had not gone to Geneva and more or less forced him to accept you with all your millions, it would never have worked. But money talks. And your instinct was right, and I was wrong, I freely admit it." He was full of a hilarity neither Jon nor Art had seen in him for a long while, obviously highly amused by the facts he had unearthed. "Which brings me to my next point," he went on. "Artie, we are going to discuss contracts. No more working for the Jonman without written deals for my new client."

Jon waved him away. "What the hell, Sal? As if it matters. Say what you want and have it made up. It will be going into one pot anyway."

"Nah, it won't!" Sal crowed. "The old man and I are setting up her own accounts, and your money will be going in it, the nest egg you put on his table when you stormed into his office. You will be a whole lot poorer by the time you take your bride to the marriage bed, my friend."

"And she knows about this? And she consents? I find that hard to believe."

Sal shook his head. Not yet, and there were one or two other things he had to do, and yes, he enjoyed working for her enormously because there was a fascinating background. A little bit like a Mafia family, they had influence everywhere, even in the political arena. Jon had better watch his back if he ever did something to bring her unhappiness.

"Makes me wonder," he concluded when he got up to leave. "That graceful mother of hers, she is from Naples, isn't she?" And again he laughed raucously. "Maybe that was a true marriage between Mafia families. Is there such a thing as a Scandinavian Mafia?"

He was on his way to the door but returned again to add, rather maliciously, "And oh, Jon? You did know she was in college when you met, yes? But did she ever to tell you where?" Dramatically, he waited for Jon to shake his head in bemusement. "She was at a conservatory, my dear famous pop star, studying piano and classical singing. Your dear, sweet hotel girl is a better musician than you can ever hope to be." With the final bombshell dropped, Sal walked out, his laughter echoing behind him through the house.

HE ARRIVED IN Halmar, and once again, for sentimental reasons, by water taxi. The lobby was quiet when he walked in, only Sven was at the desk typing away on the computer. Jon stopped and looked around, recalling his anguish when he had stood here the first time facing Solveigh and her bright, questioning stare, and how he had fumbled for the words to find out if Naomi was truly in this place. There had been no way for him to ask outright; he had been so abashed and too frightened of a humiliating scene. And then the elevator doors, the soft laughter and melodious voice that had haunted his nights for years, the deafening noise of those crashing plates, her motionless silhouette and the tautness of his heart, its uncontrolled hammering as he followed her down to her rooms, silence between them like cotton and fear like spikes in his sides.

"The mistress is in the kitchen," Sven said, "Having lunch with the girls."

They were sitting around the counter, leafing through a catalogue and eating spaghetti, a delicious garlic aroma wafting toward him from the open pot Andrea had placed between them.

"But I love pink," Naomi was saying, "or at least rose. Why can't I have pink roses on that stupid cake? And why do we need it anyway? Who wants cake?"

"It's a wedding." Andrea put a plate before her. "You can't have a wedding without a cake."

"I don't need all this." Naomi's voice sounded a little plaintive. "It's so huge. I'll make him take me to the registry office and be done with it. Maybe if I ask nicely he'll run off with me and we'll live happily ever after on a lonely little island in the South Sea with only weekly catering service for company."

"Yeah, listen to you," Christi scoffed. "Spoiled and unable to cook for yourself, relying on a caterer even on an island paradise. There will be a cake, and no mistake."

"Really, Baby?" Jon asked, "You and me on a tropical island? No people, no phones, and no clothes? Let's go."

She dropped her fork and flew into his arms so fast he staggered a little, but he caught her with delight. "Ah. So much better than last time. And no broken plates. I really hated to see those plates go to waste."

It felt so right, so perfect, to hold her close.

"I'm baa-ack," Jon announced, stating the obvious and making Christi laugh at him.

The secluded privacy of the apartment welcomed them, and when the door fell shut and the last few noises from upstairs were drowned out he once more had the notion this was a haven, a retreat for tired souls.

The piano stood open. Music sheets lay on it, not his this time, but Rachmaninoff, and some Sibelius. Gazing down at them, he realized Joshua probably did not get his talent from him at all but most certainly from his mother if she was good enough to play these composers. It was daunting.

Naomi's eyes gleamed with happiness to have him back, and she held his hands as if she feared he would leave again, tugging slightly to get his attention away from the piano.

"Greedy again, little beast?" he asked, but his eyes remained on those ominous sheets. There would have to be a serious talk, soon, before their families descended on them and more surprises were revealed.

He lifted her up and carried her up the stairs to the bed, laid her down, and looked down at her outstretched body in approval.

"I like this dress," he said as he began taking off his shirt. "It is pleasing to look at and easy to peel off. So what about the no sex thing, my sweet dove? Just some cuddling, or…?"

"Just come here," Naomi replied. "We'll find out. Maybe this once, since you've just come home."

"Come here…" Her urgent tone made him smile. "When I first came to Halmar you made me wait until night and I had to sit and simmer while you had a fine day up there with your friends. You don't have the faintest idea how that felt."

She moved against him with a deep sigh, nestling into his shoulder, her hand on his bare chest. "I was wondering and wondering. I was thinking how it would be when you returned, if I could relive the miracle of that day when you showed up here the first time. I didn't make you wait. I needed time to understand what I was doing, what was happening. I could think of nothing else that day, nothing but the certainty that I would be in your arms that night, and that once that happened I would not be able to let go of you again. A couple of times I was on the point of going down to you right away and throwing myself at you, but it was so special, so awesome, and I knew we would need time to celebrate, and intimacy, and stillness."

He tugged at the zipper of her dress. "You want me, little beast. You want me very badly."

"Yes." A sigh like a soft touch on his skin. "But no. I want to hunger for you, to yearn and dream. I want to look at you and not get you. And then, on our wedding night, I want to tremble with anticipation at what we'll do once you've taken away my bridal gown and I stand before you, finally all yours."

"Yeah." The dark, velvety voice sent shivers down her spine. "Yes, Baby. Oh, now I can see where you are going with your celibacy. Okay, you'll get your wish. But I will torture you, I promise. You'll not have a moment's peace. I'll have you thinking of sex every second of the day. I'm telling you, you will plead ever so nicely with me before then. But I keep my promises, always. I'll let you beg all you want, my sweet bride."

His hand slipped up her thigh, but she withdrew and moved away from him.

"Yes, I want you badly. God, I'm so happy to see you. But I'll make some coffee now and then you'll tell me everything that happened in the last three days."

He rose to follow her back downstairs, shirt in hand, watched as she coiled her hair on top of her head in a graceful movement and straightened her dress, and thought that despite his promise it would be he who would be doing the suffering in the following days, seeing her like that and fantasizing about wild, sweet moments and soft sighs.

"Sal met your father for the settlements, and he has unearthed a few secrets you did not care to share with me, like your education. Do you truly play this?" He leafed through the music sheets. "We will have to talk at length about these things, Naomi."

There was no answer for the longest time.

The scent of fresh coffee and the burbling of the machine filled the room, the tinkling of the cups as she took them out of the cupboard and the sucking sound of the fridge door when she brought out the milk.

Domestic bliss, Art had called it, but here they were back in the same place, and there were pitfalls without end, even though their love had grown and shifted and turned into something greater and better than they had held in their past.

"Baby, the next weeks will be turbulent, and we will not have much space to discuss these things. We need to talk about it, and you know it."

Naomi poured the coffee and added milk, stirred it and put the spoon in the sink before she moved back to him.

"There is nothing to talk about. Nothing. I have parents, and I have no siblings. My family lives in Toronto, and I have one son. What else is there to say? You've met my parents, rather forcefully as I recall, and you know our son. Some other relatives you will meet on our wedding day."

Jon took his cup and sat down on the couch, his legs stretched out in front of him, shirt discarded. "You might consider that it's rather nice to know something about the person you are about to marry."

Carefully she perched, not too close to him, and held her mug with both hands. "There is nothing to tell, Jon. I have a family like anyone else, and I broke off my studies to be with you, because I had fallen helplessly, fatally in love. What else is so important? What do you need to hear? Am I a different person because you found out I do indeed have an education?"

She gazed at him, her cheeks flushed.

"No doubts," he hastened to reassure her. "I'm just perplexed. I had to learn from Sal that you were at a conservatory, studying music when we met! Don't you think I would have wanted to know?"

Naomi turned her face away. "He shouldn't have told you. It's not his business. And it doesn't matter. And could you please put your shirt back on?"

"Ah, no. Suffer all you like. I feel very comfortable without it. And don't change the subject. I want to know, and I will make you tell me."

Angrily, Naomi put down her cup and walked to the window. It was nearly impossible to see him like that and not go over and touch him.

"Well then, come here," Jon growled invitingly, "Come and take what you want so badly. It is written plainly on your face, my love. And tell me now, is it you who plays Rachmaninoff? Why make such a secret of it?"

It was the most unbearable temptation. Instead she sat down on the piano stool and clamped her hands between her knees. "I started playing when I was six. And I'm a fair player, but not excellent like Joshua. It was good enough to get me into conservatory. But Jon…" her face lost its dreamy expression and turned serious. "If it had meant anything, I wouldn't have dropped it."

Lacking an explanation, she shrugged.

Here was the core of her life, the one thing everything else centered around, and she wondered why she had to tell him once again.

"I was always better at writing, and you know it, Jon. I'm not going to repeat it again. You were my inspiration, and after that nothing else seemed important anymore. Did I expect to meet you at that hotel? I don't know. I hoped, I guess. Did I expect to fall in love with you?" She paused and gazed at him with a wounded look. "I did not expect it. I did not even know what love felt like. All I know is, I wanted to be in your arms when I saw you there in that lobby, wanted to know how your lips might taste, and I certainly wanted you to be the one to show me…" she faltered, had to breathe deeply and close her eyes for a minute before she could finish the thought, let alone speak it out loud. "I wanted you to be the man to take me to bed the first time, see me naked, show me…" she broke off and fell silent.

He sat up and looked straight at her.

"Nothing else meant that much to me," she said. "All I wanted was to be with you, hear your music, share your life and feel your body next to mine, hold you close and know you loved me, too. It's that simple, Jon. It comes down to this." She gave him a small, tentative smile. "It still is, you know. Simple. I don't want Hollywood or glamour or fame or wealth, or traveling all over the world in private jets. Or diamonds. You and the music. That's all I need. And this is the answer you will get every time you ask."

"And now?" He tugged at her skirt to make her move over to him, but she resisted. "And now, so many years later, do you still think it's enough? This is not a decision you need to make. It was never a question of me or the rest of the world."

Naomi shook her head at him, wondering how it could be he understood so little about himself, saw himself in such a warped light that he could not recognize how strongly he influenced everyone around him, made those close to him bend their lives to suit him and his demands.

"I have," she explained carefully, "chosen to be yours. I did it then, and I'm doing it again now. There is not much room left for anything else, Jon. You fill up nearly all of my life, and the small rest that is left I need for Joshua and for breathing. It's just the way it is with you, and has always been. Your career and the road you are traveling leave little space for detours. It's either be with you or drop off somewhere by the roadside. Trailing along in this comet's fiery tail, someone called it. That's you. The comet."

Shocked, he leaned back again. "No. That is not how it is. I don't want it to be like this, and if it truly appears this way, then it needs to be changed. There's more to your life than just me, and there must be, too. You cannot give up everything else and devote your entire existence to me, Naomi."

Instantly he saw he had hurt her. He could not fathom how, but by trying to give back her independence, he had wounded her.

"And anyway, what about your family? You never told me you had all this responsibility waiting for you. You tell me you have barely enough money to pay for Joshua's education when in reality you have this enormous hotel empire in the family, and you are the heir!"

She wandered away to the deck door, this time opening it to let in the fresh afternoon breeze.

"Is this the reason why you returned early?" Her voice was brittle. "To blame me for not giving Joshua a proper schooling, or not making enough money, or not pursuing a career like you do? Suddenly I'm no longer good enough for you? Is that was this is all about?"

"For God's sake!" Jon jumped up and came over to her in three strides, grabbing her by the arm and turning her around. "This is utterly insane! You know that's not true. You know I never meant it like that! You can't center your whole life on me, you can't! There is so much more for you to do, Naomi. I'm only a man, for crying out loud. I'm not the center of the universe."

Her head was bowed, her body limp in his hard grip, and he heard soft sobs from her. Bewildered and helpless by the scene that had developed, Jon found no more words to say. Ever so slowly, as if she were coming up from deep water, Naomi raised her eyes to him.

"But you are. I can't help it, Jon. Everything else…nothing else…" A little shrug of her shoulder. "You. Forever. Even when I ran, all through the lonely years, it was only you. If this is not what you want, then I'm sorry. I never touched any of that money because I never felt I deserved it. I left my family to follow you, and I broke off my studies because being with you was more important to me. Anyway, I never meant to step into the family business. This, the Seaside, was quite sufficient for me. It was my sanctuary, my retreat from life. I needed it, here I could heal and lead a small and safe existence."

Her hand came up to rest on his chest. "I shed my life like a coat I didn't need any more once you kissed me that day by the lake. I shed it there in Geneva, and I never picked it up again."

"But, you silly girl…" It was a half-hearted attempt at reason; he knew there was no way he could argue with her single-minded logic. It was her own and just as convoluted as always, ending up in decisions that seemed like bombs dropped from high above directly on his head.

"But it makes me feel bad. I've taken so much away from you. Will you at least play some Rachmaninoff for me now? Will you let me hear? The rest we can talk about later."

Her straight, slim back and curving waist were a pleasing sight as she sat down in the place that had become his over the months. He had never wondered why a Steinway grand stood in the center of her living space, assuming it had been there waiting for him, put in that exact space for him to show up and take over.

But the thing that really blew his mind was the mastery she had over the difficult piece. She was no Horowitz, that much was true, but good enough for a concert hall any time. His own playing was not nearly that sophisticated. The few lessons he had taken when he was young had never taken him even close to a classical education. He could just imagine her as a little girl in braids and a lovely rose-colored dress with a bow in the back, gazing seriously at her piano teacher as he explained the music to her in her parents' large apartment overlooking the lake and the promenade.

The music ended. Naomi rested her hands on her thighs and waited with bowed head for his comment.

"Come," Jon said, "Come with me now, and let me love you. Come."

MUCH LATER, AFTER Naomi had called the kitchen and asked Andrea to send down some dinner, they sat amid the rumpled sheets, and while she fed Jon pieces of chicken she narrated the tale of her family.

Originally, she told him, her ancestors had come from Denmark, like so many settlers in Norway, and had developed holdings in the beautiful Gudbrandsdal that stretched from Lillehammer to the north. They had been landowners and farmers and later in the retinue of the king, and had therefore often traveled to Trondheim, the old seat of the monarchy. Because of this, the family had owned property all over Norway.

Jon asked when this might have been, and caught his breath at her staggering reply, delivered so off-handedly: sometime in the thirteenth century. He could hardly believe anyone could trace their ancestry back that far.

The family had spread out, she continued, oblivious to his astonishment, in the seventeenth and eighteenth centuries, some of the first settlers in Canada and on the American East Coast to establish hotels there. Somehow they had succeeded in their enterprises, and they held a group of hotels, nice, traditional houses with the charm of centuries and history.

Now it had come down to this: her father and his brother owned the company, and she and her uncle's son were the heirs, but she did not want a part in it, having chosen to go in a different direction. Her musical education had been meant as a reprieve, a chance to follow her own interests, before she entered business school and consequently the family business. But then—she shrugged her shoulder negligently—Jon had appeared in Geneva, and everything had changed.

And he had given her nothing, nothing at all. He had taken her with him to LA and installed her in his house and enjoyed her company, drawing solace and strength from her presence and taking all the love he could get, and had believed, in his incredible self-absorption, that life for her was just as wonderful as it had been for him. As bitter as it felt, he had to admit it was nothing better than trailing in his wake indeed.

"And now," he asked softly, "and now you consent to marry me, and you are ready to give up everything once more? What of this empire waiting for you, and the possibility to do something wonderful? What about your music?"

He received no answer, only the small shake of her head and the growing reticence.

"No wonder your father hates me so much. He wants you for different things, and here you are, throwing away your life for a useless man like me. I understand a lot better now. God, how that must have pissed him off when you returned from California, pregnant, heart-broken, and lonely. Now I understand why he was so very unfriendly when I tried to find you." He nodded in slow comprehension. "I ruined you. I plucked their beautiful, budding rose, the hope of the family and the future of their business, the talented, sweet girl they were grooming to take over some day, and then tossed her back when I was done. Or so it must have seemed to them. God, will they ever forgive me?"

The thought frightened him, and the knowledge that he would have to face her disenchanted family in a few days when he would stand before the altar to finally set right what should have been done years ago. Naomi did not react to this insight. He watched her toy with a small tomato, then lay it aside again.

"In their eyes, you are doing the wrong thing," Jon said. "They thought they finally had you back on track, managing the hotel rather successfully, your son raised and you healed. And now, just as your father and uncle think they see the light at the end of the tunnel, you let your deep, dark secret slip to Joshua and take the risk that he will try to contact me."

He shifted in growing excitement. "How devious you are, Naomi. You did this just when you knew responsibility would descend on you in the form of a hotel empire, and so you flew away again. You are truly the master of running, my dear."

From the bed between them, he began to remove the dishes and the tray she had placed there and set them on the floor.

"But here the running ends. I don't care why you run from your family or why you don't want your heritage, but I do care a lot about your running from me. I'll do what I have to do to drive it out of you for good, and I'll work on it studiously. You need such a lot of assurance, and I'm willing to give it. If feeling my love for you is what you need, then you'll get it."

THE DAYS UNFOLDED like flowers on a slow-blooming tree, one by one, each bringing something new and surprising.

Jon moved into the studio. When Naomi asked him what he planned to do up there, he replied, "Read a book. I haven't done that for the longest time."

He treated her with exquisite courtesy, never once entering her rooms without her explicit invitation and then never trying to touch her. They spent many hours together each day, taking their meals, walking along the bay, driving through the countryside. They even went to Bergen to visit the old, brightly painted Hanse buildings along the harbor.

Jon bought some more fanciful Norwegian sweaters. With a pained expression, he told her he wished he had owned something that warm when he made his torturous way from one recording studio to the next at the beginning of his career in the nasty New Yorker winter of his twenty-first year.

"You laugh," he said darkly, "but it was a really bitter winter, and I had to walk a lot because I couldn't afford the subway. You have no idea how the cold wind howls through the canyons of Manhattan."

Once again, they had lunch at the fish market, sitting at the long wooden table and eating off newspaper, and again the air was tart, only this time the breeze carried the first brown leaves with it and tossed them across the cobblestones of the open space. Triumphantly Jon brought out one of his new sweaters and wrapped it around her when she shivered, and then left his arm around her shoulder. She leaned against him, her coffee cup between her hands to warm them, and listened as he told her how he had struggled to get someone, anyone, in the music business to listen to his songs.

"You must have been very thin," Naomi remarked, as she fed him another crab.

LIKE A CIRCLE, their talk returned again and again to the subject of writing and how different it was for them, how they often had the same sentiments but found such different ways to express them. It seemed to Jon as if they were trying to unravel the mystery of creativity altogether, as if in finding the source and the mechanism of it, the workings would become easier.

Naomi shrugged often. "Just write," she would say. "Don't think so much. Shut up, listen, write. It's that easy."

He did not believe it for a moment.

She played for him. Her choice of music astounded him; no Chopin or Bach for Naomi, it had to be the difficult, intricate pieces of the late Romantics. Debussy and Ravel in addition to Rachmaninoff, and many pieces for four hands. He wondered how hard and how often she must have practiced over the years to master them, and whether Joshua had been her partner.

"You scare me," he told her one afternoon. "I would never attempt to play these. They are meant for a concert hall, not your living room. And you play them for your own amusement. Scary."

He received a bemused glance in reply, and another of her simple statements that astounded him.

"I like them. Never cared for Chopin, too boring."

So he took one of the Gymnopedie pieces by Satie, put it on the piano, and asked her to play with him.

They sat side by side on the piano bench, and he stumbled through the complicated harmonies while Naomi's fingers moved with graceful dexterity over the keys, easily catching the melancholy of the melody.

She was a good teacher, patient, and with the single-minded belief that he could do what she had mastered, telling him over and over that it was nothing, only technique, and he, musician that he was, just needed to put his mind to it. Imagine, she said, if you had no band to accompany your songs, only the piano, and went on to tell him that his own harmonies were not that much simpler, only he gave them away to let the others play instead of doing it himself.

Naomi's eyes twinkled at him wickedly, "But you thought the melodies up. So you know the chords. You are just too lazy to play them yourself."

SOLVEIGH RETURNED A week before the wedding date.

She was by herself, no Russ in tow, and for a moment Naomi felt a spark of anxiety for her friend, but it was dispelled easily.

Solveigh waved her anxious question away. "No trouble. They're still so busy with the soundtrack, and I didn't want to wait any longer to get back. I'm sure you're floundering here and need me to take things in hand."

She set down her purse on the counter and looked around.

"God, I love the jet-set life. I think they invented it for me. Oh, good, the coffee is ready."

It seemed to Naomi it had needed no more than that for life to pick up speed once more. While Christi was still pouring the coffee, Solveigh had her notebook open on the table and was discussing last-minute arrangements with Andrea, the room list for the guests and the menu for the following days, flowers for the tables and the lobby.

Helen, Sal, and Joshua showed up a day later, closely followed by her parents.

Naomi had not seen them since the day Jon had brought them to Halmar, and she greeted them with trepidation. Her father was friendly enough, even a little amused at her shamefaced hesitation.

"Perk up," he said. "We won't tear his head off. It's done. He's a good enough man, and there can be no doubting his devotion."

The band and the rest from California arrived next.

Helen leaned on the countertop next to Naomi. "They haven't changed at all. They pass through town every so often, and crowd my house for an afternoon or evening, and it's always so much fun. He is lucky to have a bunch of people who stick with him like that." She paused thoughtfully. "He is lucky. He has had the luck of the devil his whole life."

"There are drawbacks," Naomi replied softly. "He has paid dearly for his success."

That remark earned her a derisive snort from Helen.

After the band had been shown to their rooms and the lobby had emptied once more, Sal approached her with a folder and asked her to step outside for a moment where they would not be overheard.

He had managed to buy the house for her, but it had not come cheaply, and renovations would cost quite a tidy sum. All in all, though, he was rather pleased with the purchase, a good value and a solid structure.

"I'm scared," she said, "It's so final. We aren't teenagers anymore, and we should know what we are doing. We should be able to make sane decisions, but there is no sanity here, there can't be, and in all honesty I think I'm doing this against my better judgment. It's not the most sensible thing, but it seems the only one possible. It's a one-way road, for better or worse, and we're on it at top speed." Pushing her hair out of her eyes, she squinted against the sun. "And here we are again, Sal, you having to endure listening to me. You must hate me by now, all the trash I keep throwing at you. It is selfish of me, and not very nice to you. I'm sorry."

With a little smile, he shook his head. "Nah. It's okay. I can take quite a lot, and I want to see you happy."

From the mouth of the bay the mail ship made its way into the harbor. Sal watched in fascination as the tall black side of the vessel moved ever closer to the hotel until it cast its shadow onto the deck outside Naomi's apartment and even over the glass front of the restaurant, and then started its turning maneuver right by the quay wall.

Olaf stepped out and stopped beside them, looking toward the ship expectantly. His brother, he informed Sal, and the family from Toronto would be aboard. They loved to travel the slow way when they came to Halmar, flying into Bergen and then taking the trip on the Hurtigruten ship. He waved to a group of people on the deck.

The wind was brisk and unfriendly, bringing a tart bite from the mountains in the east with it, high up where winter was already taking over, and it ripped right through Naomi's cotton blouse. She shivered, put her arms around herself, and was on the point of returning inside when a taxi drew up in front of the entrance.

For Naomi, it seemed that time stood still for an instant, as if the air around her had suddenly thickened into transparent stone, making it impossible for her to move, or breathe, or speak, or even close her eyes.

It was the woman from the film premiere, Sophie, getting out of the car. Her red hair in a neat ponytail, a warm jacket buttoned up under her chin, she looked directly at Naomi and Sal, her face set in a serious, rigid mask.

Naomi felt Sal's hand grip her upper arm hard and tug at her, but she stood very still, afraid any move she made would cause a course of events to be set in motion that she would not be able to control.

Sophie came right up to her, no hesitation in her steps. "It's you, isn't it? You look different, older. Well, you can't have him. He's not yours, hasn't been for the longest time. I don't know what you did to get him back, but you need to let him go. He belongs with me, was with me until your son showed up. You have no right to him."

Her throat dry with panic, blood pounding in her ears, Naomi tried to answer, but Sal was quicker.

"Sophie." His voice did not sound like him at all, but kinder, sadder, gentler. "What are you doing here? Please leave, darling. You need to leave before he sees you."

Naomi watched as tears welled up in Sophie's eyes.

"Sal. You know how close we were. I don't know what happened. I don't know why she has such a hold on him. But Sal, please. Let me talk to Jon. Please."

There was a moment during which none of them said a word. From behind, Naomi could hear her father's voice and her uncle's deep laughter, and she tried to free herself from Sal's hand, but he would not let her go.

"Sophie," he said. "You must leave now. There is nothing for you here. Jon is getting married in a few days. He has told you that. I know he spoke to you in LA. For God's sake, go home! I assure you, you don't want to be here, it is not a good idea at all."

Instead of leaving, Sophie looked at Naomi, her fists balled at her sides.

She was a pretty, slender girl in her mid-twenties, skin clear and transparent in the way it often was with red-heads. She had lovely blue eyes. Naomi could well imagine her appeal to Jon, lively and frail-boned as she was.

"I can't let him go," she was saying in a broken voice. "I can't just give him up. I love him. God, I love him. And I know he loves me. He can't just stop loving me one day. Please, don't insist on this madness. I know he thinks he has to do this because of his son, but you could set him free. It's not too late. Please tell him he is free to make his choice, and you will see, he will come back to me. He said he was only with you because he felt it was his duty. Only his decency made him come here.

LA is his home! You can't keep him in this frozen wasteland. He's a star, he needs to shine!"

Sal felt Naomi shrink against him, her body trembling. Her father had come up to them and stopped; her uncle, a tall, white-haired man with broad shoulders and a huge frame stood beside him. Sophie, oblivious to the attention she was getting, went on: "I know it, I'm sure of it. The way he used to hold me and make love me, talking to me until I wanted to die with longing. I know he loves me." She was crying hard, her words coming out between bitter sobs. "He can't love you. All those stupid photos of you in his house, they were just him being obsessive. They meant nothing. Right up to the moment your son broke into our lives, he was with me, even the evening before he left to come here. You are too old for him! All the girls Jon dated, they were all younger than you!"

With a quick movement Sal pulled Naomi into his arms and held her tight against him when he felt her knees begin to buckle.

"Leave, Sophie," he ordered. "You know he does as he pleases. There has never been another love in his life, and I know, believe me. All of you were only passing through. Jon would never have married any of you, he had always waited for her to return. Go." And, more vehemently: "This is such a senseless stunt! You should have known better than to come here!"

Olaf and Carl watched the drama, listening to Sal with embarrassed fascination. There was movement in the lobby, laughter, a voice that they all recognized instantly.

Jon stepped outside and into a scene he thought had surely been dredged up from the darkest corner of the realm where nightmares were forged, custom-made for terrible sinners and hopeless losers. His heart froze at what he was witnessing, and his first, incongruous thought was that he was relieved his mother was not around to see.

His future father-in-law and his brother, speechless and astounded; Sophie—he had no idea where she had appeared from—in hysterical tears, facing Sal, who held Naomi close to his chest. Naomi herself was as white as a ghost, rigid with shock and quite unable to stand on her own, her hands clamped tightly onto Sal's sleeves.

A flood of relief washed over Sal's face. "There, Baby Girl," he whispered to Naomi. "He's here now. It will all be over in a minute."

There was no reaction from her.

"Sophie," Jon said.

She looked at him, wiping her face with trembling fingers. "Jon, my love, I've come to talk some sense into you. You need to come home, darling. You can't be serious about this thing here! She can't mean that much to you, it's only because of the kid, right? You should have given me the chance to have your baby, but you never wanted it. You never wanted any commitment. The young, dumb thing, never too demanding but good enough to entertain you."

It was Olaf who stepped forward and pried Naomi from Sal with gentle force and led her away into the house, followed slowly by a bewildered Carl and his family. Jon tried to turn and follow her, but Sal held him back.

"Later. Give her time to calm down. Finish this now, Jon. Create clarity."

There is a kind of exhaustion that comes with extreme emotional upheaval, a leaden, speechless kind of tiredness which makes thinking impossible and saying the right thing an unbearable chore. It was this he felt now, facing Sophie, Sal standing a step behind him as if in support.

"I'm sorry," Jon said. "I'm truly sorry, Sophie. I thought I made myself clear and that you understood. She has always been my deepest desire. For all those years, my thoughts always returned to her, and I would rather not live at all than live without her. She's the one true love of my life, son or not. My son, our son, changes nothing. I would still be here, or wherever Naomi chose to be." He drew a painful, ragged breath. "I'm sorry there has to be a scene like this. I never loved any other woman the way I love her. Nobody. And yes…" Bitter, hard words, but for Jon it was the truth: "You passed my time, that was all."

Sophie shook her head as he spoke, still crying.

"Please forget me, Sophie, I beg you. Our time together was fun, but it's over. There's nothing else to say. Please, please leave."

He tried to reach for her and lead her back toward the waiting taxi, but she drew back.

"You're just throwing me away like a piece of dirt, aren't you, Jon? It meant nothing to you. It doesn't hurt you one little bit that you're killing me like this?"

"You won't die, Sophie." A rueful smile crossed his face. "Trust me, you won't. I know. It will hurt for a while, and then you will meet someone else. Let it go. Let me put you in the taxi."

But she shook her head at him. "Norway doesn't belong to you yet, Jonathan Stone. I can stand where I please. You can't just send me off like one of your servants."

"Well, if that's what you want, go ahead. But I'm telling you, you're only hurting yourself. Go home, Sophie."

With that, he moved toward the door and the quiet lobby. Sal followed, certain that this confrontation was not over yet. He was proven right with Sophie's next words, called out to them from where she still stood in the street.

"You fool! You obsessive selfish fool! I know how to deal with you, but how long will your old flame put up with your moods, I ask you? You'll come back to me, you'll see! I'll make you come back!"

Sal felt a sudden shift in Jon's movement and gripped his shoulder hard. "No. Don't. Nothing good will come of it. There are more important things right now. You only have a few days left to set matters right, and I think you will need every minute."

"Her father, Sophie's father…" Jon said, a trace of uncertainty in his voice, but Sal shook his head.

"Don't worry about that. He's a sensible man. Go to Naomi, Jon. I'll take care of Sophie."

25

JON STOOD IN front of her door, dumbfounded by what was happening, knocking again and again without receiving an answer.

"Open up," he demanded. "Right now, Naomi. Open up and let me in. I'm done with your running. If there's something you have to say to me, do it, damn it. Don't hide behind this door and your family."

For the longest time there was no response.

Just when he had raised his fist to hammer on the wood once more, she opened it, and he realized it had never been locked. He felt like a fool.

Naomi went and stood beside her desk, about to pick up some papers, and he made himself walk in. She seemed composed enough although she was very pale and her hands were shaking.

He could see she had been crying, hard, her eyes still ringed with dark smudges, but she refused to let him get a good look at her face, fiddling with the papers instead.

"Your lyrics. What are you doing, Love?"

She did not reply, but went out on the deck and tossed them into the water, where they immediately drifted away on the choppy waves.

"Are you mad? What are you doing?" Jon shouted as he dragged her back inside, slamming the glass door behind him with a shuddering sound. She did not fight him, but once he let go of her she silently picked up more of the pages and tore them into little pieces. Outside he had stopped her, but now there was nothing he could do but watch in abject horror as the song lyrics he valued so highly were destroyed.

"No, no more!" He tried to reach for her but she pulled back from him. "Stop right now. What's gotten into you? You wrote those for me, and I won't let you destroy them. Stop now, Naomi."

"They're mine," she whispered. "And I can do with them as I please. I don't want them anymore. And I don't want you, either."

This time he did not stand by as she attempted to rip up another page. He took it from her and picked up what remained of the once thick stack.

"For God's sake, this is insane. You can't just throw away your work like that. You have tossed out a fortune, not to speak of the personal value, Naomi. You are throwing away years of your life, and for what? I don't even know why this is happening!"

"Go away," Naomi said in a very still, small voice. "I can't take it anymore. I tried to be tough about it, but I can't. Go away."

She was far away, turned inward in the withdrawn, quiet way he hated and feared.

"I'm not going away. Your family and mine are up there waiting to celebrate with us, and we need to have this out now, and be done with it. And why, for God's sake, this dramatic number with the lyrics? You are making me cry."

He tried to touch her, but she flinched from him, knocking into the glass pane behind her in a panicked attempt to avoid him. Jon stared at her in shock. He felt like his blood had stopped, freezing into painful, biting crystals in his limbs and heart and lungs. She had never done this before, retreated from him in such a final, frightened manner, and the thought flashed through his mind that in all his life there had never been a moment more terrible, more awful, than seeing Naomi leaning into the window, her arms wrapped tightly around her waist, tears slipping down her face, rejecting him.

"Naomi."

"Go," she sobbed. "Go, Jon. I can't!"

"No! I'm not going anywhere until you tell me what happened. I step out to have a cigarette, and I find you in Sal's arms, fainting with terror, and Sophie, and your father, for God's sake. There's not a single image I could dream up that would be worse than that, and I don't know what is making you go to pieces this way and destroy—" he held up the pitiful remaining lyrics— "destroy what took you sixteen years to write!"

He laid the sheets on the piano and went to pry her out of her corner.

Again she recoiled, and it was nearly more than he could take to see the fear in her eyes.

"What? My God, Naomi, what happened? What did she say to you? Why are you rejecting me like this? You're breaking my heart; you're scaring me to death! I love you, I'm desperate, and I want to know!"

She only shook her head.

"What? I need to know, Naomi, I can't fathom what I might have done to hurt you so."

The most incomprehensible answer came from her, one he could not deal with at all, an echo of words spoken before.

"Nothing." Said in the same still, deadly voice.

Naomi stood before him like a small wild animal he had hunted and brought down, helpless and waiting for the final blow, silent and hardly breathing. He wanted to hold her and take the pain from her, but by now he was too scared to reach out again, knowing he would not be able to live through one more of her flights.

So he held out his hand. "Naomi. Baby, please. Please, I beg you."

And just when he thought there could not be a more devastating statement from her, she said, "Don't touch me, Jon. Don't touch me."

A deep, sad silence settled over them, Jon trying to digest her bitter rejection, Naomi barely holding herself together. He sat down on the couch and drew a couple of breaths to calm himself and regain some small measure of composure. He was aware that their families and friends were gathering even now in the lobby and dining room, filling the hotel with the laughter and happy spirit of a wedding that had been so long in coming it seemed to most of them like the final chapter of an improbable fairy tale.

"Are you breaking up with me? What did I do? You are not even giving me the chance to set it right. You are pushing me aside, and you don't even tell me why? You throw away the love you held for me all through those long years, you toss your lyrics into the bay, and now you stand here in front of me and tell me I did nothing?"

She toyed with the few crumbled sheets on the piano as if she were thinking of destroying them too.

"Come and sit with me, at least," Jon begged. "I promise not to touch you, if that is your wish. But God, Naomi! Not even the comfort of an embrace? Not even a kiss? I know I would feel a lot better if I had my arms around you."

She did not react, almost as if it did not concern her at all.

"You are seriously leaving me. You want me to leave you. A few days before our wedding, and you want us to part? And then what? A couple of years from now, will you once again come to a concert and cry your heart out when I sing 'Secret Garden'? How do you suppose we will go on living if we part now? I know there won't be a life for me anymore. I might as well jump into the bay now and be done with it." Bitterness had crept into his voice, and the fatigue of a struggle lost.

"Well, if that's what you truly want, then I'll have to take it," Jon said, rising from the couch again. "No explanation, no solace, no love, not even shouting and fighting, which I could live with, because at least you would be talking to me. But this, Naomi? Silence and destruction, and no chance to atone? You're killing me."

He walked to the door and stood, knob in hand, waiting for her to call him back, explain her devastating behavior, but she remained silent.

"I'm not giving up." Once said, the words seemed to return his strength to him.

"I refuse to give up. We managed to love each other through half a lifetime, you in your exile, me in ignorance about what had happened to us, and I'll be damned if I let this happen again. You are not going to make this decision by yourself, and you are going to tell me what went on out there. Right now."

With that, he strode over to her and grabbed her shoulders, pulling her into his arms against her struggling. "Here is where you belong. And here you will stay, close to me, forever. I won't let you go. If you wish to keep silent, fine. But you are going to the church with me on Saturday, and you will be my wife. I'll tie you up and gag you if I have to, and drag you there by your hair, but you will be there, and you will say 'I do' when the question is put to you."

He lifted her chin with his hand and did not let go when she tried to move away, brushing his lips over hers softly, teasing the corners of her mouth ever so gently with the tip of tongue until he felt her resistance weaken.

"Yes, Baby," he breathed into her mouth when she finally opened it to his, "give in. You know I love you, you know I do. Let me kiss you now."

Relief flooded him when he felt her body lose its rigid posture and mold itself against his, but it lasted only for a heartbeat before she pulled away again.

"I can't, Jon." Spoken with deep regret, but said nonetheless.

He did not let her go completely, but loosened his grip somewhat.

"So tell me. Tell me what made you flee into Sal's embrace like that. God, he must have had the time of his life, you finally in his arms."

"This is not funny, Jon." There was so much pain and loss in her voice, it frightened him all over again. "She said something. Sophie said something that broke me, and if Sal had not been there…"

Patiently he waited, stroking her neck in a soothing motion, trying to ease the tension from her tight muscles.

"She said…" Again, one of those dreadful pauses, then, finally, heart-stopping, the kernel of the matter, the thing that had brought on this bitter crisis. "She spoke of you making love to her, and the way you made her surrender to you…the things you said to her…things I thought you had only said to me."

She tried to squirm out of his embrace, but he did not allow it.

"Ah," Jon sighed. "Jealousy. You are jealous, Baby. You think she got something that belongs exclusively to you. You hate the idea of some other woman being taken to that secret garden that is ours alone, and the ecstasy and passion."

"No. Yes. But not only that. It's more than that. It's the knowledge that despite you saying you never loved another woman, the way you love me there is at least one who feels like I do, and she is devastated now. And I feel rotten about it, and I'm thinking maybe…maybe… maybe you did wrong by that girl, and I'm not entitled at all to what I'm getting now." She paused to draw a sobbing breath and tried once more to get away from him, but he held her firmly. "It's unbearable; I keep seeing this picture of you, whispering to her, and Sophie instead of me trembling with anticipation and desire. And then you, with her, and…" She turned her head away. "And all those others. All that temptation, all the time, and they are all so young and beautiful…"

He was so relieved; it was, after all, only jealousy, no matter how she tried to twist it, and maybe some feelings of guilt and fury at him, but no more than that. His hands caressed her back and waist, and he could sense the stiffness gradually weaken in her.

"I like sex. I love it, and you know that. I'm not like you, I could never put it aside for years on end just out of pure willfulness, and I could see no good reason to, either. But there is a great difference between having sex and making love, and you know that too. You know the difference, and you know what real lovemaking feels like. You know when we really become one and leave this reality altogether, when we truly go to the secret garden together that the world goes away. And that place, that special, secret place is untouched by any other, and that I can swear to on everything I hold sacred, because I know." He sighed painfully. "I know, because I searched hard for it in every moment I spent with another woman during the past seventeen years. But I never found it. Not with any other. Not with Sophie. It's that easy: if I had, I would not be here now, pleading with you to let me take you to the altar on Saturday so I can finally be sure of the one single woman in the whole wide world who will take me to the garden when I hold her in my arms. Yes, my love, that's you. My one and only."

There was still some resistance in her, but she did not try to get away from him anymore. He made her sit down with him on the couch, settling her in his lap. He undid her hair so he could wrap it around his hand, pulling her head back a little, forcing her to look at him. Her lips had parted under his grip, and he could not stop gazing at them, so inviting and so close, begging for the kiss.

"I keep thinking, did you do this with her, too, did you look at her just like that, did she feel what I feel now, did you say the same words? Did you? Did you wish her to surrender to you like you want me to surrender to you now? Was this same look on your face when you wanted to make love to her and you could think of nothing else but naked body in your arms?"

To his surprise, he sensed laughter rising in him, even though it was bitter, filled with years of regret. "You know nothing of me yet. After all the intimacy we've shared, you still don't know me at all. Yeah, I looked at her like I'm looking at you now. And yes, I was thinking of a girl's naked body in my arms, a girl I'd held a long time ago, one who was wonderful beyond description and loved me like no other. Yes, Naomi, I've had many, many beautiful women over the years, ardent, shy, passionate, sporty, slim as willows and plump like cherries, and they came in all colors too. Some I talked into swooning submission, and others took me, aggressive and sophisticated, and others simply happened." He saw he was saying things she did not want to hear in the way she closed her eyes and tried to turn her head away, but he did not allow it. "I had strangers and left them before the sun rose; with others I stayed for a while, a few months, a few weeks. But through it all, always, there was the image of the girl I kissed in Geneva, oh, the sweetness and miracle of it. The girl I took to my hotel room a couple of nights later, so shy, so afraid, and yet so ready for me, the one who could hardly wait for me to take off her clothes and see her naked and touch her skin, and then love her, take away her virginity! I was almost in a panic, I was so afraid of hurting you, afraid that I would make you hate me from the shock, but no; I found there was abandon there, and passion, and the most tender love. I don't know why, as lovely as you were, you were still untouched, and why you let me be the first, but by God, Naomi, every single act of sex with another always had to compare to that, and they never held up." He nodded to himself in reminiscence, reliving those moments. "All the time, all through the time we were together, I was always afraid you would someday tell me you'd had enough of me and wanted to find out how it would be with a different man, if someone else could make you feel more, better, otherwise. That you would tell me you were curious how sex with another would be, and I could not be your only one. That you'd say to me…" He grinned at her sadly. "Say to me you had found out Sal was the one you really loved. There were so many who wanted you, who tried to win your attention when we were in LA. I lived in permanent fear of losing you."

"There weren't," Naomi replied a little sullenly, "I would have noticed."

At that, he laughed out loud. The tension went out of his frame and he let his free hand wander around her hips to draw her closer. "I'm not done. I have explained to you in great and sordid detail how I spent my sex life during our separation, and now I want to hear why you refused to find other lovers. And don't give me that crap again that no one looked at you and you could not imagine anyone but me."

He tugged her hair a little harder, bending her head back farther, exposing the smooth stretch of her throat. "Need to kiss you first," he whispered. "I need to kiss you real bad."

Naomi gazed at him from large, hesitant eyes. "Did you do things with all those others that you haven't done with me?"

Jon nearly dropped her.

"Did you? Did you give others what you did not dare give to me?"

His gaze wandered away from her and out the window to the bay, where the mail ship was leaving the harbor again on its way up north. The big black hulk darkened the room for a few minutes before it had passed the hotel and was well on its path to the open sea again.

"Not in any way that mattered. No."

"I did not leave you because I did not love or desire you anymore," she said after a moment's thought. "Then it would have been easy. I left you, and I took all my desire for you with me, I even dreamed of you. I dreamed of you in every manner you can imagine. I woke in the middle of the night, hot and panting, still feeling you. In my dreams, you would come to me and never ask, just do as you pleased, and I would yield, pleading, begging for you. Then I would wake, my arms empty, my body empty, my heart empty. The echo of your voice, fading in the night. It was so hard not to crawl to the phone and call the office and ask Sal for your number."

"You silly little bird," Jon said softly. "You stupid, silly little bird. And I would have been there, I would have flown to you, come here to pluck you up. I would have come straight to your bed and made those dreams come true. Naomi, why, for God's sake, why? If your longing was so great, why? Why did you do this to us, why give us all this pain?"

Naomi lay in his arms, toying with his shirt buttons, opening them one after the other, softly touching his skin under the fabric, her fingers lightly brushing the hairs on his chest.

"You had better stop." He shifted restlessly. "You might end up on the carpet after all, flat on your back, with a starved, wild male on top of you. But at least I can kiss you now, can't I? Is this terrible scene over?"

She did not answer, only sighed in something like tired resignation.

"Say you'll marry me, Naomi. Say it. Tell me you are still mine, tell me you are not going to rip our lives into shreds again. Tell me we can go back upstairs in a little while and your terrible father and his Viking brother won't chop off my head in their fury for causing you sorrow? Will I have a bride, walking up to me in a lovely gown and standing beside me? Will I?"

She freed herself from the hand entangled in her hair and climbed from his embrace, even though he was unwilling to let her go, protesting that he had not gotten that kiss yet.

"And you won't get that kiss," Naomi replied, "because I know where it would lead, and that can't happen now. I need to change and do my hair, you mussed it all up. And then we will go and meet the crowd upstairs. We will put a good face on this disaster, Jon, and we'll get married. I'm not going to send them all away again and waste all the food and flowers. Only…"

"Don't frighten me anymore, Naomi. Tell me you'll marry me because you want me, not because you can't see a way out of it. Because if that's the reason, I think I'll pass. I don't want you as my duty wife; I want you for love alone."

He watched her walk to the wardrobe, buttoning up his shirt again, the feel of her soft fingertips still on his skin, the promising, gentle touch that gave him the hope that all would be well in the end.

"You're getting me as your wife, Jon," he heard her tired voice say. "Let that be enough for now. I'll have to find a way to deal with my imagination and my guilt. It may take a while."

She returned carrying a somber, dark grey linen dress. "She said she wanted your baby and you would not give her one. There must have been more to it than just an affair, Jon, and I feel guilty for breaking it up. I should never have told Joshua about you. I destroyed her life, her hope for a life with you."

Jon nodded thoughtfully. "Yes, only there would never have been either one. No life, no baby. Not with Sophie, not with any other. It doesn't matter what she thought would happen or what she wanted. I was not prepared to give it. And making a child, Naomi, as you should know, takes two. It takes two, and it should be done in love, after wishing for it to happen."

Oblivious to his stare, she dropped the clothes she had been wearing and slowly shook out the new dress before letting it slide down over her head.

"Yes, only it didn't work that way with ours, either, right?" she said. "I don't remember us planning for a baby when Joshua was conceived."

"Ah." He rose from the couch to help her with the zipper in the back. "But then, we were in love. Every time we had sex. I loved you through every moment of it. Still do, even when you turn me around like you do now. I can't help it. Maybe, if I could, I would cut you out of my heart and be done with it, just to make life easier and not be in this state of turmoil and anxiety all the time. But I can't."

The grey did not suit her; it made her skin look bleak and brought out the deep shadows under her eyes. When she knotted up her hair and pinned it into a tight bun on her neck, he shook his head at her.

"No. Take that off. We are going to celebrate for the next few days, and you look ready to go to a funeral. Even if you feel like a sinner, put on something pretty, for God's sake. And when you have taken that off, toss it into the bay, right after your lyrics. It's the saddest, most unbecoming piece of clothing I have ever seen on you."

"She looked so young. How old is she anyway?"

Jon, busy flattening her crumpled lyrics, replied without thinking, "Twenty-four."

He looked up when no immediate reply came to see her picking up the diamond necklace he had bought for her in London. She put it on.

"You told her you had made a commitment."

"Ah." Incongruously, his first thought was that she should indeed accept the offer to write movie scripts; her timing for the dramatic was that good. The thought nearly made him smile, but he lowered his head again so it would not show and upset her again.

"Well, darling, I'll tell you something. Of course I made a commitment, didn't I? That's what I call asking a woman to marry me and giving her a ring. Come what may, I'm as committed as hell to marrying you. And now I'll even go upstairs and face your frightening family, I'm that committed."

He could see the grin pulling on her lips.

"And since we are on this commitment thing, you might say again that you want to marry me too, and from the heart, if you please. Don't tell me you locked me out all these nights and now there won't be a reward!"

26

NAOMI LEFT THE dinner party well before the others, exhausted by the stress of the day and too much champagne and good food.

After showering and combing out her wet hair, she slipped on her prettiest nightgown and wandered through the room, straightening cushions, collecting the last few pages of her lyrics and putting them back on the desk, and closing up the piano. She even lit some candles, certain that she would not be spending the night alone.

But he did not come.

The hotel grew quiet. She could see from the shadows on the deck that the lights in the dining room had gone out, leaving only the lobby illuminated.

Restlessly she wandered through the room, drawing the curtains, then opening them again. She got a glass of water and settled on the couch, listening, hoping, waiting.

Barefoot, in her nightgown, she quietly made her way up the stairs. She knew she was weak and throwing herself at him like a wanton, but she could not stop herself. He would laugh at her, and take advantage of her in a thorough and single-minded manner, but she would feel a lot better when the sun came up. The tension would be gone.

Light was seeping from under the studio door. Naomi stood for a moment, her hand on the knob, her heart beating wildly, her breath fast now that she had made her decision.

Jon lay on his bed, reading a book by the light of a small lamp. His glasses had slipped down his nose, and he was dressed only in boxers, his hair in wild tufts. He looked up in surprise when she entered, a sylph in a flowing cloud of silk, black hair falling around her like a veil, feet bare and pale under the hem of her gown.

"You shouldn't be here." Taking off his glasses, he laid the book down. "I am dangerous. If you come closer…"

Naomi closed the door behind her and walked over to him.

"How very enticing," he growled softly, the velvet tone of his voice sensual and deep as he shifted his long body to make room for her on the narrow bed. "Tempting fate, I see. Come then, fairy queen. Share my blanket."

He did not touch her as she settled beside him, but remained propped on his elbow and watched as she stretched out on her back, locks spilling on his pillow, neckline slipping, silk gliding over her body in slithering folds.

"Now, here we have the ultimate seduction. What am I supposed to do about you? I dare not touch you; I know what would come of that. I dare not stay away from you, I fear that's not what you want. You have come to torment me, and witness my turmoil. How evil, dear heart. How utterly evil and wonderful."

Her only response was a steady, dark gaze.

"If only I knew," he went on, his voice ever softer, "what you want from me. Do you wish for some caresses, some gentle lovemaking, or do you wish to unleash the wild beast here on this simple cot?"

A soft sound as she drew a breath, her eyelids fluttering, a slight movement of her hips. He looked up and down her supine form. "Ten days is a very long time. I can feel every minute of it and I am starved for you. You walk into danger willingly, my sweet dove, and you might not get away unscathed. You might get pinned down and ravished, coming here to my den in this nothing of a gown and lying down with me. I can feel the heat of your body, and how much you want me."

His hand came to rest on her belly.

"But no; I gave a promise. I will not make love to you again until you are my wife, and lawfully mine. I'll pass."

Naomi touched his chest with lingering fingertips, drawing them down to his stomach. The muscles there tightened visibly, beautifully, as her fingers trailed tauntingly lower.

"You are seducing me." Jon grabbed for her hand to stop her exploring. "Do you really want this? I warn you, there'll not be much sleep tonight once we get started."

"I want to know," Naomi said softly. "I want to know what you did to those others that you did not do with me. I want it all. You are mine, and I want everything you have to give."

He bent over her, her wrist in his firm grasp held above her head on the pillow. "And you will get it. So you will. But for now, my sweet bird, you are going to return to your own bed, and we won't spoil what we have been saving for so long. We will bear these last few hours, and then, on our wedding night, we will love until the sun rises. I've truly come into the mood of the thing, and I can see myself already, dancing with you in your bridal gown, and thinking of nothing else but how fast I can get it off you once we're alone."

He could see that she was nearly trembling with desire. "Go back to your bed, love. We would regret it, I know, even if it would be wonderful for the moment. I want nothing more than to hold you now. God, you are so desirable and beautiful. But really, I think I like the 'no sex before marriage' idea." And, as an afterthought: "And I really, really dig the 'sex right after marriage' idea."

She left him as silently and softly as she had come, and he watched her walk across the room. It was all he could do not to go after her and stop her, put her down on that rosewood table and give them both the pleasure they craved. But the door closed quietly behind her, and he was left once more in his solitude his concentration for reading gone.

"AND THE MASTER," Sal asked over breakfast the morning of the wedding day, "how is he? Nervous, excited, frightened?"

Art laughed his sharp laugh and shook his head.

"None of the above," was Art's reply. He had walked into the studio to find Jon singing to himself while he gathered his clothes, freshly showered, his hair still dripping, a towel wrapped around his hips, and Art had admired his well-muscled body. He looked like a panther, a smooth, large, wild cat, barely contained by his surroundings, a beast that needed the open space of the stage to expand and show its true nature. Briefly he wondered about the sex, and how a girl would fare when he let his restraints go. When Jon dropped his towel to get dressed—Art thought enviously that some people really did have it all—talent, fame, wealth, the perfect woman, good looks, and an impressive physique to top it all off.

"Definitely not nervous," he told Sal. "He seemed content with life and how the day is going so far. Relaxed and satisfied to have gotten his way once again, I would say."

"Yeah," Sal sighed, "But then he always does, the headstrong, lucky bastard."

"He's getting married, Sal, can you imagine? I can hardly wrap my mind around that." Art reached for another muffin after casting a furtive glance to see if Sue was around. "Jon. The Jonman can't wait to get freaking married. God, I wonder how many girls would cry their eyes out today if they knew."

Sal crumbled his croissant without eating it. "Look at who he's marrying, Art. I'm not surprised at all."

Art shot him a critical look, but Sal grinned. "And you know the beauty of it? If we had arranged a marriage for him to boost his image, we could not have chosen a better setting or wife. It's handmade for the tabloids! Long lost love, sweet girl, powerful lyrics writer, and then what? A Canadian society lady with a family as wealthy as the Rockefellers. It's too good to be true. Something like this could only happen to the Jonman. That guy has luck stuck to him like dog-shit sticks to shoes."

Just then Jon stepped out of the elevator, dressed and groomed, Joshua beside him, a duplicate of his father in elegance and style.

"Good grief, sometimes it's nearly too much to bear." Art sighed and rose to meet his boss.

Sal had often envisioned a scenario where Jon would settle on one of his many lovers and decide to get married, but there had never been one even remotely like what he was witnessing now. They gathered in the lobby, the men who had joined Jon for this day, and began their walk up the narrow cobbled street to the small white church perched on the side of the hill above the small town. Many of the shop owners and townspeople stopped to applaud or greet them in the mellow sunshine of the fine September day.

It was the custom here, they had been informed by Solveigh, that the bridegroom walks to the church. And after the wedding he would lead his bride back to show her off.

And, Sal noted with amusement, Jon's step was neither halting or measured. He strode, waving to those who called out to him but never breaking his stride until he arrived at the gate to the church. Here he paused, took one deep breath, looked around at them, then nodded and entered, all without saying a single word.

"Wow, he's excited." Art peered after him into the building. "He's not even like this when he goes on stage. He really must mean it."

Sal, on the point of pulling his cigarettes out of his pocket, was pushed forward by Russ. "No time for that now, Sal, so don't even think about it. If the bride shows up and we are not all in our places, Solveigh will give us all hell."

It was warm and light inside, the sun streaming in golden slants through the high windows, nearly drowning out the flickering candles. There were plenty of flowers, but not what Sal had expected. Despite all the wealth both families held, Naomi had picked white roses, and not the elegant long-stemmed ones but the small, wild clusters that you found wound around trellises, spreading their delicate scent through summer nights.

A wave of sadness washed over Sal when Naomi walked in on the arm of her father. She looked like a fairy queen with her entourage of friends, all of them in white, flowing cotton dresses and flower-wreaths on their loose hair. Naomi was the loveliest of all, pale, her eyes huge, black, and very serious. It seemed to him as if there was a slight hesitation in her step, but when Jon moved forward, doubt vanished from her as if the sun had melted it away like mist from a dawn meadow.

He watched her promise to be Jon's wife forever and ever in a low, somber voice, and the golden light in the church seemed to dim.

"Two heart throbs less to stir up trouble," Russ mumbled when Naomi put the ring on Jon's finger.

Art replied acidly, "Or even worse. Now they'll have a double following."

Sal stared at the cascade of locks tumbling down Naomi's back. "I think for a while there will be peace while they're busy with each other," he said.

From behind them, Harry threw in, "His fans might not like to see him as a domesticated beast."

"Oh no, they'll love him even more!" Russ swiveled around in his seat with a wide grin. "They'll be so pleased to see he can be tamed after all."

"Under the loving care of the missus, yes sir." Mirth was bubbling up in Art's tone.

She was in his arms now, kissing him to seal their contract, and kissing him just a bit longer than necessary to the sound of soft amusement from the audience on the benches. Her face was sweetly flushed when they at last turned from the altar and faced their families and friends, her earlier reticence shed like a dull skin, her chin raised and her hand tightly in Jon's. Strangely enough Sal found his melancholy reflected in more than one face. There was her uncle, the huge Canadian with white hair who had a distinctly regretful expression, her mother, who smiled with soft sadness, and her father, hiding an icy rigidity by making his way briskly out into the cool, fresh air.

She walked past him without a glance, her eyes only on Jon, walking away to jubilant music and the applause of their friends, to the lawn outside for pictures to be taken and then forward into her new life on the arm of her husband, down the street and out of sight. Sal took his time following the bridal train back to the hotel and stood for a while on the steps to the churchyard, lost in his own bitter thoughts. The parson clucked at him for pulling out his cigarettes and lighting one, but he didn't care.

In a moment he would have to go and witness their joy, watch her dance with Jon, this time lawfully his for all time.

And later, after the cake had been cut, they would vanish into the solitude of her apartment, and while all the others were still celebrating, she would give herself to her bridegroom. Here Sal's mind went black with despair.

He tossed the butt away and straightened his tie, squinting against the sinking sun, and slowly made his way to where, he was sure, he would witness his own darkest hour.

Morosely he stood in a corner of the dining room while the champagne was passed and the first speeches were delivered, Kevin's funny and full of love for his brother, Carl's somber but with a tender twinkle at Naomi, and Olaf's, brief, cool, polite. Her father pecked her cheek and shook Jon's hand, but he did it without a smile and without looking at him.

Jon pursed his lips in the way Sal knew so well. Olaf had just made a new foe, one he was drastically underestimating, made even worse by the fact that Jon had gone so far out of his way to befriend him.

Naomi drifted past Sal once, just before they sat down to dinner, and embraced him swiftly, wordlessly, leaving behind the scent of roses, but the moment was over nearly before he realized it, and she was gone again before he could react. A small blue flower had dropped from her wreath directly before his feet. He bent down to pick it up and, after an instant of indecision, wrapped it in his handkerchief and tucked it away in his pocket. Abashed at doing such a sentimental thing, he was embarrassed when he caught Art's raised eyebrow and ironic smirk, but he straightened his shoulders and stared back at him blankly.

Olaf had the good grace to open the dancing with his daughter, leading her through a slow waltz while the others stood around them and cheered. He handed her over to Jon with a flourish when he came forward, bowing to Naomi with impeccable manners, but his heart clearly wasn't in it.

It was obvious that Lucia was less than pleased with his performance. When he led her out to the dance floor she whispered to him furiously, a deep frown on her face, which made him nod and relax somewhat.

Sal noticed Russ and Solveigh in a tight embrace and Sue and Art, their heads close together, hands entwined, and felt the loneliness of his life inundate him. He turned away and stepped outside, once again alone in the cold evening breeze of the Norwegian fall night, a cigarette and a drink his only companions.

This time, she did not follow him outside to ask why he was by himself.

SEAN GAVE THEM the perfect moment to flee.

The cake had been brought out, cut, and served, and Naomi, from the threshold of the lobby, had tossed her bouquet into Sue's straining hands, and at long last the musicians could no longer be contained.

"Let's go," Jon said, and she came away with him without hesitation.

Garlands of flowers greeted them in the apartment. The soft light of candles seemed to dance in celebration. There was a small replica of their wedding cake on the dining table, champagne was chilling in a cooler. Over the bed, a bower of leaves, and more flowers over the spread and pillows of lace and rose satin.

"This is..." she began to say, and Jon finished the sentence for her, impressed at the beautiful setting: "The Secret Garden. They've built the Secret Garden for you."

"For us."

"Yes." It was so different now that the moment was here; the hot urgency had dropped from him as soon as the door had shut behind them, replaced now by a kind of awe.

Naomi was so beautiful in her white dress. It was nothing like what he had expected, no grand designer gown with layers of silk and chiffon, but a simple, straight cotton dress with a square neckline and lace on the short sleeves and the hem, some embroidery on the ankle-length skirt, and a broad satin ribbon as a belt.

He reached up and removed the wreath from her hair. Some of the blossoms came undone and rained down around her, and she laughed when one fell into her cleavage.

"We're married." Once said, the statement sounded stupid, but she smiled at him and repeated, "We are married. Now, my love, you belong only to me."

Jon took a step toward her, and the awkward moment was over.

"Yeah, and you are mine, Baby, and remember what I promised you, how it would go as soon as we were alone?"

She came willingly into his arms, her lips opened under his, her breath caught sweetly when his embrace nearly lifted her off the floor.

"Mine," Jon whispered, "*My* wife. My *wife*." He it said as if trying it on like a new suit. "At long last, my wife. And nothing, nothing will ever take you away from me again. I swear, Naomi, I'll make you so happy you'll never want to leave me, never again."

"Then, Jon," she said, her fingers on his belt, "stop talking and take me to bed. Make me happy right now."

IN THE LIGHT of a cool dawn, Jon got up against her drowsy protest, disentangling himself from her arms.

"You want your wedding gift, don't you?"

This made her sit up. "I'm getting a wedding gift?"

"Of course, silly girl. Not even I think a husband alone is enough for a woman on her bridal night." He laughed at her surprised face.

"You *are* enough for me." Naomi wrapped the quilt around her and followed him down the stairs against his protest that he would return, and please could she not just stay in bed and keep it warm?

"But I want coffee. I'll make coffee."

It was cold in the apartment. The flowers had faded overnight, the candles had burned down in their bowls, and they had never even touched the champagne or the cake. It was raining, harsh gusts of wind hurling the drops against the panes in an unruly pattern, the water of the bay in turmoil in the evil weather.

Jon, muttering about the temperature, pulled on some clothes. "Now you're getting your gift with me in a sweater. How unromantic is that?

I should have done this last night when I was still in my nice suit. Oh well."

The scent of coffee drifted through the room. Andrea had filled up the fridge with food for them; there was enough for three days, and looking at it Jon wondered if they were expected to stay in seclusion until they had eaten everything up. The thought was pleasing enough, but he doubted Naomi would have enough patience to remain hidden away for so long. It made him regret that he hadn't taken her away on a honeymoon after all.

"I have a gift for you too."

She was standing by the Steinway, a grey folder in her hand, a small smile on her face that faded when he came over to her, replaced by doubt. "When I had the idea I was very happy about it, but now I'm not so sure. Maybe we should have talked about it..."

"Mine first." He held out a blue velvet case to her, the name of the jeweler imprinted in golden letters on the top.

Her shock was an immense satisfaction to him.

These, he told her, he had found when he was out with Joshua in New York. They had gone into the shop because he had needed a new battery for his watch, no more than that, and there, in a showcase in the center of the store, with its own security guard, he had seen this and known it had to be hers.

"And don't yell at me, Baby, this had to be yours."

Big marbles of many-faceted diamonds had been set in filigree casings of platinum and strung like pearls into a chain that came to rest smoothly on her skin just below the hollow of her throat, sparkling tiny rainbows on her throat and breasts even in the muted light of a grey morning.

"Yes, just like I thought they would look on you." The result satisfied him immensely.

Naomi took the necklace off again to hold it in her hands, let it glide through her fingers, and examined it closely. "This must have cost a fortune, Jon."

"Yes." His heart soared at the expression in her face. "A fortune, and yet not nearly enough to say how much I love you."

"It's so beautiful. I think I'll never take it off again. Thank you!" She did not put it on again but just stood, touching each globe, tracing the lacy metal with the tips of her fingers, turning the stones to make them shoot their fire at her.

"And now? You said you had something for me too?" Her reluctance to let go of the diamonds made him smile.

She dithered, but then she picked up the folder again.

"Jon, I have something to tell you. I'm nearly poor again; you will have to keep me from now on, I'm afraid. But the temptation was too great."

He could hardly believe his eyes. Slowly Jon sat down on the piano bench and stared at the papers, which stated in dry, legal words that they now owned another house, and one that had such a very special meaning to him.

"You bought the Miller mansion. I didn't know they wanted to sell."

"They didn't." She smirked at him over the rim of her coffee cup. "But I sent Sal."

That house. How often, as a young man, had he stood on the promenade, staring at the Manhattan skyline, dreaming of making his fame in that city. And then, turning around to go back home, he had faced the white building on the corner and imagined it was his own. He had dreamed of being rich and famous enough to walk up, knock on the door, and offer the owners so much money they would willingly hand it over to him. In his imagination he had set up that room on the second floor as his studio, the one with the big balcony over the porch. He had seen himself stepping out into the cool evening air after spending hours at the piano.

They had sold it, Naomi told him, but she had paid nearly double its market value, and she was not sorry for it. At that price, she would not feel bad for talking them out of it.

"And if we spend Christmas with your family, we can have a look around and begin renovating what we want changed. Then we'll have two wonderful houses, one on each coast. What do you think?"

He thought it was the most perfect gift ever.

"But Baby, I imagined you would want to buy this hotel from your family maybe, and change it into our future home, right here. I expected us to live here…"

"No."

"No? But this is your home…" Fear crept up in him again for an instant before his gaze went back to the deed in his hands and he realized it was unfounded.

"Jon." Naomi caught the quilt slipping from her shoulders and pulled her legs up on the couch. "I don't need the hotel anymore. I'm done with this place." Her hands crept out of her tight wrapping to wave at her surroundings. "This is full of sadness and long, long years with only the memories of you. I lived here without you. Now I want to live with you in a kinder place."

"But your friends, your life…"

Her eyes were dark and serious when she looked up at him. "Jon, I was afraid of life. I didn't want to step out into life, didn't want to find happiness or someone else to love. I wanted only you, only a life with you. Nothing has changed." And here, a smile broke on her face that lit it up and made him move toward her. "Well, that's not completely true, of course. Everything has changed. I now have you, and my life with you. And I want summers in New York and winters in California, so I'll never be cold again!"

"Come back to bed," Jon said. "I promise, you'll not be cold."

27

ANDREA WAS ALONE in the kitchen, reading an open cookbook on the counter and eating a piece of cheese when Naomi pushed open the door. She looked up in surprise. "What are you doing here?"

"I live here. Forgotten already? Where is everybody?"

There was fresh coffee in the percolator, and Naomi poured herself a cup, inhaling the scent with satisfaction.

"Uhm," Andrea said, "Sven left for home. Christi is in the office, and Solveigh…I don't know where Solveigh is."

"What do you mean, you don't know where Solveigh is?" There was a small pinprick of unease. "And Russ?"

Andrea stared at her wordlessly.

The hotel seemed strangely empty after the last few days of celebration and partying. The tables had been set for dinner, the aroma of food wafted through the building, but there were almost no people.

"Where are my parents and Joshua? And Jon's family? The band?"

"Well, obviously not waiting for you to crawl out of your love nest." Andrea closed the book with a slam and pushed it away. "You're getting on my nerves. Go and knock on some doors if you want to know." She eyed Naomi suspiciously. "And anyway, go back to your den and your husband. You have no business traipsing around up here."

"My husband…" Naomi paused, savoring the word, which earned her an ironic glance from Andrea. "He's up in his studio, doing some of his show business stuff."

Andrea lifted a few pot covers and peered inside, stirring and tasting, adding a few herbs to one and some chilies to another. "Go away. Go get some fresh air. I'll send the girls down to set your place right, and then I'll have dinner brought down to you. No one wants to see your face today."

It was raining; the air smelled of wet earth and pines and the sea, with the tart, bitter tang of fall in it, heavy with the promise of the darkness and cold that would soon follow.

Naomi pulled her sweater closer, shivering in the sudden gale that blew around the corner of the building, whipping loose strands of hair into her eyes and bringing tears to them. Leaves danced over the asphalt of the parking lot and street, torn from the trees and driven over the ground by the wind. It had turned cold overnight, as if the weather had held its breath just long enough for them to celebrate and now felt free to release its fouler moods, taking its first serious steps into winter.

Before her stretched the vista of long weeks with Jon, here in Halmar.

An alien, in a far away place…bound by love, giving up everything else he held dear. It reminded her of the old fairy tale about a young man who fell in love with a mermaid and followed her to her father's palace deep down on the bottom of the sea, where he languished, far from the sunlight and the air, forever longing for the summer breezes in the trees. The merfolk were kind and friendly, and his pretty maid loved him truly, but in the silent hours of night he watched the waves far above roll toward the coast, and he longed for home. After some time the wish to step onto dry ground again grew so strong, he left his bride to return to his family…and here she paused, because she could not remember how the story ended. Did he live happily ever after with a new, human girl or did he go back to the sea, only to find his mermaid had died of sorrow? Or did he drown in a storm her father had conjured up in fury, seeing his daughter's misery?

"Andrea," she asked when she returned to the kitchen, "do you remember that tale about the mermaid and her human lover who went to live below the sea with her?"

Andrea shook her head in confusion, but then wrinkled her brow and thought about it. "That one I do not recall. But there is the tale of the mermaid who left the sea and her family for her human lover and married him and lived with him in a cottage by the sea. She bore him fine children, and when they were old enough she told her husband she could not stay with him any longer because she was so homesick. So she took her mermaid's cloak or whatever out of the trunk under the window—I remember that detail very clearly, isn't that funny?—and dove back into the ocean. He was heartbroken of course, and spent many evenings sitting on the beach, hoping for his love to return. Now,

I don't know if that was the end of it, but if it isn't, I don't recall the true ending."

It felt like the distant tolling of a bell, a soft resonance somewhere deep within her soul, a deep, melodic sound that welled up in her like the tide but did not recede again. The words came to her on the crest of that wave; unbidden, powerful, they roiled through her mind, clamoring for her to heed them.

Naomi was speechless as she stared at Andrea, overwhelmed by the flood of words that threatened to inundate her.

"I need to go," she said abruptly.

THE DOOR TO the apartment stood open, the maids still busy cleaning up. They were chatting while they collected the wilted flowers and dishes, greeting her with smiles and friendly remarks about the lovely ceremony. They left her then, to her own devices.

Naomi had barely registered them; she nodded briefly and thanked them, but her thoughts were far away. She was used to the fact that inspiration came suddenly to her, instigated by a word, a sound, a smell, or a fleeting image, but very, very rarely had it been as powerful as it was now, like a shout into the stillness of the night. The desk and her laptop beckoned to her, and she could hardly wait until it was up and running, using a notepad and pencil to scribble down the first ideas while she waited. She sketched out the phrases and tantalizing words that were dancing in her thoughts.

Outside, the wind whipped into the bay from the ocean, curdling the water into a white-topped grey that sucked noisily at the poles of the deck.

Somewhere deep below the sea lived that mermaid, in eternal dusk. Would she miss the light, the blue sky and the drifting clouds, birdsong and the scent of flowers? The company of a spoken word or the sound of music? Would she be captured by a voice raised in singing, a wonderful, clear baritone? Would it make her leave her abode on the bottom of the ocean and swim to the shore on a midsummer evening when the surf rolled gently on the sand and played in the shallows between the rocks? Would she sit there, hidden, bathing in water that had been warmed by the sun, listening to the song that called to her through the white night? And what would she do? Would she creep closer, to see the singer as he sat on one of the rocks, mending his fishing nets, and marvel at the strange clothes he was wearing, at his ability to stand up on two legs, and wish to know what kind of food he took out of the basket he had with him and what kind of drink he would pour from the green glass bottle? Would the sound of his voice enchant her, wrap itself around her, and make her wish for a different life, one in which she would join him in his song or share his life and be able to see and hear him every day?

Naomi was startled out of her deep thoughts when Jon said gently, "Love. The family wishes to know if we will join them for dinner or if we would prefer our solitude."

She had not heard him enter or noticed that he had come up behind her, peering over her shoulder now at the screen and the words on it.

"What are you doing?" His hand came to rest on her neck.

"I'm not sure. But as soon as I know, I'll tell you. I had this idea…" She hesitated. It seemed so preposterous. "I had this idea about a cycle of songs telling a story, an old fairy tale or myth about a mermaid…" Naomi turned in her chair to look up at him. "About how she falls in love with a human and becomes his wife and lives with him for quite a while until she finds she cannot live outside of the sea after all because she is so homesick…and I felt the plot fall together…and yes, there is a plot…Jon…" She faltered, uncertain of what she wanted to say.

"A plot?" Jon repeated thoughtfully. "Why then a cycle of songs?"

Full of amazement, Naomi watched him as his brow drew together in concentration while he read her notes again, so interested in what she was doing, and so serious. He was actually waiting for her to come up with ideas so he could have a part in them.

"Let's go and eat with the folks upstairs," he said suddenly. "Let this rest for the moment."

She tried to talk herself out of it, unwilling to let go of her thoughts, but Jon insisted and pulled her up from her chair.

"Come." He patted her behind. "It won't disappear while you eat. I promise we will get back to it soon enough. There's more to this than meets the eye, and I have a few things of my own I want to show you and discuss. But come now, little beast. We are still celebrating our marriage."

Solveigh was missing.

Russ was sitting with Sal and Harry, but there was not a trace of her anywhere, and when Naomi asked Andrea again she received a blank, silent stare in return and the unsatisfactory answer, "I haven't the faintest idea. Haven't seen her today."

There was a flutter of anxiety in the pit of her stomach. Naomi stared at her salmon, a sense of disquiet growing in her. She rose and laid her hand on Jon's shoulder. He began to push the chair back, offering to go with her, but Naomi demurred.

"Talk to Russ. There's something wrong. I know there's something wrong, and I don't want them to…" She had been on the point of saying "end up like us," but it didn't apply anymore.

It didn't apply anymore. She still had such a hard time grasping what had happened to her life. It felt as if a great wave had picked her up from the shallows where she had languished and she was now being carried away on its crest, far out into the wide, open ocean, with no horizon in sight. She had no other option but resignation in the hope that it would keep her aloft and carry her safely to a distant shore of which she knew nothing yet, a place of dreams and fantasy.

"Baby, you're doing it again." Jon watched with a mixture of awe and amusement at how she could set herself off with a phrase, or a sound, or an image, and then lose herself in the poetry that formed itself in her mind without her bidding.

"Go. Go write it down, little beast, before it gets lost. I'll see to Solveigh. Go."

Walking through the lobby, he gestured to Russ to follow him outside.

It had not been such a good idea, he realized once he stepped out into the dusk, for it was still raining and rather cold, astonishingly so, and blustery enough to make lighting a cigarette a difficult venture.

"What's up?" Jon asked after he had finally managed to get it burning. "What's eating you and your pretty blonde? Where is she?"

Russ avoided his eyes. "It's private. And it doesn't really concern you. Don't bother yourself with my problems, Jon, least of all today."

Jon digested this. He missed his jacket or one of his Norwegian sweaters; the time for silk shirts was definitely over for the year.

"Russ," he said gently, "it does concern me. We are like family, this little group of ours, and we take care of each other, and you should know that. You do know it. You are closer to me than my own brother."

"She wants to leave me. I have no idea why. Solveigh told me last night we have to break up." Russ shrugged his shoulders. "And here I had the feeling she really liked life in LA." And, a little less certain: "And me."

Jon tossed his cigarette away. "Yeah. Me too." It came out a little drier than he had intended, and to soften it, he added, "But she is such a fierce young lady, maybe you got it all wrong."

"No." Russ laughed with a bitter undertone. The wind was blowing his fine brown hair and he shivered slightly. "No, she made herself quite clear. Told me her place was here, with Naomi and the hotel, and that she had given a promise to your wife. I have no idea what that all means, but she has informed me she will not be returning to California with me. In my book, that's breaking up."

It was in Jon's, too, but he wondered where the sudden change of heart had come from. "Okay. Okay, Russ. I'll go over to her parents' house and find out what's wrong. I'll talk to her."

Russ stared at him in disbelief. "You? You, Jon?"

"Why not me?" Jon shook his head in irritation. "Wait here, I'll find out whatever there is to find out."

"Right." With a dubious sigh, Russ returned inside.

HE HAD BEEN to Solveigh's house only once before and then in passing, but he found it easily, even in the darkness.

"Open up, Solveigh," he yelled as he knocked on the door. "I know you're in there, and we need to talk."

She did not look like herself in the simple white t-shirt and jeans, the stark braid, and without her makeup and usual poise. She looked like an unhappy young woman who had retreated to the sanctuary of her parents' home to suffer.

Jon did not wait for her to invite him in but stepped past her into the narrow hallway and shut the door behind him.

Solveigh bowed her head with a sigh, showing him into the sitting room. Clearly she was unsettled by him showing up here, and she fluttered a hand in the direction of the couch to offer him a seat, but he remained in the center of the room, looking around curiously. It had been here that Naomi had put on her wedding dress and made ready to become his bride only yesterday, and Jon tried to recreate the scene, seeing her in her lacy underwear, waiting for her friends and mother to drape her gown, fix her hair. Had she been excited, he wondered now, her heart beating with anticipation and maybe some fear? Had they made some coffee before they left for the ceremony, and who had put the wreath on her head?

"I'm surprised to see you," Solveigh said. "I expected Russ to come."

Jon tore himself from his reverie. She had been waiting beside him patiently, hands folded in a way that reminded him of Naomi. She went to a cupboard to bring out some brandy. He noted that she did not pour any for herself.

"Russ is devastated."

Solveigh's shoulders shook a little, but she did not react.

"He can't understand what has happened. Will you explain to me what made you say those things to him? Why do you want to leave him now, Solveigh? I had the feeling there was something serious going on."

She arched her eyebrows. "Did he send you? You, of all people? You, running his errands?"

"He's my friend, Solveigh. He would do no less for me. Don't try to distract me, girl. It won't work."

He took the glass from her and sat in one of the upholstered chairs.

"Now, Solveigh. You picked my wedding day to drop Russ and he is heartbroken about it. I want to hear how you came to make that decision. It seems to me—" he grinned evilly—"I'm not the only one good at breaking hearts. So spill."

"You are such a conceited bastard." Solveigh sat down on the couch. "For the life of me I can't understand what Naomi sees in you."

"You do understand." He wondered whether he would be allowed to smoke in this house.

"I'm not going to move to Hollywood, okay?" Her fingers toyed with the hem of her shirt. "I promised Naomi I would stay with her. She needs me, right? She needs me to keep her sane with the life you are offering her, and she is very afraid." Solveigh glared at him. "And I won't leave her all by herself to your tender mercies."

"Tender mercies?" Jon could not decide whether to be irritated or amused. "I don't know what you could possibly mean. But we are not talking about Naomi or me. Nobody forced her to marry me, and no one forced me to come find her, either. I want to know why you are treating poor Russ the way you are. Especially after the grand time you had in California with him. At the very least he deserves an explanation, and neither he nor I will accept this nonsense about you being Naomi's keeper. She doesn't need one. So spill it, Miss Norway."

Tears pooled in Solveigh's glorious blue eyes and dropped down her cheeks, where she wiped them away with an impatient gesture.

"You, of all people. Why must it be you who sits here now? I didn't think you would concern yourself with the problems of others."

He could not for the life of him figure out why she had that attitude toward him, and it frightened him a little.

"Solveigh, I'm sitting here because I care about you. I want you to be happy, and if there's a way for me to help, then I'll do it."

By now she was crying in earnest, her hands covering her face, her shoulders shaking with desolate sobs.

"Solveigh." Jon reached for her, caressing her arm, and rose to sit beside her. "Please. Stop crying, love. Look at me. Come here." He drew her into a comforting embrace and lifted her chin with the tips of his fingers. "Now tell me. What's so terribly wrong with you and Russ?"

After a moment's resistance, she settled against him with a sad sigh and began to worry her shirt again. "I'm pregnant."

"Ah."

The sharp, sudden stab of envy surprised him, but he quickly clamped it down. "And so? What of it? I had the feeling you and Russ were on a steady course. I'm sure he would like to know. Does he know?"

But even while he was still digesting the news and mulling over the implications, the realization washed over him, making him feel defeated and very sad. Breathing became hard for a moment.

"You were making the same decision Naomi made all those years ago, right? You were going to break up with Russ and retreat back into that hotel and raise the child alone, just to be on the safe side. You don't have the courage, just the way she didn't, to stick with him and trust in him, no matter how deep the love goes?"

There was no reply from Solveigh, only the frightened, hopeless look on her face.

"What is it with you the two of you? Can't see how much we love you, and that we would rather lie down and die than let you go? We could sit here all night, Solveigh, and I could spin you a great, sad tale about how my life was after Naomi did this to me, and how hard it was, and still is, to come to terms with the fact that I never had the chance to know Joshua as a child. To watch his birth, to witness him growing up." He balled his hand into a fist in a helpless, angry gesture of loss. "I pined for Naomi. I longed for her more than I can say. It broke my heart to be without her, and nothing could heal the great wound I was dealt when I walked into that house in the pale light of dawn and found she had left me. But when I received Joshua's letter after all those years, telling me finally, finally where to find her, the greatest shock was that I had a son I had never seen, never even known about."

He went to the cupboard and brought out the bottle without waiting for her invitation. The measure he poured himself was rather liberal, but he felt he needed it; this talk was a lot more than he had bargained for and it shook him considerably. He had never spoken of his feelings about Joshua this candidly to anyone before, and it hurt in a way he had not thought possible.

"When Naomi left me, it broke my heart. But when I learned I had a nearly grown son, it tore out my soul, and it still does, and I fear it will never completely go away. The time I lost with Joshua will never return. With Naomi, now, I have a second chance, and we will make it, I know. But Joshua, his childhood, that is lost forever." The brandy burned its way through his chest, easing the tightness there somewhat and making breathing easier again.

"So please, Solveigh, don't do this to Russ. Don't take his kid from him, I beg you. Don't do this. Even if you don't want him in your life anymore, at least let him have a part in his child's life."

Solveigh had stopped crying and was staring at him.

Jon turned his back on her and stepped outside onto the small terrace of the house.

"You love her," he heard Solveigh's brittle voice from behind him. "You truly do. You must if you can find it in yourself to forgive her for this and fight so hard to make it right. No wonder you blunder about, making fantastic mistakes that result in such dramatic scenes. It's because you never gave up in your struggle to win her back."

She joined him in the wet night air, hugging herself against the cold.

"I always thought it was sheer willfulness and arrogance and the conviction that everything and everyone should bend to your wishes, but I was wrong. You love her with a desperation that is almost embarrassing to watch, and you are beside yourself with the fear she might leave you again, even now, even after you are married."

"Yes."

"You are as vulnerable as the next guy. Or maybe even more so. And here I thought you had the means to get nearly every girl in Hollywood into your bed."

Jon gave her a small, tired grin. "I do. But what good is any girl in Hollywood when she's the only one I want?" He broke off, shamefaced.

Solveigh was smart and not afraid of speaking up, so he feared the next question, knowing very well it would come.

"Jon," Solveigh said slowly. Her hand came to rest on his arm. "Jon. How could you find it in you to forgive Naomi?"

Yes; there it was, the question.

"I didn't need to forgive her. She had reasons for what she did and rest assured, Solveigh, they were grave enough. Really, it was the other way around; I had to ask her forgiveness. She ran from me and my life and hid where I would never find her, and so it is my job to make sure—now that she has consented to be with me again— sure she will never be hurt again."

GOING DOWN THE stairs to their apartment was like descending into another world.

When he opened the door, he was surprised to find Naomi still awake, sitting at her desk, staring out into the night. His voice floated back to him from the stereo. She hadn't noticed him, and he stood for a moment, taking in the picture presented to him. It must have been like this when she had written all those lyrics. The hotel asleep and deserted, she had retreated here, into her sanctuary, to regain a small piece of that other life—the one without him in it—she had led for so long.

"Baby."

"You're wet! Look at you! You should know better than to run around without a jacket in this weather!"

He laughed in surprise at her outburst. She rose from her seat and came over to him, mumbling about male stupidity and how he would catch his death, or at the very least a terrible cold, and she would have to nurse him back to health with ginger tea and chicken broth if he did not get out of those wet clothes, unbuttoning his shirt while she talked, and pulling it out of his jeans.

"Alright! Let go! I'll have a hot shower, and then I'll be fine. Stop fussing, wife!"

Dropping his clothes on the floor, he stepped into the bathroom. It did feel good, he had to admit, as his muscles began to relax under the hot deluge. He stood, his hands resting on the wall, his eyes closed, letting the water run over him, warming his cold body.

"Let me scrub your back for you," he heard Naomi's voice from behind.

"You are in danger. I can imagine how you look, all wet and slippery, your hair plastered to your skin, like a proper selkie come to me out of curiosity. I will surely steal your pelt and make you stay with me and then ravish you every night until you can't live without me anymore."

"Ah." A soft laugh. "And what makes you think I haven't come to steal you away to my castle and make you mine and take your voice from you, and the only outlet for you would be to please me day and night?"

"Take away my voice? What a dire threat." When he turned to her, she looked just as he had imagined. Wonderfully naked, her locks like black snakes over her shoulders and breasts. "Or maybe not. Maybe I'll *give* away my voice for the privilege of being your consort in your cool abode. Maybe I'll voluntarily languish there forever, without song, just for the joy of being around when you swim through the forest of algae and frolic with the little fishes."

"Frolic with the little fishes?" Naomi toyed with the soap, producing fragrant suds, which she spread on his chest and stomach. "I think not. I think I would be frolicking with my obliging mermen while you floundered around on the bottom of the sea, watching helplessly how they move inside of—"

"Yeah, Baby, don't take it too far. You're on dangerous ground now."

His muscles tightened under her caress, and he moved closer to her.

"Move inside of the algae forest, I was going to say." She finished her sentence. "I can't imagine what you were thinking. There would be some pretty mermaids to take care of you, of course, feeding you oysters and mussels and rubbing your—"

"Dangerous." Delivered in a low growl. "Very, very dangerous now. Be careful, my sweet selkie. I'd be around when you returned from your games with the puny merguys, and then you would be caught for sure. I would show you how we do it on the surface, where we get our strength from the sun and hot food."

"Overrated." A slight, negligent shrug of her shoulder and insistent hands on his body. "Vastly overrated, your human lovemaking. A mere myth to draw unsuspecting girls from the ocean to do your cooking and cleaning. Our mermen now, they don't hesitate to show some passion, and they don't waste time talking when they find a maid willing enough. They—"

Driven beyond endurance by her touch and her scenario, he hoisted her up against the tiles.

"Mermen. Right, mermen. Cold-blooded, voiceless sushi eaters. Now you are going to get a sample of how we do it, and I assure you, I'm no mean ambassador for mankind. So take it, selkie, and don't you dare refuse me."

Gripping her harder, he pressed her tightly against the wall. "Give it up, my mermaid. Yield. Yield to me and be mine forever."

"THOSE LYRICS," JON said later when they had finally found their way into bed, "I just can't get over it. They weren't yours anymore; they were mine. You had written them for me, they were your cry to me, and you had no right to destroy them."

Her hair was still damp from the shower. Her limbs moved languidly as she pulled up the quilt. He thought she truly looked like a selkie he had compelled away from her natural element, her eyes as large and dark as a seal's, her body as smooth and white as a lustrous pearl, her long, dark tendrils in sharp contrast.

There was no reply, and Jon thought she had fallen asleep. He reached over to turn off the light, ready to settle down himself, when he heard her say very softly, "I have copies on my computer. You can have the damned things if you want them so badly."

For a moment he could not believe his ears. Naomi seemed completely unconcerned as she snuggled into her pillow, drowsy eyes closing, her features relaxing into the softness of slumber.

"Are you serious?" Wide awake again, Jon shook her out of her torpor. She tried to shake him off, but he did not relent. "Tell me again! You kept copies, and you knew it the whole time?"

"Yes, now go to sleep." It was little more than a sigh. She refused to open her eyes again.

"Naomi. Talk to me. You truly have copies on that damned laptop of yours, and you tossed those sheets away only to torture me?"

Her lids fluttered. "Tomorrow. Let me sleep now. I'm tired. Getting married is very, very exhausting."

28

HER FAMILY WAS leaving. Her Uncle Carl held her hands in his. "Don't be a stranger. When you cross the Atlantic again, stop and stay with us. The time for hiding here is over now. And Naomi, come for New Year's. Come home to Kleinburg and bring your husband. Bring your friends. They should see where you come from."

The tenderness in his words nearly made her weep. "We'll come," she said.

He kissed her forehead and climbed into the car where her parents were already waiting, and she watched them drive away into the wet morning.

Jon sighed in relief to see them go. He would be the first to admit that they frightened him a great deal. Carl and Olaf were so big and blond, like Vikings. He could see them roaming the wild countryside above the fjords clothed only in furs and leather, their legs wrapped up in rags and their hair in ragged braids, crude swords slung over their shoulders as they stood with their arrow notched in a wooden bow, ready to shoot at anything that moved among the trees.

"You watch too many bad movies," Naomi told him.

IT WAS FASCINATING to watch her at her desk again. Even now, with the house still full of people, she had retreated here, truly working, not just staring out the window and dreaming, waiting for inspiration to come to her.

Quietly he sat down at the piano and put his glasses on to take another look at the song he had begun that morning. She moved and he looked up expectantly.

She was clearly searching for the right words to say. "Jon, what do I do? I don't know what to do." Her shoulders moved in something like helplessness as she struggled to express herself, a trace of impatience in the fluttering of her fingers. "I need someone to sort out my thoughts."

The outburst made him smile. "Do you think I'm the right person?"

"I don't know." She squirmed in her chair. "Since I don't know what I want, I don't know who the right person is."

He did, though. It had always been like this, and he thought it was wildly funny that she did not realize it herself. There was only one person who could sort out her creative tangles for her, and it certainly wasn't him.

"Well then, love, go find Sean. And take a walk with him."

"Sean."

"Don't get the wrong idea," Jon called after her. "You're a married woman now, remember?"

A while later he saw them strolling along the pier, wrapped in warm sweaters, Sean with his hands stuffed in his pockets, listening closely to Naomi, who was once again gesturing as she talked, her wild mane blowing in the wind.

Jon pondered the lines of her newest song, trying to find the truth in them, the relevance to her own life, theirs, but he could not find a connection. These had come, he understood, when inspiration had struck her so suddenly at the dinner table that they had made a clear thought impossible.

It was part of her charm that she refused to accept credit for her work. On the other hand, she had possessed the audacity to drop that sheaf of lyrics into his hands like the bomb they had proven to be, accompanied only by the sassy, single phrase she had scribbled on a half sheet of paper: SING THIS. He still had that note stashed away with her originals in the safe at the Hollywood office. From time to time, when he was there alone, he had taken it out and gazed at it and recalled, over and over again, their very first days together in Geneva.

That first night was bright and clear in his mind, locked away in its own precious treasury. It had been so different, so intense, so intimate and sweet, a revelation. He had been giving love for the first time, all his senses centered on the girl in his arms, aware of her every moment, his own satisfaction defined by her bliss and her reaction to him. It had been very scary, this sudden strong urge to give instead of just taking what he needed the way he was accustomed to doing. She had demanded nothing of him, letting him lead her and introduce her to this new experience, and he had done it ever so gently, taking her along until she clasped him tightly, her breath coming in hitched sobs, and she shuddered against him, gasping his name.

It was as if a veil had been torn from his eyes that night, and a whole new world had opened for him. A world where the word *love* had a completely new meaning, and he wanted to keep it forever. Not even standing on stage surrounded by the roaring of ten thousand people could match it. This had been personal, direct, theirs.

And so, when he had stood with her in that lobby the next morning, pleading with her to join him in Amsterdam and then come away to California, he had trembled in panic that she might refuse, might disappear again into her life and this city among the mountains, and his newfound feelings would have no outlet but to haunt him like a mirage for the rest of his life.

As they had.

On the flight he had tried to step back from himself, to analyze the storm of his feelings, put some distance and reality into the thing, but the closer the time came when she was supposed to arrive, the stronger the certainty became that there was no other reality. Sal had gone to the airport, and he had hardly been able to concentrate on the soundcheck, fearing—back then when cell phones were still only an idea—that he would return alone, shrug at him, and say, "She didn't show up."

But she did. He had nearly lost his composure when she walked into the hall behind Sal, a tentative smile on her face. He had known then that she had gone through the same doubts and fears, and it had made him leap from the stage and run to meet her halfway until she was in his arms.

SHE WAS TIRED; there was no other way to put it.

Back at the apartment after her walk with Sean through the blustery weather she went straight to her bed and pulled the quilt up to her chin. It was quiet in her cozy nook, and for a moment she imagined she was back in the loneliness of her old life. But it did not last long, for the door opened and she could hear his steps, the soft query, and she replied.

Jon dropped onto the bed beside her, leaning on one elbow. "So tell me. What did you talk to Sean about?"

"You'll laugh at me," she prophesied moodily, "and then I'll never talk to you again. Go away."

"No. I won't laugh and I won't go. Promise. Come on. Talk to me."

She looked up at his serious face, all the play gone from his expression.

"Tell me, Baby. Please. I know there is something brewing in you, and I get the feeling that I need to hear it." He hesitated briefly. "We are on the verge of something new, yes? Only I can't see where it is leading."

There was an awful, tearing pain in Naomi's chest that took her breath away and nearly made her cry. She felt the grief swell in her like the huge wave she had just written about, bitter, salty, inundating.

She had written those very first lyrics for him from a deep compulsion and sent them to him without thinking twice, utterly certain these were the words he was supposed to put to music and then perform. That voice, it had been the magic of the voice, it had been like the soft, warm blanket of love, the challenge of a bungee jump from a high bridge, a roller coaster ride and the wild, disturbing kiss of a stranger in the darkness of a summer night.

And here, a lifetime later, so many tears and lonely nights later, there was still the same powerful urge to give him what he wanted from her.

"Baby?" Jon asked tenderly. "Where are you? You look as if you want to cry. Why do I make you cry?"

"I never thought of loving you," she said, "when I heard you sing. Your voice, it seemed to be talking directly to me. It seemed almost as if there was no barrier, no other listener, no radio, nothing. You, and me, and the way you sang to me. I stood there in my room, helpless, struck dumb as a beast, and as excited and trembling as a teenager getting her first kiss. It felt as if you were reaching out to me. I could feel your hand on my neck, forcing me to sit down right then and there and write those songs for you, as if I was not even writing them myself. And yet, at the same time, I felt provoked, almost angry. I don't know. I wanted to smack you for disturbing me like that, invading my mind, ruining my life. Wherever I went, there was that stupid song, and that voice, calling, demanding, and yes, mocking me."

Naomi moved against him.

"And then you appear. Out of the blue, the voice has a face. And a body. And God, it belongs to the most compelling man on Earth, and he is mine for the taking. The voice that drove me into sleepless madness belongs to the one man who makes me instantly weak with desire without even saying a word, who has eyes that kill me with one look and lips that need to be kissed so badly it drives any sane thought from my head." She felt his arms tighten around her and his breath quicken against her face. "If you had pushed just a little harder, I would have been yours that first night. I ached for you; I wanted to feel you so badly. The car took me home and I cursed myself and my stupid pride, wondering if I would ever get a second chance. I did not sleep at all that night, imagining how it would be to make love to you, to lie in your arms. How you would take me to your room and steal my clothes, whispering to me in the darkness, so sure of yourself, and how you would come for me and make me yours, the first, the only one, ever. You were so decent, so very, very gentle and sweet." She sat up, which made Jon stretch out and rest his hands under his head. "Promise not to laugh. And promise not to hold it against me."

"Yeah, I promise. But I might make a little fun of you if it's too outrageous."

She slapped his arm. "Sean thinks we're creating a musical. And Jon, if we go on, if we really put together a musical, then I would like to see it on stage. Live, not a movie. And Sean thinks it's high time for your own stage production anyway."

He did not reply for so long, Naomi thought he had drifted off into a doze.

"Such a terribly long way."

It was delivered in a low, thoughtful voice, and she could not make out if there was sadness in it or only bemusement.

"Truly, Naomi, it has been such a long, long way for me to end up here in your bed and hear from you which fork in the road to take."

His head turned in her direction and he looked straight at her, wide awake and very alert. "Seems to me you always knew exactly when to push or prod me, first with your lyrics, then when you ran away, stepping back into my life just before I was ready to jump in the sea with depression, and now...now you come up with this utterly outlandish idea."

"I'm not prodding you into anything."

Disappointed, she moved to rise from the bed, but he held her back, laughing at her bristling defensiveness. "Silly girl. As if you had a chance against me. You know you can't win. But if you want a lively tussle I'll give you one, only I can't promise you will be on time for dinner then."

He brought her down and rolled on top of her, holding her wrists tightly above her head until she gave up.

"Oh yes. That's much better, you greedy little thing. Now, will you hear the rest of my answer, or do you need to wrestle some more first? I'm all for wrestling, but I'm also rather keen to finish my little speech."

"Then finish it."

"Right away, ma'am. But since I have you so conveniently under control, I think I'll do some serious kissing first, the kind that will give me pleasure. Come on, Baby, please your man."

"No! Go away!" It was barely more than a sob.

Jon did not even bother to reply. His kiss was slow and deep, brutally sensual and intimate, filled with the promise of other things, and it got the desired response from her.

"Yeah, little beast," he whispered when her body strained against his. "That's it. Show me you want me. Let me feel your need."

He let go of her, satisfied with the result of his gentle assault.

"And to think," Jon said appreciatively, "you are my wife. You belong to me, and yet you are my greatest temptation, in every sense."

"And you are my bane." Her face was flushed, her hair wild around it. "My nightmare, the cross I have to bear. I'm never safe from you and your attacks, and I always end up on my back with you doing as you please."

"Yes." he agreed with relish, "I just love it. Don't you? I know you do. Come on, get up! No more play before dinner."

He rose and held out his hand to her. She glared at him but took the offered help and followed him downstairs to the piano.

"Look, Naomi, it's all here. This is what we will do: when everyone is gone, when my mother and Joshua have left for New York, we will have the space and the quiet to work on this. We won't even tell anyone. Just the two of us, we will develop this selkie thing. What do you think?" Expectantly he waited for her reaction. It was a dream; it was more than writing songs together, it was more than writing a movie score. This combined their talents in a way that had never before occurred to him, and if they managed to complete it they would pull everyone together again, and then, and then…he did not dare to think it through, but it was there, exciting, calling to him, the beast that had been hiding from him, finally allowing him more than a brief glimpse.

Broadway.

"Baby?" His attention returned to her. For an instant he was frightened, she was once more radiating the still withdrawal he hated so much. But this time it was different, it was disbelief and awe, and a mirror of his own feelings.

"Kiss me again," Naomi said in a hushed voice. "Only do it properly this time. A little more intensity, if you please."

29

A FEW DAYS before they were supposed to leave for Christmas in New York and Toronto, Jon was on the point of calling it all off, just because he was so intrigued by the incredible quietness around them. Snow had fallen like a thick white blanket, and with it came a slowing of their daily life that made time literally creep along.

He was amazed at the leisure with which the people around him spent their dark days, decorating their homes and the little town with great care, attending church services filled with still, warm contemplation and traditional, well-worn Christmas Carols.

It was Naomi who made him stick to their original plans.

"I'm so looking forward to seeing New York with all the Christmas lights," she said one morning. "I've always wanted to dive into that hustle and bustle. You'll have to go to Bergdorf with me, Jon. I've dreamed of seeing that since I was small. And Tiffany's. And the Christmas tree at Rockefeller Center. Oh, and ice skating! Do you skate? Can we go skating? And there's this huge toy shop, I forget the name…"

"FAO Schwarz," he groaned.

Andrea had made waffles for breakfast. They had not been upstairs in the dining room for a meal for a long time, preferring the solitude of their apartment to the hotel, but the scent of cinnamon and butter had lured them upstairs early.

During the past few weeks Naomi had tried a couple of times to cook for them, but anything more complicated than instant soup eluded her. He had watched her in amused exasperation as she read the instructions on the box of a frozen pizza, her brow wrinkled, her lips moving, until finally he had taken it away from her. "Good thing we can afford to eat out most of the time or we would starve! You are hopeless. How did you survive all these years?"

"Andrea cooked. Just as she does now. I never needed to bother. In LA, it was your housekeeper. Before that, my mother or her housekeeper." It made her stop and think. "And you?"

Jon had been standing next to her with the pizza still in his hands, turning the carton over thoughtfully.

He had tried so hard to find her, listening to her father's cold and polite statements over and over that it would be useless for him to go to Geneva, she was not there, and no, he would not be told where she was.

He had never told anyone; after a few weeks of brooding he had gone to Geneva, on his own, but to no avail. Certain in the knowledge that her parents would not see him, he had hung around outside their apartment building in the hope of catching her. Her father had come and gone, picked up or dropped off by a chauffeur-driven limousine, always in impeccable suits, a leather briefcase in hand, and her mother had driven her Mercedes convertible in and out of the garage, but never Naomi. When the concierge accosted him after a couple of days, he learned that she had never reappeared there at all. He felt ridiculous and pathetic, and he kept his solitary venture to European soil an absolute secret.

Art had taken over the house in Malibu, and Jon had descended into a prolonged bout of dark depression that he first tried to cure with solitude and then with a manic swirl of Hollywood nightlife. But he had always returned to his small abode on the shore, and he had learned to look after himself.

He had learned to cook. It had been therapeutic in its own way, forcing him to concentrate on it with a certain mindlessness, following the sometimes cryptic instructions cookbooks, but he had persevered and in the end was quite adept at fixing meals for himself. He had hated eating alone and became sloppy after a while, taking the pan with him out on his small deck and eating from it while the surf crashed near his house.

"There was time enough over the years," he now replied in a light tone. "And no one cooked the pasta with shrimp and garlic just the way I wanted it." With a deft twist, he opened the pizza box. "They always put parsley in it, and God, I just hate parsley."

"You could teach me." She watched how he sprinkled extra cheese on it and put some olives on her half.

"Nah. You don't need to learn to cook, Baby. I'd love to cook for you. I want to."

"But then I'll never be a proper wife, Jon!" He did not let her take the baking tray from him when she tried, and pushed it into the oven instead.

"You want to be a proper wife?" Jon asked, washing his hands, "Really? I'll teach you to be a proper wife alright, dear heart, and it has nothing to do with cooking at all."

She was not fast enough. He caught her halfway up the stairs to the loft.

THE NEIGHBORHOOD LAY in silent dusk when the car pulled up in front of Helen's house. Joshua opened the door. He gave them a critical look up and down and yelled into the house, "Grandma, the jet-setters are here!"

"And good day to you, young man," Jon replied, pleased to see how well he had settled in with his family.

"Well, don't let them stand out there like strangers," Helen shouted back. "Bring in the luggage, if they have any. Knowing your father, he's probably only planning to stop for a cup of coffee."

"Thanks, Ma." Jon called, "The luggage is at the hotel already. We only dropped by for brief hello and then we'll be gone."

Helen came from the kitchen, drying her hands on a towel. She wore jeans and a fan t-shirt of Jon's, her silver bob covered with a kerchief..

"You're early," she said crossly. "I haven't changed yet and dinner isn't ready."

Jon grinned at her. "Nice shirt, Ma. I didn't know you were a fan of mine."

"You can't have your old room back," Joshua announced when they had joined Helen in the kitchen. "It's mine now. I threw out some of your old things, too."

Jon sat in one of the chairs around the big oak table and took the coffee Helen held out to him. Naomi had vanished somewhere in the depths of the house to find Valerie, and he could hear their voices echoing down the hall, laughing, calling to each other and to the girls.

The phone rang, there was trampling on the stairs and the sound of a TV when a door was torn open suddenly and then slammed shut again, some more shouting and more wild running.

Kevin and Sarah would come for dinner, Helen announced, and they would have to make plans for the next few days. How long were they going to stay, and would he go out and get a tree tomorrow morning and put it up?

"If you know how to do that, I mean."

"Mom, please." He wanted her teasing; he wanted the noise and the disorder and the bustle, and he wanted to be in the middle of it, letting the feeling of family and belonging wash over him and wrap around him like the wrapping on a Christmas gift.

The kitchen smelled wonderful. Roast beef, potatoes, and fresh cookies all mixed together to form an aroma that could only be called home. The windows were hung with garlands of evergreens and red bows. There was the reindeer figure on the sill he remembered from his childhood, and the bowl with the tiny ruby apples his mother always bought for the season, and another with nuts and dried apricots.

"Where do you want the tree, Ma?" Jon had moved to the living room.

Helen had placed lit candles on the mantelpiece and hung up the stockings.

"By the fireplace. And you might as well go to the attic and bring down the decorations. But don't drop anything, you hear me? And don't fall off the ladder!"

"Won't, Mom."

For the life of him, he could not understand why he had given up on this and not returned home at least for the holidays once in a while.

"What do you think you're doing?" Valerie asked from behind him as he started up the rungs of the attic ladder. "You'll break a leg for sure."

"And hello to you too, sister dear. I'm doing the chores my mother gave me. Where's my wife?"

"Your wife," she snorted, "is not your lapdog, and I would strongly advise her not to climb up after you. If you break a leg we'll hire a nurse and put you up in a private hospital room where you can rant and whine, but if Naomi breaks a bone we'll have to deal with your hysterics here all day long. I'd sooner jump into the Hudson than endure that." Valerie held the rickety ladder for him until he had vanished in the darkness under the roof. "Nice butt, brother. You sure take care of yourself."

"Val, go away and do something useful. Polish the banister or something equally important."

This, he decided when he stood in the dim, musty space of the attic and dusted off his hands, was fun. It was loving, easy, heart felt fun.

"Are you hiding from your family already?" Naomi's head appeared through the opening. "This is a dead end."

She looked around curiously while he searched for the box with the decorations that his mother wanted. "Attics are a treasure trove. There's always history hidden somewhere. Will I find interesting things from your past if I dig deep enough, do you think?"

"Probably." His voice sounded muffled from the corner he was in. "Embarrassing stuff that will tell you more about me than I ever wanted you to know. So no, don't start digging."

She opened the door of an old wardrobe.

There were clothes in plastic coverings inside, but then she realized they were his stage shirts, neatly washed and pressed and labeled, one after the other, a hundred of them at least.

"I think I'll pass on the youth stuff and look at these instead."

There it was: deep, dark red, beads on the sleeves and the breast, the collar too wide and the waist too narrow for current taste. but beautiful nonetheless. That kiss, it was still so vivid in her mind, the hot rhythm, driven on by Sean and the bass drums, the stadium thronged with people, the warm Mediterranean summer night, her excitement and turmoil at finding herself standing there at the side of the huge stage, and Jon. Jon, moving with the music, his guitar in his hands, making love to the audience, young, unbridled. In that shirt, with the impossible embroidery, he had sung "Secret Garden" in public for the first time. The world had taken notice by then, and he was on the point of stepping from popularity to utter stardom. Even the tasteless thing he had worn in London was there, the last in the line, a sort of cowboy shirt, mortifying in its blatant appeal for attention.

"I would like to take this one back home." She brought out the red one. "Do you think Helen would mind?"

He came over to look at what she had unearthed.

"God. Geneva. I kissed the loveliest girl in that shirt, and I had my mind on her through the entire show. But she tells me that's not how it works! I'll never forget that sentence. Such a put-down, and from a young thing who should have fallen at my feet right away!" He took the shirt from her.

"And here. The one you wore in London last winter." She held it out to him. "Put it on for me?"

"You do have a penchant for torturing yourself," Jon said slowly. "Why would you want to relive that night? I know you were hurt, Baby. And I remember being very sad when I sang 'Secret Garden.' I was almost ready to give up."

Somewhere deep in her chest was a pain, it was true, but it was a pleasant kind of pain now, encapsulated in warm reality.

With a shrug he acquiesced and pulled off his turtleneck.

"I thought it was rather nice." He peeled the covering from the show shirt. "Colorful and easy to recognize even from the furthest seats, high up under the rafters. I climbed all the way up to the highest rows before the show to get a view of the stage, and I tell you, it is far, far away." He paused. "I climbed up there and stared down at my stage while you stood outside with the fans. God."

"By then I wasn't standing there anymore. I had gone to pick up Joshua and have tea with him. I had seen what I had come to see." She held his sweater to her face to catch his scent. "I had seen you, getting off the bus, and you were just as desirable and wonderful as ever. I wanted you. I wanted you back, and I wanted to forget you, but my mistake! Being in the same city with you was too much. Seeing you there, in front of me, seeing you on stage, singing our song…oh well." She tried a smile and failed. "We know what happened next, right? I couldn't keep my big trap shut and had to spill my dirty little secret to our son."

"I only wish I had noticed you in that group," Jon said. "I would have plucked you up, my dove, and Sean would have had to do the soundcheck because I would have been too busy showing you in words and deeds where you belong."

He had buttoned up the shirt and was adjusting the cuffs and collar, standing very straight, his feet slightly apart and his shoulders back, taking the commanding stance he always had on stage.

"Jon."

He looked up to see tears in her eyes. "It's okay, Baby. Everything is okay now. Come here."

Seeing him in that shirt had undone her; it had thrown her back to that cold, unfriendly day in London and the feeling of hopelessness and terrible grief and Joshua's biting remarks.

He was holding her close, his lips in her hair, stroking his hands over her shoulders and back. "These stupid shirts. I didn't know my mother kept them up here."

Naomi, though, was shaken by the imagination of what might have happened that night in London if she had walked up to him, and by all the wild emotions she had lived through that day.

"Look at it this way, love. If you hadn't come to London for that concert, you would never have decided to tell Joshua. You needed that incentive, you needed the fresh pain. You needed to see I was still a living, breathing man and not just a picture on a CD cover." He took her face between his hands and gazed into her eyes. "You're still punishing yourself. You still relive the past and stir it up, but it only brings pain."

"That's not it." Shamefacedly she tried to free herself from his embrace.

"What then? Here I stand in my stage shirt and you go to pieces, and it's not because of our lost past?"

She shook her head, unwilling to speak up.

"Oh, there's a secret here! Come on, spill, little beast!"

She sighed. "It's seeing you in the shirt, remembering how you looked then, on stage. I wonder what would have happened if I had truly come up to you."

He laughed softly at those words. There was a large crate against the wall, and he pulled her over and made her sit down with him.

"Listen well, little beast, I'm going to tell you the whole London story."

From downstairs they could hear the doorbell and Kevin's voice booming through the stairwell, Helen calling for them, Joshua's footsteps in the hallway, but Jon shouted down, "We'll be down in a minute." Then he turned back to Naomi. "This is how it goes. Where do I see you? Outside, with the fans, or at the beginning of the concert?" Again he stopped briefly. "Sean is telling me about some new arrangement or other, I'm a bit grumpy because the coffee was lousy and there were no cinnamon rolls at Starbucks."

"Lousy coffee at Starbucks?" she murmured, but he shook his head.

"Don't interrupt. Okay. I glance toward the fan group because someone shouts a greeting and waves, and God, all those women in their ugly clothes and their flat, ungainly shoes! What's this all about? Am I not worth a little more consideration, for God's sake? Here I travel across continents and oceans to bring my music to these people, and they show up in parkas and sweaters? Why do I take the trouble to outfit the band and myself and drag around a makeup artist and a costume specialist if my fans don't give a fart how they look? No, but wait—there's a gem! But there's this red-haired lady with a rough German accent in front of her, and hell, she is one ugly woman! The glimpse I just caught, it reminds me of someone, it reminds me of my lost love, of the one I loved beyond sense and reason and who still burns in my heart, the girl I'm always looking for. In every city and at every concert, she's the one I hope to find, and here, on this drab winter day in London, it happens, finally. She's well hidden behind the fat German, but it's enough for me to step forward."

Jon looked larger and even more vibrant than in real life in the colorful, embroidered shirt, even up here under the tired light of a single bulb.

"So I step forward," he continued, "and the German smiles at me angelically. Gosh, but she has bad taste in lipstick! Red hair and orange lipstick? Please! But right there behind her, hiding from me, hiding…"

He toyed with her rings, lost in his own fantasy for a moment.

"She has not changed over the years. She's just as lovely and sweet as she was, and I want her, I want her back, God yes, that one glance is enough for me. I can see in her eyes that she has come here to ask exactly that question but is unsure of herself and of me. This time, this time I'm going to hold on."

She leaned into his shoulder and rested her head under his chin.

"The ugly German watches, they all watch, as I make a fool of myself right there outside the venue, as I ask her to please, please come with me, give me the chance to show her I love her still." He shrugged slightly. "Ah, here it comes! She does follow me inside, but she keeps her distance, she has her doubts. And I want her in my arms, I need her, I've missed her for so long, I need her to hold me and make me real, so I take her to my dressing room even though Sal is after me and wants us to do the soundcheck right now…I tell him to go to hell. I tell him to do whatever he pleases but to leave us alone, let us settle this, give me the time to set things right…and she still has not said a word and just stands there. I can feel she wants to run. But I won't allow it. Oh no, not this time."

He looked down into her face.

"Not this time. This time, I'll make sure she wants to stay with me, stay by my side. I'll love her as hard as I can and then some more. I'll love her day and night with every breath I take, and I'll see to it that she'll never regret it. And the longer she's there in my dressing room, the greater the urge becomes to touch her, to feel her in my arms and make all those lonely nights vanish. So..." His lips pursed in thought. "So I reach for you, and your body is warm and soft, and you smell so good, and you permit the kiss, you let me kiss you, just like you did when I found you in Halmar. You are back in my arms, and I want you, God, I want you so much I'm reeling from it. I want you right away, want you like crazy, want the kind of loving I've only ever had with you, yes, Baby."

She toyed with the embroidery on his shirt, listening to his heartbeat and his breathing while he held her, lost in his thoughts.

"Go on. Don't stop now just when it's getting interesting."

He laughed. "Greedy. Really, little beast? Here, in my mom's attic, with all the dust and old stuff? Okay, well then. But I warn you, we will have to go down soon, and I don't want you panting at me. It will be a while before we are alone and I can do something about it."

It was nearly enough already.

"If that had really happened," Jon picked up his narration, "I guess I would have hesitated. It would have been nearly civilized."

They could hear Helen's voice from below, asking in irritation where they had gone off to.

"There's only the couch," Jon went on. "Are you willing, little beast? What happens when I touch you? Do you retreat, do you refuse me?"

She bit her lip.

"Yeah, that's what you say now." Drawled out to perfection, picking up her mood and playing with it, using his verbal power on her.

"So I kiss you some more, and I can feel your blood heating up there in my arms, I can feel you come alive under my touch, responding to me, and now it's too late to stop anyway. We don't even need to speak, it's only building passion and the growing urgency."

Her hips moved invitingly.

"Stop that. Don't tempt me like that. Oh God, I don't want this quick number in the dressing room at all. I want you on a big bed, naked, feeling your body against mine. But it will have to do, just a brief reclaiming, and maybe a promise of what is to come. And yes, that's how it used to be. This is how it always felt. I reclaim you, put my mark on you in such a way that you will not want to run again."

With another brief kiss he put her back on her feet and slapped her rump playfully. "No more talk. I'm all talked out anyway. I wonder, what would happen afterward? What would you do or say after that number?"

Naomi thought for a moment, then gave him her best insolent shrug.

"I know exactly what. You would not have gone on stage in that shirt for sure. I would have seen to that."

INCREDIBLY, IT WAS Naomi who complained about the cold.

It was, she stated, different from the cold in Norway. Here, it was dark, wet and dirty. The wind howled through the canyons of Manhattan and brought out the really ugly side of winter. There was nothing of the grandeur or the meditative stillness the bay offered when frost and ice turned the water into a slate-grey sheet and fog and snow shrouded the mountains.

The dense, evil-smelling clouds of fog drifting up from the grates above the subway were an endless source of fascination to her. She made up stories about monsters and fairy creatures living in the darkness beneath the city streets until Jon told her there were indeed people living in the tunnels.

He had, he said a few days after Christmas, an appointment, just this one business appointment, and he wanted her to come along. Naomi was still in bed and didn't feel like going out in the cold again. She pulled the covers up over her head and grumbled.

"Come on, Baby," he coaxed. "I'll buy you breakfast. I'll buy you scrambled eggs and smoked salmon and fresh scones."

The blanket flew back. "Scones?"

Jon threw up his hands. "Why do I have a wife I can bribe with food and not with jewelry, I want to know?"

Wherever they were going, it wasn't far. The car took them past the park and then onto Broadway, south toward Times Square.

"The Shubert?" Naomi asked in bewilderment when they stopped.

Jon shrugged, but she could see the glee on his face.

They were welcomed by a fair-haired, elderly, but extremely agile man who introduced himself as Stan and gripped her arm while he talked in a seemingly endless stream about the theater and the current show. He was the manager of the place, he informed her, and extremely pleased by their plans.

Right now they were in a rehearsal session, and would she care to take a look? Would she like to see the backstage area? And when did they think they wanted to start their production?

Naomi looked at Jon in confusion. "But you don't even know what we're going to write."

Stan laughed at her. "Are you crazy? The world has been waiting for this! After so many years of wasting his talent on love songs, Jonathan Stone has finally come around to writing real music." He stopped in his tracks. "It's like this. He is lazy. Somewhere down under all that pop music is a really great composer. Yeah, he can sing, too." A deprecating wave toward Jon. "But honestly, there are so many good singers out there. Composers? A handful. The music he wrote during the last fifteen years or so never sounded right. It was either too big, or too country, or too jazz, or too whatever else, never really great. And you know why, my dear?" Stan pushed his face toward Naomi until she shook her head.

"Because, in effect, he writes musicals all the time."

"But…" Naomi tried to say, and he shook his finger at her.

"Ah, no buts!"

She was so confused by his breathless lecturing she hardly appreciated the huge auditorium when he led her into it.

The stage was crowded with dancers warming up for the rehearsal, musicians were tuning their instruments, lighting technicians were busy in the rafters, climbing amid the rigging like monkeys and shouting to each other. In the first row a small group was deep in discussion, their heads close together over a couple of clipboards, while a girl with dense red curls was using the time to practice a song.

Naomi stood next to Stan. The hall lay before her in half-light. Above them, the balconies rose into the dark of the ceiling.

"But," she tried again, "you don't know anything about me."

Stan's shout of laughter echoed through the space. "Not know you? It is my job to know people like you, my dear! You are the one who wrote the lyrics for the movie album, right? Of course I know you. Everyone knows you."

Stan led them down to the edge of the stage and introduced them, chased off one of the young men to get coffee, and then began to quiz Naomi about their plans again. She answered hesitatingly, unsure of herself and the situation, casting beseeching glances at Jon, but he had settled down in the fifth row to watch the proceedings onstage with great interest.

"You could have your pick of musical composers," Stan was saying, "but I'm sure you are aware of that. What a pity you chose to marry Jon, I bet he insists on exclusivity. Otherwise I would introduce you to some interesting people with, I am certain, interesting results. There are too many who aspire to singing as it is. The creation of the music, that's a different thing. And creating a musical, that's true art. It's contemporary opera! The culmination of music and stage performance, it demands many talents in one performer! Singing is nothing!"

Jon laughed out loud. "Yeah, Stan, tell me all about it! The next thing you'll ask me to do is swing from a branch while I sing and wear nothing but a loincloth!"

Stan regarded him critically. "No. No Tarzan for you, even though I am sure the ladies would swoon to see you nearly naked. Phantom of the Opera, though, that I can visualize. Or Dracula? A pity there's no James Bond musical yet, that would be the ideal role for you."

"He's too nice for that," one of the others interjected. "No cynical edge."

"But he looks grand in a tux," Stan contradicted. "And I'm sure he's really good at ordering martinis."

"Nah," Jon called. "I hate driving English cars! Have you ever seen Bond in a Porsche? Won't work, guys! And really, all those girls! Too much bother."

Of course, Stan stated, she knew which play they were preparing, and she nodded.

"Soundcheck, Baby, nothing else!" came Jon's voice from behind. "Only they have to dance, as well. God, I'm glad I only need to sing."

"Your man is ridiculous," Stan said sternly. "He could never compete with any of them on the stage now!"

"I can too, as long as we talk about performing and not jumping across the stage." Jon came to stand with them. "And I don't even need your orchestra to do it, Stanley Farmer! Don't mess with me!"

"Well then, I dare you!" Stan stared at him belligerently. "Get up there and show us what you can do without your band and all your electronics!"

"Boys," said the red-haired girl, "we are trying to work." She eyed Jon dubiously. "Are you someone we should know?"

"Good grief!" Stan slapped her back and shoved her toward the stage. "Janet, don't talk if only trash comes out of your mouth. You're ruining your career with your ignorance!"

Naomi sank down into a seat and folded her hands in her lap to watch the scene unfold. It felt almost like being with the band before a concert again. There was the same kind of excitement and exhilaration, the nervous agitation and hectic pace, the all-pervading scent of coffee and the hint of illicit cigarettes in some dark corner, the dust in the beams when the engineers tested the spotlights, snatches of music from one instrument or another, and the one voice that made all others fall silent when it was raised.

He did not even go to the center of the stage but sat down at the piano that stood at the side for practicing and began to play and sing along, effortless and quite strong enough to fill the space without a microphone.

The troupe had stepped aside and stood listening quietly.

Naomi saw the wide grin on Stan's face and the satisfaction among the others who stood around him. But when Jon stopped and tried to rise from the bench, Stan yelled, "That wasn't even your own song! You cheated! I thought you were here to impress us with your newest compositions, and you serve us that old Broadway crap? Come on, Jon!"

"Stan." Jon's voice was modulated so well he didn't have to raise it at all to be understood. "You are a piece of shit and a manipulative asshole. If you want to hear me sing, buy a ticket to my next concert. I'm done playing the performer for you. Let your dancers practice and come to lunch with us."

Silence greeted his words, but a wide grin was spreading across Stan's face as he raised his arms in a gesture of benediction.

"Yes, my friend! Say it out loud! Listen up, my striving children, here you have the voice of heaven! A good thing, Jon, you did not decide to become a preacher. You could convince nuns to pray to the devil if you put your mind to it."

"You will never forgive me for that poker game, will you?" Jon came back to them, a feral grin on his face.

"Never, my friend," Stan agreed. "Come on, buy me lunch at the Russian Tea Room and tell me all about your great idea. Don't forget the lovely lyricist."

THEY SETTLED INTO one of the niches of the restaurant and ordered lunch. Naomi felt like a schoolgirl as they gossiped about other Broadway shows. She could imagine herself in this setting; she could see herself living and working here, and Jon, too.

"What poker game?" she asked during a lull, and Stan laughed.

Jon's arm came around her shoulder.

In Las Vegas, he said, one New Year's Eve, he had given one of those notorious concerts that had become a tradition over the years, and afterward, just before midnight when the audience had dispersed into the various clubs and bars to celebrate, he sat in his dressing room by himself and took a break before he went to join the others.

Even though he didn't say it, she heard the meaning in his words quite clearly. Loneliness.

There had been a knock on his door, and "this funny bird stuck his head in. A pale, blond guy in a pink shirt and a blue tie, and asked if we really played poker all the time, and were we as good as the rumors said. I was so surprised to see a stranger walk into my dressing room, I couldn't come up with a reply right away. It took me a moment to even ask him how he had managed to get past the security and into the backstage area."

"Yes, well," Stan interrupted. "He's not the brightest bulb, is he? He should have known who I was."

Unfazed, Jon went on, "At that time, he was the show manager for one of the big hotels, and he could go where he pleased in Las Vegas. And that night, he decided what he pleased was to come over and play cards with a singer."

Naomi had the distinct impression that there had been more to that meeting than a round of poker, but she kept silent and waited for the two men to unfold their tale.

"Of course," Jon said, "he couldn't play at all. Sean had stripped him before I lit my second cigarette."

"I had come, you see…" Stan said as he stuffed a blini heaped with caviar into his mouth, washing it down with champagne, "to tell him what a nerd he was. Wasting his time on ridiculous shows in Las Vegas, prostituting himself to a raucous crowd instead of working seriously."

She could hardly believe her ears.

"He was selling himself so far under worth, and please, dear girl! Those shirts! Why did you never stop him?"

"When was this?" Naomi asked.

"When? Oh, five years ago or so." Stan signaled to the waiter for coffee.

"I had watched him for quite a while by then, and it seemed to me he was drifting off, spiraling away from his true potential. It had been going on for some time, but that New Year's Eve my patience ended. I could not just stand by and let him slide any longer." He pushed his plate aside and snatched the last piece of blini from the silver platter. "We played some poker that night and I offered him a story that had come to my desk a few days earlier. It would make a nice basis for a musical, but he refused, saying something like he didn't have a writer anymore, and his own lyrics were only good enough for little songs. Pathetic."

Jon listened silently, his eyes wandering through the curtained windows out onto the street, as if the conversation did not concern him at all. Naomi looked at his profile. Here was another glimpse into that long stretch of dead time.

"The inspiration was gone," he said softly. "The urge to do great things wasn't there. My voice was somewhere else. My thoughts were somewhere else, and I could not hear them." He took a deep breath and seemed to shake off his melancholy with it. "But not any longer. Now, everything is as it should be."

"Well, then," Stan said as he stirred his mocha, "no more excuses, and no more dithering with trash."

"That trash, Stan," Jon growled, "has made me richer than you will ever be. So it can't be all that bad. Anyway, you should decide: is it trash, or are my songs musical hits out of context? Make up your mind, you crazy man! They can't be both."

31

SHE WANTED A new dress. There would be a ball on New Year's Eve at her uncle's house, with many people, important people, so they went shopping together. "That one," Jon suggested, pointing, outside Dior, "the one with the pearls." He could see her in that blue satin dress with the wide neckline and tiny sleeves, its skirt nearly as wide as one Scarlett O'Hara would have worn. And, he promised, he would not allow her to fuss this time. If he was going to show her off as his wife to Canadian society, she was going to sparkle and gleam. They were going to see that he kept her in style.

She didn't protest, but let him do as he wished.

He played outrageously with her, trying on one evening suit after another, asking her which one she wanted him to take off for her later, much later, after the party was over and he had her alone again.

Reluctantly and still not convinced it was what she truly wanted, Naomi bought herself a new riding habit for the hunt on New Year's Day, while Jon watched the proceedings with much interest and a steady stream of comments. The riding boots fascinated him, and while she tried them on with the help of a shop assistant, he asked if they had to be that tight, that high, made of that kind of leather, and how was she supposed to get into them later on her own?

Naomi stood before him in breeches, a brown blazer, and those boots and explained rather absentmindedly that the groom would attend her.

"You have your own stables." It was more of a statement than a question. Jon found there was very little she could surprise him with anymore. Maybe, he thought, if she told him her family owned the London Eye, maybe that…

"Well, in a way. There is the hotel, you see, in Kleinburg, at the other side of the park, with the golf course, tennis courts, and the stables… it's kind of a resort."

"But the CN Tower," he asked, "that's not yours yet?" He decided he needed a drink very badly when she said, "Well, no, but I think my uncle did think about the restaurant for a while. It was too much trouble. The elevators, you see, the upkeep…" Her mind was not in the discussion or, he knew, she would have reacted differently.

"And London? Which hotel in London is yours?"

Live Monopoly. It was the craziest thing, marrying a dreamy-eyed girl for love, and then finding out she was a princess of Canadian society.

"None," he heard her say. "In London, truly none."

She eyed him speculatively. "But the idea is not bad. I wonder why we don't have one there? I'll have to ask Carl."

"You freak me out. You truly do. So what happens? We go to Toronto and you say to Carl, 'Listen, Jon asked about London, and hey, I think we should do it! Let's buy the Mandarin Oriental and call it Carlsson House'?"

"Well, not the Mandarin. That's too large for our concept. But, yes, that's how it would go."

"I give up." In desperation he threw up his hands and left the store to smoke a cigarette outside on the sidewalk.

He picked the subject up again when they were on their way back to Helen's. "And here? In New York?"

"A small house, near the Park, off Madison," she replied.

"What do you mean by a small house?" Jon asked and received another of those unwilling replies. "Small. Like the St. Regis."

"Small, Naomi?" he repeated stunned. "Small?"

It occurred to him that even though she never talked about it and professed to have no interest in the business at all, in truth, she knew everything about her family's properties.

"Paris Hilton is not so reticent about her heritage."

"She's blond and has nothing else to do. Me, I'm not going to spend my family's money if I'm not prepared to work for it, and since I don't want to, the whole thing is not my concern." She did not look at him. "Jon, you just don't know what you're talking about. You think it's glamorous and prestigious and it makes me into something more, or better, or whatever. But in reality, if I were to really take on that job, you would see almost nothing of me anymore. I would be traveling, visiting the different hotels, and I would have to spend a lot of time in Toronto." She smiled sadly at him. "I would have my own jet. No more cruising in rented planes. And I would probably have to move to Kleinburg. Stop talking about it already."

"You know," he commented after a long while, "You are like a gift wrapped in many layers of tissue. I get a glimpse of what's inside when I remove one. Every time I peel one off, I see something new, something that was hidden before, but the whole thing is still a mystery."

Naomi did not respond. For the time it took the car to cross the river and make its way along the promenade to Helen's house, she remained silent and thoughtful. When they stopped, she said, "Jon. It's like this. There is this huge family business with all these obligations and responsibilities, and I've known all my life what was waiting for me once I was old enough. Everytime a boy approached me, I was never sure if he was seeing me, or my family's wealth. That is why, when we met, I was still a virgin. I know you wondered. Then you came into my life, and you loved me for me. You wanted me, and you never asked, you never gave a damn about where I had come from or who I was. For you, it was only me, Naomi. You took me with you to Los Angeles, and you saw the songwriter in me, you valued me for my lyrics, not for what came with me." She took his hand in hers. "When I followed you to Hollywood, I didn't know I would give it all up. I wasn't happy with what was planned for me, but I was prepared to take it on, after a time." She paused and smiled at him so sweetly it turned his heart over. "And then I realized I didn't want it at all. I wanted to be with you, and lead a life filled with music, and love, and laughter. I wanted it very much, Jon. I wanted to spend my life with the man who did not care at all who I was."

Jon had the weirdest sense of displacement, hearing the echo of his own words. "We are," he said with slow realization, "we are the same. We were both looking for the same thing, for the person who would love us for ourselves, who could see through the trappings and disregard them. You did not care one whit who I was, you treated me like any other man who wanted too much too fast. I loved you the moment I saw you."

She nodded gravely at him. "So you see, you may be a superstar, but you hold my love, if only for that one reason: because you wanted me for myself. Not Olaf Carlsson's daughter, not the hotel heiress, just me, Naomi."

It was so ridiculous in its own way, he laughed out loud.

"Seems to me we are well matched, then. Two neurotics who want nothing more than honesty, and here we are, killing ourselves with the fear of losing the other, when in truth each of us knows we really found what we were always looking for. I understand your reticence a lot better now, but Baby, it doesn't matter. Flaunt your hotels at me all you like. I know what's really important is you and me."

HE BEGGED HER to let him do it his way.

She was his wife, and he would not travel to her ancestral home as her entourage. It was his duty to provide for her, and he was proud to do it, to show her off to the world and show how well he cared for her.

Doing it his way meant picking up the phone and giving orders to the office in LA, she realized soon enough, and then expecting everything to be arranged exactly as he wished. There was no sense fighting it. What seemed like arrogance was only the visible part of his deep longing for privacy and security, and she had come to accept it.

"Your hatred of the world frightens me sometimes," Jon said when the plane taxied toward the runway. "Why don't you take what it offers you so generously, why don't you take what I offer?"

"You," Naomi said, taking the blanket the flight attendant held out to her, "are like a piece of forbidden candy. Sweet, colorful, juicy, expensive, and found only in the most exclusive stores. But you give girls a toothache just like any other piece of sugar."

"Tell me, Baby," Jon said after they had been served coffee and sandwiches, "tell me about yourself. We'll be in your hometown in a short while, and after all this time I still don't know who you are."

"What is it you want to hear? You know me better than anyone else."

"Except Sal, the bastard," he growled. "I recall you sitting with him in Geneva, and you shone like a star down there while I had to stand on the stage and do the soundcheck and couldn't be with you. He stared down your neckline the whole time, and I was in agony, fearing he would make a successful pass at you and I would be left with empty arms, would have to see you walk away with him and maybe even wave gracefully in my direction before he took you to his room, to his bed, whatever, had the chance to make you his before I even had kissed you again. And Baby, I was dying for that kiss. My lips were still tingling from that magic moment by the lakeside, and I wanted to find out very badly whether I had imagined it or if there was a true miracle happening there. I wanted to undo that outrageous braid of yours that stroked your breast with every move you made, and I wanted it to be me who opened your blouse to reveal those lovely, rosy mounds and taste that peachy skin." He reached for his coffee cup. "In that hallway, when you said those terrible words to me, God, how I wanted you. I wanted you right there against that wall. It nearly fried my brain. It's a good thing you were so reticent, or the couch in my dressing room might have been witness to that burning passion. And oh, what a pity that would have been, you being what you were, my sweet, sweet virgin, my wonder, my lovely revelation." Jon sighed and took her hands, "You taught me, Naomi, that true bliss is giving pleasure to someone you love, and not seeking release. I'm never as happy as when I see you smile for me."

She had to take a few minutes to digest his words before she could speak again.

"You always return to that day. You are such a hopeless romantic, and I marvel at what you saw in me. I was just a naïve young girl in jeans and a cotton blouse."

"You were the sweetest vision, my darling. You were like an answered prayer, shaped from the mist for me, only for me." He paused briefly as if diving back into his memories. "I know that's the reason I never really cared about your background. The gods sent you to me, and so I knew it was right, I knew you belonged with me and nowhere else, and that was it."

"Jon."

She turned his hands over in hers, his modest gold band glinting in the overhead lights of the jet, and kissed his palms tenderly. "It was the other way around, and it is too delicious to recall that moment, I know. It was you who had come across oceans and mountains to pick me up and take me away, my mystery man, finally in flesh and blood. The echo of my yearning dreams, the arms I had longed for in my empty bed without even knowing it, the kiss that woke me from my mindless innocence. You, on that stage, while I talked to Sal, you think I could have noticed any other? Sal had it right, you know. I did not even realize they were there. Your presence was so overpowering, you filled all my senses. I felt you close every moment."

He felt the light shiver running through her body, reliving that day.

"I wanted your touch. Your kiss. Your hands on my body, on my naked skin, opening me up, oh…I wanted to know how it would be to feel a man, suddenly I wanted it more than anything else. When you held me against that wall in the hallway I ached for you, I prayed for you to go on, to overwhelm me. At last I was ready for a man, and it had to be you. God, I wanted to see your body, even then I dreamed of opening those shirt buttons and running my fingers down your chest. But more than that, I wanted it to have meaning, be special, last forever. Not a quickie in the hallway. But later, the next night, I couldn't wait, I counted the hours and the minutes until that door closed behind us and I finally had you all alone, all mine. You were so beautiful, so sure of yourself, and then so surprised, and suddenly it seemed you were a different man, gentle and patient and mindful not to hurt me, and God, Jon, when I felt you pushing, so slowly, I wanted to die with pleasure."

The chime woke them from their memories.

Naomi made the driver take them the long way, following the Gardiner Expressway down along the lake toward downtown, and as always, her heart opened when the skyline spread out before them, the tower reaching toward the sky, the great stretch of water vanishing toward the horizon, and the many high-rise buildings glinting invitingly in the pale sunlight.

"Your hometown. And still I don't know much about your life here. Where was your school? Where did you play, and where did you go for ice cream with your girlfriends? Who stole your first kiss?"

Jon pointed to the arena where he had performed on his last tour through Canada, calling it an overheated monstrosity, but the people had been very kind and the audience extremely appreciative.

He did not tell her how he had walked those streets, alone, gazing into every woman's face that even faintly reminded him of her. How he had hoped to meet her here, in her hometown. He had been nearly desperate, but Toronto was a large city, and he had no idea where to look. His search had nearly driven Sal to a nervous breakdown.

"I was not here then," Naomi was saying softly. "I've not been here in a long, long time."

He knew this now, of course, but then he had not. He had imagined the crowd in one of the malls parting, revealing the one image he wanted to see so much: Naomi, unaware, moving toward him, and he would catch her, hold on to her and make sure she did not run, not until he had his answers. Or, a nightmare vision, her on the arm of a strange man, loving laughter in her face for someone else, happy, and he, just a forgotten image from a past she had long laid to rest, seeing him there amid the bustle and going past him without a second glance, recognizing but dismissing him completely, gone forever. The thought almost killed him even now.

"You searched for me. You thought you would find me here."

Jon turned his head away and pretended to watch the scenery, but she persevered. "Don't look away, you miserable man." She tugged at his jacket. "Speak to me. You did, didn't you? You crept through Toronto hoping you would run into me, guessing I would be here, with my family. Confess!"

Grudgingly, he nodded.

"Jon. Look at me."

"Baby, don't torture me like that. You know it. I wanted to know, I needed to find out what had happened to us. I wanted you back so badly. All the time, every day, each morning when I opened my eyes and late at night before I went to sleep. And yes, I hoped. Over the years we were here six times, and every time I looked down at the audience I hoped to see you. I wandered through the city and prayed to run into you. Here I had that hope, wild as it was. But I always came away with my arms and heart still empty."

She laid her arm around him and her head his shoulder.

THE CAR HAD left the city behind and passed through a rural area, deep in snow. The sky was dusky even though it was still early afternoon when they entered the small town of Kleinburg.

"Here?" Jon asked, impatient to see where she had grown up.

"Not much farther."

A cold tightness closed around her heart as they drew closer to the Carlsson property. She had been back a few of times—never for longer than three days—unable to bear the house or the feelings it brought back of that time when she had sought refuge here.

"You fled everything." Jon was gazing out of the car window. "My God, I made you run from every place you knew. I made you hide in a strange country, among strangers, pregnant with my baby. I made you face that all by yourself, and you, so young, so fragile."

They turned through a huge gate onto a narrow road that wound through a dense forest of snow-laden trees.

It occurred to him they had been driving for quite a while.

"Is this all your property?" Jon asked perplexed, "Where are we going?"

"We're here." Her voice sounded distant and tired.

The trees opened up to reveal a large park laid out in English fashion, expansive stretches of lawn interspersed with little copses, a fountain in the center of a circular planting, and behind it, fronted by a tiled driveway, a huge, three-storied manor.

"You're kidding me," Jon breathed. "Naomi? This is not a house. This…you grew up here?"

"We all did." She smiled unhappily. "It's been my family's home for two hundred years, more or less."

"Baby, your secrets are all so deep and well hidden. You drive me crazy, Naomi. I must be the stupidest man in the world, because even though I should know better by now, I still find the truth hard to accept."

"Then don't!" She grabbed his jacket and held him back as he started to climb out. "Please, Jon. Don't get out. Let's just turn back and go home and pretend it was only a joke! I don't need to be here, and I don't want you to change your perspective of me. Please."

"No, love." He shook his head at her. "The running days are over. For you, and for me, too. We are going to face this together, and you will show me the room where you slept after you left me, and we will explore every corner of this monstrosity together until all the ghosts are laid to rest."

The great winged door flew open to reveal Lucia and Olaf, beaming and waving, happy to see her again so soon, talking at the same time, embracing Naomi tightly and shaking hands with Jon.

"Jon, I'm overjoyed," Olaf said, "that you let her step back into the family. And in New York, you should reside in our hotel until your house is ready. There's a family suite there. I have never understood Naomi, insisting she prefers anonymous places, even in London."

"London, dear heart?" Jon murmured. "Didn't we talk about London? Monopoly again?"

"Well no," Olaf amended. "Not exactly London, but Oxfordshire. Only a small house."

"Haven't I heard those words before."

Naomi squirmed, but had the good sense not to speak up.

WANDERING THROUGH THE manor, he asked her how many people worked there for the family, but Naomi did not know.

And how many of her relatives lived here permanently?

Her uncle and his wife, their son with his family…there were not many left.

Her parents, when they chose to spend time here, and sometimes the Danish branch came to visit.

"All those youngsters at our wedding. Where did they come from? Why is it so important for you to take over the business? There seemed to be a lot of younger folks."

But not the direct line, she explained. Her family was very traditional in that. They liked everyone in the family to work in the business, but only direct descendants would inherit it, and that would be her and her Uncle Carl's son.

Naomi opened a door at the end of a narrow hallway on the third floor, far away from the bustle and the rest of the guests.

"Here."

It was secluded, a quiet room looking out over the park and the forest, with not much more than a big canopied bed, a wardrobe, desk, and chair. The floor was covered in a thick carpet, and on the bed was a quilt that looked well used and old. The en suite bathroom was small.

Jon tried to imagine it, Carl and his wife bringing Naomi here after her flight from LA. Helping her to climb out of her clothes and into bed, drawing the blue curtains to give her peace, letting her settle in.

She had slept, she told him as she stood by the window. She tried to drown in sleep, shocked and frightened, so lonely.

"You left me alone," he heard her say, and for the very first time there was a trace of accusation in her voice. "You left me, Jon. I was barely twenty-one, and I had only you in that crazy place, and you left me alone. I can't remember any other time in my life when I was that scared."

He felt something like elation at her tone. It was such a huge relief to see her angry at him at long last, to see her replace the grief with accusations. "Yes, I did. I left you alone in that house that night. I didn't even think about it. The party just followed me to jail."

Her hand tightened in the velvet curtain. "When we were in Geneva, before you left for Amsterdam, you promised you would take care of me if I came away with you. You promised I would never come to harm. But you broke your promise."

"Yes," he said again, "I know. I was stupid and thoughtless, and there is no way to excuse it."

"I never wanted to leave you."

Jon decided not to give her comfort this time.

"Your indifference nearly killed me."

This he could not let pass.

"I was never indifferent to you!" He took her shoulder to turn her around. "I was thoughtless, mindless, selfish, and arrogant, that I will accept. But Naomi, I was never indifferent."

"All those words are nothing but a circumspect way to say indifferent. Say what you like, but you had what you wanted. You were so secure in the knowledge that you had a sweet little toy, you could afford to be careless."

It was hard not to allow the hurt she was causing him to show in his expression, but he thought he succeeded rather well.

"You left me alone," she repeated. "And you will never be able to understand what it felt like to be all by myself in that house surrounded by the debris of the party and not have the faintest idea of how life was supposed to go on for me."

Impatiently she wiped the tears from her cheeks. "I felt betrayed. Why didn't you call Sal? Why didn't you think to have someone look after me?"

"Because," Jon said very deliberately, "I was drunk and drugged and I didn't give a damn about anything at all. I can't even recall worrying about you."

It was delivered without any emotion, cool and dry, and it made her catch her breath. He nodded. "Yes. I've been waiting for you to be angry at me for so long. It's about time you laid the blame on me. Now I feel a lot better. Go on; tell me how you really felt. I never believed all that stuff about me not being responsible for the misery of our lives."

They had been over it so often, but she had never thrown it at him like this.

"I hated you! Is that what you want to hear? I hated that I loved you, and I wanted to burn you out of my heart. I wanted the memory of you gone! I was furious at you for leaving me alone, not only that night, but all the time, treating me as if I were just another piece of furniture in that house of yours. Do you realize we only did things that you wanted to do? Didn't you see that it was you who always made the decisions? When you went to jail with the others, I finally found the strength to go, Jon."

She was magnificent in her anger, her fists balled at her sides and her eyes blazing, hair flying wildly with each movement. The words she was saying broke his heart, but he was ready to take them in and absorb them and help her find healing here, in the room where she had hidden from him.

"I came here, and I told my uncle I wanted to go to a place where you would never, ever find me. And I told my father to tell you, if you should come searching, that I was dead."

"Yes, Baby." He sighed bitterly. "And he did. Olaf seemed to find real joy in doing that."

This shook her out of her fury. "He had no right to say that to you."

Jon laughed despite the dire situation. He gazed out at the snowy stretch of lawn, trying to picture the house and the land around it in summer, or even in early fall, when the maple trees and oaks would be in flaming glory.

"My love. I didn't believe him. I knew you were alive. I'm sure I would have felt it if something had happened to you. I'm certain. You see, there would have been a lot less music in the spheres."

Speechless, she stared at him.

"And see where we are, Naomi," Jon said between the kisses he planted on her lips. "Everything is well, and there are no shadows left. I'll never let you go again, and I'll make very sure you won't want to. I promise, my love."

SAL CALLED. THEY were on the way, but this could not wait. It had happened, just as they had hoped. The movie soundtrack had received a Grammy nomination. Naomi could hear laughter and Solveigh's raised voice in the background.

"I suppose this means I have to take you out shopping again," he grumbled teasingly. "And that is such a chore, knowing how much you hate it. Maybe I'll just wrap you in a bedsheet for the Grammys. They look great on you, and they're cheap."

"But Jon. Doesn't it mean anything to you, a Grammy nomination, the whisper of Academy Awards?"

He dropped onto the bed and watched as she unpacked the glorious blue silk gown she had bought in New York and spread out the wide, billowing skirt. He could already see her dancing in it, the material swinging around her legs, her waist narrow and supple in his arm.

"Of course I'm pleased, Naomi, and you know why. We find each other, and even in the midst of all the turmoil of bringing our lives together, we are able to shape a grand a piece of songwriting. Proof that we belong together is what it is: we are surely meant for each other."

"You wrote superb songs with Sean. And I sincerely hope you did not have to…"

"Ah, watch what you're saying! Don't paint pictures no one wants to see!"

Shaking her head, she took her cosmetics into the bathroom.

"Tonight, sweet thing," he called after her, "tonight we'll be here in this bed! Here, where you tried to sleep me out of your memory, we're going to make new memories that will keep me forever in your mind and your heart."

He found he rather liked this simple room; it had the same quiet, withdrawn atmosphere of the apartment in Halmar. It came down to this, over and over again, the great mystery of her life and the way it had centered around him all the time, either with him or trying to let go of him.

"And Russ and Solveigh. I wonder. Have they set a date yet? Did she tell you where they want to get married? Just think, Russ getting married, and to a European, too! Incredible, the way our lives have changed, and all because of that letter! How I wish I could relive the day of that concert in London, only this time I would find you among the crowd." He folded his hands under his head.

"You are the most maudlin and sentimental man on Earth. You really like those bittersweet memories, don't you? You wallow in them."

She climbed up onto the bed, creeping up along and over his body, her hair falling forward over her shoulders, watched by Jon with growing excitement, but when he tried to reach for her, she pushed him down again.

"Gives me ideas," she whispered into his mouth, pulling back when he tried to kiss her, "Gives me strange, dark ideas of a strong man bound to my bed, forced to please me again and again."

Jon lay quite still and listened to her with an amused sparkle in his eyes.

"Yes," she continued softly, her fingers once more on the buttons of his shirt, "forced to please me."

Silent laughter rippled through him, but he did not move. Naomi had opened his shirt and was stroking his chest and the curly hair there. "Oh yes, mine, all mine."

He reached up to cup her breasts through her blouse. "Like apples, so smooth, so round and firm, delicious, sweet to the taste. Come here, Baby, come to me, let me free them from all these clothes." The amusement had vanished from his tone, replaced by the roughness of growing urgency, but she moved away deftly.

"No. We need to go down and greet our guests. No more play."

Quite easily he toppled her over and held her, kissing her deeply.

"God," he breathed, "the way I want you. Will it ever lessen I wonder, will this dire need ever pale? I could dive into you now just to hear you sigh, see the brightness in your eyes that tells me you want me just as much."

Naomi moved against him, on the verge of losing herself to him.

"And your lips, how am I supposed to refuse that invitation, how do you expect me not to kiss you? I can feel your blood boiling for my touch. My God, how do you expect me to rise and face the world, with you, here, softening in my embrace, willing, pleading for love?"

"Sal. Russ and Solveigh. Artie and Sue. At the door, in a few minutes."

He let her go unwillingly. "Why is it that you mention Sal first? Pure provocation, little beast."

For a moment, she couldn't move but simply lay there on her old quilt watching watched him button up his shirt and run his fingers through his hair.

"Now get up yourself," he ordered. "You are spread out there on that bed of laments like seduction poured out of a dream, and you expect me to be the cool-headed one? Pull down your skirt, comb your hair, and wipe that look off your face, or Sal will think it is meant for him!"

33

"SLAP ME SIDEWAYS till I cry," was Art's comment when the car left the forest and the vista of the house and park opened before them. The windows were lit, the Christmas decorations around the fountain illuminated, and the door was ajar to welcome them.

Sal was not overly surprised. The size of the house was more than he had calculated, but not by much. A wonder, he pondered idly, she did not act like more of a society girl. He recalled their conversation that day in Geneva while Jon was doing the soundcheck, glaring at them from the stage. Even then there had been the sleekness of wealth and good grooming about her, the ease of a cosmopolitan. She had been reticent and a little doubtful, visibly shaken by the impact of her encounter with Jon, but never frightened by the circus around him.

And here she was now, his best friend's wife, stepping out onto the broad stairs, waving and laughing, clearly happy to see them. The image was ruined for him when Jon came up behind her.

"Good God," Art sighed. "Isn't this as it should be? Don't they look like the lord and lady of the manor?"

"Yeah, he would like that," Sal grumbled evilly. "Bastard. Lording it over the Canadian peasants, striding over his acres of land in the morning light and accepting the homage of his adoring subjects."

Solveigh and Sue giggled as the limousine stopped in front of the entrance.

"Riding a huge, white horse, probably," Sal went on in a sepulchral voice. "Riding crop in his fist, the poor sods groveling and kissing his highly polished boots as he distributes advice and bread. And yeah! The buxom maidens running from harvesting the maple sap to offer themselves up to the charismatic leader…"

Jon pulled the car door open. "Welcome to the land of maple trees and pretty girls," he said, and drew back in surprise when Solveigh and Sue broke down in hysterical laughter.

Sal looked past him at Naomi. He wondered briefly whether it had been a mistake to come here and see her in this setting where she belonged; she looked so contained and serene.

"Welcome." She hugged him briefly and kissed his cheek, allowing him to inhale the flowery perfume he always associated with her alone, and hold her close for a precious instant before she was gone again.

The flight had been worth it, seeing her in that red dress he liked so much, her hair flowing in the cold Canadian wind, and with the prospect of New Year's Eve and dancing with her. Surely she would not deny him a dance.

They had been given wonderful rooms overlooking the park, with the offer to have their evening clothes pressed and a snack if they were hungry, but he had declined, needing a moment to collect himself before he changed for the night.

SAL NOTICED WITH interest that there was little difference between this and a grand affair in Hollywood. There was a live band, huge buffet, opulent flowers and a host of service personnel. He stood at the bar in the great hall, drink in hand, and watched the guests arrive. All of them were very well-dressed, the women in lovely gowns, the men in tuxes.

Olaf paused near him for a moment and snatched a glass from a passing waiter. "We do this every year. It's nice to see this old house in its glory. This is how it is supposed to look, and it was my deep wish that with Naomi the family would bloom. But now…" He downed the martini. "Now it seems it will be going to the dogs. Her cousin, God help me, is a stupid, arrogant asshole who cares more for his bloody Polo ponies than the business, and his wife, the lovely Rita, knows the fashion stores better than her home." Morosely he glared at the flowers on the table. "Naomi, she received all the careful grooming and education. We had a prospective husband chosen for her, someone who would understand our ways and support her in her profession, but, well, things went differently."

Sal was scandalized. "Is this how things are done here? You choose partners for your children? You tell them what they are supposed to do with their lives?"

Olaf glanced at his watch, an expensive gold piece. "Yes, well. We try to keep things together and pass it on to our heirs, just the way it has been done for generations. Now, with Naomi out of the picture, there is the danger that it will fall apart."

"Surely you know," Sal replied, piqued into defensiveness, "how good she is as a songwriter? She told you, didn't she, that she's been nominated for a Grammy?"

"A Grammy?" Olaf repeated derisively, "What's a Grammy?"

"It's…" Sal sighed in resignation. "Probably not important to you."

"It's the least that husband of hers can do for her after she's thrown herself away for him." A spark of anger marred Olaf's civil appearance. "My daughter, married to a bloody American showman. It's impossible." He wandered away.

Sal stared after him.

"Oh, good grief," Art said from behind him, "Look at that. The queen and her superstar. They sure know how to make an entrance, don't they?"

"I don't think it's intentional. She just looks like that." He did not want to turn around, afraid to see her in glory again.

"Right." Art barked a dry, ironic laugh and slapped Sal on the back. "You are one besotted idiot, Sal. Snap out of it!"

They were coming down the broad stairs together, Naomi's arm hooked through Jon's, and she was laughing at something he had said to her.

In the blue ballgown, her hair done up with the ends bouncing in curls around her shoulders, she seemed radiant in a manner he had not seen before. It was as if she had settled into herself and their new life, and allowed herself happiness at last. The dress was beautiful and hung well on her, accentuating her bare shoulders and neckline.

The band stopped their muted playing when Carl stepped up to the microphone to welcome his guests and open the ball.

"Who are we seeing here?" Jon asked, returning to Sal when Carl took Naomi away to meet people, but received only a shrug as answer.

"All Canadians. So no one important." Art grinned cynically.

"Isn't that the mayor of Toronto?" Jon pointed out a man about their age with reddish, graying hair and a short, sturdy figure. "I remember him from our last visit. He came backstage, didn't he?"

"Is he still the mayor?" Sal enquired. "My, but you have a good memory, Jon!"

Jon waved him away and explained that he had been very friendly and interested and had confided he was a great fan.

He was busy watching Naomi make her way through the room and greet the guests, stopping to talk for a few minutes sometimes, her gown gleaming like a beacon. She seemed familiar with most of them and was welcomed by all with surprise and enthusiasm, some even with an embrace and a kiss. From time to time she turned and smiled at him, assuring herself he was close.

"You look like a band of spies," Sue said, "Like James Bond times three on enemy territory, checking out the bad guys."

"And how do you know," Jon growled, "we aren't the bad guys?"

"Aw, Jon." Sue laughed at him. "No one in the whole wide world would buy that. Give up that illusion right now, my friend."

"Strange." He sighed. "Someone in New York said much the same to me the other day. Oh well."

CARL COULD NOT find any faults in his niece's American husband. His behavior was as impeccable as his clothes, and an accomplished dancer who had the good manners to ask his wife's mother for a slow waltz.

"You are biased," he said to Olaf when he caught him watching her dance with Jon. "You are still prejudiced, despite what you see with your own eyes. You gave her away to him, Olaf, and told her to be happy. Now she is, and to such a degree that she can return here and into society, and still you are not pleased. In all those years she never came here, and now, married, she does."

Olaf grunted in reply but folded his arms defiantly.

"Olaf," Carl pressed, "give in. Make peace with yourself and with your daughter. No amount of money is worth that. Here is the chance to bring her back into the family, and you are wasting it with your pride."

He paused to observe the dancers, Naomi secure in Jon's arm, holding her skirt with one hand to prevent stepping on it, the silk swaying around her.

"It's not pride, and you know it. It is a waste, a terrible, senseless waste, to see her like this, when she should be living here, running the business, at her age, and married to Seth." Olaf gave his brother a cold stare when Carl touched his shoulder.

"Please! You know as well as I do she would never have married him. I mean, look at him, Olaf, and then look at Jon! Plans are just that Olaf, and they get upset by life!"

"Goddamit all, Carl," Olaf hissed through his teeth, "Don't give me that sentimental crap! She preferred marrying into show business to doing the right thing."

"She preferred," Carl said quietly, "hiding in Halmar for half her life to living without him, Olaf."

He turned toward the waitress, but his glance fell on Lucia, who had been listening to them silently, gazing at her husband thoughtfully, leaning back in her chair as if she wanted to put distance between them.

SHORTLY BEFORE THEY went downstairs for the ball, Naomi handed Jon a battered red folder and a photo album.

This room, Naomi disclosed, was where she had grown up. He would be sleeping in her childhood bed, under her old quilt. There were no more mysteries, and nothing much had changed.

In the folder were her tentative first tries at rhyming, short, rugged lyrics lacking the fluid elegance of her later writing. The album was filled with pictures of a little girl in pigtails and a young teenager with the ubiquitous braid, riding, with friends, in a school uniform with a pleated skirt and dark blue jacket, and out on the terrace at the back of the manor, lounging on a deck chair in a bikini, staring insolently at the photographer over the rim her sunglasses, a fashion magazine on her knees, maybe fifteen.

"Ah," Jon had breathed, gazing at the snapshot, "Good thing I didn't meet you then. I would have gone to jail. No way would I have been able to keep away from you, dear heart. I would have snatched you up so fast. Look at the expression on your face! If that isn't provocative I don't know what is. Who took this picture?"

She said she couldn't remember, but he didn't believe it for a moment and made a mental note to find out. He wanted to know who had been worthy of such a sultry look. He found it difficult to tear himself away from the vision of that young, lithesome body stretched out in the sun.

Fifteen, which would have made him twenty-two, the year he had moved out to LA. He would have fallen like a star from the sky for that girl. He would have ruined his career for her, just to get that kind of glance. She was perfection, and totally unconscious of it, which made the picture so much stronger. That braid, and the way it hung over her shoulder and breast, literally forcing the eye to follow its trail and consequently stare at the soft skin of her cleavage and the swell covered by the scanty red top, the long, shapely legs crossed at the ankles, toenails painted pink, waiting to be touched.

"Stop staring," Naomi had said sternly and taken the album away from him. "You child molester. Give it back."

He had done it unwillingly, firmly resolved to get a copy of that photo for his studio.

"You looked just like that when we met. You still look like that."

"Hopefully not." Naomi had put the book back in its drawer.

As a child, she had looked just the way he had imagined her: sweet, joyful, without a care in the world, cherished.

This was all, she had informed him, that was left of her here in Kleinburg. Maybe, if he felt like it, they could raid the attic like they had done in Helen's house, but there were no stage shirts hidden away here.

THE CLOCK CHIMED in the New Year.

The big doors were thrown open and the fireworks began. Most of the guests streamed outside to watch the spectacle, but Naomi shook her head. "Go. I don't care for the cold."

Sal remained behind too. For a few moments they sat silently side by side, listening to the sounds from outside.

Sal cleared his throat. "I'm a curious old shark, as you know, Baby Girl, and I really would like to know."

Naomi raised her head to him, her hands folded over her skirt. "What, Sal?"

"The man you were supposed to marry. The one your family wanted you to marry. Is he here tonight? I would really like to know who they picked for you." He grinned at her. "Just curiosity. And maybe comparing him to who you chose yourself will be fun."

She glared viciously at him and turned her head to where Jon was returning from outside in the company of Toronto's mayor, talking to him.

"No." Sal leaned forward so she could not avoid him. "Tell me it's a joke. Please, I beg you, Naomi; you know you will never live this down. Tell me you're kidding!"

"I hate you," she hissed, flustered now. "Go away. Inviting you of all people to come here was the worst mistake of my life."

Jon tried to introduce the mayor, but Naomi interrupted him.

"Hello, Seth."

"Naomi, dear," Seth bowed slightly to her. "Haven't seen you around in a long time. Married, are you?"

With interest, Jon watched the slow blush creep up on her face and Sal's wide smirk and wondered what they had been talking about in the short time he had been gone. He had the impression she was extremely uncomfortable, and furious at Sal.

"Yes." It came unwillingly and with lowered eyes.

"Why don't you sit with us for a moment," Sal said, patting the chair beside him. "I recall you were very kind to us when we were here for a concert some years ago."

Naomi, her lips clamped together tightly, listened to them talking about when the band had passed through, but she refused to take any part in the conversation, only glaring at Sal from time to time.

"Naomi and I, we were nearly engaged for a brief while. Did she tell you? But we were very young and she preferred to go to Europe with her parents." Seth raised his glass to her. "There was the understanding that she would return in a couple of years or so and become my wife. Only she vanished."

"Ah." Mirth twinkled in Sal's in his eyes.

"Understanding?" Jon asked. "Really?"

"Well, yes." Seth did not seem very concerned. "But not to worry; I've overcome my broken heart." He eyed Naomi with appreciation. "I always had the feeling she was aiming for something more spectacular. She had that air of extravagance."

"That is so not true." Naomi's anger was barely contained. "And you know it, Seth."

"I know you never thought I was good enough for you," he replied. "You never wanted to marry me anyway."

"And that's not true, either." She rose and shook out her skirt. "I'm leaving now. I hate being talked about like this, and if you want to go on, do it without me."

"Hey, which part of that is not true?" Sal called after her, but she made her way across the hall and up the stairs without looking back.

SHE WAS IN bed when Jon entered the room a good while later. He turned on the bedside lamp, but she pulled the blanket over her head. "I'm not going to talk to you. You'll imagine all kinds of weird things, and I'm not going to start the New Year with a hateful discussion."

"Who said anything about a discussion?" he asked softly, highly amused by her angry defiance. "All I want to know is this, dear heart: did the extraordinary Seth take that picture of you in the red bikini? Did he receive that impossible look from you?"

Furiously, she threw back the quilt and glared at him. "You! You only have one thing on your mind, all the time!"

"Well, did he or didn't he? Come on, sweet bird, spill your secret!"

He took off his jacket and pulled the tie open, moving through the room noiselessly.

Naomi sat up and leaned against the headboard, her mind gradually calming as she watched him. Whistling under his breath, Jon hung up the dress she had dropped on the chair.

"It was Seth, yes. And it was the summer before I turned sixteen."

That day, it had been hot and humid like it often was in July. School had ended for the year and the vista of long, lazy weeks stretched out ahead of her. She had put on that bikini and flounced out onto the lawn with her mother's *Vogue* to find some peace. It had irritated her that the color of her nail polish did not match her bathing suit, but she hadn't had the energy to change it.

The magazine had been boring; there wasn't even a crossword puzzle in it, and nothing captivating about new music or books either. Seth had shown up unannounced in the middle of the afternoon. His father was a high-profile lawyer in Toronto and owned a big firm; in fact he and his associates were retained by her family, and that was why everyone was looking to their possible union with so much favor.

"They never said it directly. But it was always, 'Oh, look, Seth is here; Naomi, why don't you go riding with Seth; oh, maybe Seth would like to see that movie, too'." She paused and shook her head. "I was sixteen, for crying out loud. I didn't even know what my favorite color was, and my family was pushing a future husband in my face."

"And how old was he?" Jon asked without looking at her, busy peeling off his shirt.

There were special, small things that were terribly arousing, like the smooth way the muscles in his shoulders moved when he undressed, or the way the hair on his chest tapered to a fine line over the taut stretch of his stomach. She felt quite warm under the quilt and moved her legs restlessly, which made Jon raise his eyebrows and shoot her an amused, sidelong glance.

"Easy, Baby. You know what happens when you get too excited. It'll be over in a minute, and who wants that?"

But he did turn to face her when his hands reached for his belt, feet well apart and hips thrust forward, unconscious of his very male, aggressive stance.

Naomi felt her heart hammering furiously and sweat prickling between her shoulder blades.

"So how old was your suitor?" Jon repeated.

"Back then? Twenty-four. He was working on his law degree."

She wanted him. She wanted the talk to end and to be in his arms.

"Patience, little beast. First, I want to know. They left you alone with a man of twenty-four? You, looking like that, on the verge of becoming a woman, the essence of seduction, and they handed you over to Seth?"

The trousers came down.

"Come on, tell me. Was it Seth who took that photo? Or someone else?"

"It was Seth. He was nice. I liked him, he was like a big brother. He used to buy ice cream for me and take me riding."

"But," delivered in the voice that reminded her of dark, melted chocolate, "you didn't desire him, right? You didn't feel like you're feeling now, right, Baby?"

He came over to her and wrapped her hair around his hand, talking into her mouth. "You didn't crave him, the way you do right now, with me, right? You weren't willing to plead with him to stop the talk and not wait any longer."

Her mind was racing with lust when he laid her out on the sheets, his fingers expertly opening the ribbons on her thin muslin nightgown.

"And I bet when he saw you poured out like that in your sweet little bikini, he wanted very badly to find out what you were hiding."

His hands slid lower on her body, over her hips and thighs.

"He wanted it more than anything else, I'm sure. And he'll never get it. Never. No other man will ever find out how it is to hold you, not Seth, not Sal. No one will ever feel the passion of your love."

"AND NOW," JON said a lot later, freeing himself from her embrace, "now that picture belongs to me. I'm going to take it away from you and pretend you were searching for me even then. That gaze can only have been meant for me."

She watched him remove the album from the drawer, and the folder with her early lyrics as well, and stow them away in his suitcase. She did not demur.

35

SAL WAS WAITING for them at the airport with the limo; sunglasses pushed up on his head, tanned and very relaxed. "Welcome back to LA," he said, grinning broadly at Naomi's warm sweater. "You won't need that here, you silly Scandinavian."

The sunlight was blinding, and the sun-soaked air felt like warm oil against her winter-parched skin. She felt like she could just strip off her clothes and lie down on the tarmac, limbs spread wide, and drink in this flood of spring and ease her tired muscles after the long flight and their final weeks in the cold of Norway.

Against Sal's protest she had opened the car windows to let in the soft air, waving away Jon's dry comment that she might as well hang her head out the window like a dog, but please keep her tongue in. He was pleased to see her delight in the weather and her easy, playful mood.

Sue and Art had moved out of the Malibu mansion. The house was still and empty, spotlessly clean, as pristine as if it had never been touched by others. The studio was once more a working space, even if it was still missing Jon's personal things. In their bathroom, everything was white. Towels, rugs and shower curtains were all brand new, there was lavender and rose soap in the dishes, bath oil on the corner of the tub. Jon looked over her shoulder for a moment.

"Here." He stepped inside, laying the hair clip on the side of the sink, right where he had picked it up that morning. "I'm returning it to you now that you've come back to me."

Naomi stared at the cheap old thing, a smudge in the virginal space, surprised he had kept it all this time.

"No," Jon said. "Don't say it. Don't tell me you're sorry. Tell me you love me. Tell me you'll never leave me again. Those are the words I want to hear."

Their bedroom looked just like it had last summer, with flowers on the table and a choice of drinks on the cupboard, the cream quilt folded over the bed, gossamer lace curtains blowing lazily in the breeze.

"I'll never leave you."

Her voice drifted toward him from where she was standing on the roof garden, looking out over the glittering sea. She had begun opening her braid and combing through her hair with her fingers, the wind catching tendrils away from her and curling them around her face.

"I'll always love you."

Those were the promises he needed to hear, over and over again, to drown out the constant fear.

"I never stopped loving you," Naomi said, stepping back inside. "And you know it. I would certainly not be here now if it weren't for my love of you. In that, nothing has changed. California without you was never on my agenda."

"Falling so madly in love while on tour in Europe wasn't on mine," came his quick reply. "And I know you are doing things you vowed never to do again, like being here with me in Los Angeles. I know I promised you would never have to come back, and that I would stay with you in Halmar always. You never wanted to set foot in this house again, and yet we are going to live here once more. I know, Naomi, what you are doing. Don't think I haven't noticed."

Slowly she sat down on the edge of the bed. His tone was so sincere and heartfelt, there was neither the lover's charm nor the tenderness of their more intimate moments in it.

Jon stood in the center of the large room as if it were his stage.

"We've never really talked about it, I know what it means that you consent to be here with me, to leave your old life behind like that. Even when you came here with us last summer I knew what it meant for you, and now, here, preparing for the tour, it is even more."

"As if I had a choice. As if there were an alternative for me."

A furrow appeared on his brow. "You might have," Jon offered pensively, "stayed behind. You knew I would return to you. You could join us for the kick-off in London. I would come over to see you as often as I could, Naomi."

She was unbuttoning the cotton top, revealing a lacy bra underneath.

"No, there would be little fun in that. Now that I have you back, I don't want to be apart from you again. And so," she looked up at him with a tiny smile, "and so I'm afraid you will have to lug me around with you wherever you go."

He went for her then.

"I would have," he whispered to her later, "I would have taken you off that deck chair so quickly. Your stupid magazine and those sunglasses, they would have ended up on the ground, and you, my sensuous hussy, would have found yourself on a bed of leaves under those maple trees and learned soon enough why you are not supposed to look at men like that. Sweet sixteen, and I would have robbed you of your innocence on that hot afternoon. Oh yes, Baby, I would not have waited for an invitation."

Naomi was lying on her side, listening to him with half-closed eyes, the setting sun casting a coppery glow on her skin, her hand under her cheek.

"Had you come across the lawn that day instead of Seth, I would have taken off that top myself to seduce you. I would have made you follow me into the woods and found a hidden place for us. I would have had you, lover boy." A dreamy smile curled her lips. "I would not have waited for you to start your seduction routine. You would have been mine right away."

"And yet." His hand wandered over her hip in a slow caress. "You told me—oh those bitter, bitter words—that's not how it works, when I had the first chance with you. Eternal regret, I hold that moment in my mind in eternal regret."

"You are such a wimp."

Her body stretched under his touch.

"You had the choice to ignore those words, and you didn't. You opted for suffering and waiting, remember? You chose to obey. Your doom, lover boy, because it showed me your weak spot."

"I have a weak spot?" His grip tightened considerably. With one deft move he had her flat on her back. "Really, a weak spot. Now I need to know what that might be."

A slow, hot flush crept over her throat and face as she tried to reach his lips for a kiss, but he drew back just far enough so she could not touch him.

"Your weak spot," she managed breathlessly, "is your love for romance. And I gave you romance by putting you down and making you wait. There."

NAOMI BARELY LOOKED up from where she was lounging on the couch when Sal and Art walked in the next morning.

Sal stopped to stare down at her. "Well, are you ready to step out into the public eye next week? You know you can't hide here any longer."

She did not reply.

"And do you have a proper gown?" Sal went on, ignoring her cool silence. "You know you can't show up in one of your cotton thingies on the red carpet."

He eyed her suspiciously when she did not reply and only held out her cup to Jon to get it refilled.

"You know how important it is how you look, don't you? They'll see you not only as a nominee, but also…"

"Yes, I know." She held up her hand wearily. "As his wife. Don't I know it. Shut up, Sal."

"You did not answer my question. What are you going to wear? I'm your manager, and you pay me a lot of money to push you."

"I pay you a lot to look after my interests, Sal."

He opened his mouth to snap a sharp reply but drew back when Jon shot him a glance.

The room had not changed much since Art and Sue had lived here, and yet it was completely different. Sue had allowed the comfortable, slightly negligent atmosphere of a well-used house, but Naomi kept it airy, the surfaces cleared and clean, spare in the graceful Scandinavian manner. The flowers on the table were pale roses, the cushions on the couch had been replaced, no longer a mixture of colors and shapes but cream and very light green against the beige leather.

"I know where I want to go," Naomi was saying, but not to him. "And I'll do it tomorrow. Alone, sadly, since Solveigh can't seem to find the energy."

"Right, Babe," Jon replied without even looking her way.

Sal was on the point of intervening, fear for her safety surfacing, when he saw her pick up the phone and instruct her new bodyguard, Stewart, ending with, "I'll be ready by ten, and I don't know how long it will take. Better plan on the day."

"You'll be getting a lot of attention, for a number of reasons, so get used to it. You know you will have to look and act your best. No mumbling, and no hiding behind the Jonman. Dress up, look sharp, dazzle the world. I know you can do it!" Sal said.

"I don't have to do any of those things, Sal, if I don't want to. I can choose to put on a simple black silk suit and stand beside Jon and smile, and no one would give a damn. No one can force me to even accept a Grammy. Leave me alone."

"You—" he started, but now Jon interfered.

"Sal, it's okay." He offered him a coffee. "Don't fuss."

"Why is this so important, Sal?" Naomi asked, sitting up finally to face him. "I've done almost everything you wanted. I wrote the lyrics for the soundtrack, I came back here last summer for the recording session, and now I'm here, am I not, because of the stupid Grammy? It's only a useless statue, for heaven's sake, one more thing to dust!"

She did not see Jon draw his shoulders together, standing behind her with his back turned, but Sal did. Her easy dismissal of the award had touched a nerve, but there was no reaction from Jon toward her.

"It doesn't mean anything to me." She reached out to touch Jon's arm as he leaned over to give Art his coffee. "I know that it's important for Jon. But for me, there are things that count a lot more."

Gentler, smiling at her husband so sweetly it nearly broke Sal's heart, she added, "That's why I'm here, Sal. Not for the Grammy, not for a possible Oscar, but because of him."

"Oh for God's sake," Sal murmured.

"And for him, never fear, I'll dazzle the world. I would never demean him by showing up in anything but the best. You can stop the arguing already."

Sal caught the serene expression on Jon's face and decided to call it a day.

SHE FELT RIDICULOUS and completely out of place in the huge, silent car as Stewart drove through the town. Over breakfast a short discussion had ensued, and with a phrase he used unconsciously, Naomi understood that at least half of Jon's concern was not for her safety but also that she would feel at ease in LA. Curiously enough, this strengthened her resolve to go out on her own. She had to prove to herself and to him that she could survive quite well here without his protection and without Solveigh or Sal in attendance.

"Don't be afraid," she said to him before she left. "I lived alone for so long, I think I can survive a shopping trip."

"You know that's not how this is done." Jon had followed her outside to where Stewart was waiting beside the brand-new Rolls. "You are going to get a gown for an official event, you should be taking your manager, your assistant, your best friend to hold your purse while you try on dresses. Then have lunch at a chic place and let yourself be photographed by at least a dozen paparazzi, and later throw a fit because you weren't wearing any makeup and your hair wasn't right, and because you were seen eating real food! Ah, and you need one of those ugly little dogs that can be carried around in a pink purse!"

She had only huffed in reply, which had made him laugh. But he won, at least, her promise to meet him for lunch.

HARRY'S WIFE HAD recommended a Lebanese designer to Naomi. He was, she had said, relatively unknown, his store not in the most fashionable part of town, but he had an extravagant flair that might appeal to her.

Naomi, stepping into the cool, plush interior of the shop, realized she had come to the right place. She knew Solveigh liked to call her a drama queen, and here was a heaven where she could play out that role. She regretted being alone now; the choice was so great, and each dress was more beautiful than the last. When the manager asked her when and where she was going to wear it, she took a long time replying.

At last she gave in. "To the Grammys."

The man nodded, his lips pursed. His name, he told her, was Jamal. He came from Beirut himself, and the designer was his cousin. Quite candidly he added that he had no idea who she was, but he wished her to look better than any other woman, and if she would allow him to advise her...

There was a white dress with gold embroidery that Naomi liked a lot. Jamal nodded, but took it from her again. "It would look wonderful on you. And maybe you want to buy it for some other occasion, but not for the Grammy. You want to stand out. Here." He picked a flaming red silk gown with a flaring, ruffled skirt. "Wear this, and you will stand alone. And get your hair cut."

Scandalized, Naomi opened her mouth to protest, but he shook his head.

"Not short, but just so it reaches your shoulder blades. Get it layered and wear it loose. Get rid of that braid. You are too old and too young for it."

She accepted the fragrant mocha he offered her, and the oriental pastries, and sat on the couch while he showed her more gowns, shawls, exquisitely embroidered jackets, and little evening purses she could dangle from her wrist. A couple of times Jamal glanced toward the waiting car outside and Stewart, who had taken up his position beside the door.

"Will you be going to the Oscars as well?" When she nodded reluctantly, he said, "Then you can wear the white and gold."

But Naomi had her own ideas. Did his cousin, she asked, come to LA from time to time? She had something in mind. She wanted a dress made especially for her.

Jamal sat, his legs crossed elegantly, and regarded her over the rim of his dainty cup for a while. A faint scent of patchouli intermingled with the cardamom aroma of their coffee, the light from the heavy crystal chandeliers reflecting lazily on the polished surface of the small glass table between them. "You are going as a guest to the Grammy?" It was asked as circumspectly as he could without being outright rude.

"Yes and no."

He waited politely.

"I'm a nominee."

"A nominee for the Grammy? Then I have to ask. Who are you? Which song?"

"With my husband. My husband is the composer."

She had no idea why she was telling this dark-skinned stranger about herself at all. He was watching her acutely with his velvety Mediterranean eyes, toying with the tiny silver spoon he had used to stir his coffee.

"What did you have in mind for the Oscars?" Jamal asked, and as she told him, his face lit up in mischievous joy.

"Yes. I can see that. I can see my cousin beaming with delight already. Drink another coffee. I will call Sayed now."

There was a dark green gown she had been eyeing during their conversation, the brocade skirt interwoven with gold threads and embroidered with pearls along the hem, a gown for a harem princess. She was turning in front of the large mirrors in it, a couple of shop assistants tugging the rich folds into order, when Jamal returned and stopped, looking at her with appreciation.

"My cousin, the designer, will be here next week. If it pleases you, he will see you right after the Grammys."

In the end Naomi bought more than the three gowns. She felt wonderful in the precious materials, the luscious colors, the rich decorations, every pearl and thread applied by hand, Jamal told her, in a small village in the mountains of Lebanon, high up where the famous cedars grew and snow fell in winter.

"The red dress," Jamal said as she pulled out her credit card, "I'm giving to you. You will be asked which designer you are wearing, and we would be proud if that name is ours."

36

NAOMI HAD ALWAYS stood to the side with Sal while Jon walked the red carpet, fielding questions and posing for pictures, but this time, her hand firmly in his, she was by his side, aides around her telling her where to stand and where to look, directing the questions put to her, indicating when she could move inside for a pause before the presentations began.

Solveigh never left her side. When Naomi was separated from Jon, who had to give an exclusive interview to a magazine, Solveigh whispered, "Powder room. Blessed silence."

But when they made their way in the door, they discovered nearly every other woman attending was already there, putting finishing touches on impeccable makeup and hair that seemed plastered into place.

Around them were many famous faces, female singers and musicians who had been nominated, which made her realize she had not bothered to ask who her rivals were, or if there would be anyone performing their song tonight. She was certain Jon knew every detail of the evening's program, that he and Art had left nothing to chance and he had not involved her to take some of the pressure off her, but she saw she was laying a burden on him that he did not deserve.

She rose from her comfortable nook and straightened her skirt.

"I'm going to join Jon," she informed Solveigh, who pulled up her eyebrows in surprise. "He shouldn't have to do everything alone."

She had seen him like this before, alone on a couch, speaking to the reporters in his slow growl, reacting only to the questions he wanted to answer and simply ignoring the others, so cool, so intimidating, exquisitely polite and charming, yet distant and curiously unapproachable.

He saw her even though she was standing in the shadows, and gave her a small, quick smile before he returned his attention to the reporter's questions.

He seemed so isolated, facing the world on his own terms. His bodyguards stood in the background; his manager and his producer, listening to the interminable requests, monitored the procedures while he stood in the limelight, but he was out there alone.

She moved forward, head held high, and Jon, forgetting what he had been about to say, jumped up and took a step toward her.

She sat down beside him, her hands folded neatly in her lap, and smiled brightly into the camera.

Later, when their names were called, she strode up to the stage with him, accepted the award, kissed the presenter on his cheek, and spoke a brief but very polite greeting into the microphone before dropping into her chair again and taking the offered champagne from Sean, her hand still shaking but firmly clasped around the little statue.

THREE DAYS AFTER the Grammys, the glamour and glitz seemed like a distant memory. Jon greeted Sal at the door with the dour words, "Leave me alone. Bother Naomi if you need someone to talk to. I'm working," and left him standing there in the entrance while he retreated to his studio, uncombed, unshaven, in run-down loafers, a cigarette between his lips, and squinting malevolently through his glasses at their manager.

Sal found Naomi in the kitchen with her blouse untucked, her jeans rolled up, and her hair still wet from the shower, padding around barefoot on the tile floor. Their recent Grammy was sitting ignored on the kitchen counter.

Sal glared at her.

"What's wrong with you people?" Sal asked, taking a steaming mug from her. "Your husband slouches through the house like a bum, you leave your award sitting in the kitchen, and here I am with your tickets for the Oscars and all you can do is shrug your shoulders?"

Unbelievably, she really shrugged, setting a ham sandwich down in front of him. "We knew, right? We've known for quite a while. The question is, are we going to need those tickets, or are we going to sit up front with the other nominees?" A pensive look crossed her face. "I hope so for Jon, I think he wants it a lot."

"Of course he does, you stupid woman!" Sal cried. "Who wouldn't, except maybe for you?"

Again the shrug. He wondered how Jon dealt with the cool dismissal and the blatant provocation she could express with that one small gesture.

"And your man?" The sandwich was delicious, plastered liberally with mayonnaise. "What's he up to today?"

"Don't know exactly." Naomi planted herself on the kitchen counter, her feet dangling next to his knees. "I think he woke up with a new tune in his head and felt the need to try it out."

"Aha." Sal had run out of words for once.

The serenity was almost too much for him. It was a much better defense than her withdrawal or anger.

"If you like," Naomi suggested, "we could take a walk on the beach. I've not been out yet today, and it's such a lovely morning."

He followed her and waited on the porch while she went into the studio to tell Jon. Another thing he would never have dared to do—intrude on him when he was working—having learned quite early in their career that Jon hated nothing more than being interrupted when he was composing. But he heard Jon laugh at something she said, a few bars of music from the piano and a brief, derisive comment from her, an outraged cry from Jon, followed by more laughter from both, and something that sounded suspiciously like a slap on a female rump.

"Take Stewart, Babe," Jon called after her before she closed the door again. "Don't go alone!"

"I'm taking Sal. He should be good enough."

The beach was quiet and empty, impressive waves thundering on the wet sand before dying in sizzling foam at their feet. Overhead, the sky had the pastel tint of clear air, the breeze quite tart, reminding them that it was still only February.

"I used to imagine," Naomi said, looking back toward the house, "that the sky was a big bowl covering the West Coast, encapsulating every acre west of the Rockies. Every time I come here it feels as if I'm leaving Earth and going to a different planet altogether. Why is life so different here, Sal?"

She picked through the debris, collecting stones again, wiping them on the hem of her shirt only to toss most of them back into the sea.

"Life here is soft and warm, but treacherous, like a bog. As long as you're young, successful, and famous everyone is your friend. If your star sinks, you can clean their toilets again. It's all about fame, Sal, and how often your face is on the billboards or in the tabloids."

Sal held out a flat pink shell to her and she took it from his hand, scrutinizing it closely before cleaning it.

"To some, it means everything. Did you see your designer yet?"

She had, she told him, and yes, her gown for the Oscars was even now being made in Lebanon.

"Something nicely flamboyant again? You do have a sense for drama with your dresses." It was meant as a compliment, but she drew her brows together briefly, so he hastily added, "Beautifully dramatic, and with style. You are an eye-catcher when you step out in public."

They followed the gentle curve of the beach, strolling leisurely close to the water, Sal with his hands deep in his pockets, awkward and searching for words that did not come, Naomi intent on her finds.

"Jon kept my little stones," she said suddenly. "I found them at that hovel where he was living. He had them lined up on the railing of the deck. He held on to them all that time, Sal."

He'd known, of course.

Soon after Jon had moved, Sal had stood right there on the deck, the high tide roiling under his feet, and picked up one of them, mindless, and tossed it into the sea in a wide curve, just for the fun of seeing it fly, and Jon had nearly thrown him right after it in a sudden rush of fury. He had yelled at Sal, ordering him to never touch them again, never; if he valued his life and his job, they were not his to touch.

"They're only stones, for God's sake," Sal had said, but the answer had been, "They were *hers*. They aren't just stones. They are mine now, and you don't throw them away."

He had stared at the lively water as if he wanted to jump in to retrieve the worthless pebble, as if Sal had taken a part of his body from him and tossed it into the surf.

"I wrote some lyrics about them when we came here last summer," she was telling him, "but he's still toying around with them. Don't know if it will ever be a song. He keeps dismissing ideas, as if he can't find the right kind of music. It was only a little piece of nonsense."

He followed her silently back to the gate where Stewart was waiting.

AS SAL HAD hoped and Jon had expected, there were a handful of nominations for their movie, including two for the music.

"Ah, here we go," Sal had crowed when he came to them with the news two days after their walk on the beach. "Now we're back in business!"

Jon, reclining on the couch with his feet on the table, had muttered, "Never left it, I think."

Naomi had barely looked up from her magazine.

They were nominated together for the song, and Jon for the film score, and she could see how deeply he was pleased with this. She had called her parents to tell them about the honor and the upcoming event. Her mother had congratulated her very nicely, adding she was glad her change in life had brought her more fulfillment than just love. Her father had been less kind.

"It's nothing, Naomi," had been his words. "Like smoke. One day you're famous, the next day you're dirt. Don't waste yourself. You know your place is here, always."

It had felt like a cold blast into her warm and sunny life.

Carl was delighted. He was glad, he told her, that everything had worked out for her so beautifully, and that her son had been able to develop a meaningful relationship with his father.

"That's all that matters. You have your life back now, after all those long dark years you punished yourself. I'll be sure to watch the awards show, and maybe I'll even see you on the red carpet."

37

SAL WAS NERVOUS. They had a tight schedule, with a set slot for their limousines in the long row of arrivals outside the Los Angeles Shrine Auditorium. They needed to get across the city to get there, and he hated the fact that they were all standing in the hall of the Stone house waiting for Naomi.

Jon, as usual, was completely relaxed. He had brought out his case of Cuban cigars and offered them, along with a good measure of deep golden bourbon, saying, "Stop fussing, Sal. You know she'll be down in good time."

Jon nearly dropped his Cohiba when he turned to see Naomi descend toward them, head lowered and hands gathered over her chest.

Jon paniced briefly, the dire thought that she had decided not to go, wasn't dressed and was here now only to tell him. Then he realized she was made up and her hair set, and what he had at first glance taken to be a bedsheet was in fact an exquisite satin gown.

He recalled how she had come to him that morning after their first night together in Halmar, warm, wrapped only in a sheet, the scent of love still on her, while he was sitting at the piano. That had brought home to him, more than anything else, that she was his again. And now, on the cusp of her own success, she was returning it to him. Jon's heart flooded with adoration at the statement her gown made, and at the beauty of it.

HER HAND TIGHTLY in Jon's, Naomi walked along the stretch of carpet between the throngs of people on both sides. Cameras and reporters from all over the world shouted to them to step closer for a few words, or to let them take a picture. Art and Sal had a hard time shepherding them along without stopping too often.

In the lobby they were greeted by Harry and his crew.

Solveigh breathed nervously. "My God, Naomi, isn't this exciting?"

"It's another crowd, and I hate crowds. This one is better dressed than most, but it's still a crowd." Naomi wondered how some of the women would ever make it to the washroom in their elaborate gowns. There were too many varieties of perfume intermingling, the babble of hundreds of people and the constant roar of the onlookers outside added to the deafening noise.

"How do you feel?" Sal had come up behind her. "Where is your speech? I can't see a place to hide it on you, not even a small evening bag."

"Do I need one? I don't think so."

Sal laughed out loud. "I don't know. Are you good at impromptu speeches? You probably are, but can you deliver when you're standing up there facing the multitude?" He let up when he saw her waver and added, in a gentle tone, "Don't worry. You don't have to say anything at all. Just look moved and distressed, stammer a thank you, and you'll be fine. They don't expect grand words; in fact the more you seem unable to speak, the greater the impact."

Her eyes wandered back to Jon, who was looking her way, a small grin tugging at his lips, his eyebrows arching in question. He said a few words to an interviewer and then came over to her, taking his hands out of his pockets and straightening his jacket.

"Darling. How about it, do you want to take your seat yet? Or would you like a drink first? There's still time."

IT WAS EXCITING, and she was nervous when the nominees for Best Song were announced, the wish to win rising inside her. She wanted that trophy with all her heart, and it grew into a desperate yearning when the envelope appeared in the presenter's hand and he opened it, reading the names on the paper to himself before he spoke them into the microphone. Her palms were damp with nervous anticipation. The winner had been announced, but she couldn't hear over the roar in her ears.

"Come on," Jon was saying. "Let's go and get you that little naked man. We did it, Babe."

Sal was hugging her tightly, kissing her lips, Harry shouting with glee, and Jon, as cool as could be, pulled her along up the stairs to the stage, where she stood, dumb and mindless, while he accepted the award and spoke graceful words to the public. She held her statuette in her hand, staring at it in disbelief, until she was prodded gently by the presenter and had to face the expectant audience.

"Thank you," Naomi managed, her voice brittle with fear, then rapidly stepped back again, seeking shelter beside Jon.

There was some good-natured laughter from the crowd as the music welled up and they were ushered backstage, where the press was waiting for the first interviews with the newly honored artists. Someone put a glass of cool sparkling water in her trembling hand, and she sipped it gratefully while a makeup artist fussed around her, applying powder and fresh lipstick, and, to her horror, eyeliner on Jon, too. He saw her staring and gave her a sultry, hooded glance, grinning insolently when she blushed.

The spotlights centered on them, hot and glaring like dragons' eyes, the cameras zoomed in with their huge lenses looking like black holes into the nirvana of the world. Briefly she wondered whether her parents were watching, seeing her here with the Oscar clutched tightly in her hand, the proof of her accomplishment, a celebrated star in a moment of transitory glory next to her glamorous husband.

The movie itself did not win the award for Best Picture, but Jon, together with Sean, won for the score. This time she could observe from her seat how he climbed those stairs with the smooth elegance of an entertainer, kissed the young actress holding out the prize to him, and addressed his audience with his killer charm.

"What a great honor"—he held up the award—"to receive two of these in one night." After a small pause, he went on, "We strive to put what we feel, what the film makes us feel, into the music. We were lucky because we had the opportunity to work in a place where…where the setting was just right for this soundtrack. The landscape and the people around us were inspirational, creative, and very kind." He broke off and looked down at her, smiling softly. "Working with my wife was the best piece of good fortune, as the result shows. She won too, tonight, and I'm afraid she's so happy with that little guy that she'll put him on her bedside table and I'll have to look at him every morning when I wake up from now on, which is heavy competition."

A tinkle of laughter greeted his words before he turned serious again.

"There's little more to say, except thank you, love."

THERE WAS A brief moment of indecision, because Jon had to give a live TV interview that Art insisted on. "You don't have to come," he told her, "it won't take long. It's a matter of ten minutes. You could go ahead to the party at the Vogue if you want. Sean and Sal will go with you. I'll join you right after."

"Yes," Solveigh pressed, "let's do that, Naomi. I'm ready for some decent food."

Naomi realized she had barely seen Joshua all night long, and now, unable to make up her mind, he came breezing past with a group of teenagers and called, "We're off to Harry's place, Mom, there's be a party there. Staying overnight! Bye!" Before she could even respond, he was off again, climbing into a spacious van with them and Harry's wife, who waved to Naomi before the door shut behind her and they drove off. Solveigh needed another short trip to the washroom and returned inside, followed by a bemused Russ.

"About Joshua," Sean remarked. "You don't have to worry one bit. He's found his crowd, it seems."

"Alright," Naomi decided, "we'll go ahead to the party. You go do your interview, and we'll see you later."

Jon nodded slowly and wrapped his arms around her. "Come here. One kiss, and then I'm off. Don't get any fancy ideas, and no making out with your designer while I'm away."

Sal watched how she flowed into the embrace, the hand holding the trophy on his shoulder, how she let him kiss her deeply despite all the people standing around them, forgetting everything but his presence for that moment. A couple of cameras flashed, catching the image of the star and his wife in that instant of intimacy, making Sal move forward, but Jon released her again and walked away toward the waiting limousine without looking back. Her car moved up to the end of the short walk across the carpet, still lined with a thick throng of spectators waiting to see the winners leave, calling loudly to catch their attention. People from inside the theater stood out in the warm evening air, chatting idly. Overhead, helicopters from the LA TV stations were filming the scene, broadcasting everything live.

Stewart got out and came up to escort her, meeting her halfway across the carpet.

"What a night." Sal sighed. "A year ago I wouldn't have bet a penny this would happen, but you surprise me all the time. And what are you going to do with that thing now? Put it on your bedside table?"

He never got an answer.

Naomi dropped beside him, silently and as quickly as a stone, faster than he could reach out to catch her, before he could even begin to understand what had happened. There was a sort of tumult; he felt more than saw Stewart move as swiftly as the wind to block them from the public, security running from the entrance, but it was too late.

She was looking up at him with a puzzled frown, her arms spread out, hair wild around her, the white dress like a sheet around her immobile body, the Oscar statuette just out of reach. At first Sal did not grasp what he was seeing, and he stood, wondering why her white gown seemed to dissolve into the red of the carpet, until she gasped and more blood came from her mouth, nearly choking her. He heard a shot and a cry and saw Stewart crash like a felled tree, scattering panicked people.

Sean regained his wits first. He was on his knees beside Naomi, trying to support her head, talking to her as calmly as he could.

"We need a doctor!" Sal yelled, finding his voice at last. "Quickly, we need help!"

Howling sirens tore through the incredible noise surrounding them, more shots rang out, the helicopters descended dangerously close, trying to capture the wild scene.

Naomi's hand came up ever so slowly and gripped Sean's shirt weakly.

"Jon," Sal heard her whisper. "Sean, please…"

The guards made way for the EMTs rushing up to them from the building. More people were streaming out, Hollywood celebrities staring in shocked silence as their worst nightmare played out before their eyes. Sal sank down beside Naomi, helpless, a terrible dark fear rising in him as he saw the blood spreading, soaking his trousers, her life pumping out of her.

"Hang on," he begged. "Hang on, darling. Look at me. Help is here, my love, please look at me. Look at me, Naomi, don't leave me!"

She obeyed, her tired eyes closing, her fingers slipping from Sean's shirt, leaving crimson streaks behind. They were pushed away by the medics. Police had taken control and were quickly and efficiently dispersing the crowd and chasing away the reporters.

It was, Sal thought wildly, like a scene in a very bad movie. All that was missing was a too-pretty female cop in high heels parading in to take over. He could see Solveigh running toward them, her face white as chalk, screaming something he could not understand. Russ was behind her, trying to stop her from getting closer. He saw more ambulances stopping, their teams running to help Stewart and injured bystanders, and he heard the awful, hectic whining of the AED and the brief order to step away before they shocked Naomi.

"Come away, Sal," Sean said. "We can't help, and we need to think what to do. We need to…" he wiped his brow, painting a crimson smear on it.

Sal stared at it, and at the stains on his pleated evening shirt.

Her blood. And still he could not wrap his mind around the awful thing that had happened.

More uniformed men were crowding around Naomi, pressing the contents of infusion bags into her veins, putting an oxygen mask on her, taking her blood pressure, trying to stop the bleeding, trying to save her life.

"This is not real," he told himself, but the flurry of action around that outstretched body told him differently. Sal realized the EMTs had stopped working on Stewart and were covering him with a sheet, and that a limp woman's form in a green gown was being lifted onto a stretcher. Just when they were about to push her into the Coroner's van, he saw the mane of red hair.

"Please God, no."

The men stopped and let him lift the blanket from Sophie's bloody face.

She seemed incredibly young and vulnerable, her eyes open and blank, the lips parted, the wound in her throat where she had been shot a horrible, shredded gash in her freckled skin. Her dress was drenched; there was so much blood that Sal nearly retched.

From the building, Harry was running toward them his face a grim mask of fury and shock.

"Sal! Wake up, man!" he shouted, "Has anyone called Jon?"

"I'll do it." Russ' hands shook so badly he could hardly hold his cell phone, let alone dial the right number, but he managed after a few tries, gathering his wits enough to not call Jon directly but Art.

Sal reeled with the impact of the situation.

"Will she be okay?" he called after the medics, but there was no answer. Solveigh was holding the Oscar statuette, hugging it tightly against her breast as if it were a newborn, Russ beside her, steadying her when she stumbled, and Sal blanched when he finally reached Art and tried to tell him how their dream night had become a terrible nightmare. Sean, wiping at his face, sticky with the dried blood, gazed in horror at his fingertips. The large stain on the ground glistened in the floodlights.

38

SHE WAS STANDING on black sand. Black, oily waves were rolling in at her feet in gentle swells that did not break but just retreated again silently. The huge open sky above her head was black too, with dark gray clouds like curtains hanging in it, illuminated by a small, distant, golden sun hovering close to the horizon. Its light cast a dim glow over the water. The air was neither warm nor cold, there was no wind, no scent, no sound, no movement other than the dreamy black ocean.

There was no thought, no pain, no sorrow, no will at all, only a calm, unquestioning acceptance. She was completely alone, solitary in a still universe, waiting, listening, waiting.

"SHE HAD A second cardiac arrest during transport," the surgeon told Sal. "We're taking her to the OR now. It will take quite a while, so you should all go to the waiting room at the end of the hall. We'll keep you informed. Is the family here yet?"

Sean gripped the sleeve of the doctor's green scrubs before he could rush out. "We need to know. We need to know now. How bad is it? Her husband will be here in a moment, and we have to tell him something, for God's sake. The man will go insane!"

The doctor took off his glasses to rub his eyes. "It's bad. I can't say how bad yet, but she lost a nearly fatal amount of blood and her heart stopped twice. She went into shock and had to be resuscitated, but she is strong and young. Tell him we're doing everything we can."

He extricated himself from Sean's grip with a wry, brief smile and disappeared behind the milk-glass doors of the operating suite.

"I'm scared as hell." They looked at Sal. "He'll be here any minute, and what will we say to him? How are we going to tell him what happened? How are we going to explain that she may not..."

"Don't!" Solveigh still had the Oscar in her lap. "Don't even say it, Sal. It cannot happen, it won't. She will be okay. She will be fine. That doctor will come back and tell us it's a clean wound, and she's not badly hurt, and in a few days she'll be well again." Tears spilled down her face and dropped on the bright silk of her dress. Helplessly, Russ stroked her shoulder, but she sobbed inconsolably.

"I'll do it," Sean said quietly.

It had been Sophie, standing among the guests, who had shot Naomi, and then, when Stewart came toward her, she'd shot him too. The police had shown them the small gun she had held in her dress pocket, a lady's weapon that seemed too frail to release death. Stewart was not at the hospital now; his body had been taken to the morgue, just like Sophie herself, killed in the ensuing melee with the police. A couple of bystanders had been wounded as well, and they were in the ER right now. Outside, they knew, the media was gathered, waiting for a report, and Jon had not yet arrived.

Sal had a good understanding of how it would be when he did, how he would react, and the knowledge had his stomach in a tight knot.

"We need to…" He had to clear his throat before he could go on. "We need to protect Jon, Sean. We have to get him into a separate room and keep him there until we know…until they tell us…until…"

"Forget it." Sean shook his head. "No one will be able to contain him, Sal. He will tear this building apart if they don't give him any hope. God."

"I just can't grasp it." Solveigh's voice was rough with despair. "Why? Why would she do such a thing? Now? After all this time? They've been married for six months. He married Naomi, he married her, he made his choice, and now…"

"You aren't going to understand this. There is no understanding."

Sal had no more cigarettes, and smoking was forbidden in the hospital, but he patted his jacket pocket anyway as if everything would be all right if he could just find one small piece of normalcy to cling to. All he found was the paper ring that had been around his Cohiba, the one he had smoked with Jon and Art while they were waiting for Naomi to join them. He stared at the colorful, flimsy thing in his fingers, recalling the easy mood of that moment.

"I don't want to understand it," Solveigh cried. "I want it to go away! I want to make it undone, Sal! We came all this way here, and she never wanted it, she was so afraid of coming here and only did it for him, and now look, now she's—"

"She's not dying, damn it!" Sal rounded on her. "I was right beside her, I was talking to her, damn it, she was laughing at me, she was unafraid and beautiful, and she was radiant and happy, and—"

Sean slapped him hard on the shoulder. "Stop it. Right now, Sal. We need to keep our wits about us for Jon."

"Yeah." He wanted to cry, to find a dark, silent corner where he could hide and nurse his broken soul instead of going out, as he knew he would have to in a short while, to face the press and their questions.

"Russ," he said curtly, "come on. We need to start working. As long as Art isn't here, it will be you and me. First, we need one hell of a lot of security. The hallway must be closed. No one needs to see him break down."

As he would.

The door opened and they swung around, but it was Harry.

"I haven't told Joshua yet." With a deep sigh, he dropped onto the bench beside Solveigh. "He's at my house now, but I think I'd better call Grace before they see it on TV."

"He should be here anyway," Sean answered. "And soon."

THE WATER WAS very still, tepid. She drifted on her back, her arms outstretched, her dress a floating, billowing mass around her. Above her, the sky was a beautiful, rosy opaque, like the inside of a seashell, gleaming softly in the pale light of the early morning sun. Long reeds grew from the bottom of the large lake and stood in swaying tufts around her, rustling in the fragrant, cool breeze. In the distance, still partly hidden by a bank of fog, she could see the contour of a small island. Dark cypresses rose from the chalky stone, casting stark shadows on the towers of rock that loomed over them. She thought she could make out a gate somewhere near the center, half open, beckoning, inviting her to step through and find peace, and forgetting, and oblivion.

JON BURST THROUGH the swinging doors like a violent storm, Art on his heels.

"What happened? God damn it, what happened? Where is she, where is Naomi?" He reeled back when Solveigh broke out in loud, helpless sobbing.

It was Sean who took his arm and said calmly, "Come with me, Jon. I'll explain."

But Jon could not take in what he was hearing; his brain simply refused to process the information behind the words, the horror was just too great. He heard phrases like *cardiac arrest, blood loss* and *operating,* and even *death.* He nodded gamely when Sean asked him if he understood, but it was not true.

"Stewart is dead? Dead? He was killed?"

"Yes."

"But Naomi? What happened, Sean?"

Sean sighed and repeated his terrible report.

"I want to see her now."

"She's in surgery, Jon. And the way the doctor put it, it will take some time. She was gravely injured. We will have to wait."

"No, I won't wait." There was a nurses' desk close by, and he went there and put his fist down on the counter. "My wife. I want to know, right now. I want to see her, and I want to speak to a competent physician."

The woman behind the desk tried to calm him down, but he only shook his head at her excuses. "No, I'm not taking any of that crap. You go and get someone out here who will tell me what's going on this instant, or I'll go in there and find out myself!"

"Jon." Sean tried to pull him back but was shaken off impatiently.

"Where is she now? What are they doing to her, why can't I see her?"

"Sir," she answered, "they are trying to save her life. You can't do anything right now, but I assure you, as soon as there is news you will be informed."

"Save her life?" Desperation made his voice break. "Save her life? Is she dying? Is Naomi dying?"

Sean had never seen anything like the sudden, naked fear on his friend's face as Jon wheeled around and made for the shut doors that led into the OR suite.

"Jon," he called after him, but it was Harry who grabbed the silk lapels of Jon's tux and slammed him into the wall, knocking the breath out of him.

"Stay here, you fool! And calm down. You're not helping her, and you're not doing yourself any good, either."

For a moment, it looked as if Jon was going to hit Harry, but he sagged against him instead.

"Sit here." Harry pushed him down on a chair next to a huge potted palm. "I'll get you some coffee."

He scrutinized the others: Solveigh, her lips drawn and pale, Russ, his arm around her, Sal, dazed and disoriented, Sean, withdrawn and very still, and Art, trying hard to gain control. "Hell, coffee would be good for all of us." He signaled to the nurse, who nodded gratefully and picked up the phone.

The hallway grew very quiet the longer the night wore on.

Grace arrived with a bewildered, frightened Joshua, who immediately sought out his father, bringing a small spark of life to Jon's ashen face for an instant before they both sank back into the fear that surrounded them like a grey cloak. Around three in the morning Joshua fell asleep, his head on Jon's knee, covered by the jacket Art had taken off and draped over him.

"It's taking so long," Jon whispered to Sean. "Why don't they send someone out to tell us how it's going? At least inform us what her injuries are? I don't think I can take much more waiting." For the first time ever, he looked his age; there were deep lines around his mouth and dark smudges under his eyes, worry and fatigue in his expression.

"I'll go," Sean offered, but Jon shook his head.

"No," was his weary reply, "I need to do this myself."

Carefully he shifted Joshua from his leg and rose, stiff and exhausted, and left the room. Sal and Sean followed him anxiously with their eyes.

The nurse phoned, and a few moments later a doctor came out to see him. Jon's heart turned to ice at the sight of the man in his green scrubs, the front liberally splattered and smeared with blood. The surgeon wiped his brow and yawned, but collected himself quickly. It was very bad, he said, and they were still working on her. The bullet had passed through her body and splintered the lowest rib. That in itself was not too bad, but the bone splinters had pierced her lung and liver, and they had to remove parts of both. They had repaired the liver now, but the lung was giving them trouble. Her heart was very weak from the enormous amount of blood lost. And she had a head injury, a hematoma, from the fall, which they would try to remove before her brain was damaged.

"So far," he concluded, "We've had to give her thirty units of blood, but I fear we aren't done yet."

"But she'll be okay?" Jon hardly dared to ask. "She is going to pull through, right?"

The physician hesitated for a moment. "There are six surgeons in there, the best we have, and we are the best in the state. She is a strong woman." Again he waited before he added. "Get some sleep, if you can. It will be several more hours."

Jon needed to be alone.

The lobby was quiet and nearly empty at this time of night, but outside an ambulance passed by with howling sirens toward the ER entrance. A couple of white-clad men, medics or doctors, were standing near the door, talking and laughing at something. There was a TV mounted to the wall in a niche with a couch, and he settled there to watch the images flickering over the screen. A solitary woman was nestled in the corner; her head leaning against the beige upholstery, a crumpled handkerchief in her hands. She gazed at him from red-rimmed eyes and looked away again quickly, as if she did not want to notice him.

The TV was set to a local news channel, showing the accidents and disturbances of the night: a number of police cars chasing a white pickup along the highway, a house on fire in one of the suburbs, and then, a report on the shooting at the Academy Awards.

Horrified, Jon watched it happen. He saw Naomi walking beside Sal, Sean trailing behind, and how she dropped to the ground. He saw Stewart rush over to help her and then collapse. Sean, falling to his knees beside her, the crush of people, the panic in the crowd, medics, police, sirens, flashlights, and in the center of it all, Naomi. Then the police honing in on the crumpled form of a woman and dragging her away, her red hair spilling over their hands, more blood, more rescue attempts, someone trying to help Stewart, and again, Naomi, being reanimated now, the paddles on her skin, Sean, stepping away, red stains on his shirt, and Harry as he stormed toward them. The entire gruesome scene had been recorded. The famous star's wife, gunned down after the awards show—and what a juicy, sensational morsel of drama it was.

"You should be with your wife."

Surprised, he turned to the woman in the corner. She was regarding him tiredly, kneading the piece of cloth in her fingers.

"Your wife," she repeated as if she was speaking to an uncomprehending child. "She needs you. Why are you sitting here? Go back to her."

"She's in surgery," Jon replied. "I can't do anything at the moment."

"But when she wakes up you should be there. She should see you there by her bed."

The surrealism of the entire situation made it nearly impossible for him to collect a sane thought, let alone lead a coherent conversation.

"I don't think she will wake up very soon." He unbuttoned his jacket and leaned back, tired and battered, fear churning in him like bile. "If at all. God."

There was a slow nod. The woman was not unattractive, maybe in her mid-forties, his own age, dusky-skinned and with an ample but well-defined body, her hair still black with a few single white strands that looked strangely interesting.

"My husband just died. He was watching football, and then he died. He was fifty-two, and apparently healthy. Then he gets up to get himself a beer and drops dead on the kitchen floor, just like that. Never knew what hit him. They brought him here, but it was too late. I don't want to go home. There's no one there."

"No children?" he asked, and she shook her head.

At least, Jon thought, at least he had that. If she did not survive the night, there was Joshua, and Jon knew he would give up everything and retire to share his son's life. Shocked by his own thoughts, he jumped up and rubbed his face.

"You're right. I have to go back."

Only when he had reached the elevators did Jon have the sense to turn back and call: "Thank you. Take care!"

But either she did not hear or did not care, for there was no response.

The early morning routine had returned to the hospital hallway before those ominous doors to the forbidden area opened again, disgorging a group of physicians who looked as exhausted as those waiting for them outside.

"You can see your wife now," the same man who had talked to Jon earlier said. "The nurse will take you in."

Jon felt the others draw closer to him, building a circle of support.

"We've done everything we could," the surgeon went on. "She has lost half of her right lung and about as much of her liver. Her heart is still volatile, very weak. The hematoma has been removed, and her brain should be okay. For now, we've put her in a drug-induced coma, and we'll keep it up for a while."

"So she will live?" Sean pressed Jon's arm to steady him when he swayed, relief flooding through him.

"If there are no further complications, yes. But she is critical, as you can imagine, with those injuries, and she has a very long period of healing ahead of her."

"Oh, thank God," Solveigh breathed, and then broke out again in ragged sobbing.

"The family," Sal mumbled. "We forgot to call her family. Jon, go see her. I'll do it, don't worry."

THE SAND ON the beach had changed. It was brilliantly white and as soft as down. It was warm under her feet, comfortably warm, just like the fragrant breeze rustling through the dense green trees farther up on the land and the few stray palms standing near the water. The shore followed a gentle curve into the distance, where it ended in a rocky headland with a huge blue moon rising above it, so close that its body could be recognized as a sphere. The ocean shone a deep improbable turquoise, turning to a paler shade with the surf, while the sky was lusciously violet, so dark it was nearly black. Great glittering wheels of stars turned in a slow, majestic dance, galaxies spinning through space like spiderwebs of light, rows of pearls and lacy concoctions, sugar candy. Music came from them, a slow, low hum overlaid by a sweeping, elusive melody that seemed, impossibly, to combine a multitude of tunes into one complex, many-layered score, a cosmic symphony she heard and understood, even followed under her breath, and which seemed to run through her entire body like a second stream of blood.

"The music of the spheres," she heard a voice say. "Listen well."

She turned, but no one was there. She was all alone in this eerie, beautiful landscape, but she was no longer so deadly tired, and she felt aware of herself for the first time in an eternity.

"Open your eyes," the same voice ordered, "and look."

This seemed a ridiculous thing to do. She thought her eyes *were* open, because she was seeing the beach and the sky, but she did as she was told.

It was surprisingly hard, almost as if she had to push through her own flesh, but the landscape opened up before her and pulled her in.

She was in a hospital room, like the kind you see in the movies or on TV, with many blinking and beeping machines, and a glass wall to a nurses' station. She knew it was her lying in the bed with all those monitors, hurting. The body she had dropped into was a vessel of pain, tied down by tubes, needles, and bandages.

A man was standing beside her, his head lowered and his hands helplessly by his side. He seemed familiar; seeing him, she felt comforted and safe, but she could not remember who he was. There were tears on his face and he was whispering something to her. She wanted to tell him not to be so sad and not to cry, but once more the terrible fatigue swept over her.

The man raised his eyes to look at her.

"I'm so sorry, my love," he said tenderly. "I'm so, so sorry. It's my fault. I was selfish, I wanted you here and you came, and now this terrible thing has happened. Please come back to me, Naomi. Please, Baby."

He sounded so heartbroken and lonely that she wanted to reach out to him and promise that everything would be all right, but she could not.

"I'll take better care of you," he was saying. "You will never, never get hurt again, but please don't leave me. Baby, you know I need you, and Joshua needs you. Please, we have only just started our lives together. There's so much living still to do…"

She sighed tiredly. The beach beckoned, and the lovely music.

JON REFUSED TO leave her side again.

"Go home," Sal urged. "Take a shower and get some rest. She's in good hands. I'll stay here with her until you return."

But he would not budge. She might wake up, and he wanted to be there, did not want her to find herself alone in that horrible hospital bed and think that he had deserted her.

"Don't be stupid, Jon," Sal said. "As if she would ever think that. And anyway, she's sedated. They won't let her wake up for a few days. You know that."

Joshua was upset and scared, but he calmed down when Jon told him he had seen Naomi, that she was sleeping now and was going to be okay, but it would take some time.

"Joshua," Jon explained, his arm around his son's shoulders, "I promise, I will not leave her alone for a single minute. Go with Grace and Harry and try not to worry. Sleep and eat, and in the afternoon come back and you can see your mom."

Russ had taken Solveigh away. Art and Sal were downstairs talking to the press.

Two nurses were with her when Jon returned, checking the machines and IV bags and changing her position carefully.

"Her hair is clotted with blood," one of them whispered to him. "I'll come back later and wash it. For now, we'll leave her alone."

They brought him breakfast, and later in the day lunch, but he only managed to choke down some tepid coffee, which he drank while he sat at her bedside.

She was not breathing on her own; the tube taped to her lips seemed incredibly brutal to him, an invasion of her dignity and privacy.

He listened to the low hiss of the oxygen and the beeping of the heart monitor, watched the blinking lights, and fell into the uneasy sleep of exhaustion, his head awkwardly on a corner of her blanket, her fingers in his.

THE NURSE WAS back with Naomi, washing her hair with sponge, when he returned from a quick shower and changed into the fresh clothes Russ had brought for him.

Very carefully, she was picking up every strand and lock, patting it gently to remove the grime and blood. He stared dolefully at the basin she had on her knees, the water in it turning a dirty red.

"I watched the show," the woman told him. "Your wife was so pretty up there on the stage. I nearly cried because she was so moved by the award."

"She never thought she deserved it. Somehow she never realizes how good she really is at writing."

The nurse nodded silently, and he had the impression she had no idea what he was talking about. "I need fresh water," she said. "It's so much."

More clotted blood came out of the long tresses.

"But she will heal? She will be well again, right?"

The woman looked up at him. "You know I'm not able to answer that question. But from what I can see, her chances are good, if nothing untoward happens."

"Like what?" Jon pulled up the chair again and took Naomi's cool hand in his. There was no reaction when he pressed it slightly.

There was a brief hesitation. "Like another cardiac arrest, an infection, or inflammation. Something like that. You should talk to her doctors."

"But she is out of immediate danger?"

"You need to ask the doctor," she repeated.

SAL AND ART cast furtive glances at each other. A couple of times Sal considered interfering, but in the end it was a family matter, and they had no business being present when Naomi's father bore down on Jon, shouting bitter accusations at him.

"You!" Olaf threw at Jon with all the pent-up fury he had been harboring. "You are nothing but temptation and danger, a womanizer and a seducer, and I'm taking her back home to safety. You will never see her again, and this time I'll make sure of that. Screw around all you like and let your lovers kill each other, but Naomi won't be one of your victims again, you bastard!"

Lucia tried to pull him back, but he shook her off.

"You think throwing all that money her way will make things better? You think those useless trophies are of any importance? They mean nothing at all!"

"She'll not go anywhere," Jon responded just as vehemently, "until she can make that decision herself. You're not going to move her against her will."

"As if you have a say in that!"

Sal had the impression that Olaf was ready to hit Jon, he was that angry.

"Well, I do. I'm her husband, and as such I get to decide what happens with her, and not you. She will stay here in safety until she tells me otherwise."

"In safety!" Olaf stepped up closer to him, his fists balled by his side. "Safety? You let her get shot by your former mistress? Right out on the street too, and she has to suffer the indignity, on top of everything else, of being seen helpless and half-naked by the world while she lies bleeding on the pavement!"

Jon fell silent, his head lowered before the onslaught.

"We took care of her safety, Olaf," Sal intervened. "Believe me, we did, even against her will."

"So it's her fault now, is that it?" Olaf rounded on him. "She put herself in the way of that gun?"

"Please stop this," Lucia broke in. "Listen to yourselves! Shame on you all, fighting like this, when the only thing that matters is Naomi's recovery."

She left them standing in the hallway and went in to Naomi, who was still sedated and motionless.

FIVE DAYS HAD passed since the incident. Hollywood had outwardly returned to its routine, but those inside the business knew that this was an illusion. Harry and Sal had come down on the Academy with the force of their lawyers, threatening to pick the organization apart for making it possible for someone to bring a gun inside.

"How much do you want out of it?" Jon's attorneys had asked him, but he had replied he did not give a damn about the money; he wanted Naomi healthy, and he wanted to make sure nothing like this ever happened again to anyone.

"Donate whatever you get to the hospital," he told them. "They've earned it, they saved her life."

Having her parents in the house was ordeal enough.

Olaf prowled the grounds like a suspicious wolf, examining every corner of the estate and the fence to the beach.

"Come with me," Jon said after watching him a while, and took him upstairs to their bedroom. Olaf stood on the precious carpet and gazed at the lovely, tranquil surroundings, the fine furniture and the paintings on the walls, originals by Canadian painters he knew only too well, and the framed photographs on the shelves of her small family and her parents. On her dressing table, velvet cases with famous jewelers' names imprinted on them, a couple of them open, as if she had toyed with the things before she left; crystal flacons of perfume, silver hairbrushes, and in the wardrobe a rainbow collection of evening gowns, shawls and furs, rows of expensive clothes and shoes. Even now, with Naomi in hospital, there was a large bouquet of fresh roses on the table, the cleaned and polished Oscar statuette next to it. The roof garden had become a lush paradise over the last few weeks, with oleander and jasmine, just like the garden below, comfortable furniture and even a broad daybed. It was the home of a cherished princess.

"This is Naomi's private place," Jon said quietly. "She loves this room, this patio, and she feels good here, Olaf. She likes this life, believe it or not. I did not take very good care of her when she lived here before, but this time I'm making sure there's nothing missing, nothing she could possibly want for. Not in things, not in love, not attention or security."

Olaf did not reply. He had seen the silver Rolls with the tinted windows and listened to Amparo, the housekeeper, who told him it was Naomi's car, that she never went anywhere without at least one guard, and every trip she took was monitored and planned.

"I don't know anything about the procedures in this weird society of yours here in Hollywood, and I don't want to. Your life is a waste," he stated sourly when he and Jon returned to the living room, where Lucia was waiting for them, ready to go to the hospital again.

Jon nearly lost his patience then. "My life," he replied, "is what I've made of it. It's obviously good enough for many, many people, and it has made me very wealthy and beloved by many. But in the end, it's my job, and it does not make me into something other than human. I'm just another man, Olaf, and I love my wife and my son. Providing for them, looking after their well-being, that's what I try to do as well as I possibly can."

Olaf snorted.

"I don't have time for this," Jon said coldly. "I want to be back with my wife. If you wish, you may go on degrading me; I don't care anymore. But you might keep in mind that you are insulting your daughter's choice and questioning her decisions. You think she is good enough to head your business but too stupid to choose a husband for herself? That says a lot about you."

He walked out without looking back. "I'm leaving. You can ask one of Naomi's bodyguards to take you wherever you want in her car. I don't think she would mind."

Jon did not care at all that he had been as offensive as possible as he drove off by himself.

40

SHE KNEW THIS place. The meadow stretched down a gentle slope to a narrow beach, the tall grass and the wildflowers sending off the fragrance of summer, the memory of a hot day under the sun. The light of sunset was in the sky to the west, but above her head, stars already blinked in the black of night. Small waves toyed with debris, casting them on the sand and picking them up again with their next visit, replacing, burrowing, pushing.

One stone stood out, a fist-sized thing shaped vaguely like an egg, with turquoise veins shot through it. She picked it up and wiped in on the shirt she was wearing.

"Poor little stone," she thought. "I'll take you home with me."

"Don't move," the man in the green scrubs said. "Wait. Stay calm, all is well. Breathe now. There."

It felt as if he was pulling out her lungs, forcing a painful cough from her. Hands supported her and wiped her lips, held her when she retched miserably, weakly.

"It's okay," he said again. "You're doing fine, just fine. Good morning, Mrs. Stone."

She gazed up at him, puzzled and disoriented, unable to think or speak or move, but he patted her cheek and smiled.

"You had us worried, but I think you're going to be just fine."

His face vanished from her vision, but she felt his fingers on her pulse and checking the needles in her arm before his steps receded.

She was tired and thirsty, and filled with the certainty that somewhere terrible pain lurked.

"Naomi, love."

That voice she knew. It was wonderful, warm and dark, intimately familiar, comforting.

Someone came and gave her some water. It felt incredibly good, cool and soothing, but they only let her drink a few sips before it was taken away again.

"Easy," the nurse murmured, "Not too much or you will get sick. Your stomach needs to get used to it again."

A hand touched hers, took hold of it ever so gently.

She wanted to hear that voice again and remember why it was so important to her, and she wanted to see the face that belonged to it, but moving was so difficult and she was exhausted.

"Baby, I'm right here. Don't be afraid."

Gentle fingers brushing her brow and face, trailing the line of her jaw and chin, a caress she knew well and took comfort from.

"Sleep," she heard him say. "I'll be here when you wake up. Promise."

Jon thought his heart was going to burst with the hot flush of relief when her grip tightened on his for an instant before she drifted off again with a small sigh.

THE SCENT OF coffee woke her. Her stomach churned with hunger at that smell.

She wanted some very badly, but before they would give her some she would have to open her eyes and make it clear she was conscious. Briefly, during the night, she had been awake. Jon had been sleeping in the chair by her side. Naomi had understood at last where she was, and with some careful fingering had found the bandage on her body, a longish strip of cotton covering an area about twenty inches in length on her right side. The real hurt, though, was deep inside her, knife stabs with every breath, accompanied by a nearly killing fatigue. Her limbs felt sore and her back cramped.

But worst of all was that she felt dirty, unwashed. Naomi hated the stickiness on her skin and the foul taste in her mouth, as if she had not cleaned her teeth in a week.

Since the tube had been removed she had not yet spoken at all. Her throat felt raw and full of mucus.

"Coffee," she croaked, which resulted in a rather terrifying coughing spell. Someone came to hold her upright until it subsided. This made her feel better, as if her sluggish circulation responded to sitting up.

"Coffee?" the nurse repeated, "Not yet. But you can have some tea, if you like."

Jon was standing at the foot of the bed, watching her anxiously, almost as if now that she was awake he was afraid to approach her. The doctor who came to check on her tried to send him away, but he only shook his head and waited for the verdict.

"Well," it came, "You seem to be doing well. Your heart is still weaker than I'd like, but with time you will regain your strength."

They were left alone after that.

Naomi was so very tired. She couldn't remember ever having felt like this, so exhausted that every movement brought giddiness and a wave of nausea. Even lifting her hand seemed too much.

"It hurts." She whispered.

This seemed to wake him from his trance. "Baby."

"Stewart is dead," Naomi said softly, "Right?"

Jon returned to the chair where he had spent the last five nights in vigil, praying for her life.

"Yes." It was so good to hold her hand and feel her fingers curl around his after the many hours when they had lain cold and limp on the sheet. "You were attacked."

Her face was pale and drawn, her lips dry and cracked, all the glossy beauty of the awards night gone, only the bare, stark outline of skin on bone left, a frail memory of who she really was.

"It is a terrible thing, I know." It had to be said, but the words were not easy. "And it's my fault, I know it's my fault. But Baby, I tried to make so sure you would be safe, I never meant you to come to harm, you know that, Naomi. Please…"

From outside, they could hear the impatient voice of Olaf arguing with the nurse, demanding to be let inside. Naomi looked toward the door.

"We will talk about this later, Jon," she said. "I'm so tired. How sick am I really? Tell me, before my father comes in. I don't think I can bear him."

Haltingly, he described her injuries to her, deeply upset when she began to sob softly and then turned her head away from him.

"Naomi, love, you will be well again in no time. Please trust me. I'll do everything to take care of you, and I'll take you home as soon as possible. We'll hire a private nurse and make you comfortable in your own room. I'll cancel the tour and we can stay home, or even return to Halmar. Hell, we don't have to go anywhere else ever again if you want to retire. I'll give up the music and stay with you. But please, Baby, don't turn from me. You know you are more important to me than anything."

"Oh, shut up."

He leaned back, his heart breaking over her rejection.

"Your father wants you to return to Kleinburg with him."

Even that he was willing to do if it would help her; he could let her go, in the hope that one day she might decide to return.

"If you want that, I'll…I'll…" He could not say it though.

"You never learn."

Here it came, the verdict he dreaded more than everything else.

"You are so quick to give up on me." Naomi looked at him again. "You would send me away just to ease your conscience, wouldn't you?"

"No!" He wanted to grab her shoulders and shake her, shake that notion right out of her, but all he did was take her hand again and hold it tightly. "No, Naomi, giving up is the last thing on my mind! God! But what am I supposed to do? You were on the brink of death, you nearly died! I left you alone to go to that stupid talk show. I didn't look out for you, and look what happened! I feel guilty as hell."

"Atoning, again." Her voice was so weak. "You are so good at atoning, Jon. And what if *you* were lying here now, so badly hurt? Do you think I would let you go? Do you think I would let you retreat and leave me alone?"

She had to smile at the way he perked up with those words.

"Take me home, you punk. Why did I spend all that money and effort on the roof garden if I can't use it now?"

Before he could think of a reply, she had drifted off again, her hand in his.

Olaf was outraged, and this time he showed it without restraint.

"You do this on purpose. You think you can keep us away from her long enough to convince her not to go back home with us."

Olaf could not see Lucia's face, but Jon did. "Lucia," he said quietly, but she raised her hand in resignation.

"She will listen to me," Olaf went on. "And she will come back home with us, where she can heal and live in safety and peace. And you will drop out of her life without fuss. I'll see to it that you'll get your blood money back, but my daughter is history for you."

Jon took a step back. "I have borne your attitude with good will and endured your slander without reacting to it for Naomi's sake. But Olaf,

I'm not willing to take any more of it. This is hard enough for all of us without fighting over her like two mad dogs. My priority is to see that my wife gets well again, and happy, and I'll do everything to make sure of that."

"You can't make her happy. That's the truth of it, the one she refuses to see and you are too stupid to accept. You are good enough for an affair, and for giving her a fatherless child, but not for a lasting marriage. You're just not good enough."

It was almost amusing. Jon could not recall anyone telling him anything similar during the past twenty-five years, and here he stood and had to take it from his father-in-law.

"I'm forty-five," he replied, "and I've made a name for myself quite successfully. I've won the love of the most wonderful woman on earth, and just because you happen to be her father I'm not going to throw that away, Olaf." He was about to turn away but then thought better of it. "If it costs me my life, I'm going to make this marriage last. I'm not going to have you try to turn my wife against me and then hide her in some obscure corner of the world again. It was not me who destroyed her life, it was you. I would have made it right for her if you had given me the chance to talk to her then."

"And then what?" Olaf threw at him. "You would have seduced her again and she, stupid child that she is, would have followed you back to this hell hole here."

The elevator door opened to reveal Sal and Solveigh.

"You call your own daughter a stupid child?" Jon asked, dark fury rising in him at the man's attitude. "I've had it with your low opinion of me, but even more than that, I've had it with your attitude toward Naomi." To Lucia, a lot gentler, Jon said, "I offered to let Naomi go with you to Toronto if she wanted some distance and peace from me and our life here. She refused."

"He's only afraid." Lucia looked from one to the other, her hands clenched around her pursestrap.

"Aren't we all?" Jon took Solveigh's arm. "I'm going down to the cafeteria for a coffee. So now you have time to try to convince Naomi to go to Toronto with you. Good luck."

Sal got them coffee, which Jon nursed uneasily, his mind in turmoil, his thoughts up there in the ICU.

"Can't wrap my mind about it. I just can't understand it." Now that she was out of immediate danger and had not turned away from him, Jon found he could at last put his attention to what had actually happened.

"There's nothing to understand," Sal replied. "A woman's jealousy became hate, and that hate got twisted into insanity. It's not your fault, or anyone else's. People get ditched all the time without killing their rivals. Actually, you were a lot more decent with her than with many others, Jon. I recall a number of girls being informed by instant message."

"As if you haven't done that yourself." Jon cast a furtive, embarrassed glance at Solveigh.

"Sure I have. We don't need the grand opera for every playmate." He shrugged. "Come off it, Jon. The way she showed up in Halmar? That was stalking."

Jon was not as sure as Sal. "You only call it stalking because it's me we're talking about. If it were someone else, you'd probably call it romantic and lovelorn."

This was the part that had him so worried. Naomi would not see it as stalking. She would recognize the desperation and hurt in Sophie's actions and feel guilty about her death. And Stewart's.

"Conceited as always, Jon."

They both looked at Solveigh full of surprise, but she only grinned mirthlessly. "That was not romantic behavior, that was sick. Traveling across continents and oceans to win back a lost love? That's what I call manic."

Jon leaned back in his chair, shocked by her words. "But I did that, Solveigh. That's exactly what I did to get Naomi back. Am I a stalker, then, in your eyes? I would have done anything to find her."

Solveigh pushed the glass of milk in front of her away, eyeing their coffee enviously. "No, you're not, and Naomi is not one whit better than you either, hiding away from the world and then sneaking out on her own to see your concert in London, Jon. You deserve each other. And richly. Maybe you should be put on a deserted island together and left there for all eternity so you can play out your drama to the hilt without involving half the world. But where would be the fun in that, right? No audience."

Sal was aware of the fact that the restaurant was gradually filling, it being near lunchtime and people taking a break. Some were looking their way, and there was a certain amount of whispering, but no one had made their way over to their table.

"We should go," he suggested. "We can continue this talk in private. This is a little too public."

But the scene they found right outside the ICU was no less public and a lot more dramatic. Grace had arrived with Joshua, who had seen his mother briefly and was so relieved to find her awake and out of immediate danger that he finally allowed his pent-up fear and anger out, and it hit Olaf full blast.

"You are not going to take her away from us, Grandfather, you won't!" he was yelling across the hallway. "It's not Dad's fault someone else was out to hurt Mom!"

"I mean well, Joshua, and I want to give you and your Mom back the peace you had all your life; before…before…" Olaf tried to reach out to him, but Joshua drew back and even swiped at his grandfather's hand.

"But I want to be here. And I know that mom wants to be here, too. She is happy here. She likes it here."

"And how would you know? You're too young to realize what your mother really needs."

Jon would have sworn there were tears in Olaf's eyes.

"I know she goes through the house singing, and I know she is never sad or angry here. Even when she yells at me for some reason, her heart is never in it and the laughter comes right back. Mom was having so much fun, and we are a family! We belong together, even if things get rough!"

A lengthy, embarrassed silence followed his words.

Lucia was close to crying again. It tore Jon's heart, but he refrained from any comment and only touched Joshua's hair briefly before he returned to Naomi.

She was awake and aware but still connected to a number of machines and the beeping heart monitor that drove him crazy with its rhythmic sound. Someone had changed her bedding and made her more comfortable, but she was still as pale as the sheets.

"My father," she said. "He is making a fuss. He's just scared, Jon."

"Yes."

He sat on the corner of her bed, ignoring the chair and the nurse who tutted softly. "It's my fault. I know it, Baby. I pushed you out into the public eye, and this happened to you. It would never have happened if we had stayed back in Halmar. Maybe you had it right all along and this life here is not meant for you. God, I hate myself for bringing you here. It was one of the first things you said to me after I found you, that you never wanted to come back. And I compelled you. I made you come, you did what I wanted, and now you suffer the results of my stupid ideas." When she did not react, he pressed on, desperation rising like bitter bile in his throat. "It's true I wanted more for you. But you never really asked for it, you were content with your life—"

"Who said that?" Naomi interrupted him softly. "I don't think I ever said that."

Surprised, Jon stopped and looked up at her. There was a faint smile on her exhausted face. Her breath was short and sounded painful; her words were clipped and forced.

"But you had built so much for yourself." Her fingers in his, he wondered what had happened to her rings.

"Nothing, Jon." Her voice was barely more than a whisper. "You still don't understand, do you? There's nothing. Safety is nothing. If I had been killed out there, at least I would have died happy." A tug on his hand to pull his attention away from his black thoughts, then, "Where's my Oscar? I hope someone thought to pick it up. I want that thing very badly."

"You…" he began, but he couldn't think of anything sensible to say.

41

COFFEE. SHE WANTED coffee, she complained, and something to eat. She was starving, and all they were offering her was tasteless mush and that abysmal herbal tea. She wanted a shower and proper clothing, or at least a decent nightgown, and a room with a window, not this glass-fronted chamber. Her querulous demands lightened Jon's heart. The nurses brought her a thin broth, which she sipped gratefully, mumbling that as far as she had been told her stomach wasn't injured, and she wasn't eating with her lung, was she?

"But your liver, dear," the woman reminded her. "That needs to be watched. You can't process everything."

"My liver," Naomi replied tartly, "is telling me that it needs coffee to function properly. And some shrimp."

Jon laughed. He was so relieved to see her spirit returning. He wanted to rush right out and get her the best shrimp the town had to offer, bring a chef to prepare them at her bedside, along with whatever else she craved, just to make her smile again.

"Slowly," he said. "You'll get everything you want in good time."

She dozed off soon afterward, her head turned away from him, the deep fatigue of her injury etched plainly on her face. He had to clamp down tightly on the impulse to just pick her up and carry her home to the safety and comfort of her room where he could wrap her in her silk quilt and pamper her back to health without Olaf's blistering wind of hate whipping everything and everyone in sight.

"I think I was dead."

He had fallen into a light sleep in his chair and woke at those chilling words. Naomi was looking at him from dark, deep-set eyes, but she reached out for him and tugged his sleeve.

"I had the weirdest dreams." A rustling breath, then, "And I couldn't remember, Jon. I couldn't see a reason to return. One time I was here, and you were crying and promising all kind of things and loading yourself with guilt, as usual…" A small smile slipped across her dry lips, but it vanished quickly.

"It hurt so terribly. There was only pain, a burning, screaming pain in my body, and I could not stay."

"You weren't awake, love. Not for a moment. You were sedated so heavily, it was impossible for you to be awake. It was just a dream." Her words scared him badly.

She pondered this for a while. "No. I was awake. I must have been awake. For the life of me I can't think why I would bring your guilty tirades into a dream."

OLAF WAS BITTER, and he told her so in no uncertain terms.

She should never have come back here, he said, standing at the foot of her bed, and she should never have told Joshua who his father was in the first place. She should have remained in Halmar, where they had put her at her own request and where she had been leading a meaningful life instead of playing the wife of a Hollywood star. He brushed away her argument that Joshua had a right to know his father, and Jon his son, stating that there were plenty of children in the world who never knew the identity of their fathers and were perfectly happy.

Naomi listened to him with growing exhaustion and impatience. His attitude upset her more than she could say, and she felt insulted by it. She was much too weak to argue with him, but Olaf did not see her distress and went on with his harangue even after her eyes had dropped shut.

"Let me take you back home. You will be so much better off in Kleinburg, Naomi. You know this is not the right place for you. You know it. And he…" Olaf said with enough anger to wake her up again, "he is nothing but trouble. Was then and is now, no matter how many precious jewels he puts on you."

When no reaction came from her, Olaf added, "Damn it, Naomi, one of his former girlfriends gunned you down! She wanted you dead and out of the way, and how many others, do you think, will come up with similar ideas? You will never be safe, you will never be able to lead a normal life! Darling, please come home with us."

There was sweat on her brow, and her breath came laboriously. "His ex-girlfriend?"

"Yes, the same one who made that horrible scene right before your wedding, the one who made you nearly drop at my feet when I had to lead you down to your apartment and safety, and you were crying so hard you could barely see. That one, Naomi. She was the one who shot you."

"Sophie?"

Olaf shrugged. "How should I know? The redhead. She was killed, they shot her. Didn't your husband tell you? Did he think he could keep the truth from you? Two people died, Naomi, and you barely escaped with your life, and all because of him!"

She stared at her father, her hands gripping the blanket.

"You're throwing away your life. Naomi, I want to protect you! We protected you from him for years, and the minute you allow him back in you nearly get killed!"

Naomi tried to reply, but there was just not enough strength left in her. Her lips moved, her head dropped back against the pillow, and then all hell broke loose as the monitors sent off their alarms and medical personnel came running, pushing Olaf out of the way to get to Naomi.

THE NURSES TRIED to keep Jon back when he tried to storm inside, but he would not have it. Fear gripped his soul when he saw the group of doctors bent over her still form, paddles in the hands of one, a large syringe in another's, a third listening to her pulse carefully.

"Yes," came the verdict, and that needle plunged into her chest. He had stepped into a wild, claustrophobic nightmare, a scene from a bad TV show. Gradually the frantic signals of the monitors silenced one by one, and the nurses and doctors in the room moved away from Naomi until only one physician remained to watch her closely.

"Your wife," he explained once the immediate danger was past, "had another cardiac arrest. We can't figure out why yet; she seemed to be doing so well. Did something happen to upset her? She needs rest and quiet, even if she looks strong to you. It will take her months to heal, Mr. Stone, and she will need all the care in the world during that time, and absolutely no distress."

Two nurses returned with a fresh gown to replace the one she was still wearing, handling her ever so carefully, whispering calming words even though she was barely conscious, her breath a cruel, rasping sound in the stillness of the room. Naomi's skin was grey and damp, her lips and eyelids had a bluish tinge, there were purple smudges under her eyes and once again needles in her arms.

"Baby," he whispered, uncomprehending and frightened to his bones. "Baby, what happened? I was ready to get you a big pot of Starbucks."

Tortured tears slipped across her face as she looked up at him.

"I think I'm dying, Jon," he heard her breathe. "I won't make it. Please, let me die. It hurts so much."

He sank down beside her, stunned into speechlessness by her words. All his dreams seemed to end here in this stark, impersonal hospital room with these hissing machines and blinking screens, and the life force seeping out of his beloved like spilled light. Tentatively he reached out to touch her cold hand, but there was no response, not even the slightest movement or pressure, only a passive acceptance, as if it were something she had to endure to get his permission to move on. She had turned her head away and drifted off, into what he did not know— sleep, unconsciousness, or simply a rejection of a world that was too full of pain and sorrow.

One of the doctors returned to Jon. "I've been told that your wife had an altercation with her father before this new crisis. This must not happen again, Mr. Stone." He paused for emphasis. "She will not survive otherwise. I suggest you ban all visitors. This is not good, not good at all."

It did not take Jon long to make his decision. He plucked the cell phone out of his pocket.

"Solveigh," he said, "I need you."

"Hang up, Jon," was all she replied after listening for a minute.

Kevin, he wanted Kevin. He wanted her home where he could close the gates and keep the world out. She would be in her room, or the roof garden on that large daybed, and he would be with her all the time and pamper her back to health himself.

Her doctor was scandalized when Jon informed him, but he did not budge.

"It has nothing to do with your hospital. I want those two nurses who've been looking after her, and anything else she might need, and it will not be your loss, I promise."

He did not leave the small hallway outside her room again, making sure no one but her medical staff entered. No one dared get close to him.

After he had asked Sal to see to transportation for Naomi, he found his father-in-law and took a deep breath.

"You'll not get close to Naomi again until she asks for you explicitly. You will not see her now, and not for a long, long time. If it were my decision she would never see you again." He looked past Olaf at Lucia. "I'm sorry, Lucia. But Naomi's heart stopped again. She nearly died, and I have a good idea why that happened. You can go in with me now and say goodbye, but then you'll leave. I'm through with your family." In turning, he added, "And don't even think of contacting Joshua. I'm going to have the lawyers get a restraining order against your husband and anyone else in your family."

"You cannot do this. She is our daughter, and Joshua is our grandson!" Olaf took a step toward him, but Jon only raised his hand in a bored gesture.

"Now, Sal."

"Right away, Jon." Sal moved aside, the phone already in his hand.

Nothing, Lucia learned bitterly, that concerned her son-in-law was done until he ordered it, and he was very good at ordering people around without seeming to do so. He did it quietly and courteously, using "please" and "thank you" a lot, but in the end he was still dictating his terms to the world. He was impressive, a self-assured and world-wise man with only one thing on his mind: saving his wife. Ignoring Olaf completely, she followed Jon inside to Naomi's bedside, only to see her unconscious with no chance to bid her goodbye.

"I can't allow this, Lucia. She will decide for herself what will happen eventually, but until she does, nothing in her life will change. If she wants to leave me once she is strong enough to make up her mind..." The famous voice cracked on those words. "If she pulls through, I'll do anything she wishes, I promise, but right now, I'm the one who says what will be done."

The dark, intense eyes came to rest on her, and Lucia drew back a little from their scrutiny. "I'm sorry, but she doesn't deserve Olaf's attitude, Lucia. I don't deserve it. I admit to many mistakes, but alienating her from you is not one of them. Please leave now."

And she did.

SOLVEIGH, HER GROWING belly contained in wide jeans, appeared at the hospital a few hours later. She had, she reported, chartered a plane to bring over Andrea and Christi. The hotel would be shut down, compensation made to the guests who had booked for the next few weeks and alternate lodgings found for them. Russ would pick them up from the airport himself and bring them right over. Kevin was on his way too.

Joshua would be returning to New York and school in a few days, with strict orders not to go anywhere without a phone and his bodyguards.

"Your Mom will be fine," Jon promised. "You know I will do everything to make it so, Joshua. She is receiving the best care in the world, and once she is back in her own house, nothing evil or disturbing can touch her. She'll be back to her old self in no time."

42

THE MOSS WAS so soft under her feet, the air cool and earthy, almost moist, and it was quiet as a church. Somewhere above, the sun was shining, casting rays through the foliage of the huge, strange trees that rustled ever so gently in the lazy wind. There were deep, dark pools of water among the gently rounded hummocks, rocks like the bent backs of dwarfs digging for jewels under the ground, and tiny white flowers in the folds of the forest floor. It was the most tranquil, beautiful place, even lovelier than the white beach under the stars. Jon was walking beside her, patiently, matching his pace to her slow, halting steps.

"Can I stay here a little longer," she asked, "and not return?"

But he shook his head. "No, Babe, we have a life that needs to be lived. Didn't you want coffee?"

The word still echoed in her mind when she opened her eyes to morning sunshine over the ocean and the unmistakable scent of her favorite brew. She had the distinct memory of being moved and carried, of having slept in Jon's arms, the imprint of his embrace still on her body, and she needed a moment to realize she was not in her hospital room anymore but in her own bedroom.

"Don't," Jon ordered when she tried to move. "Wait."

They helped her sit up against the cushions, and she looked into smiling faces she had not seen in a while; Christi, Andrea, Solveigh, and Amparo, a steaming mug in her hands.

And then, after more than a week of nothing but water and gruel, her first sip of coffee. Naomi fought when Amparo tried to take the cup away from her again, nearly growling at her, to the amusement of her friends, but Amparo was adamant, promising chicken broth later.

"Toast with butter and strawberry jam, please!" Naomi begged, but again she got a negative reply.

First, dry toast. Then everything else. And slowly, slowly.

They chased Jon out and helped her to the bathroom, slowly, carefully, where they let her use the toilet discreetly and then sat her on the rim of the tub to give her a sponge bath and wash her hair.

Naomi nearly sobbed with relief when the clean nightgown slipped over her head and Solveigh rubbed her hair dry. Christi put lotion on her feet and the dry skin on her legs and arms, and held her when she swayed with exhaustion.

She was made to walk all the way out to the patio, where they settled her on the bed under the canopy so she could look out to the Pacific and into the hills. They sat with her and chatted like birds, excited to be in Los Angeles and in Jon's huge mansion by the sea.

Kevin had arrived and come to look at her, checking her bandage and her vitals and pronouncing that he was pleased and did not really understand all the commotion, since she seemed well on her way to recovery.

The surgeon who had operated on her came by and smiled in approval.

Downstairs, to Jon, he said, "I didn't expect your wife to rally at all. We thought she'd be dead after that last collapse. Now, I'm very hopeful." He dithered before he went on, "In a way, she's an invalid now. Her health will never fully recover, and she'll never again be as robust as she was. But the scarring will not be too bad. With luck, only a thin white line will be visible down her side."

"An invalid?" Jon repeated incredulously. "We were hoping for another baby, and we have the tour ahead of us. God, we had so many plans… Our life was just beginning!"

"Well, not in the immovable, wheelchair way," Kevin threw in. "But she will never be as strong as she used to be, Jon, and a lot more fragile." He fell silent, then added slowly, "At some point, depression will set in. You need to be prepared for that. Right now she is still too preoccupied with her physical problems, but when that wears off she will start to think about the whole thing, and the reaction will show."

These predictions were hard to believe, seeing her propped up on a heap of silk cushions, her friends around, feeding her little pieces of toast, chatting and laughing, Solveigh braiding her hair, Amparo bringing a huge bouquet of roses sent by Jamal and placing them in a vase by her side.

Naomi smiled at Jon when she saw him standing in the doorway and asked the others for some privacy, which they granted readily.

"I feel terrible," she said when he sat down on the corner of her bed. "You haven't kissed me since the Oscars and I miss it."

"I've kissed you plenty, you greedy thing. Only you chose to sleep through it. I kissed you last night when I slept beside you, and you didn't even notice. Sleeping Beauty would have woken from the many kisses I planted on you, but you didn't. Must be losing my touch." To prove his point, he put his lips to hers softly.

"That's not a kiss. That's nothing. No wonder you couldn't wake me. I mean a real kiss."

"Ah, Naomi." Very carefully he took her in his arms and kissed her again, his tongue playing over her teeth and inside her mouth.

The nurse came, and Jon rose to make place for her.

"You don't seem to need me at all, my dear. You have a whole posse of people here to look after you. You will be spoiled and pampered so much you will get used to it and never want to rise again from your lair. But up you go, and some exercise, please."

She was extremely wobbly, but Naomi made herself walk around the patio once, guided by Jon, his strong hands holding her up as she moved slowly to the balustrade to look out at the sea.

"I want to be on the beach," she said querulously, "and in the garden."

"You will," he promised. "Just have a little patience."

"I want shrimp, too. Real food."

"Shrimp, no." The nurse laughed at her. "But it's good to hear you ask for them. How about some chicken?"

Naomi grumbled. Anything, as long as it wasn't tea or broth.

When they had settled her down again, she wanted clothes and not a nightgown, or at least something that felt a little more like clothes.

Jon promised he would see to it, and left her to drive downtown to Jamal's store and ask him to come along later in the day and bring her some comfortable, light things that would make her feel good and dressed at the same time.

CHRISTI AND ANDREA, unaccustomed to the balmy climate of California, sat perched side-by-side on one of the benches and watched in wonderment how their old boss was treated like a queen by the people who came and went—Sal, Art and Sue, Harry, Sean, all of them staying only minutes, leaving again as soon as she showed signs of flagging. She slept often and was always demanding food, specifying what it was she wanted, and to their amusement, complaining bitterly when she did not get it. Everything at the house revolved around her and her health, and it was done with light hearts and a lot of laughter.

This gave Jon the space to regain his own inner peace and find the time to ponder his own role in the dramatic events.

He rose early in the mornings to wander along the beach, collecting debris and shells. The solitude cleared his head and allowed him to gather the strength he knew he would need once her attention turned outward again.

He felt quite certain that he had done Sophie no wrong, feeling it was his right to end a relationship when it became senseless to him, with or without anyone else waiting behind the scenes. Sitting on the warm sand of the beach, he tried to recall the time when he had allowed her into a segment of his life, waiting, watching, judging, wondering if maybe she was the one who could fill the awful empty space in his heart.

Many had come and gone from the little beach house, some for a few hours or a night of heated sex, but for none of them, not even Sophie, had he taken down the pictures of Naomi on his shelves.

Tenacious, obsessive bastard, Sean had called him one day, as if Naomi's pictures were an old battered mug or teddy from his childhood that he could not bear to part with, but he had hung on and looked at those photos every morning after coming down the stairs from his bedroom, often with someone else still asleep up there. And she had gazed at him from those silver frames, a question in those deep, dark eyes and an invitation in the shape of her mouth. Most often, seeing her image there, he had sent the girl upstairs on her way in a cab, because there was always something lacking and he felt ashamed of his own frenzy.

There were moments when he thought his imagination and his memory had made a lot more of Naomi than there really had been, but then that instant by the lakeside came back to him and he knew with bleak certainty that it did not really matter whether it was fantasy or dreadful truth. It was what he lacked, what he needed.

He had met Sophie at a party at her father's house, a well-known movie director and friend of Harry's. She had caught his interest because she had not—unlike all the others—tried to catch his attention but stood alone, seemingly unconcerned, disinterested in the great singer who had come into the room like a star falling from the sky. Jon was so used to having the attention turn to him wherever he went that this piqued him, and he had gone over to her and talked to her, only to find out why she had not looked his way.

The reason had been funny and eased his suspicious mind: she had been wondering if she had turned off her stove, and she had been worried. On the spur of the moment he had offered to drive her over to her apartment to check, and they had ended up, of course, in her bed.

To this day he had never found out whether it had been an extremely clever plot on her part or not, but that was immaterial.

Sal had warned him at some point, warning him about his wild life and ever-changing partners.

"You'll catch something," he had said, "You'll come down with AIDS if you keep messing with everything in a skirt."

But he had always been so careful. He didn't want to get any of them pregnant because maybe, some day—and he was not too old yet to stop hoping—she might come back. Somewhere in the world, on one of his tours, in one of the strange cities, she might be there. So in the end, and without a second thought, he had placed that brief call from the airport.

"Listen," had been his words, "I'm going away. I won't be back, either. The things you left at my house, my housekeeper will pack them up and deliver them to you. We had a good time, but I need to move on."

It had been rather rough. There had been tears and pleas on the other side of the phone, and he had, couched in well-rehearsed and slick words, said some soothing things, but in the end he had hung up on her.

Over. Just like that, he had decided it was over. Time to say goodbye, and not a moment of emotion wasted.

43

JAMAL BROUGHT HER a stack of flowing silk kaftans in a rainbow of colors, comfortable, cool things she could easily wear over her bandages, with shawls woven from the finest cashmere, lined in velvet or fur to keep her warm.

"You are all treating me like I'm an old queen," she said. "But don't bet your money on a fast demise. I want to live a good while longer yet."

In addition to her new clothes, Jamal brought a huge assortment of Lebanese dishes from his favorite restaurant and was about to spread them out on the table when Kevin came out onto the patio. "Oh no! No foreign food, for heaven's sake! You'll kill her!"

"He won't," Naomi lamented. "I want to eat that!" For good measure she slapped her blanket in a show of frustration, which had them all laughing.

"Darling," Kevin cautioned, "Garlic, olive oil, spices, and onions? You poor liver will do somersaults. Please, none of that."

But in the end he let her take a few bites, glad to see her with a good appetite.

JOSHUA CAME FOR a week. He had convinced his teachers to let him go and made Helen buy him a ticket, and he showed up at the house unannounced. Happily he sat on the end of Naomi's bed, his legs crossed, stealing food from her plate until Jon slapped his wrist and then went down to the kitchen to get him something.

Jon was glad he had come. When Joshua had walked out onto the patio, Naomi's face lit up in a way he had not seen since before the shooting, and it gave him hope.

For a few days life felt nearly normal again, and when Harry's kids dropped by to pick Joshua up for a day on the beach his heart lifted, and he could almost envision a happy future. Their young laughter seemed to echo through the house when they drove off, leaving a trail of sand left behind in the hall, and the fridge well raided.

AT NIGHT, WHEN they were alone, Jon held her when the pain came and breathing was hard, and he was with her when the nightmares started, when she woke from sleep sweaty and crying, disoriented, clinging to him in fear.

It had taken eight weeks for the traumatic impact to finally come to the surface. Her mind had waited until her body was nearly healed before it opened the door to that dark abyss, but then it came with a vengeance.

She could not talk about it.

She tried to explain, lying in his arms, but the words just would not come. Instead, tears streamed down her face and bitter sobs wracked her body, and Jon, helpless against her torment, tried to soothe her as best as he could. He tried to figure out if it was her own injury that troubled her or whether she was beginning to think about the others who had been hurt that day, or even if the struggle with her father depressed her now, but she was unable to articulate her turmoil, answering only that she was sad and afraid.

"Of course she is," Kevin explained when he talked to him about it. "Jon, she nearly died, not once but a number of times. She has looked over that wall, been halfway across it even, and she has not returned from there completely yet. There's a shadow on her soul. No person endures what she endured and remains unscathed."

Solveigh made her walk around the roof garden every day, but the spirit she had shown in the beginning had changed to listlessness.

Sean, lugging his portable keyboard up the two flights of stairs to play for her, was greeted with no more than a silent glance, and when Jon came with his guitar to join him, she closed her eyes to listen but turned her head away.

Strangely, when she found it in her to talk at last, it was Art she turned to.

Sean and Sal, with her when she was attacked, she avoided, not even looking at them when they came to see her, almost as if she were ashamed they had seen her prostrate on the red carpet, bleeding. Toward Jon she was completely silent.

"I was dead," Naomi said suddenly one afternoon when she and Art were alone.

Art raised his head to look at her. She looked like a fairy in the shimmering robe she was wearing, stretched out under the canopy of the daybed, frailer and paler than she had ever been, her movements languid and passive.

"You are alive. You can't have been dead."

"No. I was dead." Wincing, she tried to sit up straighter. "I remember everything, Art. I remember Sean kneeling beside me, his shirt stained all red, and Sal talking to me, and then it suddenly all stopped. It was so peaceful, Art."

Shocked, he put his coffee cup on the table and folded his hands between his knees.

"In the ambulance, I heard the paramedics giving their report to the hospital, saying they didn't think I would still be alive when they got there. I heard the sound of the defibrillator before I drifted off." She fell silent, picking the skin off a fresh fig before she nibbled the red, seedy flesh. "I was aware and yet not, and there were many moments when I never wanted to return to this life. It was so much easier to just let go, just drift off, not feel, not think, not see Jon's distress or my parents' anger."

Float, silently and softly, and then dissolve into oblivion and forgetting.

"I heard him cry, Artie. In the deep of the night, when no one else was around, I heard him cry and talk to me, and I didn't want to return because it hurt so much. I wanted him to go away and take his sorrow elsewhere."

Art thought she looked exhausted in an alarming way, as if she had given up the fight. "Maybe you need some distance," he suggested carefully. "Maybe your father was not so wrong, Naomi. Maybe you would heal better somewhere else."

But she shook her head. "No, Artie, I need to be here. If I run away from my nightmares again, I fear I would never find the strength to return."

"She was a lunatic, Naomi. There's no other way to put it. Millions of people separate every day all over the world, but only very few go out and shoot someone because of it. Sure, it's heartbreak and pain, but Baby Girl, you can't make anyone stay if they don't want to." Even softer, he added, "Least of all him, the Jonman. He is single-minded and obsessive, and he always wanted that true love thing, stupid romantic that he is."

Art moved away so he could light a cigarette without bothering her.

"You shouldn't think about his former girlfriends, Naomi, not for a moment. He's just not that kind of guy. Where girls are concerned, he's as old-fashioned as you can get. Single-minded, I tell you. Don't worry."

She toyed with the tassels on her cushion, her eyes lowered.

"I feel guilty, Artie. Guilty as hell that she had to die. And Stewart. God, Stewart. He died because of me. He died because it was his job to protect me."

When she struggled to rise from her couch, Art tossed his cigarette over the balustrade mindlessly and rushed to help her up, holding her around the waist until she stood on her feet. He was shocked by the way he could feel her bones under his hands, so different from the lush, glowing woman they had all admired at the Oscars. Now she seemed like a wounded little animal.

"You need to get back into shape, Baby Girl," he said. "So you will have the stamina for the tour."

Together they strolled to the other side of the patio where they could look out toward the hills.

"I don't know that I will go, Art."

The girls were looking after her very well. Her hair was glossy and groomed, her skin soft, her hands and nails perfectly manicured, but the spark had gone out of her.

"Of course you'll go! He won't do it without you, and you know it. Hell, they're only doing it because you wanted to see them on stage again."

They could hear Jon's voice from inside, and Sal's, both of them laughing at something, Sal nearly crowing with delight, and then they stepped out into the sunshine.

"Baby, you're up!" Jon called happily, "Why don't you come downstairs. We can all sit on the terrace and have coffee together."

Naomi turned toward him slowly. "I want to go out, Jon. I want you and Sal to take me out."

They all stared at her in surprise when she told them she wanted to see Stewart's family. She wanted to tell them how sorry she was, and how bad she felt about his death, maybe take something, anything, to emphasize how terrible she felt. No press, no uproar, just a very private, quiet, brief visit.

"Naomi," Art interrupted, "everything has been done. We were there at his funeral, Jon was there to see them himself, and of course they received compensation. You should know your husband better, dear."

"There is no compensation for a lost life."

"Well, of course there isn't," Sal agreed. "But at least his family won't have to worry about money in the future."

She hardly dared to ask. "Did he have a family of his own? Children? A wife?"

Jon shook his head without looking at her. "Of course not, Naomi. We don't hire guards who have kids. I don't. And believe me, they're paid well. They know what they're getting into. Baby, they are bodyguards. They are supposed to save your life, even at the cost of their own if necessary."

"We know you feel guilty," Sal added, "and it's a very fine trait, darling. But in the end, their job is a lot like a policeman's, or a firefighter's. They protect and save people, only they get a much better salary."

"How much?" she wanted to know. It did feel a little twisted, but she wanted to know how much her life was worth in terms of security.

Sal shook his head at her with a small, ironic smile.

"I won't tell you, because I don't want to weigh your life in coin. Rest assured, Stewart could afford a very nice house in the hills and a couple of pretty expensive cars. His bank account was quite feisty, and with the millions Jon put on top of it, his relatives are now among the wealthy."

"But he's dead, because of me."

Jon rushed to help her when she swayed on her feet. He led her back to her bed.

"I want to do it. I want to do it myself, Jon. I need to apologize to them, need to…"

"Yes, love, I understand. But it's been weeks now, and you would be tearing open the wound again. He's buried and everything is over, everything. I will take you if you insist, but you would only rip it open again, for his parents, and for yourself, too." He hesitated, then added softly, "I went to see his mother myself. If it means anything to you, I felt the need to ask for forgiveness too. She was very bitter, and she told me it was his own fault; he had chosen this profession, after all. Please don't do this to them, and us."

Her fingers tightened on his briefly.

They were still without their rings. The hospital had returned them to him, washed and in a little plastic bag, but when he had taken them out he had seen the residue of blood among the stones. The dress he had refused. He had even refused to look at it, too afraid of seeing the huge blood stains on the cream satin, too scared to relive those terrible moments. He had requested a video tape of the shooting and had watched it over and over again at night when she was asleep, torturing himself with the pictures and the deep guilt of having left her there, turning away after that kiss without looking back before getting into the waiting car. Sophie, Sal said after sitting with him through one of those viewings, had been out to get Naomi, that much was clear. She must have been in that crowd of guests even when Jon walked past, and she had let him go by unharmed.

"But the hate that girl must have cultivated," Sal had said in an almost admiring tone. "Just think of it! A year later, and she's still out for vengeance!"

"And how…" Jon hardly had dared to voice it. "How could she get a gun in there? I know it was a small and she had it in her dress, but Sal, that place is supposed to be safe. They have the tightest security you can imagine."

But he knew, of course. No one spoke about it because it was a shameful fact, but everyone knew, and Jon pitied her father more than he could say. She had come with him, and everyone knew his face. No one had bothered to check the lovely daughter of the celebrated Hollywood director for a weapon.

"You could visit his grave, if you want," Art suggested to Naomi. "Would that help you?"

She shook her head. "Your suit," she said to Sal. "I remember you knelt beside me. Your suit must be ruined. And Sean's."

They stared at her.

"Yes," Sal found the courage to answer. "I threw it away. I'm sure Sean did the same." A lot more than a pair of trousers had been ruined that night, he thought ruefully, so much more, seeing her there, pale and thin, her eyes dull, listening to Jon's careful half-truths and side-stepping.

They had succeeded in keeping the media hype away from her, but it would not work forever, and he feared the moment when she found out how heavily she had hit the headlines despite their maneuvering.

"You didn't expect us to keep them, did you?" He said it lightly, but he knew there were traps hidden in this discussion.

She nodded, her fingers fidgeting with the embroidery on the quilt. It was a new nervous habit he did not like to see in her at all.

Slow, silent tears spilled onto her cheeks and she turned her head away.

"Right, folks." Sal rose, motioning to Art. "Let's move, Artie. We need to go. There's work waiting."

"Don't you have to go too?" Naomi asked, but Jon settled down next to her and shook his head.

"I'm tired. You might as well go along with them, Jon, I'll rest now."

It was offered in a listless, grey tone.

"I'm not going anywhere," was his light reply. "If you need rest, then I'll stay right here and stare at the sky for a while and watch you sleep. Maybe it'll do me some good too. I'll think about what I want for dinner tonight and whether I'll take the girls shopping and spoil them to the hilt before they return home. I'll dress them up and get them at least five purses each; that seems to be a big item with you females. Maybe I'll even get them some pretty bracelets or something. And then I'll take them out for lunch to a place where they can be sure to see some famous faces, and I think I'll introduce them to some of the hot, smooth actors too, so they'll have something to brag about."

He paused, his hands folded behind his head.

"Hell, I'll ask Harry to organize a party for them and ask a few people over, give them the entire Hollywood treatment for a few days. Can I borrow your Rolls?"

Her reply was slow in coming. "Sure. Whatever."

It was not the reaction he had been hoping for.

"You might come along, you know."

Kevin had told him, the morning before, that there was really no good reason for her to stay sequestered in the roof garden. She would tire easily, true, but medically she was ready to pick up her life again, if she did it slowly and carefully.

"In every respect," he had added and eyed his brother circumspectly. "But gently, Jon. No wild trysts, please, not yet. Although a little loving would surely be good for her."

"Wild?" Jon's voice had been brittle with mirth. "Don't know what you mean, wild."

"Are you telling me, brother of mine, that all that energy you bring to the stage is pure show? Come on! Even my Sarah fantasizes about how it would be with you in bed. She imagines you're a real stud." He had eyed Jon with some irony.

They had been standing in the kitchen, Jon leaning against the counter, a mug of coffee in his hand, dressed in a black silk turtleneck and slacks, unshaven, and grinning broadly at Kevin's unspoken question.

"Never more than three at once, Kev. Too much bother. They talk all the time, and my capacity for listening is limited."

"You jerk!" Kevin had nearly tossed his breakfast at him. "Stop with bragging already!"

Jon had shrugged. "Well, the wife seems pleased with the performance, so I guess I'm good enough."

This had been a new experience for them, bantering about sex, sharing a few confidences without being too serious, a moment of brotherly closeness in lives that had barely touched at all in years.

"Yeah, good, right, I bet you had a lot of practice before you decided to settle on one, too. So don't brag! If I were in your shoes I would have taken advantage of the situation too, and all those sweet offers."

"Sure. Had to stay in shape. My wife is a stern mistress, and she knows how to punish me swiftly and harshly if I fail."

Kevin's shout of laughter had echoed through the entire house.

"COME ALONG? SHOPPING with the girls?"

At least she had not told him no right away, Jon registered with some relief.

"I need you, Babe. Need you to want to live again. You're letting go, Naomi, and I can't bear to watch you drift away. Tell me what to do to make you want to live, Baby."

"I'm alive." No more than a sigh, and a very resigned one at that.

Her eyes were huge in her pale face, her skin almost translucent after her weightloss and the long time without proper exercise and sunshine. She was wearing one of the loose robes that did not show her contours, a beautiful silk thing in a deep purple that slid over her arms and left them bare when she reached up to push her hair back.

"But Babe," he argued gently, "alive means more than just living. I want you to get dressed and go downtown with us. It's high time you returned to life, and to me. I want you wanting me again, loving me. I want our life together back. We were doing so well before this happened, and I really, really want that back."

"Later, Jon."

Only that, later.

Unaccountably, a hot fury rose in him.

"No. Not later. No more, Naomi, I'm not going to watch you waste away! You've languished here for over two months, and that is quite enough."

Against her protests, he picked her up from her bed and carried her inside. She was as light as a child and it felt like holding a struggling bird, but he did not let her go.

"Oh, fight all you like. At least it shows me there's some will left in you yet." He put her down on her feet in front of her wardrobe and opened it for her. "Here. That thing is coming off now, and you're going to dress properly. And then we'll take the girls out for dinner. Go on. Either you do it yourself or I'll do it for you, but it's going to happen."

His anger was not directed at Sophie and at the blow she had dealt them. Whatever he might have felt in terms of guilt or commiseration was dead now, burned out of him by the sudden surge of rage, born of desperation at seeing Naomi retreating into the shadows a little further every day.

"But you have to go away. I don't want you to look." Her hands pulled the silk of her gown tightly around her body in protection, but it only showed him quite clearly how thin she was.

"Are you crazy? I'm not going anywhere, and you'll drop that thing right now. You're my wife, and I'm looking at you all I like! Go on, toss it, or I'll help you, but then we won't be going out for a while yet."

"I won't!" She retreated a couple of steps from him, but her voice had gained a trace of steel he rather relished. "I'm ugly now, and damaged, and you'll never look at me the same way, you'll always see that scar and think of what happened, and…and…"

He was upon her so fast that she stumbled.

"That does it. Dinner will have to wait, I fear."

He had not seen her naked since the night before the Oscars—the girls had taken care of her and always chased him away—but now she stood before him, shivering a little, her hands knotted together in shame, and it shocked him how she had wasted away during the past weeks, despite their care and Andrea's cooking.

"Baby, you need some proper attention, and I'll give it to you now. I'm going to drag you back into life, by your hair if I have to."

Gently, gently, he laid her down on their bed and held her against his body, caressing and exploring the new curves and contours.

Naomi held on to him as if she were fighting for her life.

"Going to bring you back now," Jon growled in her ear. "We're alive, damn it all. Let go, love. Let it all go now."

HIS FINGERTIPS FOLLOWED the ominous trail down her side, scar tissue, red under his touch. He knew there was a daily routine with a salve to keep the skin soft, and he also knew, from Kevin's explicit reports, how extremely circumspect the surgeons had been, despite the severity of her injury, to restore her to at least superficial normalcy.

"But I am ugly now, Jon." Naomi gazed down at her own body in disgust and sorrow. "Why did they have to cut me open from top to bottom? It looks like a zipper!"

There were no gentle words of comfort; she was right, and nothing could change the bitter facts. "It does look a bit like a zipper, but that's only now. It'll get better. And I don't mind one little bit, darling. You are definitely not ugly." Jon pulled up the quilt. "You were wounded, but that doesn't make you ugly and it doesn't diminish my desire for you, you silly girl. As if I care about a little scar."

His hand grabbed her arm tightly when she tried to pull away, shame creeping into her eyes again. "Oh no. You're not going anywhere. If I have to, I'll keep you here in bed until I've driven that notion out of you, my pretty thing, and then I'll take you down to Valentino and have them outfit you with all the scanty clothes they have. You're not going to hide yourself away anymore."

It was delivered in the cool, hard voice she dreaded, but Naomi knew the tone was not really directed at her but at her sorrow and at Sophie, poor, dead Sophie.

At last she found the words to pour out her distress.

Jon, sitting up against the headrest, held her tightly against his chest while she talked and cried and dozed through the night.

"Yes," he admitted when she asked, "you were dead. Well, not really dead, or you wouldn't be here now." Those words nearly choked him. "Your heart stopped a couple of times and they had to bring you back, but Baby, you lost so much blood, and you were so terribly hurt, and... hey Babe, I'll go down to the kitchen and find us something to eat, what do you think?"

There was no immediate reply, so he turned to look at her, a tinge of alarm pulling at his senses, but there was nothing wrong. She was sitting in the middle of the bed, the sheet gathered in her lap but otherwise naked, her hair wild and astoundingly black against her skin, regarding him thoughtfully. The first light of dawn was creeping in through the open balcony door and casting a bluish shine on her, enhancing the ethereal impression.

"You look just like you did when I first brought you here. Exactly like that, Naomi." He could hardly say it. "You're still the girl I found so long ago, you haven't changed one bit. I love you, Baby, so much. Are you truly hungry?"

"Yes, but not for food."

WONDERING, MARVELING, BREATHLESS with desire, his chest burning with a frightening, intense love, Jon sat on the bed and watched her get dressed for dinner at Harry's.

Naomi had needed a rest, but she had been in a good mood when she retired for a couple of hours, kissing him and gently pushing him away when he wanted to follow her inside.

"I can see it in your eyes, little beast. Ah, and how sweet that is! I see you looking at my mouth and your face goes all soft with longing." Just like that time in the hallway in Geneva where he had held her cornered against the wall, leaning toward her, one hand beside her shoulder blocking her escape, their bodies not touching but very close, the air between them simmering.

She loved it, he could hardly fail to notice, loved him to charm and seduce her, talk her into surrender in his dark, sweet drawl, his lips close to her face so his breath stroked her skin. "Let me into your room. Let me in, sleep with me. Let me make love to you. You won't be disappointed; I know how to do it in a way that will make you faint with ecstasy."

Her eyelids had fluttered and her lips had parted so invitingly, but once more, to his absolute delight, her reply, delivered in a low, cool voice, had been, "That's not how it works."

"Beast." But he let her go with a light slap on her rump and a regretful sigh.

"THAT LOOKS GOOD on you, you thin stick," he commented now when she slipped on one of the dresses she had bought on their shopping trip with the girls.

Naomi pulled her hair up in a saucy ponytail. "Shut up. I'm doing what I can, alright?"

The exhausted tone surprised him. "Well, you're not eating, love, and I don't want you to stay like this, weak and wan. Hell, how will you ever be able to give me a spirited tussle again if I have to be afraid of breaking you in two?"

"Think of something else for a change." Naomi fished for a pair of sandals that would not slip from her bony feet as soon as she took a step. "Oh, bother." Resigned, she sat down beside him, her hands in her lap, still barefoot. "I'm so tired, Jon. I can't keep pretending everything is alright. I try, but it's just not working. Maybe my dad was right, maybe I should go to Kleinburg for a while. Maybe I really need to step away from it all."

"No." His reply came swiftly, panic in his voice. "No, Baby, please. You know what will happen if you do that. You won't come back, you know it. You won't come back to me, you'll leave me forever. God, Naomi. Please. I'm begging you. Please don't leave me now."

He watched her gaze travel to the Oscar statuette on the table, right next to the Grammy Award. "You were happy here before this happened, we were happy. You had fun, you loved it. You're depressed and scared now, but darling, it will come back, the fun and the joy, I promise."

They had been to Tiffany's, where he had bought some trinkets for the girls. While he was picking out a ruby pendant for Solveigh he observed how Naomi brought out her rings and weighed them in her hand and then returned them to her purse, but he had refrained from a comment then.

"Your rings," he now asked, "don't you want to wear them?"

She only shrugged, and it nearly broke his heart.

"Naomi, don't you want to be married to me anymore? Do you want out? Is that it?"

Silence settled over them, Naomi, her head bowed and her hands folded in the material of her new dress; Jon, his eyes closed, dreading her next words.

How naïve, he thought bitterly, to assume that some lovemaking would bring her back to him, would make her forget the hurt and the fear. "What do you want me to do?" he plodded on, grief settling deep into him. "What can I do to make it easier for you?"

Gently he reached for her hands and eased her stiff fingers into his.

"You can't unmarry me. I won't let you. I know you love me. Look around you—all this is yours, and me, I'm part of it. I'm all yours, Naomi. God, there is no other who could take your place! You know that!"

"Unmarry is not a word, Jon." A slight pressure, a tentative sign. "You can't have me unmarry you, you silly bastard. But…"

"But, Baby?" he interrupted. "There's a 'but'? Don't kill me, Naomi."

"But," she concluded sadly, "I just don't know how to go on. I don't know how to pick up the pieces, Jon. Even Halmar, even that's tainted now. I'll always think of Sophie and that scene outside the hotel and feel terrible about it, how desperate she was. She surely did not deserve to die over you."

"Die over me?"

"Of course she died over you, Jon. She died because she wanted you and knew no other way to get you but to try and kill me. Can't you see?"

THEY WERE ALL, it seemed, waiting for her.

Heads swiveled when she entered Harry's house; silence descended on the large group of guests.

Grace came to meet her and kiss her cheek and lead her to a couch in a quiet corner. "Here, love." She pressed a glass of champagne into her hand. "You can't imagine how good it is to see you here again, and looking rather well, too."

For a little while she was left alone, but then a strange, almost ceremonious parade began as one after another well-known Hollywood faces approached her and asked after her health, wished her a speedy recovery or commiserated, inquired how her work was coming along or what her plans were for the future, some of them only chatting briefly about the weather or the food, some not even looking at her, as if she was the realization of something they did not wish to be confronted with at all.

One of them, the host of the show Jon had appeared on after the Academy Awards, Jake, sat down beside her. "You know, you're an icon now, you've made movie history. That shooting will be in the chronicles of the Oscars for all time."

It was said in his usual darkly humorous manner, but Naomi could not really see the funny side of the affair. She started to turn away, but he laid his hand on her arm. "No, dear, I wasn't making a joke. Quite the contrary."

He made a serious effort to appear respectable for once.

"Nightmare stuff." Jake shook his head at her. "Absolutely, Naomi, a nightmare. It's what every one of us fears more than anything else. Ever since John Lennon no one has felt safe. The innocence is gone. We try to live as normally as possible, but you know yourself how restricted we really are. So in that place where we feel reasonably safe, on that well-guarded red carpet, none of us looks for danger, right? And you were assaulted there. Pure nightmare. You embody something now that no one here wanted to see or experience, ever, and that is why they look at you with such mixed feelings. We are sorry for you because you were hurt, we are angry because it was possible to hurt you at all, and we are scared, because if it can happen to you, it can happen to any of us, anywhere, and that makes life so much more precarious. Who can tell? Maybe on my way home, when I'm stopped at a red light, the guy in the car next to me will shoot me. Because his wife laughed too hard at my latest stupid joke, or because he felt personally insulted by it, or just because he's in a foul mood and thinks killing a famous person will make him feel better." He fished the olive out of his Martini with expert fingers and popped it into his mouth.

"But this was personal."

This made him laugh and turn his big frame into a position that allowed him to face her.

"Ah, personal, a lover's tiff. That's what you think? Then why choose that particular spot? She could have caught you in so many places, on the beach, shopping, during lunch somewhere. Why pick that exact spot and time? No, this was meant to be a spectacle. She wanted to go out in a blaze. Curious, isn't it? She let him pass by, but you she tried to kill. She was stalking you, not him, so it's something to do with you and not him at all."

Jon was standing with a couple of musicians. He was gesticulating animatedly with the hand that held his cigarette and shifting from one leg to the other, listening to some inner rhythm, his shoulders moving with easy grace as he talked, his voice low but still strong enough to be heard over the general murmur.

"I don't think," Naomi replied, "she was stalking me at all. She wanted me out of the way so she could get him back. She wanted him back very much."

Jake's ample body shook with his deep laugh. He nearly spilled his drink when he sat up straight for emphasis. "Well, of course she did! Who would want to let go of such a precious catch? Just think, all the prestige, the notoriety, the wealth, the attention! But relationships end all the time. That was not all of it. You are very sweet to think it was only a jealousy thing, Naomi." His eyes narrowed in curiosity. "Can you really be that naïve, that untainted? No one angles for a star like your man without wanting the whole cake. I find it hard to believe anyone can even see him as a normal person without everything else that comes in that package. The fame, the glamour, the trophies. Catching someone like Jon means harnessing the beast of show business, taking advantage of all that it has to offer, and good luck with the ride! But that's what they see, and it's what they want. Don't tell me you wanted something else?"

She did not reply right away. "I guess I *am* that naïve, I just fell in love. I didn't care much about the fame."

His laugh bellowed through the large room, causing many heads to turn in their direction. "Bless you, child. And I think I will even believe it. But no!" He became very serious again as he returned to his original question. "Whatever you may think, this was not about Jon. It was about you. You were the main target, and I have the feeling it was because you were the embodiment of her dreams."

Harry found his way to her soon after and asked what Jake had been talking about, a little worry in his voice, but she waved it away.

Exhaustion had been creeping up on her over the past hour, and, incredibly, a crazy hunger for meat, as if her body was telling her what it needed. Garlic bread, too, and pineapple, preferably barbecued, all washed down with a tart white wine.

"Harry, do you think they have some steaks ready yet? I'm starving."

Fatigued, Naomi leaned her head back against the upholstery and closed her eyes, the noise of the party humming in her head. She felt trapped, caught in a dark, cavernous labyrinth where she was getting more and more lost with every turn she took. The commiserating looks were a burden, the words of pity a constant reminder of her deep-seated guilt, the alertness to her misery a bondage without respite.

By the time Harry returned, the girls had come to sit with her for a while, starry-eyed and breathless to find themselves in the company of so many faces known only from movies or magazines, the glamour still working on them despite Solveigh's acid comments.

Jon was hovering. He refrained from staying with her all the time so she wouldn't feel like she was under observation, but he was never far away and seemed tuned in to her, ready to be by her side as soon as she needed him. Even now, his back to her, talking to others, he seemed to be harkening backward. Critically he had watched as Harry brought her food and how she picked at it without really eating anything, her appetite gone again as soon as it was in front of her. He was on the point of turning to her, but Sal was quicker.

"Stop fussing, for God's sake," he told her bluntly. "Just feed your face. You look like a bulimic supermodel. All you need is a stash of cocaine to complete the picture. Are you planning to go down the drain like so many other females in Hollywood?"

Naomi felt like throwing the plate at him, but Solveigh added, "I think she likes the way she looks now, as thin as a piece of paper and paler than vanilla pudding. Me, I think she looks like crap, but whatever."

Out of sheer defiance, Naomi cut off a big piece of steak and stuffed it in her mouth.

"Oh, okay." Sal leaned on the backside of the couch, staring down at her fork. "I guess the rest should be thrown away. You don't want to overdo it, dear. Maybe your man likes the tuberculosis look on you."

"Shut up. Leave me alone, Sal." She attacked the potato on her plate.

"You're not getting the invalid treatment from me, honey. Beg all you like. I want to see you up and running before we move out on tour. We can't be dragging a zombie along."

"Sal!" Solveigh shot him a scandalized look, but he shrugged at her.

"What? She wanted a tour, and she got it, got her way once again, and now she had better deal with it, shot in the gut or not. We can't very well cancel all those venues and hotels again."

"Of course." The lobster was good, even if it wasn't quite as tasty as prawns. "Why should I be content with less? I need grand hotel hallways and lobbies for my grand scenes, and you should know that by now."

Everything, everything, Sal realized ruefully, had changed. No matter how hard they tried and how convincingly they pretended, deep in his heart he felt that the life had gone out of her and she was barely keeping herself together. They could push her into defiance for a little while, but the sadness always resurfaced, and the resignation. Step by slow step, she was drifting away from them, and he wondered if Jon had noticed, if all the good spirit he was displaying just now was nothing more than an act.

45

HE WOKE JUST before dawn to find her gone. For an instant, a cold fear gripped him, but then he saw her standing outside by the balustrade, her nightgown stirring in the cool wind.

Naomi did not turn when he stepped up to her but gazed at the ocean silently. A stillness had settled around her like a cloud of mist, as if she had drawn all her pain and sadness together to put distance between herself and the real world.

"I wish I could go back," she said into the silence of the early morning, "I wish I could go back to that black beach I saw when I was in a coma. It was so peaceful. No fear, no joy, no pain, no music. Everything floated away from me, all my sorrows, all my thoughts, even my love. No desires, no memories."

He knew then.

"I'm going away." Slowly she looked up at him. "As hard as I try, I can't find myself here anymore. It's as if my soul poured out of me along with all that blood, leaving nothing but a shell that's pretending to be me."

"Baby, no." Jon tried to reach out to her, but she drew back as if she had already left inwardly. "Where will you go? I'll go with you."

"You can't." Delivered in a soft voice that killed any argument before it could even be spoken. In the eerie grey light she stood before him, her head bowed, the selkie, returning to her cold abode.

"I feel like I'm dead, Jon, and I don't even have the solace of that peaceful place. Everyone is staring at me and wants me to be my old self again, but I can't. I'm not that person anymore."

"But you are. You will be. I know you will be again, the spark is there, you only need more time, more time to heal. Please, Naomi, give yourself more time. We'll go away together, we'll...hell, I don't know, we'll go anyplace you want and take all the time you need, but please, don't leave me!"

She might as well have pushed a blade right through his body with her next words.

"At least this time you'll know it wasn't your fault. You'll be able to rest easier." She walked past him back into the bedroom, without another glance, without the promise of a touch.

He watched how she took out a small bag and packed her old clothes in it, things she had brought from Halmar but nothing she had bought while they were together. None of her jewels, not even her rings. There was not a lot. It made him think of his own hasty journey, and how he had climbed from that jet in Bergen and walked into the freezing winds of winter, and about that other dawn so many years ago when he had found her gone.

"You know I will not survive this. Naomi, if you go, I'll not survive."

For a moment she stood before her trophies, even touched the Oscar briefly, but then left it standing in its place and wandered out to the patio again and sat on the day bed where she had spent so many days recuperating.

The sun had begun its rise behind the hills, touching the trees with tentative rosy fingers and casting the first golden light onto the sea.

"And will you come back to me? Will you come back to our life together or is this the end? Are you ending everything now?"

He sat down beside her and took her hand, afraid she would pull away and take the last trace of hope from him. Her hand lay in his limply, all life gone from it again.

"I don't know, Jon."

"You don't know?" Amid all the fear and pain, he felt a small bud of anger bloom in his chest. "You don't know? After everything we've been through, after all the obstacles we've overcome to be together and make this right, you sit here and tell me you don't know?"

There was no reply. She got up again and began to walk slowly through every room in the house, ending up in the studio. Jon followed her. It made him recall the many times he had imagined her on the morning after the drug raid, when she must have drifted through the house much like this, all by herself, just as lost as she seemed now.

"You are not alone." he said out loud.

She was standing beside his piano, the sheet with the song he had been working on in her hands, one of the pieces intended for the selkie musical. Her hair was back in a braid, she was in a linen dress and sandals, ready to leave, and to Jon it seemed as if only her body was still present, her soul had left long ago.

"You are not alone like you were back then. I'm here. I didn't desert you this time, and I'm not going to. You don't need that black place you were talking about to find healing. My love, I'll take you away from here and find us a place where we can heal together. To hell with the tour and everything else. We can sell the house and move away and you'll never, ever have to come to California again. And I promise, with all my heart, that I'll never ask you to, not even for a day. Please don't leave me."

She held up the paper to him. "This is new. You didn't show me."

"It is new, yes. I'm still working on the musical we wanted to put on stage. I haven't given up on life." It sounded like an accusation, but he didn't care anymore. It felt as if his well of pain and sadness had dried up. He could just not drag any more out of it to share her misery.

"I'm going to make coffee. I want coffee. If we are going to have this discussion and you want to go, I at least want some coffee to go with all the drama." Without waiting for her reply, he went to the kitchen and turned on the machine. "So you want to go." Jon called across the living room to her. "And what do you think will be better then? You'll have your family hide you away again in some obscure place like before, rending your heart, killing yourself with your longing for me, listening to me sing, and then what, Naomi? Ten years from now you'll stand outside a venue again in some city and watch me walk by? And sit in a concert and cry your eyes out and then go home and mourn? Is that what makes you really happy? Is that what you really crave?"

To his surprise, she came and stood in the door to listen to his bitter tirade. Jon felt ridiculous in his pajama pants. Angrily he banged down two mugs on the counter top. "Here. Drink some coffee, for God's sake. Don't stand there like a stranger. And answer my questions."

She sat down without comment.

"So tell me, where to this time? Norway is out of the question; you've used that one up. And if I know you, it will have to be someplace cold and harsh, right? No gentle breezes for you. You really need the drama and the sorrow to feel good, don't you? You can't allow yourself ease and happiness. You think life has to really suck to justify your existence. Well I'll tell you a secret, Naomi: that's not how it works."

That made her look up from her cup and gaze at him in surprise.

Jon opened his mouth to tell her again how sorry he was and how guilty he felt about everything that had happened, but to his astonishment he found he needed to say something else entirely.

"You're breaking my heart, and you know it. You know I would gladly lay myself down and let the world roll over me to make you happy, and still you want to go. Well, here it is, Naomi: I'm at the end of my rope. I've done everything imaginable to make you want to live with me. If all that isn't good enough, then I'm sorry, because there is no more. This is who I am. Go on and tell me you don't love me. I want to hear you say it before you walk out of this house for good."

Naomi blinked at him, for the first time that morning with something like a spark of life in her eyes. Jon felt the strong urge to grip her by the shoulders and shake her hard and then drag her back upstairs to their bed and drive all those dark thoughts out of her for good.

"Jon, how am I supposed to live with the shame and guilt of those deaths?"

"Who said you had to live with the guilt?" He nearly shouted it, exhausted to death by the recurring discussion and the reminder of his own failings. So many nights when she had been asleep he had mulled over Stewart and Sophie's deaths and his role in them, so many times he and Sal had discussed it, but the conclusion had always been the same. There was no guilt. He was not guilty.

"You're not guilty of one damn thing, Naomi. And I'm tired of repeating that." He needed more coffee, and he really wanted a cigarette, but there were none close by. "Or maybe yes, you are guilty. You are guilty of making me suffer like hell over and over again with your doubts and fears and silences. And I've had it." The moment the words left his lips he was sorry. She had paled considerably during his speech, and now she lowered her head again so he could not see her face.

"You were shot," Jon went on, a little calmer. "And I bear the guilt for that without you having to tell me. For some reason or other I did not manage to break up with my last girlfriend in such a way that she could get over it. My fault. But not yours, Naomi." He leaned forward, his hands on the table right in front of her, furious at himself for his ranting, furious at her for the hurt she was delivering again. "Do you really think," he said in a cold, dead voice, "do you really think any woman in the world could make me stay with her if I didn't want to?

Even you, my dear, not even you could make me stay if I didn't love you beyond all reason. With the choices I have, why should I care about any one woman for longer than I have to? I didn't leave Sophie because of you, Naomi. I left her because I was not in love with her at all. And I left her because a better adventure was waiting for me." He drew a deep breath. "You. Because, my love, you are the adventure of my life. That is all. The beginning and the end of it."

Without another word he left her there, in the kitchen, and returned to the bedroom to dress. If he had to stand in the door and watch her go, he didn't want to do it in pajamas; he needed some dignity at a moment like this.

From outside he could hear the voices of her guards, then the deep rumbling of the Rolls as it was brought out of the garage, and suddenly, despite all his harsh and dire words, he felt the desolate fear of returning downstairs and finding her gone. All her things, her lovely gowns, the shawls and jewels, none of these were missing, she had just left them behind, shed them like a glittering skin she did not need where she was bound.

The entrance stood wide open when he returned downstairs. Naomi was outside at the bottom of the stairs, talking to Amparo, the light of the morning framing her and shining through her skirt. Jon debated going down to her to plead with her again, but then he decided he would not treat himself to another painful spectacle. Slowly he walked away and closed the studio door behind him. The music. In the end, the music had always rescued him in his darkest moments.

Like this, just like this.

She had walked out of the house that morning too. A car had been waiting for her and she had vanished from his life.

His thoughts wandered to the tour looming before him like a giant snow-covered mountain, the booking for the Shubert where they had wanted to stage the musical, the house in New York, and Joshua.

Wasted. Jon did not know how to deal with these matters yet. Tired, he decided that he would have to go and close the front door, since she probably wouldn't have returned from the car to do it.

He opened to the door to the living room.

Naomi gave him the ghost of a smile.

"I'm hungry for an omelet. Will you make me one?" she said softly.

If you enjoyed

THE DISTANT SHORE,

be sure to catch
Book II of The Stone Trilogy,

UNDER THE SAME SUN

Coming in Fall 2012

An excerpt follows.

chapter 2

HE'D BEEN HOLDING the apple in his hand the entire time it took the bus to cross London. Beside them, the river was a golden band shimmering in the late afternoon sun, with a few ships collecting ripples in their trail like lace on a satin gown.

Quite successfully, he'd ignored the chatter of the others as they commented on the sights and on how excited they were to be back in England, back on the road, and made plans for the next day when they would have time to explore.

His fingers gripped the apple like a good-luck charm, the promise that all would be well, something to dispel the loneliness.

Jon had felt that loneliness like a terrible ache on the bus ride to the venue, like a deep silence settling into his heart. Alone in his hotel room that morning, he'd stared at the curtains blowing in the morning breeze, the other side of the bed empty and cold, untouched. He listened to the sound of the birds in the park across the street, remembering when they had been in London together for the first time. It had been a day much like this one, maybe a little cooler. He remembered opening his eyes and seeing her black locks on the pillow, a pale shoulder partly covered by the sheet, and he knew it was the day he would propose. How nervous he had been, afraid she would refuse! But she had agreed, and after breakfast he'd taken her out and bought her a ring. The elation of the moment when he'd put it on her finger had come back to him when he'd retraced that walk this morning. He had stood outside Tiffany's, still closed, and felt the crazy urge to bend down and run his hand over the pavement, trying to find a memory of her footsteps there. Furtively he had looked around, but no one had taken any notice of him. The stream of early-morning pedestrians had parted around him, ignoring him as if he were no more than a garbage can that had been put in the wrong place.

Later, returning to the hotel, he'd stood in the lobby for a moment and observed the group of fans hanging out there, waiting for him and the band to show up, but their attention was focused toward the elevators, and for some reason he could not explain, this had made him feel even lonelier, as if he had dropped off the world the moment she'd gone.

IT HAD BEEN three weeks.

Three weeks since he'd let her go, watching with a heavy heart as she left their home, fleeing from their life and the aftermath of the shooting. He had tried to talk her out of it, had made her breakfast and hoped with every fiber of his heart that she would change her mind, but seeing her sitting at the kitchen table, head lowered in defeat, hands folded in her lap, omelet untouched, he'd told her to go. Very softly, so his voice wouldn't crack, he'd told her to leave and find her peace. Naomi had looked at him, a small spark of hope in her eyes, and he knew it was the only thing to do.

She had not said where she was headed, and he had been too afraid to ask, too afraid to hear from her that it was none of his business and she would not be returning anyway. He had stood in the door as the car pulled out of the driveway and vanished into the early Los Angeles traffic, and then he stepped back inside, alone, desolate.

The house had seemed dead without her, an empty shell, and he had wandered through the many rooms, listening to their lonely echo. At last he'd found enough energy to make coffee, and while he was standing in the kitchen, dolefully watching it drip through the machine, the phone had rung.

"I'm at the airport," Naomi said, her voice as normal as if she'd been calling from a shopping trip, asking what to buy for dinner, "I'm going to New York first, to see Joshua, and then I'll go to one of my family's hotels on the eastern shore to rest a bit."

Jon had offered to join her, first to visit their son and then in her exile, but she had declined. She needed some time alone, to heal, and to regain her peace. And yes, she had promised, she would be in London when he started the tour.

SO NOW, AS the bus took drew close to the huge arena, he closed his hand around the smooth surface of the apple.

"Your fans," Sal said from behind him, "are faithful as ever. Do you feel like giving some autographs today?"

"Sure." Jon didn't care one way or the other. In fact, he didn't even care about the concert. It had been meant for her, and she wasn't here. He had dreamed of going on the stage, but never mind the ten thousand people in the audience; he wanted to sing only for her.

Once off the bus, he took the pen Sal held out to him and began walking toward the group of fans. Sal, Russ and Art were by his side, security surrounding them all. Jon was so used to doing this, the smile fell into place even before they had walked halfway across the parking lot. He was aware that he was still wearing the same shirt he'd put on that morning when he had gone on his little excursion downtown, and that it was a bit rumpled, not exactly suited for public snapshots, but he didn't care.

Many of the fans in the crowd were wearing t-shirts with his picture on them. Somehow he had never gotten used to seeing his own face on other people's clothes, and he even tried to get out of seeing the merchandise for the tours. When Sal pressed him, Jon would say he was not a piece of flesh for sale.

To which Sal would reply, "But you are, my friend. That's just what you are. The solace of their lonely nights, the dream boy they talk to over their solitary breakfast, the guy they want to take along when they buy underwear at the discount store." Sal could, after all their years together, say this like a mantra, always with the same acid inflection.

And now he was staring at a sea of middle-aged women in blue shirts with his face on their chests. As he stared in despair, he noticed a speck of red hidden behind the matrons holding out CDs for him to sign, and his heart skipped. He tried to see around them, take a closer look, and then she stepped forward.

He had, he realized bitterly, not expected to ever see her again. And yet here she stood, in a dress much like the one she'd worn that day he'd asked her to marry him, her braid falling over her shoulder, unchanged. Her lips curled into a small smile when she saw his stunned expression, and she moved forward to take his hand when he held it out.

"Forgive me," Naomi whispered, so low only he could hear it. "Forgive me, and please take me back."

There was nothing to forgive. He wanted somewhere quiet where they could be alone, if only for a moment, and he wanted the fans gone so he could kiss her right there and then.

She pressed his fingers slightly, the corners of her mouth twitching. "Don't stare, Jon. Let's go."

He heard the murmur of discontent from the waiting group of fans, but he couldn't be bothered. There would be no more autographs today.

RUSS LED THEM inside, where they were greeted by representatives of the venue, the British tour management, and the press, but Jon waved them away and asked for his dressing room.

"Later," he told them. "I promise.."

Sal stayed behind to answer some of their questions, and Jon closed and locked the dressing room door, relieved they would have at least a few minutes of solitude before he had to go and join the sound check.

"You're here," He said.

Again she smiled. "Of course I am. I promised. Did you forget?"

It was so hard to believe that she had really come. "And you stood out there with the fans. Just like you said you did last time, only then I walked by and didn't see you."

"Yes." She sat on the corner of the dressing table and picked up the eyeliner. Carefully she pulled off the cap and drew a thin line on the tip of her finger. "I could hardly wait for you to find me. I was afraid you'd decide not to give autographs at all and I would have to call Sal to let me in. Then my surprise would have been wasted."

Jon could hardly speak. Her composure was too much to bear, her cool, sensible words as close to a taunt as she had ever attempted.

"I'm rested," Naomi went on, a little gentler. "I needed a break."

The morning she had left came to his mind again, how she had sat at the table, staring at the steaming eggs like a prisoner, a captured animal, miserable, defeated and hopeless. He had let her go, sent her away, even though it broke his heart.

"I never wanted to put pressure on you," he said. "Never. I only wanted to see you healed and well. I wanted our life back." He balled his fists, his fury at what had happened to her boiling up again. "I wanted you to forget and be your real self again, not that broken husk on the verge of death."

"I am myself," Naomi said softy, "I'm okay now."

It was a lie, Jon could see. She looked incredibly tired, and she was still too thin. "You should have stayed where you were," he said. "It's too early for you to come back." He could hardly believe what he was saying. "You need more rest."

Instantly he could see he had hurt her badly. Naomi lowered her head. She laid the eyeliner back on the table and stood up. With a shaking hand, she smoothed down her dress and tugged her jacket into place.

"I'm ready to cry, Jon. I've come all this way, I flew overnight to come to you, and you don't even want me. I thought you had forgiven me, but it seems you are still angry that I had to go away for a while to gain some peace, when in truth all I wanted was to be with you." She looked up at him, her eyes brimming with tears. "That was all I wanted. I couldn't wait to be back with you again."

"But baby…" Jon wanted to kiss her. He wanted it so badly he could feel his lips tingling, and he reached out to her. "Baby, I'm so happy you're here! I can't begin to tell you how much I've missed you, how desolate I've felt without you, how scared I was that you'd never come back. Don't you know how much I need you? But Naomi—"

"No buts, Jon. No more buts." She pulled him to her and kissed him deeply.

He wanted to drown in that kiss, wanted her body close to his and feel the soft warmth of her skin under his hands. Three long weeks she had been away, and to him it felt like an eternity.

"I missed you so much," Jon breathed into her mouth. "You have no idea. I wanted to go after you, find you and stay with you wherever you were hiding. I wanted to give up the tour, everything. Nothing makes any sense if you're not there."

From outside, he could hear Sal's voice, not yet impatient but loud enough to remind him of where he was supposed to be.

"They're waiting for me," he said, but he didn't let her go. It felt too good to have her in his arms again.

Naomi pushed against his chest. "In a moment, Sal is going to crash through the door, and that would be so awkward. I'll be right here, darling. Give me a minute to drink a cup of coffee and then I'll join you, I promise. But I'm just off the plane and I need to freshen up a bit before I meet the rest of the group."

"But how will I be sure?" It sounded a little plaintive, and it made her smile.

"You'll just have to trust me, I'm afraid. I'll make Sal take me to hospitality and get me a backstage pass so I can move around without being a nuisance." She rose on her toes. "But first, one more kiss."

Jon did not want to let her go, too afraid she would be gone when he returned from the sound check. He wanted to keep her right there with him; he'd done it before, taken her with him onto the stage and sat her down next to Sean on the piano bench, just to make sure she wouldn't vanish. He was very tempted to do it again now, but he was sure he would meet resistance.

There was a sharp knock, and he sighed.

"Go," Naomi urged. "Don't make them wait. I promise not to go anywhere."

"I can't." His hands dug into her hair, loosening the braid, freeing the locks. "How can I, with you here, after not having you in my arms for a month?"

"Three weeks, Jon. Don't exaggerate so. We talked on the phone all the time." But she didn't try to pull away.

"The phone," he mumbled against her temple. "Can't make love on the phone. Can't feel your breath on my skin, can't touch you. Can't see you when I wake up."

Her body softened against his, but only for a moment. "Jon."

"Ah, Naomi, you're breaking my heart. All I get is a moment's solace, and then you send me off again. I've hardly had time to say hello to you."

"And little wonder." She undid her braid to put it in order. "You were too busy kissing me to speak in proper sentences."

He had been on his way to the door, but now he turned and shot her a dangerous glance. "I haven't even begun kissing you, my dear. Just wait until we're back at the hotel."

FOR THE FIRST time in his life, Jon didn't want to get onstage.

He made his way slowly, carefully. At the bottom of the narrow stairway that would take him up to where he would make his entrance at the beginning of the concert, he stopped. One hand on the handrail, he looked back, dithering.

Sean had started the band. They were rehearsing the orchestral intro, a short piece from the movie soundtrack that had won them an Oscar only a few months ago. Jon could hear Sean giving directions to their sound engineer, Russ and Sal fiddling with the recording computers at the side of the scaffolding, and lighting people climbing along the crossbeams like monkeys. Their rope ladder dangled down onto the stage, almost exactly at the spot where he was supposed to be, right by his microphone stand.

Someone had set up his guitars for him, but not in the right order, and he cursed silently. His attention wavered. Part of him wanted to go back to Naomi so he could look at her and have her in his arms, but this bothered him.

Over the years they all had developed a routine full of small rituals. Now that someone had broken one of his, the obsessive part of him that lived in the music was upset. Calling for Sal, Jon jumped up the few steps. He pushed at the ladder hanging in his way and pointed at the guitars, a harangue on his lips. But Sal was already there, putting the instruments in their place.

"You are insufferable," Sal grumbled. "You clearly can't stand being here, so go back and smooch some more with the wife. Don't dump your sour mood on us."

Jon didn't reply.

"You've wasted fifteen minutes," Sal said. "You have another forty-five for the rehearsal, and then the press and the fan clubs will be here. You know we promised a press conference."

As if he didn't know, after a quarter century in the business. This was the first show of the tour, and they needed a good write-up. Everyone in the music world would be watching this concert. Everyone who was still thinking about buying a ticket for later performances would be watching too.

"Yeah," Jon mumbled. He still didn't feel like playing, let alone singing. Naomi had said she wanted coffee and would join him shortly, but she wasn't here yet and it made him restless. "Let me just check if she's alright."

Sal sighed. "For heaven's sake, Jon. She doesn't need a babysitter. But fine, let me go and see what she's up to. Just please, go do your job."

Without waiting for a reply, he left.

The guitars were well polished, not a single fingerprint on their glossy surface, just the way he liked it. Lovingly, Jon ran his hand over the koa twelve-string, its bold grain and coloring like the curly auburn hair of a lovely woman. It was an old friend, as old as his career. How well he remembered playing it in the sun-drenched open-air stadium in Geneva all those years ago when he had met Naomi, and the turmoil of his feelings when he realized she was the one and only, the one girl he wanted for the rest of his life.

Beside it was the ebony acoustic, his lover, custom-made for him ten years ago. He had seen the black wood in the workshop, the fine, wavy red stripes like the highlights in Naomi's hair, and he had known he wanted it. The sound of the instrument, when it was delivered, had first surprised and then almost hurt him. It was soft, melodious, with a sweet, mellow timbre and an echoing, haunting quality that reminded him so much of her he could only bear to play it when he was alone.

Now, of course, everything was different. She was back in his life and he could easily pick the guitar up during a concert, could even play their most intimate song, "The Secret Garden," on it and not cry.

Sean launched into the opening chords.

Jon raised his head to look at the high ceiling, listened to the song and let it inundate him. He wanted to stretch out his arms and float on the melody, feel it carry him like a wave. It was his music, the extension of his soul into the real world, a shining cloud that always surrounded him, the fabric of his existence.

He picked up his twelve-string, swung it over his head, settled it into place against his body. The guitar pick in his raised hand, he waited for his cue and then dove into the ocean of his creation.

READING GROUP GUIDE

1. In the beginning of the story we see Jon, a famous rock star, living in a small house in an unfashionable part of LA. What drove him to live there when he owned a mansion in Malibu?

2. Jon tells Sal about his first meeting with Naomi and how he fell in love with her immediately. Do you believe in love at first sight?

3. When Jon leaves California to find Naomi, he insists on going on his own. Why was this so important for him?

4. Naomi agrees to marry Jon as soon as he proposes, but later she has doubts. What is her greatest fear?

5. Jon takes Naomi shopping in London and lavishes her with expensive gifts. Is there a deeper meaning, or was this just fun day on the town?

6. Naomi told Joshua he was the result of a brief affair after a concert, but when he and Jon meet, Jon explains that he and Naomi had been lovers for three years. How does this affect Jon and Joshua's father/son relationship?

7. After Jon accepts the offer to write the movie soundtrack, he reads the book the movie is based on. He and Naomi then have a discussion about how far they would go to save their loved one's life, and Naomi asks Jon if he would be prepared to kill her to spare her suffering. Why do you think Naomi and Jon had such different reactions to this question? Was it just a male/female response, or something unique to their relationship? How far would you go for love?

8. How does Art's arrival in Halmar change the atmosphere, and why? Do you think Art satisfied Naomi's misgivings?

9. Why did Naomi pick Art to talk to when she was finally ready to discuss the night of the drug raid, rather than someone she is closer to, like Solveigh or Sean?

10. Naomi never confronts Jon after overhearing him talking to Sophie at the Hollywood party. Why not?

11. What do you think of Jon's mother and sister? What about his relationship with them?

12. Why do you think New York holds such a strong appeal for Naomi?

13. It is Sal who unveils Naomi's secrets. Why didn't she tell Jon about her family and their business?

14. When Sophie shows up at the hotel and makes a scene, Naomi reacts by throwing away the lyrics she'd written. Jon thinks she is just jealous of Sophie. Do you agree? If not, what do you think were the reasons behind Naomi's behavior?

15. Once she and Jon are back in LA, Naomi seems to accept her new life and even enjoy it. What made her change her mind about living there?

16. The ending of the book is ambiguous, and we don't know if Naomi stays with Jon or not. What do you think will happen?